NEIGHBORHOOD THREAT

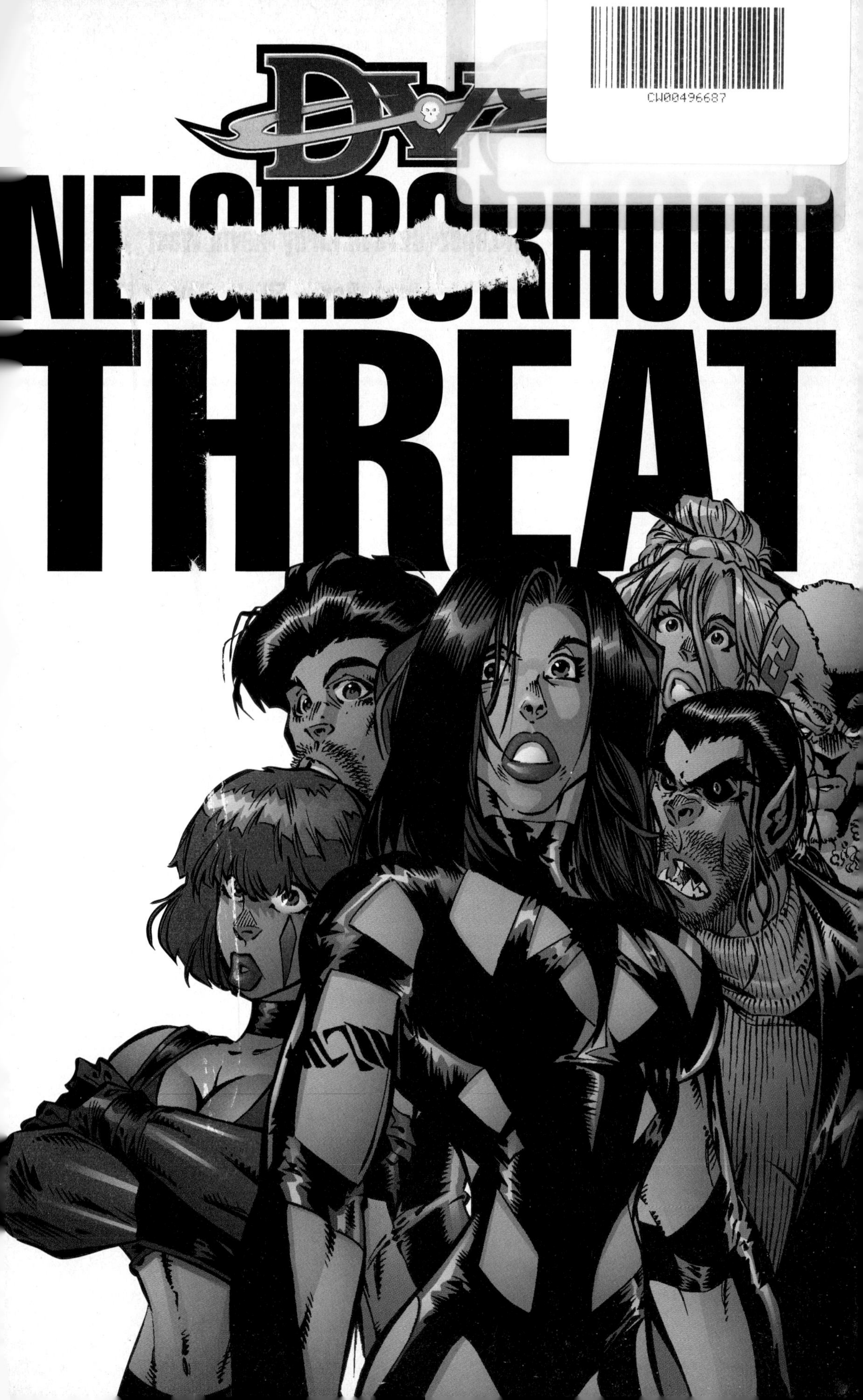

Warren Ellis writer

Humberto Ramos • Michael Lopez • Juvaun Kirby • Kevin West pencillers

Sal Regla • Troy Hubbs • Mark McKenna • Randy Elliott • Dexter Vines
Saleem Crawford • Luke Rizzo • Chuck Gibson • Mike Miller inkers

Wendy Fouts • WildStorm FX • Bad@$$ colorists

Mike Heisler • Amie Grenier • Bill O'Neil letterers

DV8 created by **Jim Lee, Brandon Choi,**
and **J. Scott Campbell**

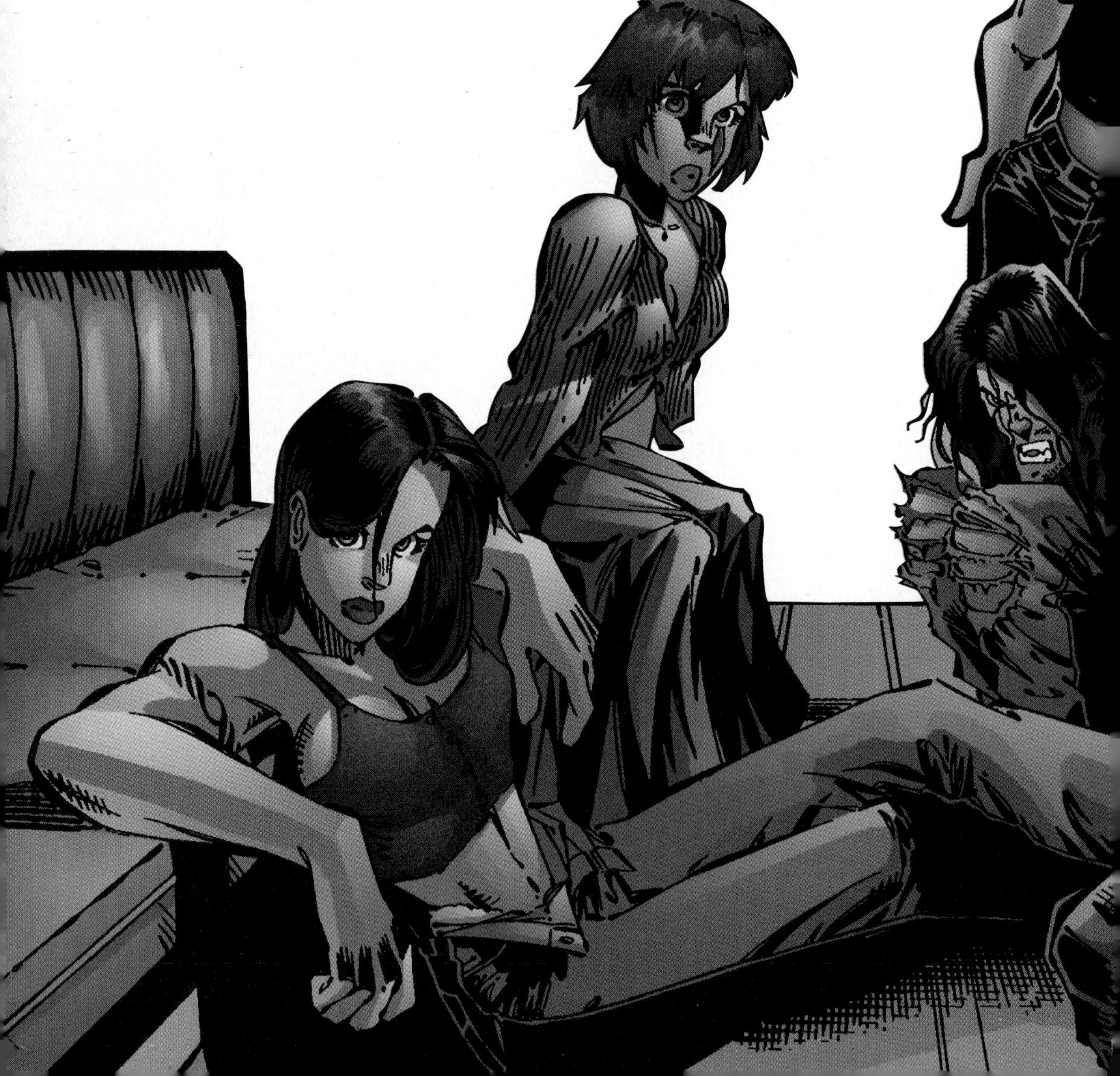

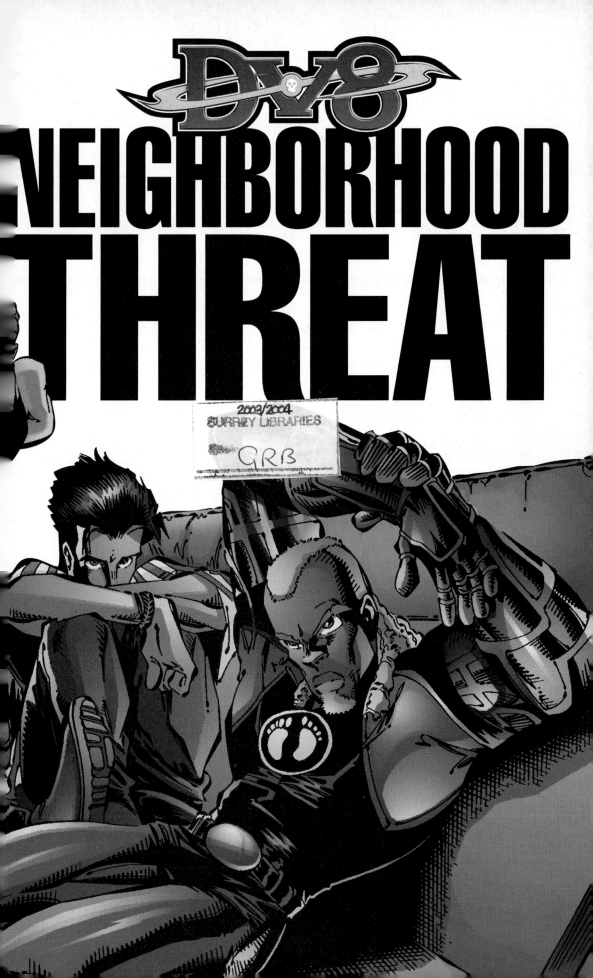

DV8
NEIGHBORHOOD THREAT

DV8: NEIGHBORHOOD THREAT
Published by WildStorm Productions. Editorial
offices: 888 Prospect St. Suite #240, La Jolla, CA
92037. Cover, introduction, and compilation
copyright © 2002 WildStorm Productions, an
imprint of DC Comics. All Rights Reserved.
Originally published in single magazine form as
DV8 #1-6 and DV8 #1/2. Copyright © 1996,
1997 WildStorm Productions. DV8, all
characters, the distinctive likenesses
thereof and all related indicia are
trademarks of DC Comics. The stories,
characters, and incidents featured in
this publication are entirely fictional.
WildStorm does not read or accept
unsolicited submissions of ideas,
stories or artwork.

DC Comics.
A division of Warner Bros. -
An AOL Time Warner Company
Printed in Canada. First Printing.
ISBN: 1-56389-927-2
Cover illustration by Humberto Ramos and Sal Regla.
Cover color by Wendy Fouts.

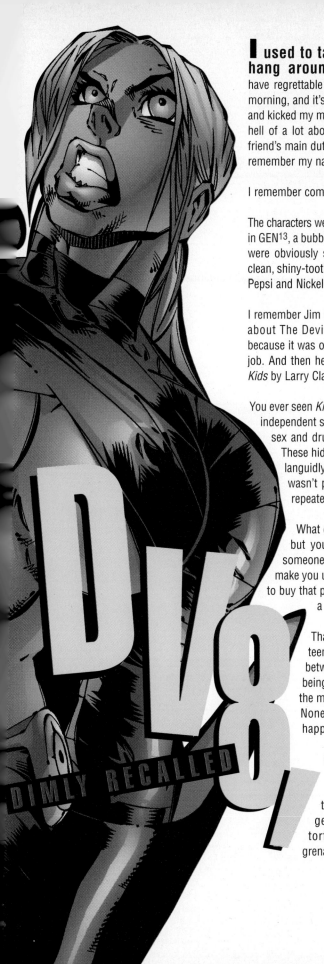

DV8
DIMLY RECALLED

I used to take drugs, get drunk every night, hang around bars looking for bad women, have regrettable sex and wake up naked in trees at four in the morning, and it's incinerated my hair, buggered my cell structure and kicked my metabolism to death, so I don't remember a whole hell of a lot about how I came to write DV8. I mean, my girl-friend's main duty when I wake up in the afternoon is to help me remember my name.

I remember coming up with the title, if that helps.

The characters were called "The Deviants," and had been introduced in GEN13, a bubbly Britneyoid soap-opera super-hero comic. They were obviously supposed to be the Dark Side of the squeaky-clean, shiny-toothed GEN13 kids, but the whole thing was a bit too Pepsi and Nickelodeon for them to have any actual bite.

I remember Jim Lee phoning me. He wanted me to write a series about The Deviants. I kind of made a few groaning noises, because it was obviously going to be a kind of bland and sugary job. And then he said a thing. He said, "Did you see the movie *Kids* by Larry Clark? We want this book to be like that."

You ever seen *Kids*? It was a real hand grenade into the American independent scene, back in the mid-nineties. Remember when sex and drugs were about rebellion for kids? Not in *Kids*. These hideous, ethically deformed and doomed kids were languidly ruining their lives as a way to pass the time. It wasn't perfect, but when it was right, it was like being repeatedly hit in the head with a hammer.

What do you do when you're convinced you're special but you have no life? And, in those moments when someone else agrees that, yes, you have a talent — they make you use it for the equivalent of being sent up the road to buy that person beer. Just grinding their heel in your soul a little more.

That was DV8. A bunch of severely damaged teenagers with no visible lives, their days split between marking time until suicide looked good and being forced to undergo deadly missions that were all the more frightening for their apparent pointlessness. None of this "we are a family" crap. They just all happened to be on the same train to Hell.

I remember saying I'd launch the book for them. I remember the first issue was the best-selling comic of its month. I remember enjoying the thought of bubbly little GEN13 and *X-Men* readers getting it and being introduced to drug use, torture, dominant sex and incest. Just a little hand grenade, but one I enjoyed pulling the pin on.

— Warren Ellis
The Nursing Home
May 2002

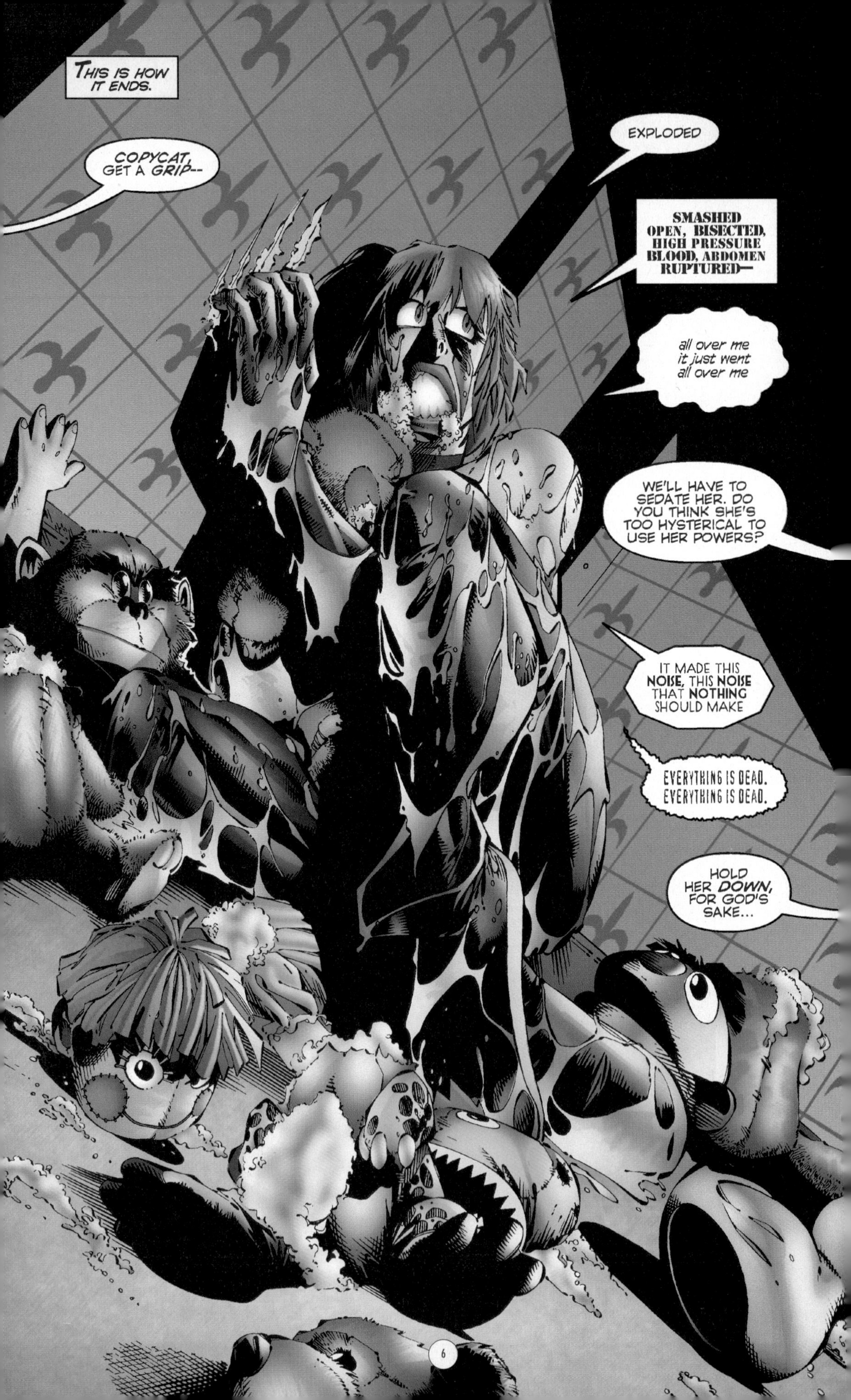
THIS IS HOW IT ENDS.
COPYCAT, GET A GRIP--
EXPLODED
SMASHED OPEN, BISECTED, HIGH PRESSURE BLOOD, ABDOMEN RUPTURED—
all over me it just went all over me
WE'LL HAVE TO SEDATE HER. DO YOU THINK SHE'S TOO HYSTERICAL TO USE HER POWERS?
IT MADE THIS NOISE, THIS NOISE THAT NOTHING SHOULD MAKE
EVERYTHING IS DEAD. EVERYTHING IS DEAD.
HOLD HER DOWN, FOR GOD'S SAKE...

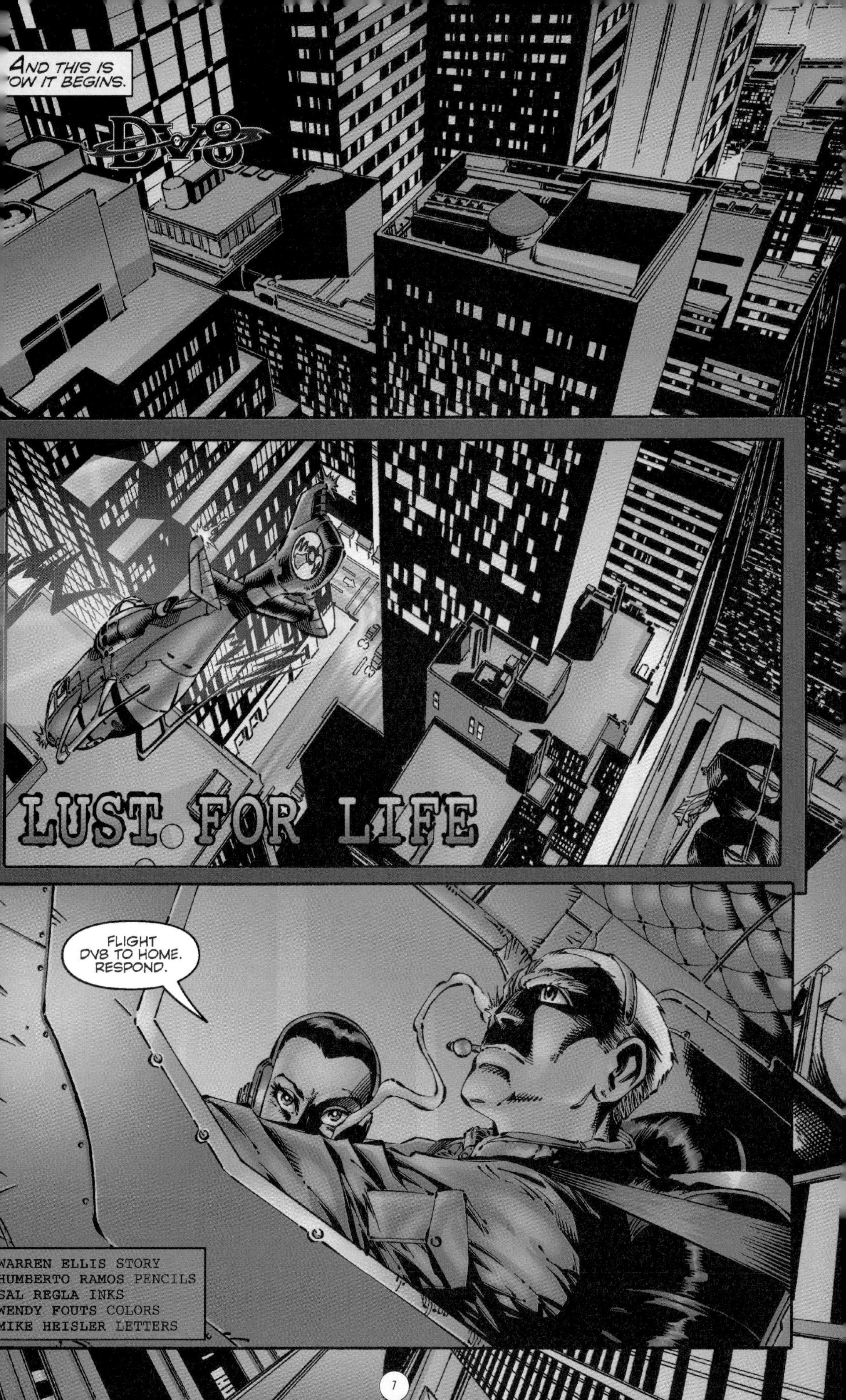
AND THIS IS
OW IT BEGINS.
DV8
LUST FOR LIFE
FLIGHT DV8 TO HOME. RESPOND.
WARREN ELLIS STORY
HUMBERTO RAMOS PENCILS
SAL REGLA INKS
WENDY FOUTS COLORS
MIKE HEISLER LETTERS

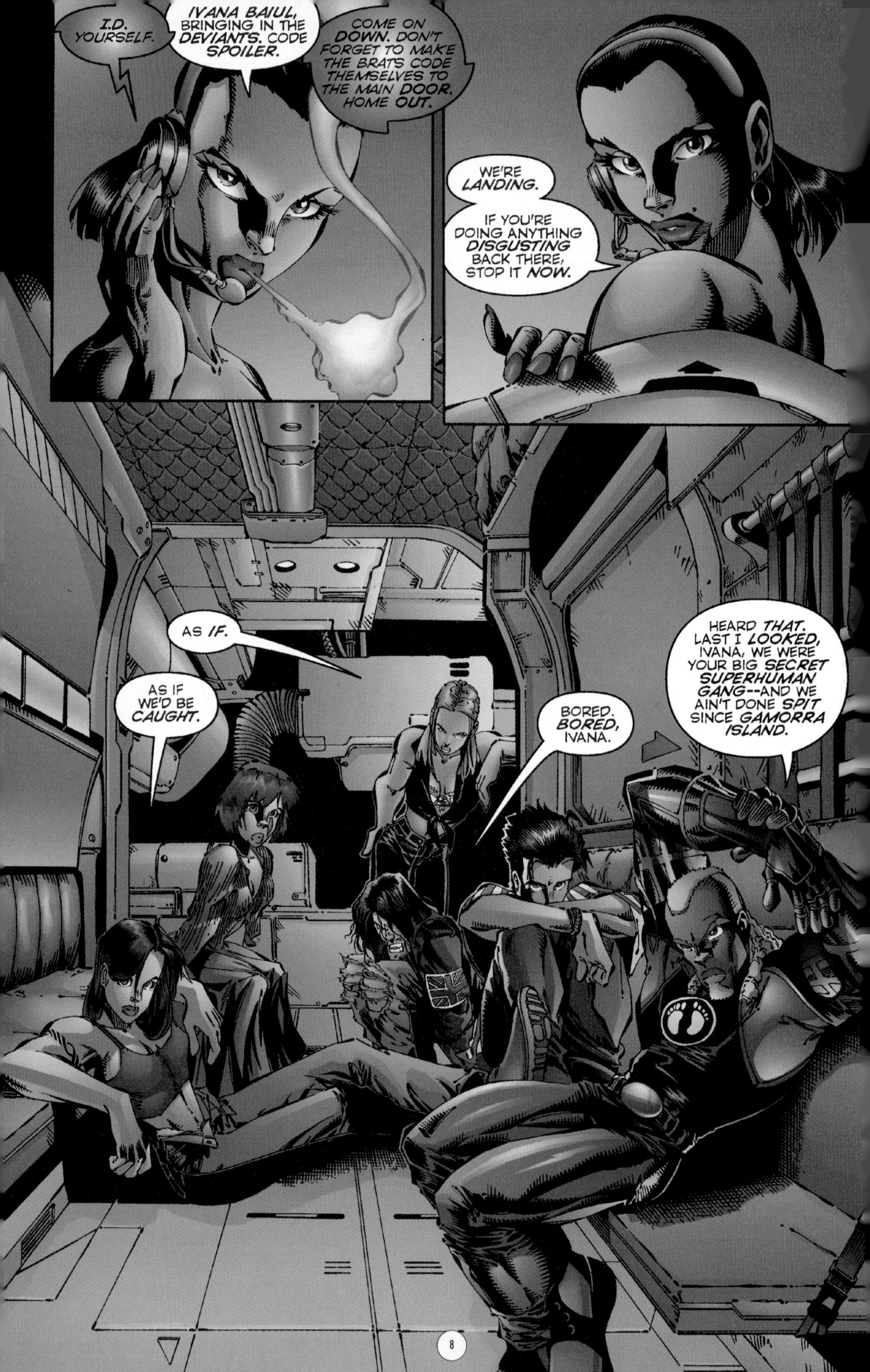
I.D. YOURSELF.
IVANA BAIUL, BRINGING IN THE DEVIANTS. CODE SPOILER.
COME ON DOWN. DON'T FORGET TO MAKE THE BRATS CODE THEMSELVES TO THE MAIN DOOR. HOME OUT.
WE'RE LANDING.
IF YOU'RE DOING ANYTHING DISGUSTING BACK THERE, STOP IT NOW.
AS IF.
AS IF WE'D BE CAUGHT.
BORED. BORED, IVANA.
HEARD THAT. LAST I LOOKED, IVANA, WE WERE YOUR BIG SECRET SUPERHUMAN GANG--AND WE AIN'T DONE SPIT SINCE GAMORRA ISLAND.

"THE MISSION ON GAMORRA WAS YOUR *FINAL TEST*, LEON.

"NOW WE KNOW THE TEAM HAS A *USE*."

HEAD FOR THE *ELEVATOR*. FLOOR *SIXTY-SIX*, CHILDREN. THE *PENTHOUSE* FLOOR. *REMEMBER* THE NUMBER--IT'S OUR NEW *HOME*.

WE'RE NOT GOING BACK TO THE *TRAINING ISLAND? REALLY?*

OH, GOD, COPYCAT'S DOING HER *HAPPY LITTLE MUPPET* BIT AGAIN...

NOBODY ANYWHERE ON THIS PLANET *LIKES* YOU, FROSTBITE. DOES THAT *BOTHER* YOU?

OKAY: TO *ENTER*, YOU NEED TO *TELL* THE *DOORLOCK* WHO YOU *ARE*. PRESS *THUMB* TO *PAD* AND LOOK AT THE *SCANPLATE*.

DULL. STUPID. BORED.

9

LOOK AT IT *THIS* WAY, MICHAEL: IT'LL HELP YOU TO *NOT FORGET* YOUR OWN *NAME*, AS YOU DID LAST WEEK AFTER STEALING MY *VODKA*.

MICHAEL HELLER. CODENAME *EVO*.

SATISFIED?

CODED.

RACHEL GOLDMAN, CODENAMED *SUBLIME*.

AND THERE'S A LIE IF *EVER* I HEARD ONE. IVANA, CAN WE CHANGE HER NAME TO *DADDY'S GIRL?* OR MAYBE *NOSE CANDY?*

DIE OR SOMETHING, *EVO.*

CODED.

HECTOR MORALES, *POWERHAUS.*

IS THIS THING TAKING *PHOTOGRAPHS?*

Umm...*GEM ANTONELLI,* I GUESS. AND *COPYCAT.*

AND SEVERAL *OTHERS.* YOU'RE *NEVER* ALONE WITH *MULTIPLE PERSONALITY DISORDER,* EH?

CODED.

OH. *OH.* THE DOOR'S OPENING, IVANA. DID WE DO SOMETHING *WRONG?*

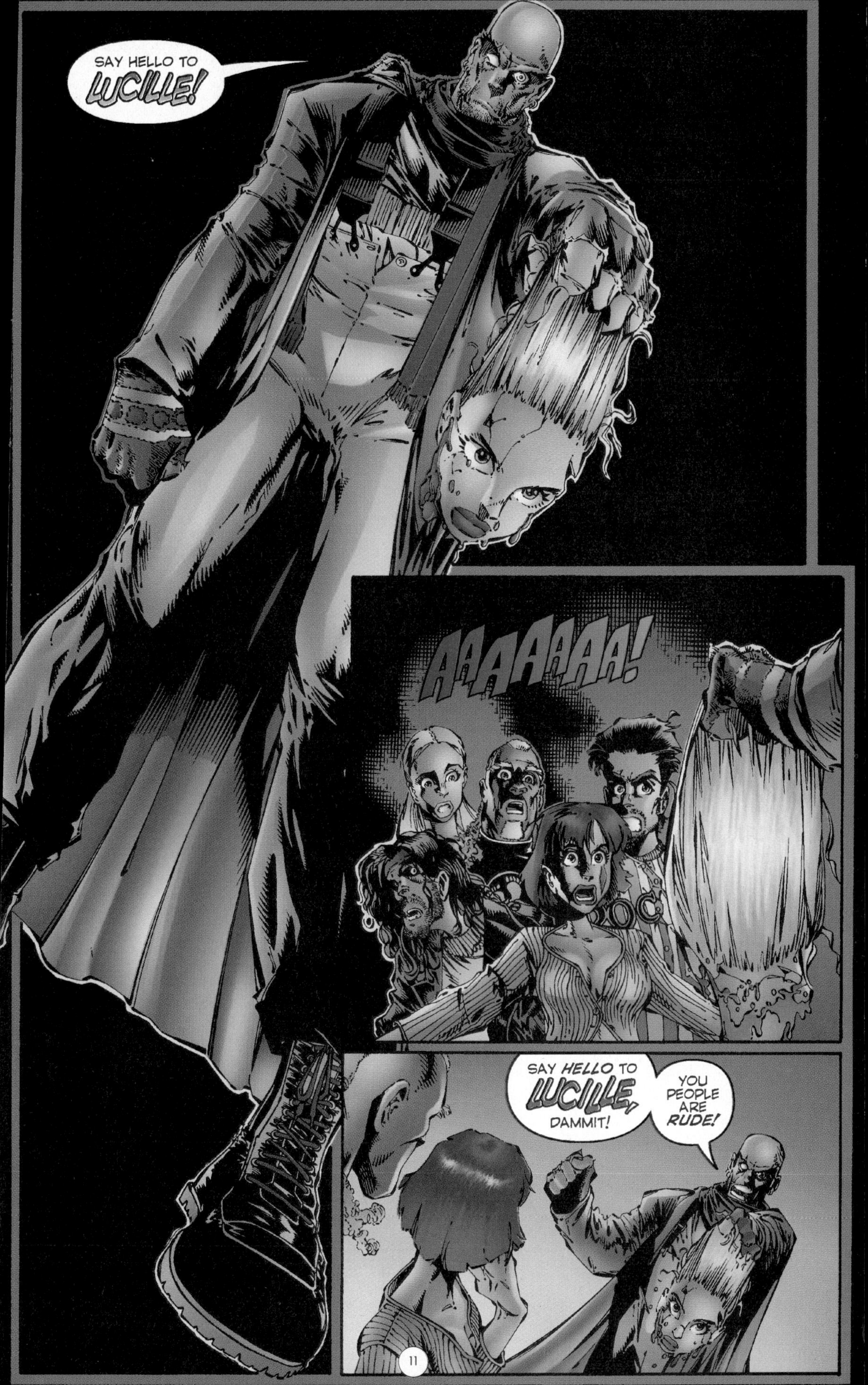
SAY HELLO TO LUCILLE!
AAAAAAA!
SAY HELLO TO LUCILLE, DAMMIT!
YOU PEOPLE ARE RUDE!

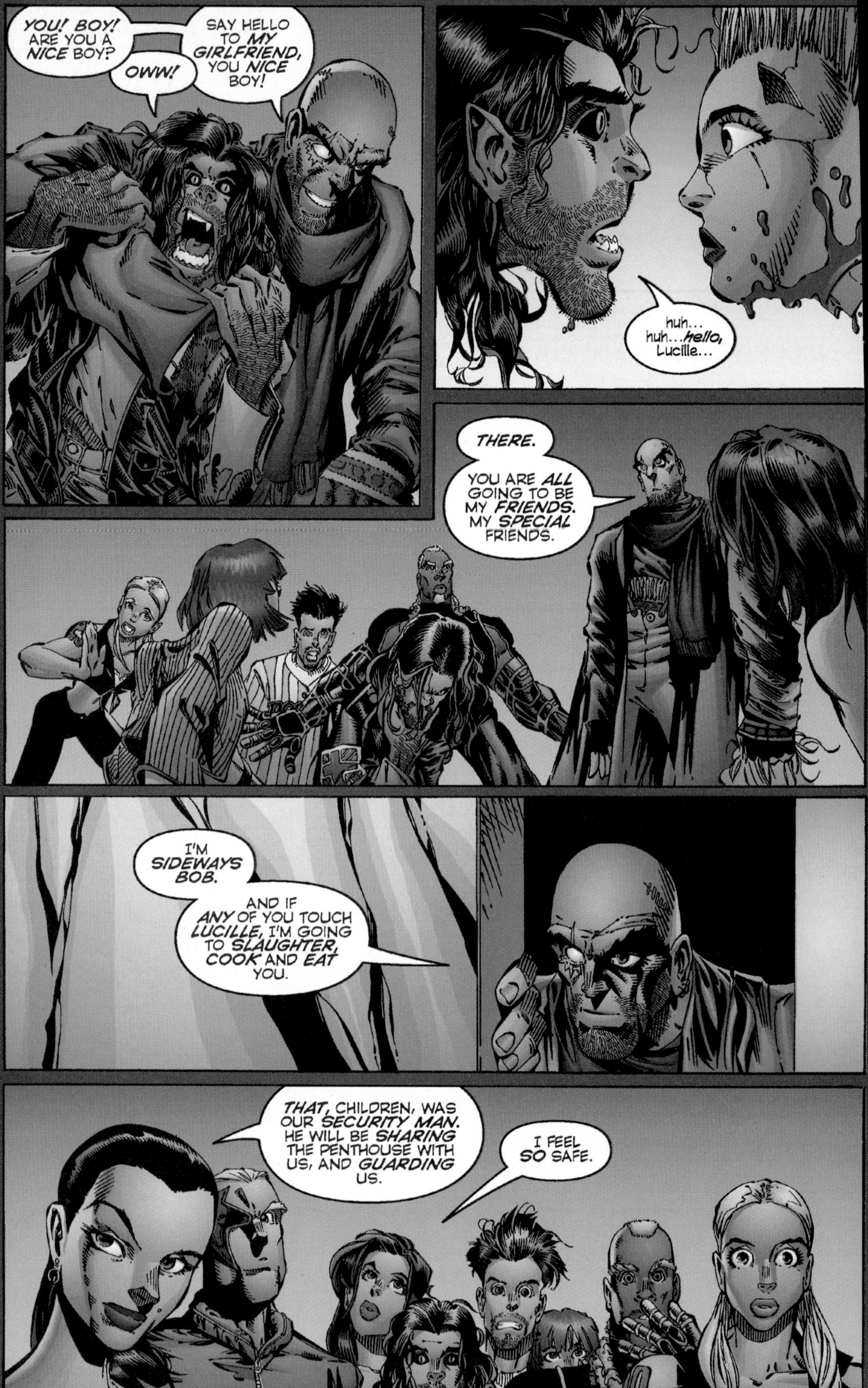
YOU! BOY! ARE YOU A NICE BOY?
OWW!
SAY HELLO TO MY GIRLFRIEND, YOU NICE BOY!
huh... huh... hello, Lucille...
THERE.
YOU ARE ALL GOING TO BE MY FRIENDS. MY SPECIAL FRIENDS.
I'M SIDEWAYS BOB.
AND IF ANY OF YOU TOUCH LUCILLE, I'M GOING TO SLAUGHTER, COOK AND EAT YOU.
THAT, CHILDREN, WAS OUR SECURITY MAN. HE WILL BE SHARING THE PENTHOUSE WITH US, AND GUARDING US.
I FEEL SO SAFE.

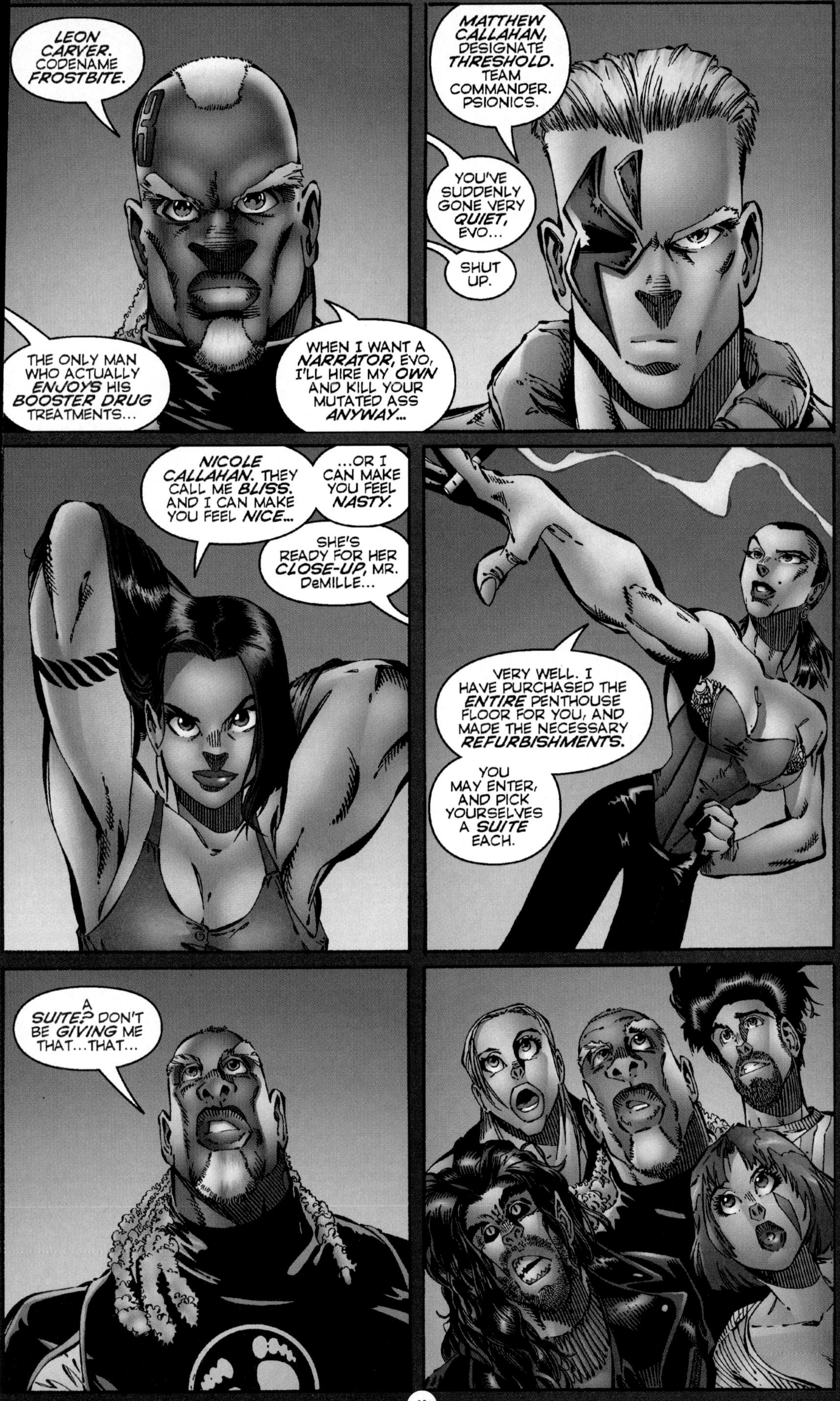
LEON CARVER. CODENAME FROSTBITE.
THE ONLY MAN WHO ACTUALLY ENJOYS HIS BOOSTER DRUG TREATMENTS...
WHEN I WANT A NARRATOR, EVO, I'LL HIRE MY OWN AND KILL YOUR MUTATED ASS ANYWAY...
MATTHEW CALLAHAN, DESIGNATE THRESHOLD. TEAM COMMANDER. PSIONICS.
YOU'VE SUDDENLY GONE VERY QUIET, EVO...
SHUT UP.
NICOLE CALLAHAN. THEY CALL ME BLISS. AND I CAN MAKE YOU FEEL NICE...
...OR I CAN MAKE YOU FEEL NASTY.
SHE'S READY FOR HER CLOSE-UP, MR. DeMILLE...
VERY WELL. I HAVE PURCHASED THE ENTIRE PENTHOUSE FLOOR FOR YOU, AND MADE THE NECESSARY REFURBISHMENTS.
YOU MAY ENTER, AND PICK YOURSELVES A SUITE EACH.
A SUITE? DON'T BE GIVING ME THAT...THAT...

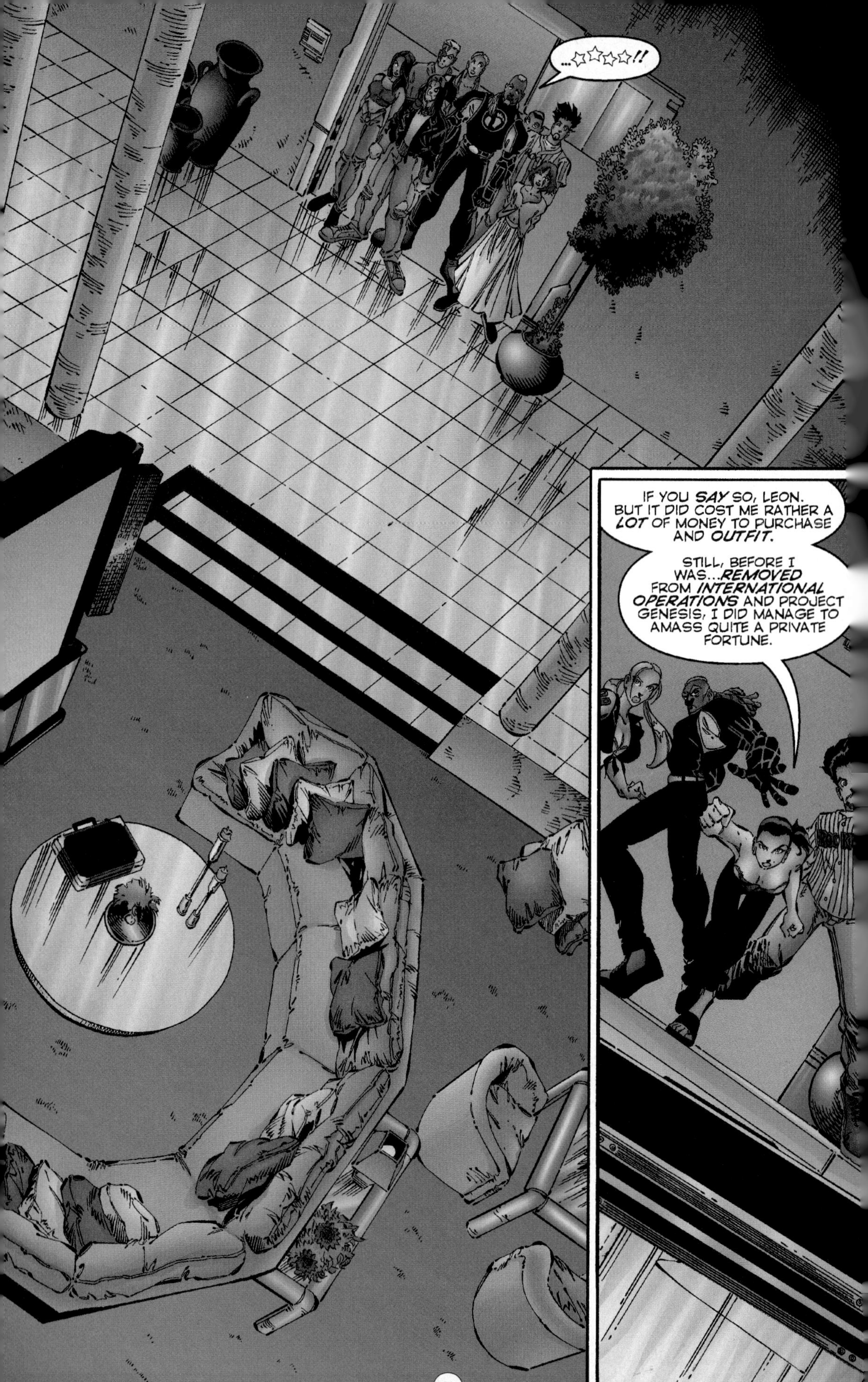
...☆☆☆☆!!
IF YOU SAY SO, LEON. BUT IT DID COST ME RATHER A LOT OF MONEY TO PURCHASE AND OUTFIT.
STILL, BEFORE I WAS...REMOVED FROM INTERNATIONAL OPERATIONS AND PROJECT GENESIS, I DID MANAGE TO AMASS QUITE A PRIVATE FORTUNE.

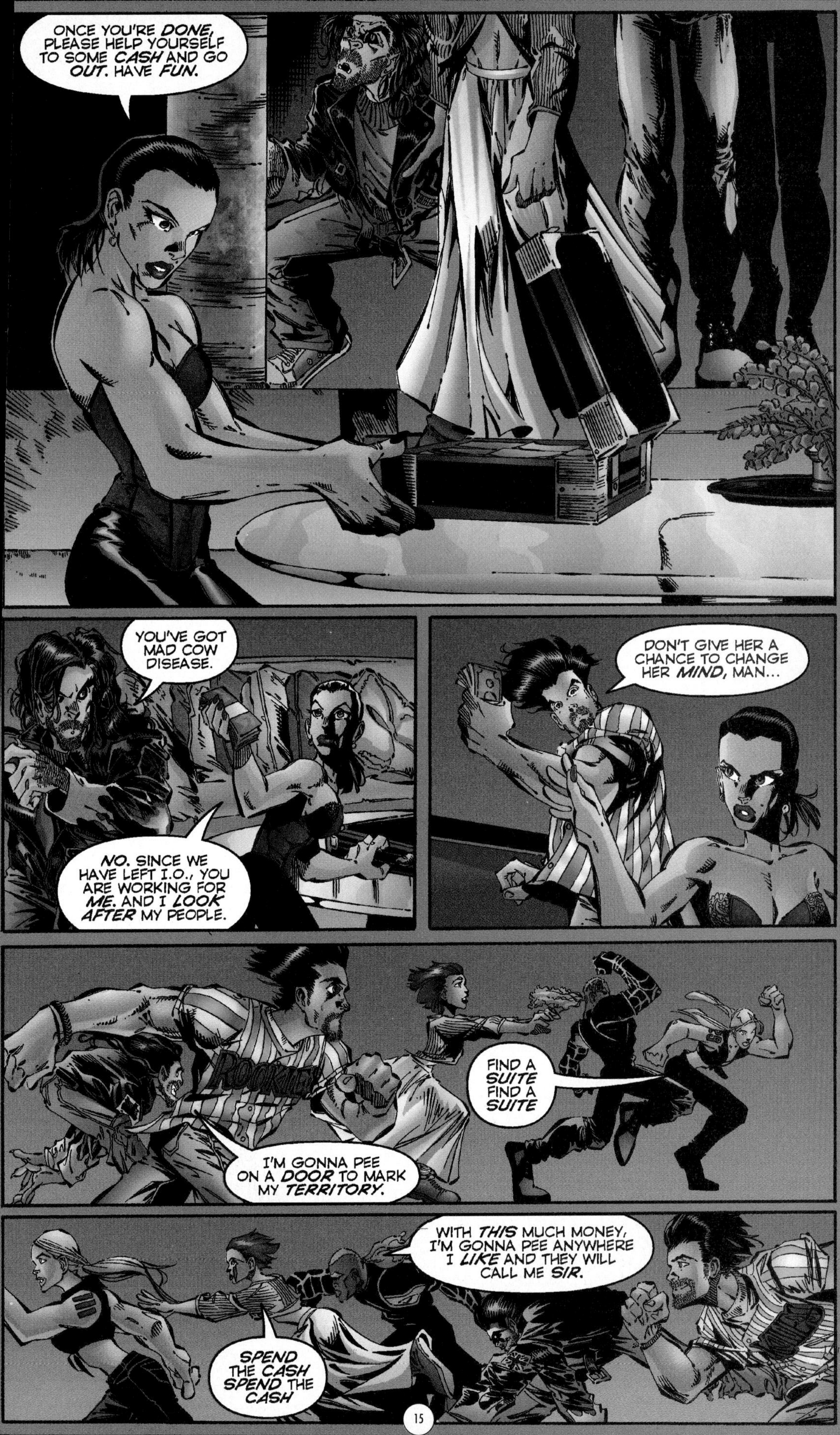
ONCE YOU'RE DONE, PLEASE HELP YOURSELF TO SOME CASH AND GO OUT. HAVE FUN.
YOU'VE GOT MAD COW DISEASE.
NO. SINCE WE HAVE LEFT I.O., YOU ARE WORKING FOR ME. AND I LOOK AFTER MY PEOPLE.
DON'T GIVE HER A CHANCE TO CHANGE HER MIND, MAN...
FIND A SUITE FIND A SUITE
I'M GONNA PEE ON A DOOR TO MARK MY TERRITORY.
SPEND THE CASH SPEND THE CASH
WITH THIS MUCH MONEY, I'M GONNA PEE ANYWHERE I LIKE AND THEY WILL CALL ME SIR.

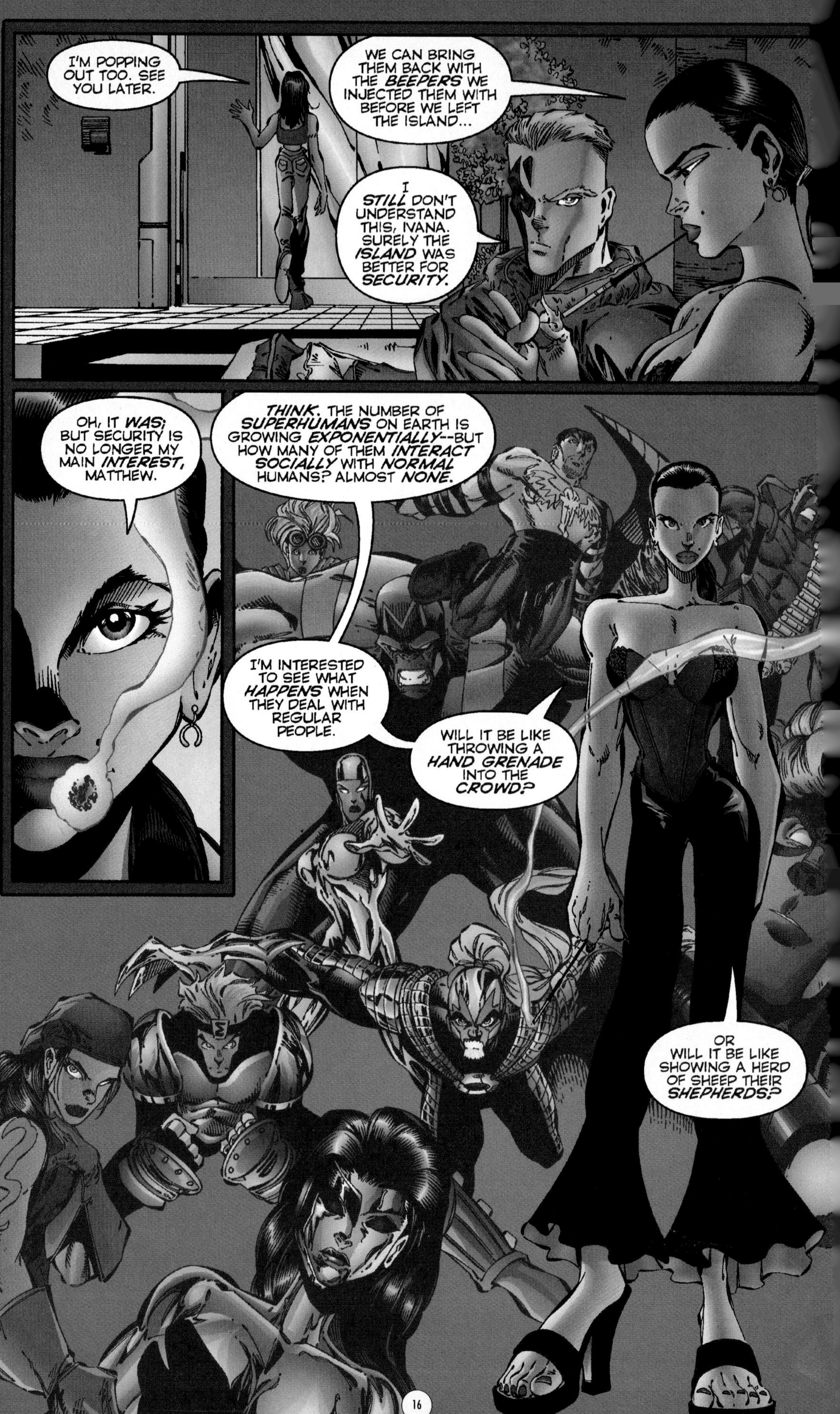
I'M POPPING OUT TOO. SEE YOU LATER.
WE CAN BRING THEM BACK WITH THE BEEPERS WE INJECTED THEM WITH BEFORE WE LEFT THE ISLAND...
I STILL DON'T UNDERSTAND THIS, IVANA. SURELY THE ISLAND WAS BETTER FOR SECURITY.
OH, IT WAS; BUT SECURITY IS NO LONGER MY MAIN INTEREST, MATTHEW.
THINK. THE NUMBER OF SUPERHUMANS ON EARTH IS GROWING EXPONENTIALLY--BUT HOW MANY OF THEM INTERACT SOCIALLY WITH NORMAL HUMANS? ALMOST NONE.
I'M INTERESTED TO SEE WHAT HAPPENS WHEN THEY DEAL WITH REGULAR PEOPLE.
WILL IT BE LIKE THROWING A HAND GRENADE INTO THE CROWD?
OR WILL IT BE LIKE SHOWING A HERD OF SHEEP THEIR SHEPHERDS?

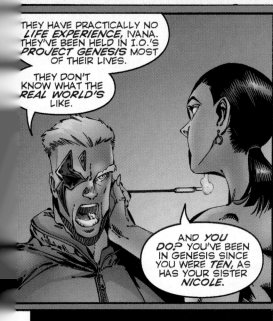

THEY HAVE PRACTICALLY NO *LIFE EXPERIENCE*, IVANA. THEY'VE BEEN HELD IN I.O.'S *PROJECT GENESIS* MOST OF THEIR LIVES.

THEY DON'T KNOW WHAT THE *REAL WORLD'S* LIKE.

AND *YOU* DO? YOU'VE BEEN IN GENESIS SINCE YOU WERE *TEN*, AS HAS YOUR SISTER *NICOLE.*

THAT'S *DIFFERENT.* I'M *OLDER* THAN THEM. I *KNOW* I'M SUPERIOR TO THE OUTSIDE WORLD.

Hm. WELL, WE'LL SEE, WON'T WE? I THINK IT'LL BE A *FASCINATING* EXPERIMENT.

MAYBE ONE OF THEM WILL *KILL* SOMEBODY. *THAT'D* BE INTERESTING.

HI. LOOK WHAT I FOUND AT THE *NIGHTCLUB* AROUND THE CORNER.

NICOLE, YOU'RE *DISGUSTING.*

AND *THAT'S* WHY YOU *DREAM* OF ME, BIG BROTHER. WE'LL BE IN MY SUITE...

AND THAT'S JUST *NICOLE.* SHE'S *PREDICTABLE.*

GOD *KNOWS* WHAT THE *REST* OF THEM ARE UP TO...

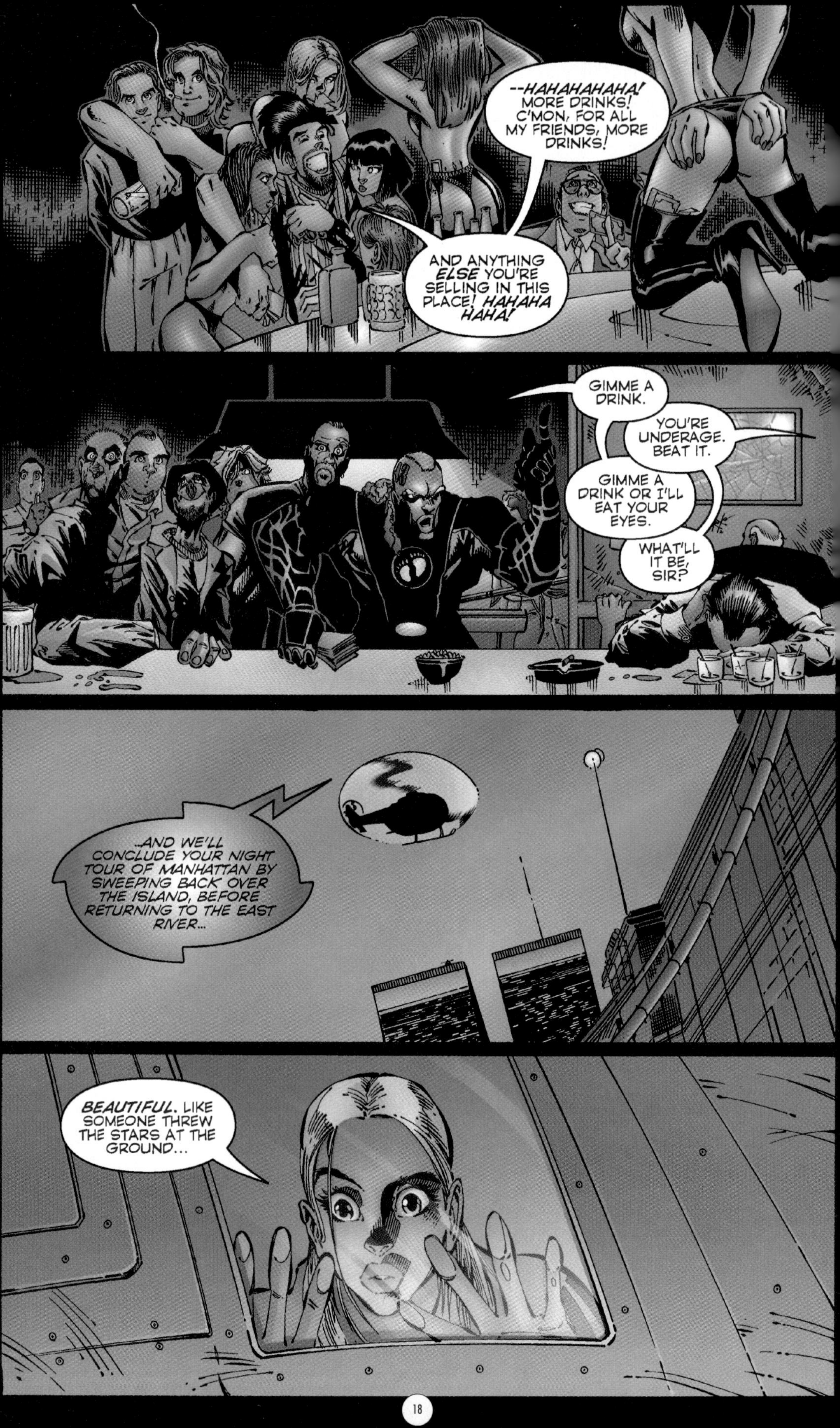
--HAHAHAHAHA! MORE DRINKS! C'MON, FOR ALL MY FRIENDS, MORE DRINKS!
AND ANYTHING ELSE YOU'RE SELLING IN THIS PLACE! HAHAHA HAHA!
GIMME A DRINK.
YOU'RE UNDERAGE. BEAT IT.
GIMME A DRINK OR I'LL EAT YOUR EYES.
WHAT'LL IT BE, SIR?
...AND WE'LL CONCLUDE YOUR NIGHT TOUR OF MANHATTAN BY SWEEPING BACK OVER THE ISLAND, BEFORE RETURNING TO THE EAST RIVER...
BEAUTIFUL. LIKE SOMEONE THREW THE STARS AT THE GROUND...

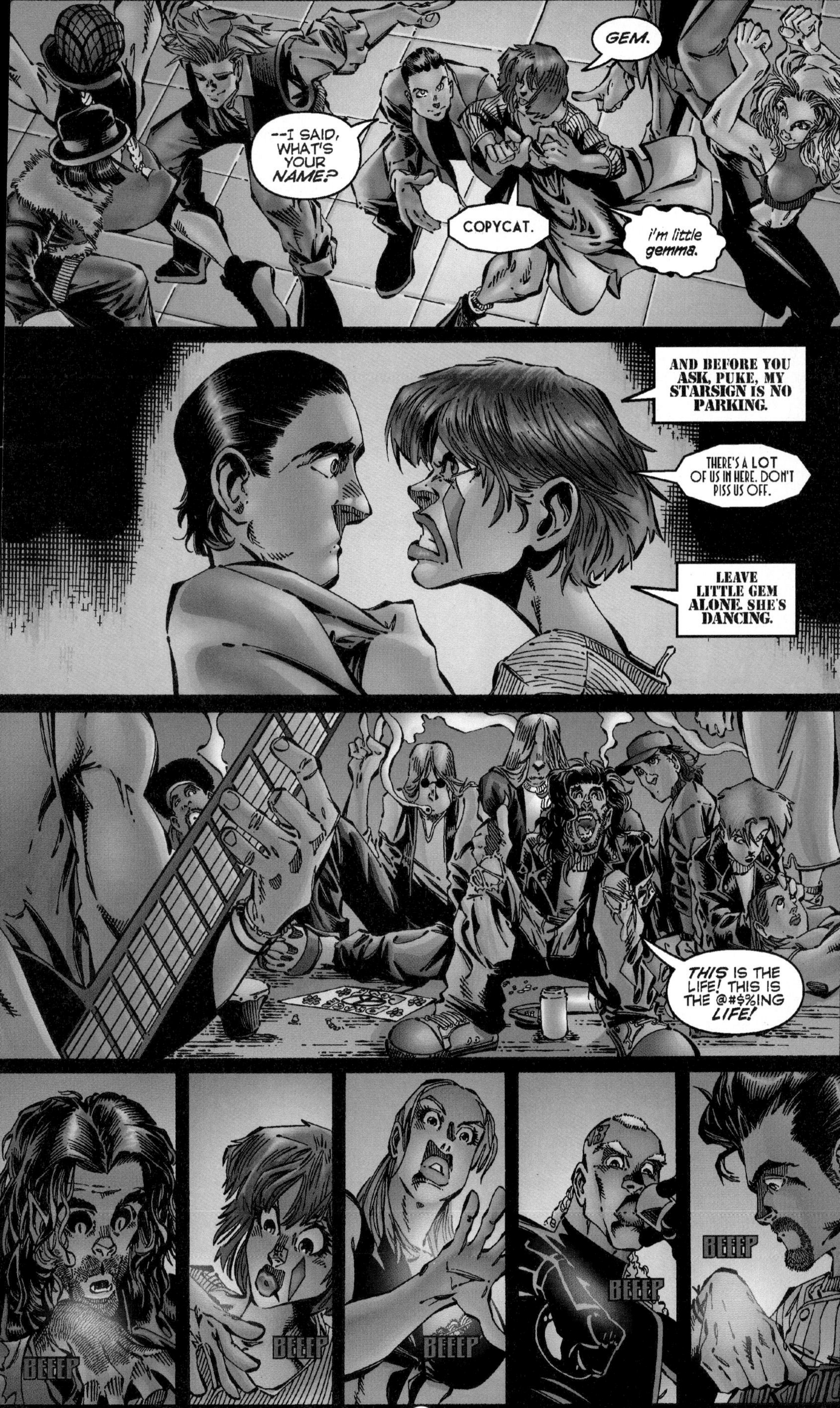
--I SAID, WHAT'S YOUR NAME?
GEM.
COPYCAT.
i'm little gemma.
AND BEFORE YOU ASK, PUKE, MY STARSIGN IS NO PARKING.
THERE'S A LOT OF US IN HERE. DON'T PISS US OFF.
LEAVE LITTLE GEM ALONE. SHE'S DANCING.
THIS IS THE LIFE! THIS IS THE @#$%ING LIFE!
BEEEP
BEEEP
BEEEP
BEEEP
BEEEP

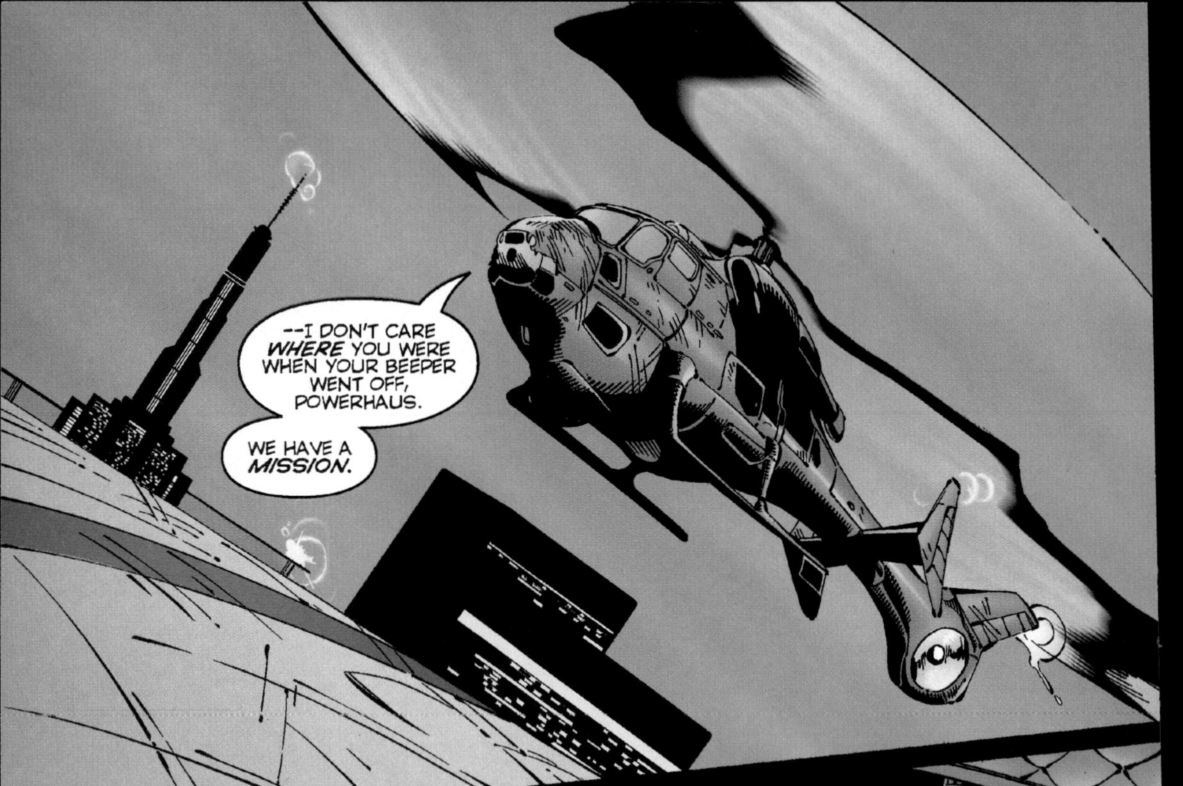
--I DON'T CARE *WHERE* YOU WERE WHEN YOUR BEEPER WENT OFF, POWERHAUS.
WE HAVE A *MISSION.*

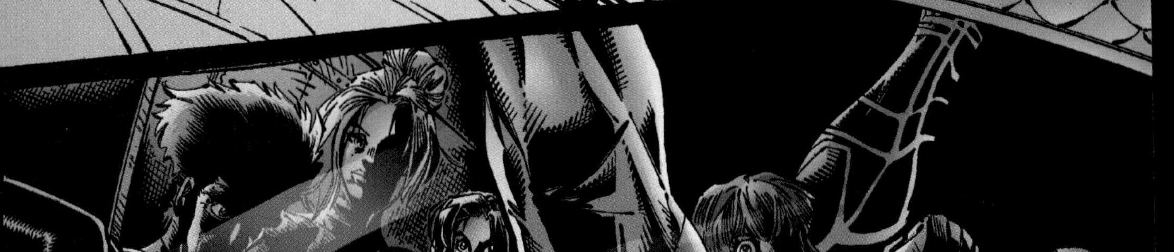
WHILE YOU WERE OUT, *IVANA* LEARNED OF A SITUATION IN *UPSTATE* NEW YORK.
WE ARE PROGRESSING DIRECTLY TO A *C.I.A. SAFEHOUSE* IN THAT AREA. THEY *HAVE* SOMETHING IVANA *WANTS.*
BEFORE THE *COMPLAINTS* START: YOU WERE INTENDED FOR USE AS A *SPOILER FORCE* AGAINST *OTHER INTELLIGENCE AGENCIES.* THIS IS WHAT YOU SIGNED *UP* FOR, CHILDREN.

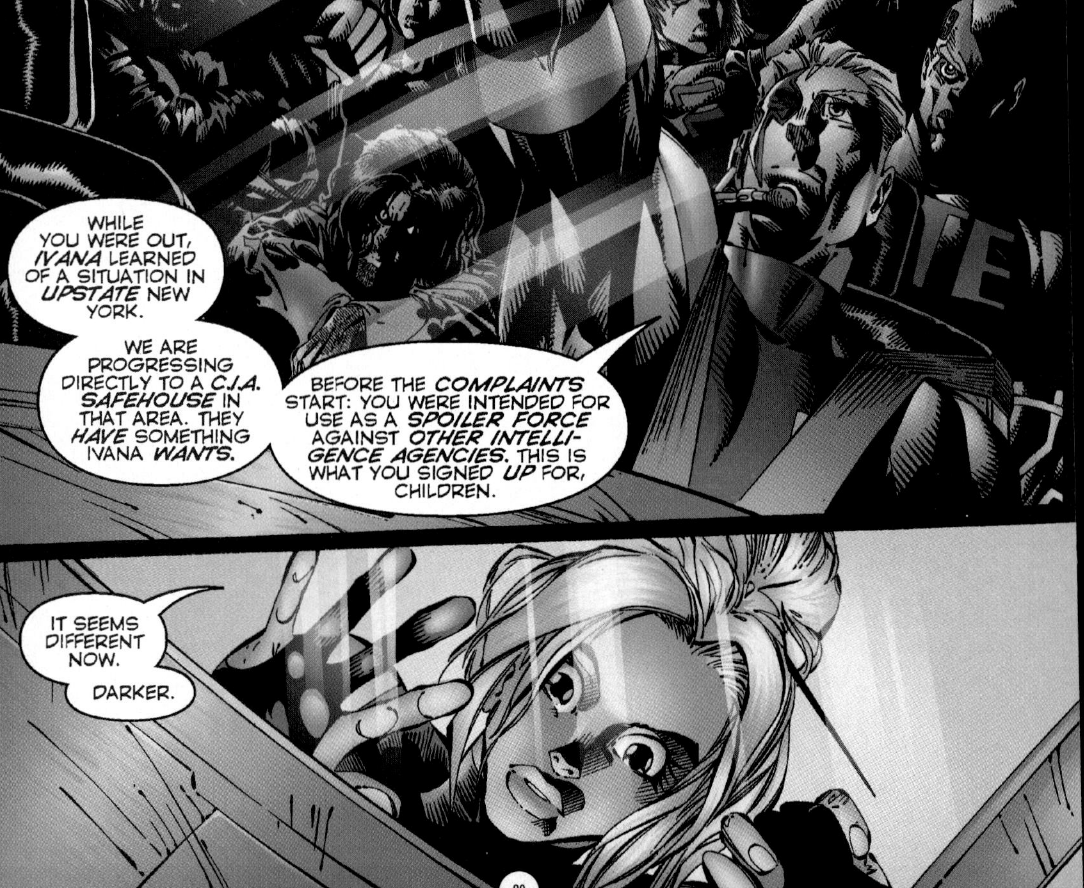
IT SEEMS DIFFERENT NOW.
DARKER.

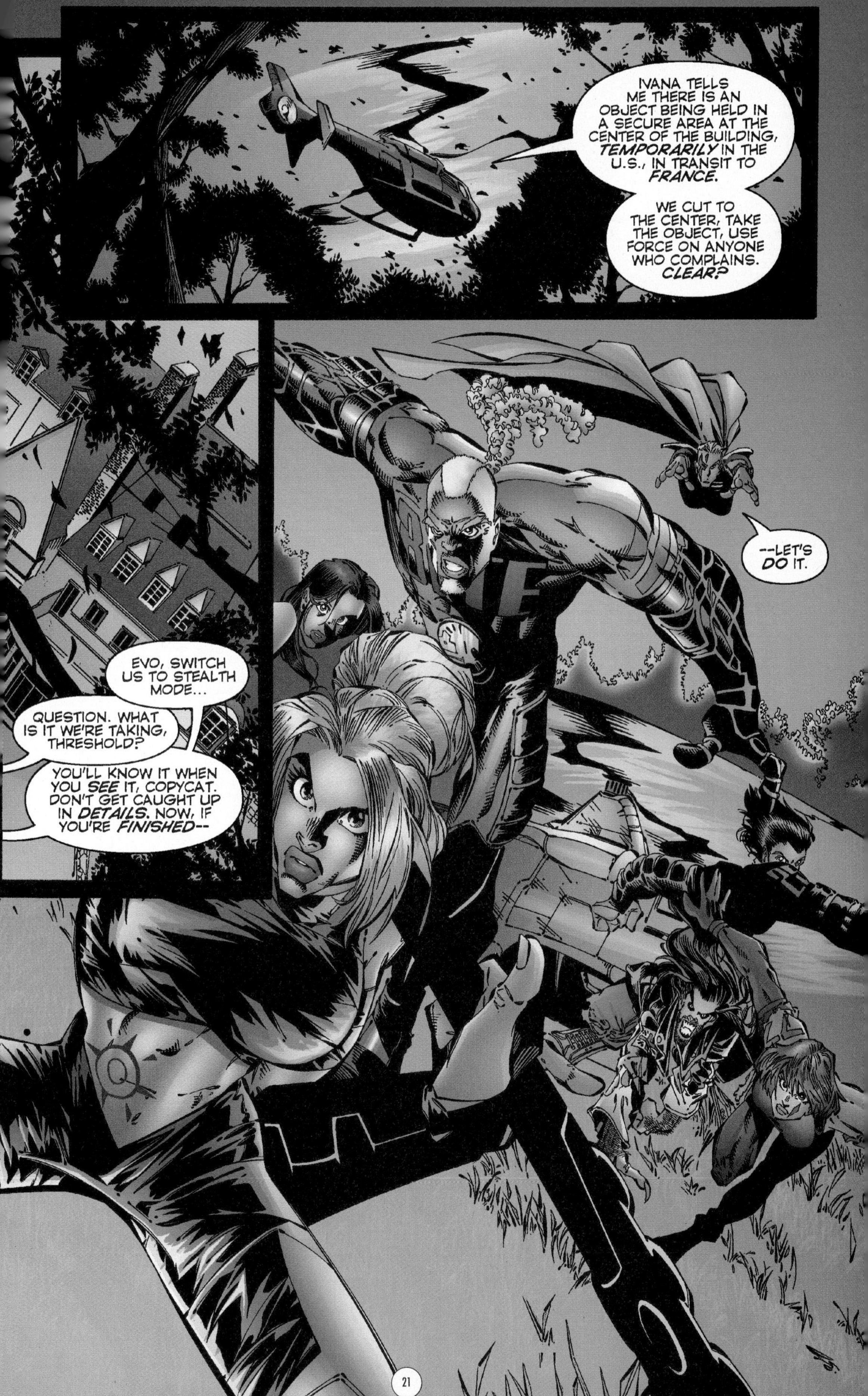
IVANA TELLS ME THERE IS AN OBJECT BEING HELD IN A SECURE AREA AT THE CENTER OF THE BUILDING, TEMPORARILY IN THE U.S., IN TRANSIT TO FRANCE.
WE CUT TO THE CENTER, TAKE THE OBJECT, USE FORCE ON ANYONE WHO COMPLAINS. CLEAR?
EVO, SWITCH US TO STEALTH MODE...
QUESTION. WHAT IS IT WE'RE TAKING, THRESHOLD?
YOU'LL KNOW IT WHEN YOU SEE IT, COPYCAT. DON'T GET CAUGHT UP IN DETAILS. NOW, IF YOU'RE FINISHED--
--LET'S DO IT.

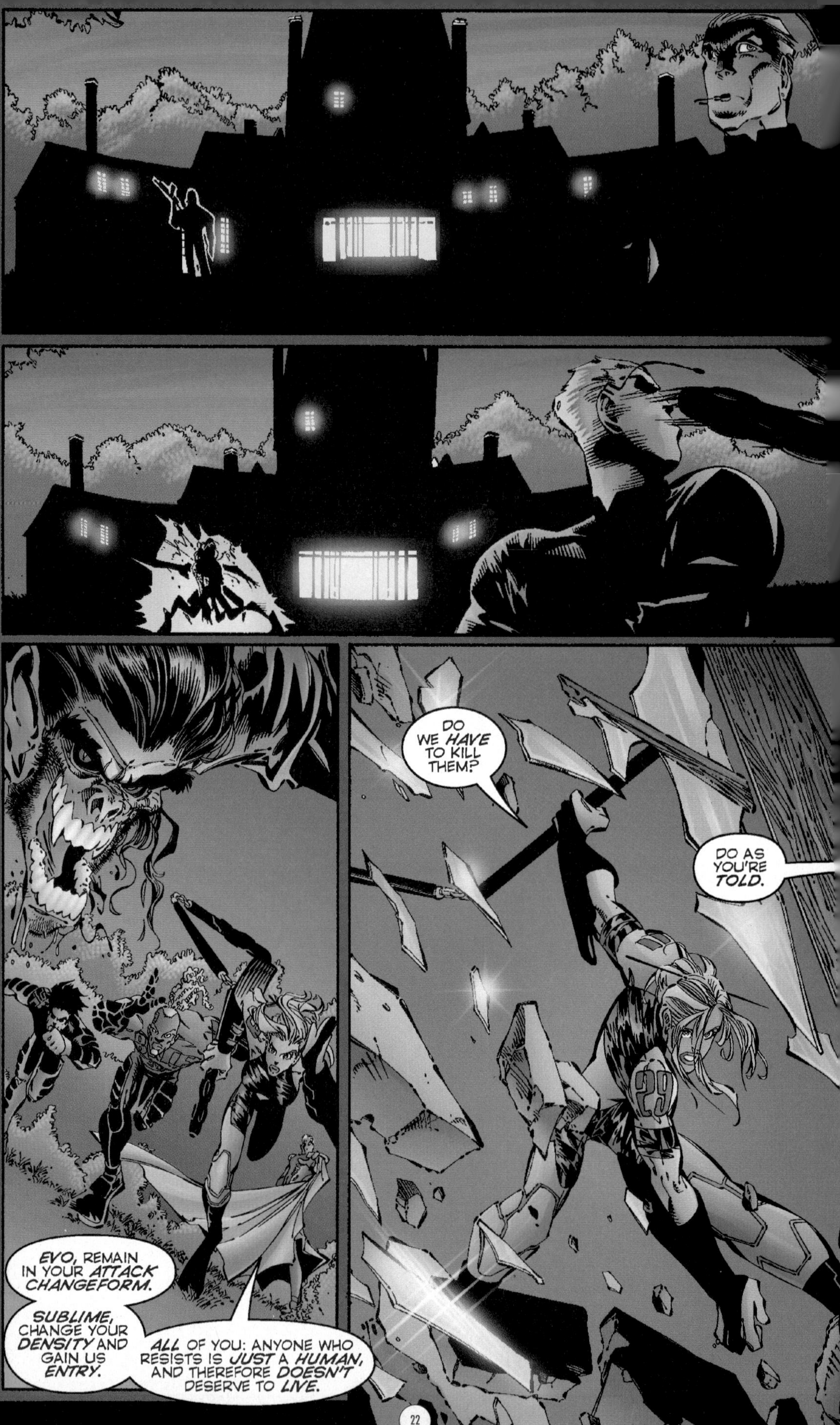
EVO, REMAIN IN YOUR ATTACK CHANGEFORM.
SUBLIME, CHANGE YOUR DENSITY AND GAIN US ENTRY.
ALL OF YOU: ANYONE WHO RESISTS IS JUST A HUMAN, AND THEREFORE DOESN'T DESERVE TO LIVE.
DO WE HAVE TO KILL THEM?
DO AS YOU'RE TOLD.

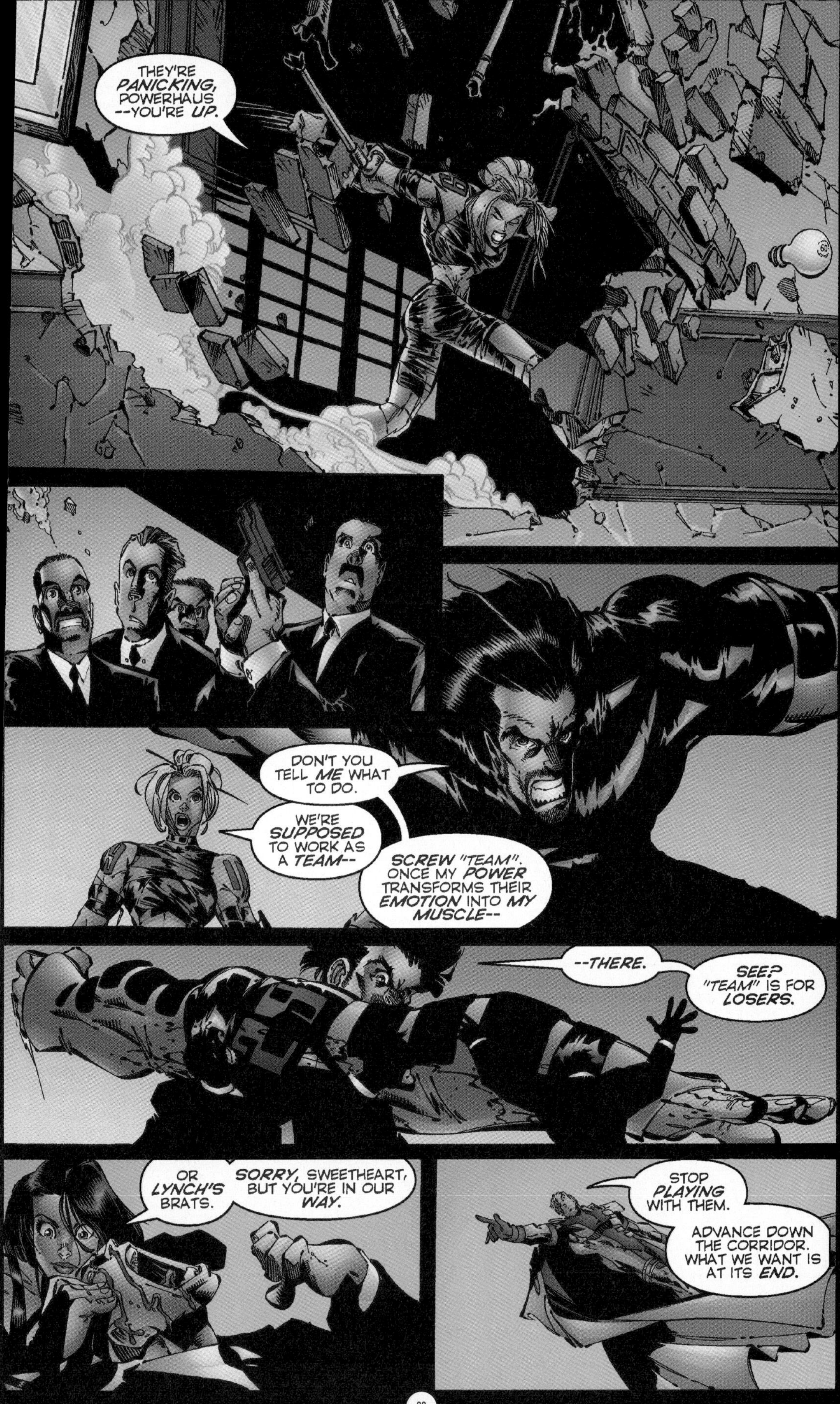
THEY'RE PANICKING, POWERHAUS --YOU'RE UP.
DON'T YOU TELL ME WHAT TO DO.
WE'RE SUPPOSED TO WORK AS A TEAM--
SCREW "TEAM". ONCE MY POWER TRANSFORMS THEIR EMOTION INTO MY MUSCLE--
--THERE.
SEE? "TEAM" IS FOR LOSERS.
OR LYNCH'S BRATS.
SORRY, SWEETHEART, BUT YOU'RE IN OUR WAY.
STOP PLAYING WITH THEM.
ADVANCE DOWN THE CORRIDOR. WHAT WE WANT IS AT ITS END.

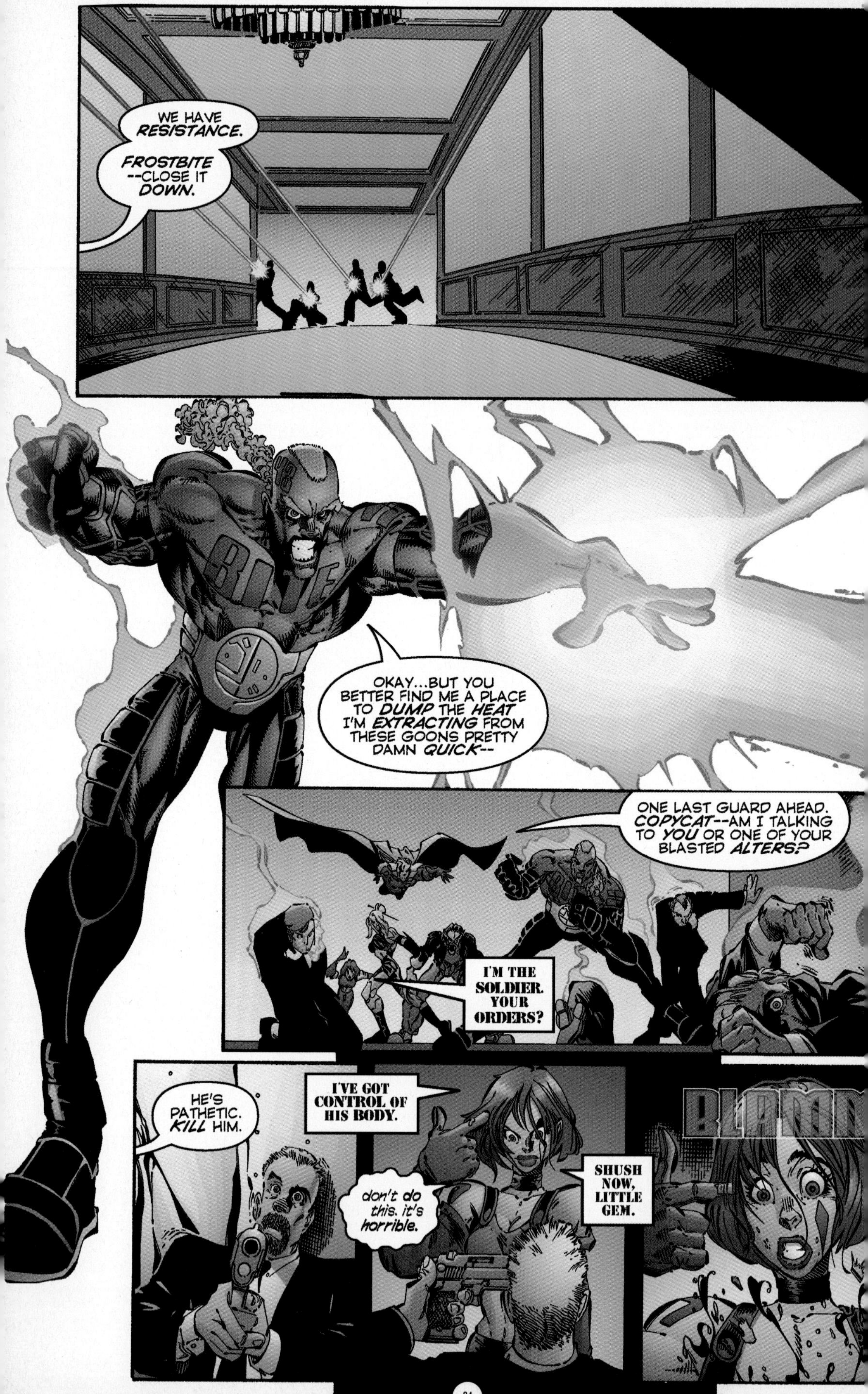
WE HAVE RESISTANCE.
FROSTBITE --CLOSE IT DOWN.
OKAY...BUT YOU BETTER FIND ME A PLACE TO DUMP THE HEAT I'M EXTRACTING FROM THESE GOONS PRETTY DAMN QUICK--
ONE LAST GUARD AHEAD. COPYCAT--AM I TALKING TO YOU OR ONE OF YOUR BLASTED ALTERS?
I'M THE SOLDIER. YOUR ORDERS?
HE'S PATHETIC. KILL HIM.
I'VE GOT CONTROL OF HIS BODY.
don't do this. it's horrible.
SHUSH NOW, LITTLE GEM.

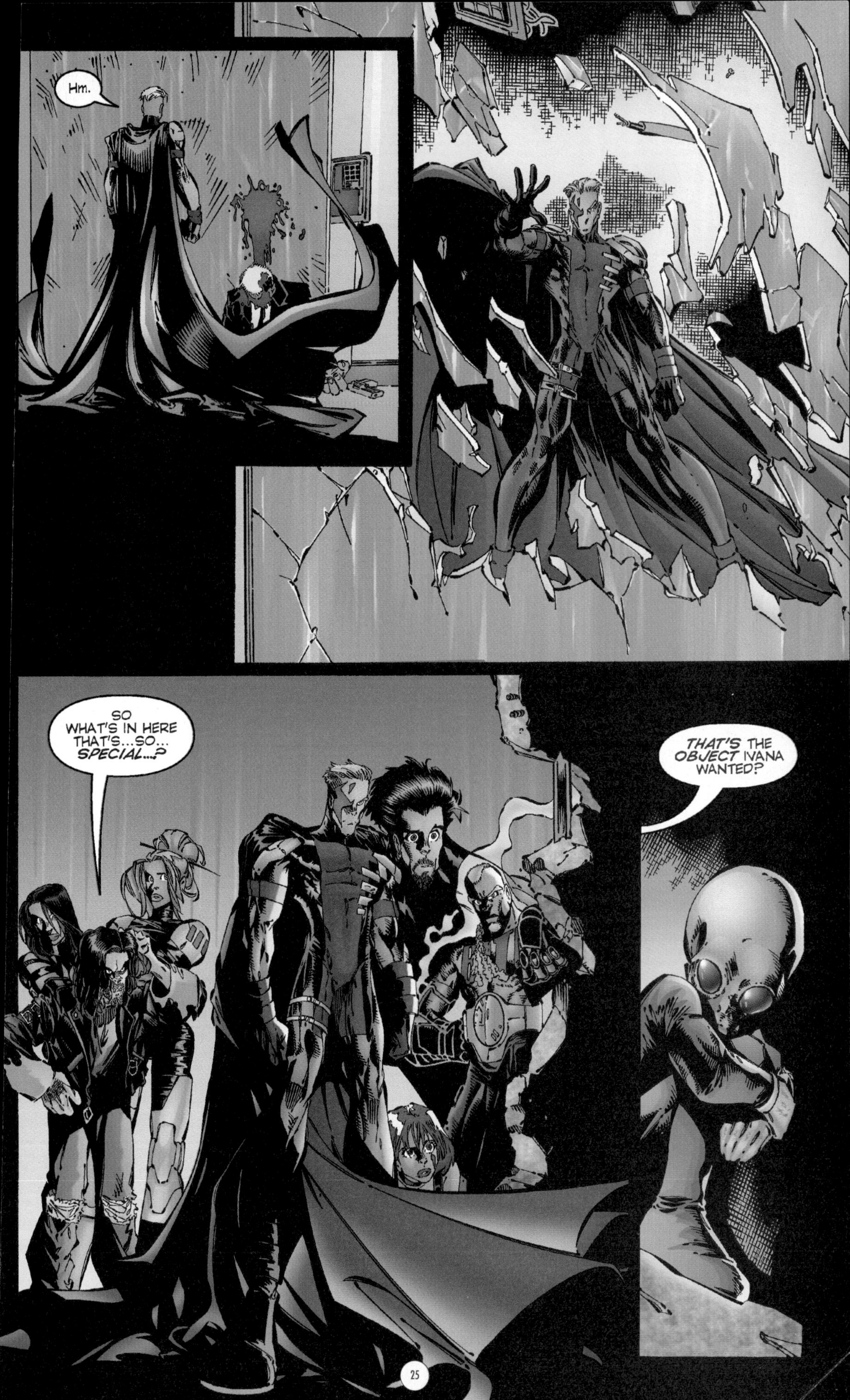
Hm.
SO WHAT'S IN HERE THAT'S...SO... SPECIAL...?
THAT'S THE OBJECT IVANA WANTED?

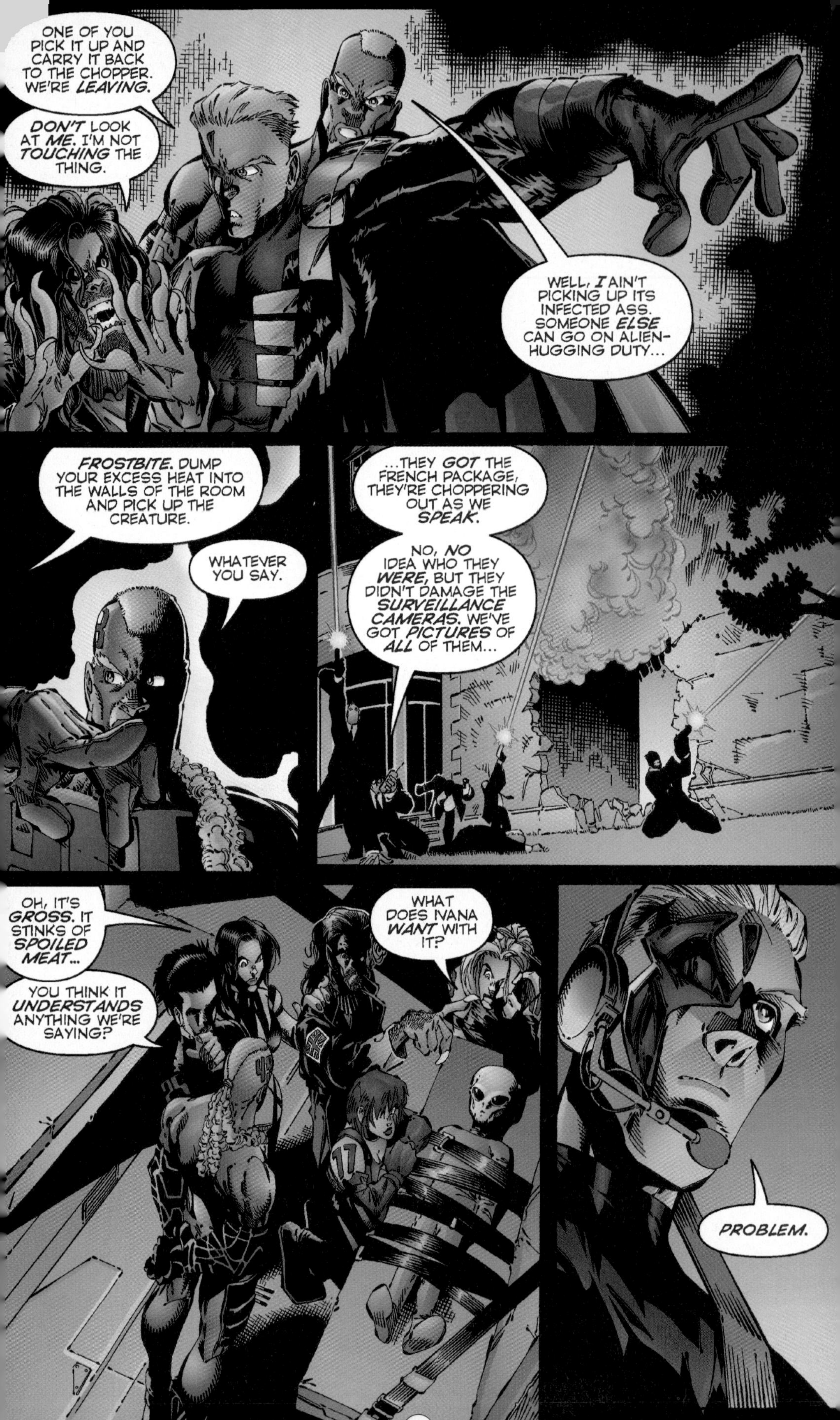
ONE OF YOU PICK IT UP AND CARRY IT BACK TO THE CHOPPER. WE'RE *LEAVING*.
DON'T LOOK AT *ME*. I'M NOT *TOUCHING* THE THING.
WELL, *I* AIN'T PICKING UP ITS INFECTED ASS. SOMEONE *ELSE* CAN GO ON ALIEN-HUGGING DUTY...
FROSTBITE. DUMP YOUR EXCESS HEAT INTO THE WALLS OF THE ROOM AND PICK UP THE CREATURE.
WHATEVER YOU SAY.
...THEY *GOT* THE FRENCH PACKAGE, THEY'RE CHOPPERING OUT AS WE *SPEAK*.
NO, *NO* IDEA WHO THEY *WERE,* BUT THEY DIDN'T DAMAGE THE *SURVEILLANCE CAMERAS.* WE'VE GOT *PICTURES* OF *ALL* OF THEM...
OH, IT'S *GROSS.* IT STINKS OF *SPOILED MEAT*...
YOU THINK IT *UNDERSTANDS* ANYTHING WE'RE SAYING?
WHAT DOES IVANA *WANT* WITH IT?
PROBLEM.

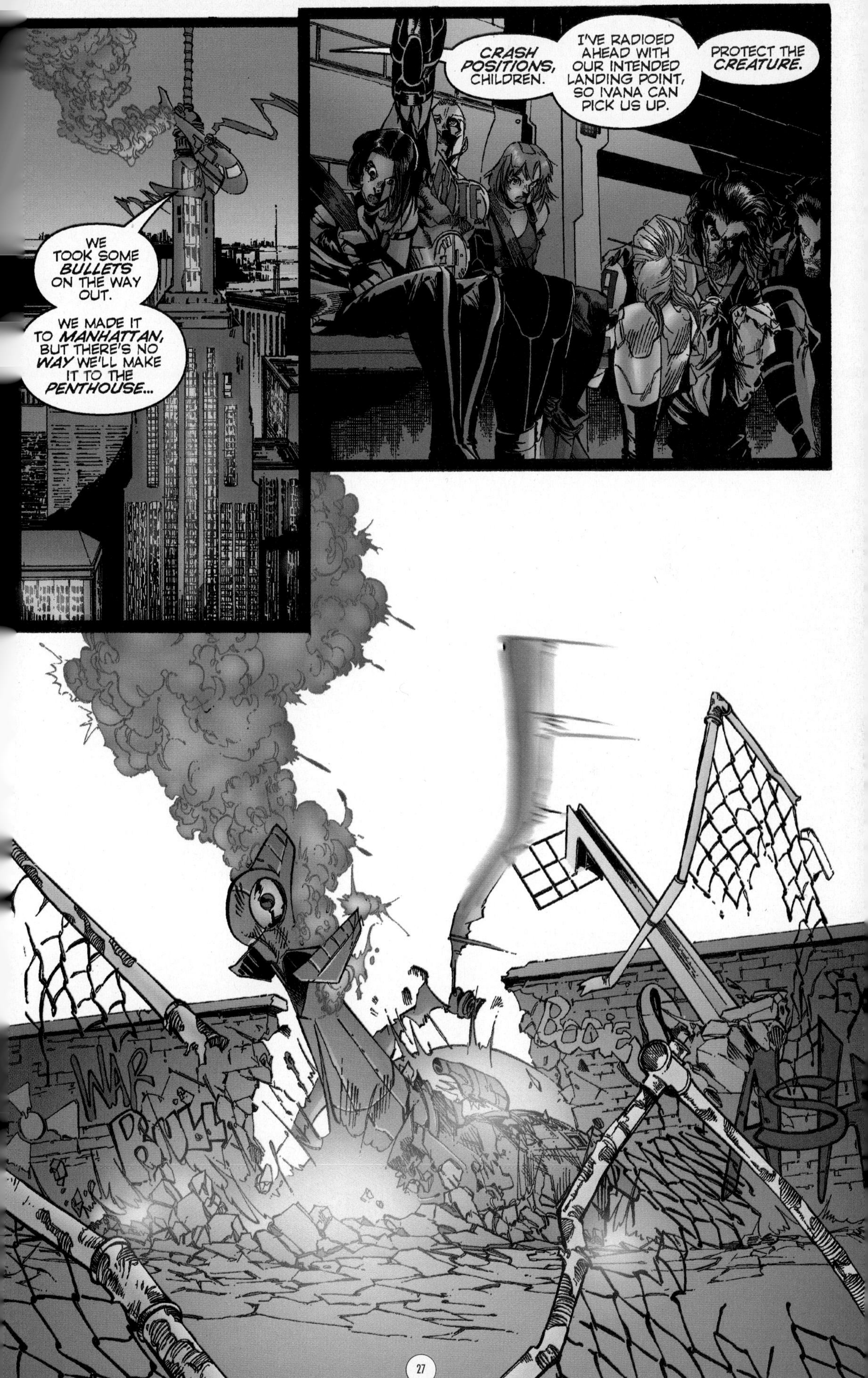
WE TOOK SOME *BULLETS* ON THE WAY OUT.
WE MADE IT TO *MANHATTAN*, BUT THERE'S NO *WAY* WE'LL MAKE IT TO THE *PENTHOUSE*...
CRASH POSITIONS, CHILDREN.
I'VE RADIOED AHEAD WITH OUR INTENDED LANDING POINT, SO IVANA CAN PICK US UP.
PROTECT THE *CREATURE*.
WAR
Booie

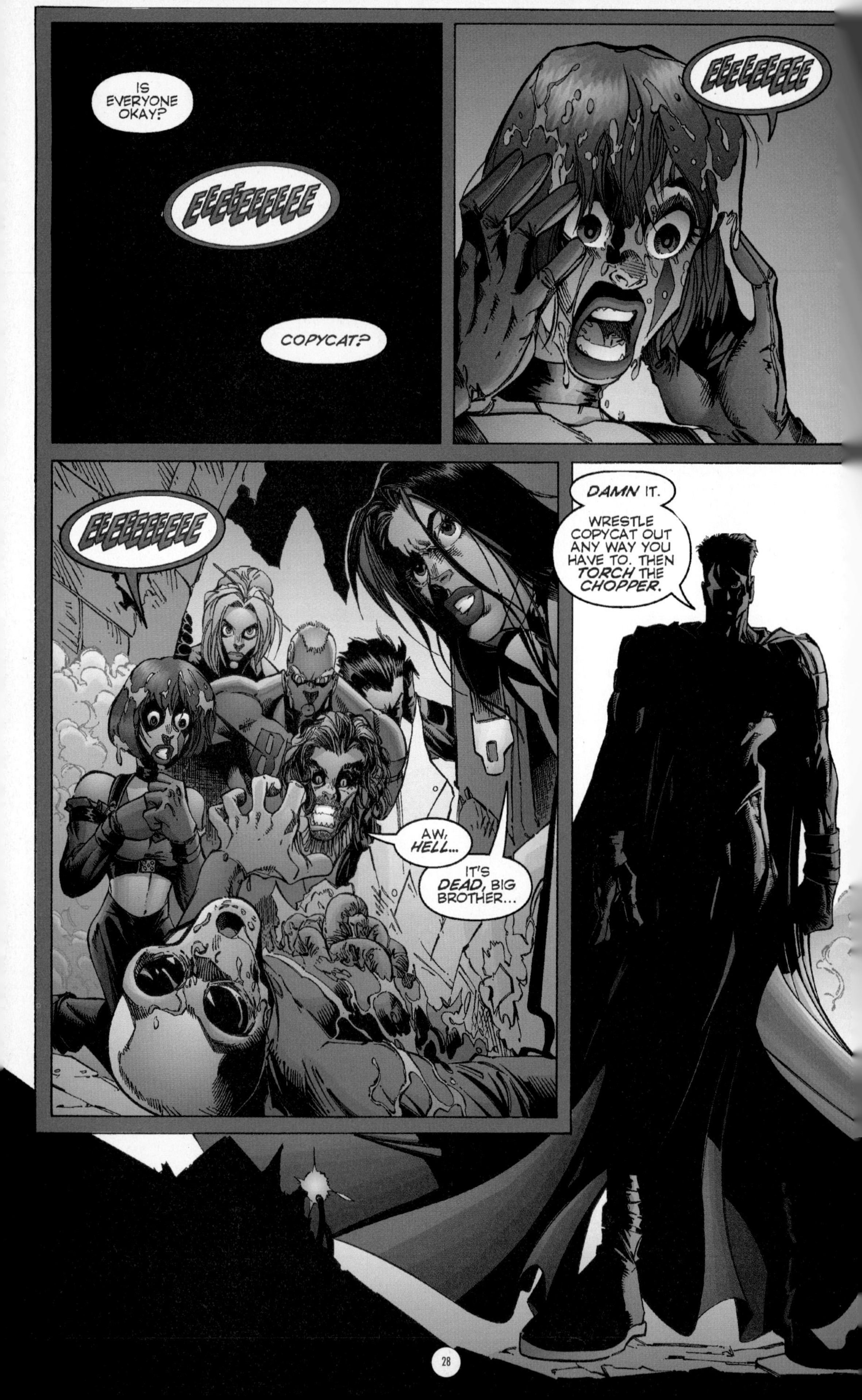
IS EVERYONE OKAY?
EEEEEEEEEE
COPYCAT?
EEEEEEEEE
EEEEEEEEEE
AW, HELL...
IT'S DEAD, BIG BROTHER...
DAMN IT.
WRESTLE COPYCAT OUT ANY WAY YOU HAVE TO. THEN TORCH THE CHOPPER.

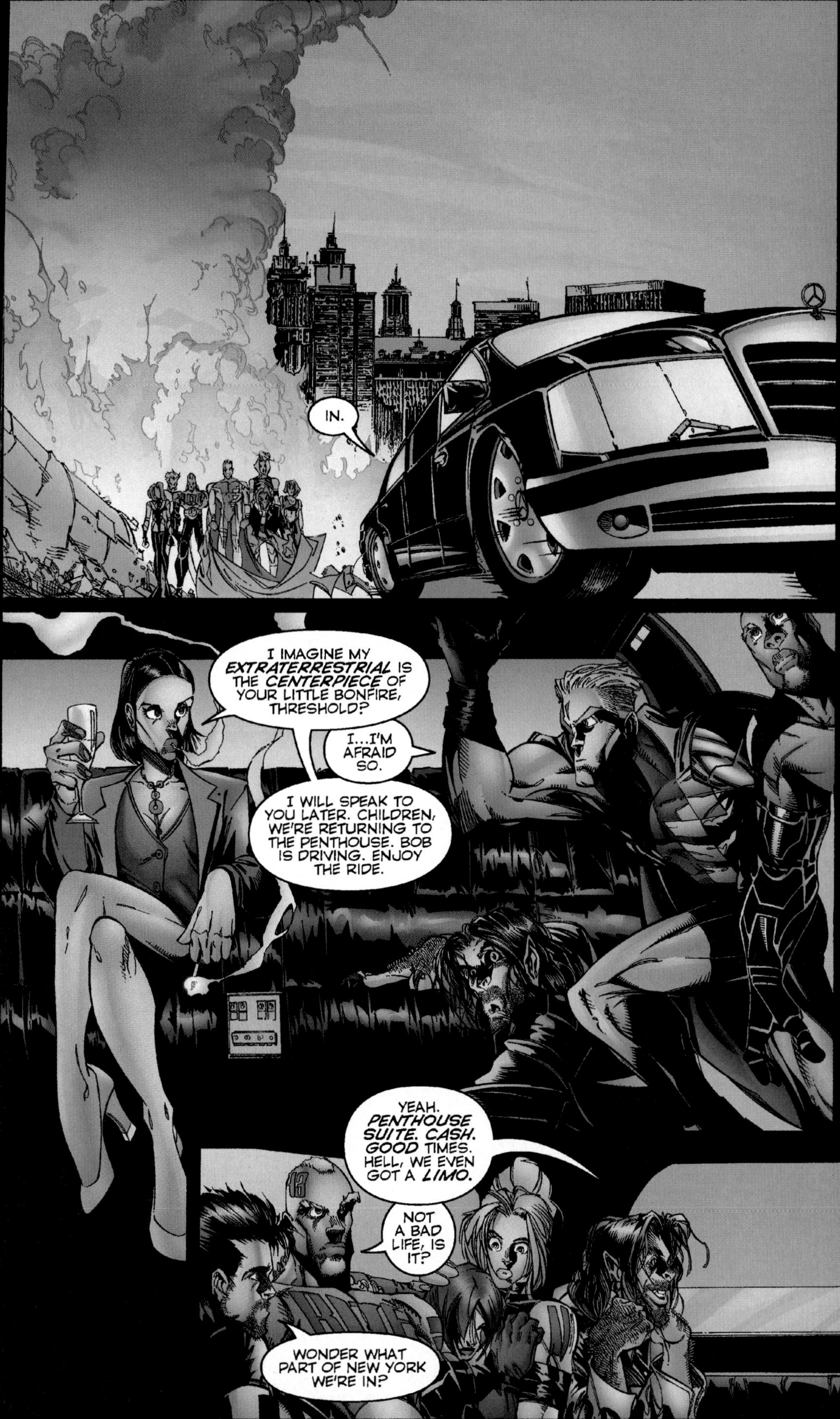
IN.
I IMAGINE MY *EXTRATERRESTRIAL* IS THE *CENTERPIECE* OF YOUR LITTLE BONFIRE, THRESHOLD?
I...I'M AFRAID SO.
I WILL SPEAK TO YOU LATER. CHILDREN, WE'RE RETURNING TO THE PENTHOUSE. BOB IS DRIVING. ENJOY THE RIDE.
YEAH. *PENTHOUSE SUITE. CASH. GOOD* TIMES. HELL, WE EVEN GOT A *LIMO.*
NOT A BAD LIFE, IS IT?
WONDER WHAT PART OF NEW YORK WE'RE IN?

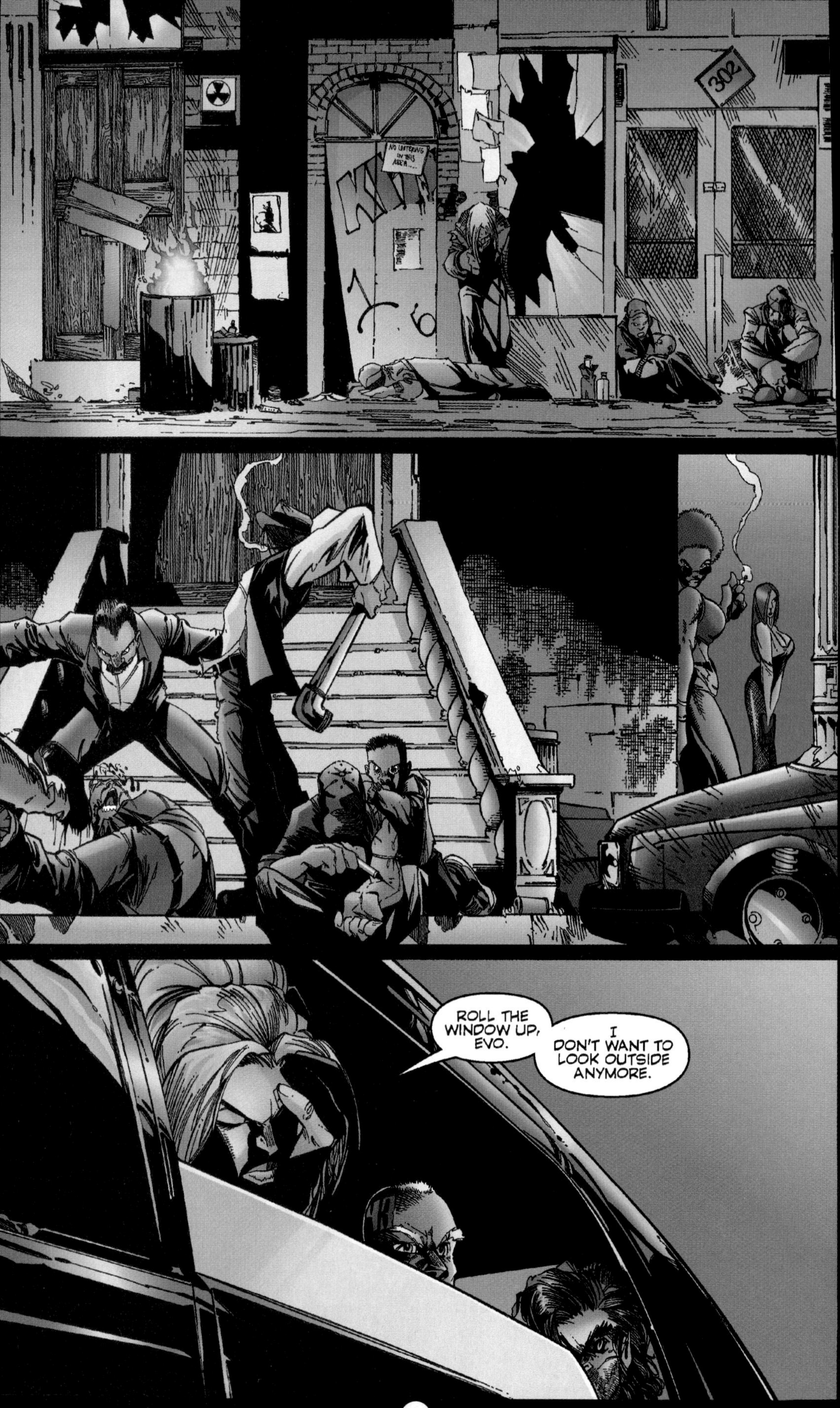
302
ROLL THE WINDOW UP, EVO.
I DON'T WANT TO LOOK OUTSIDE ANYMORE.

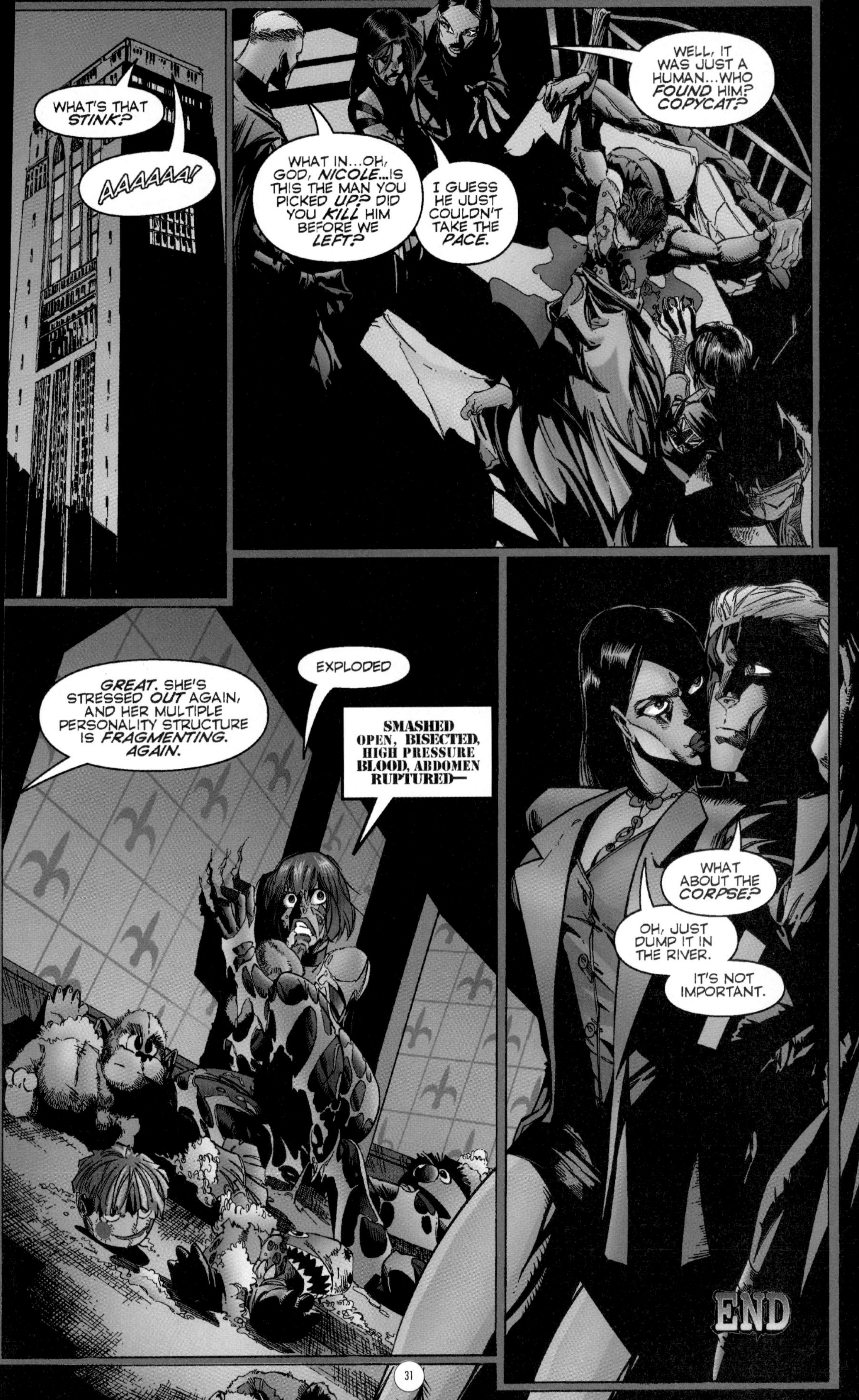
WHAT'S THAT STINK?
AAAAAA!
WHAT IN...OH, GOD, NICOLE...IS THIS THE MAN YOU PICKED UP? DID YOU KILL HIM BEFORE WE LEFT?
I GUESS HE JUST COULDN'T TAKE THE PACE.
WELL, IT WAS JUST A HUMAN...WHO FOUND HIM? COPYCAT?
GREAT. SHE'S STRESSED OUT AGAIN, AND HER MULTIPLE PERSONALITY STRUCTURE IS FRAGMENTING. AGAIN.
EXPLODED
SMASHED OPEN, BISECTED, HIGH PRESSURE BLOOD, ABDOMEN RUPTURED—
WHAT ABOUT THE CORPSE?
OH, JUST DUMP IT IN THE RIVER.
IT'S NOT IMPORTANT.
END

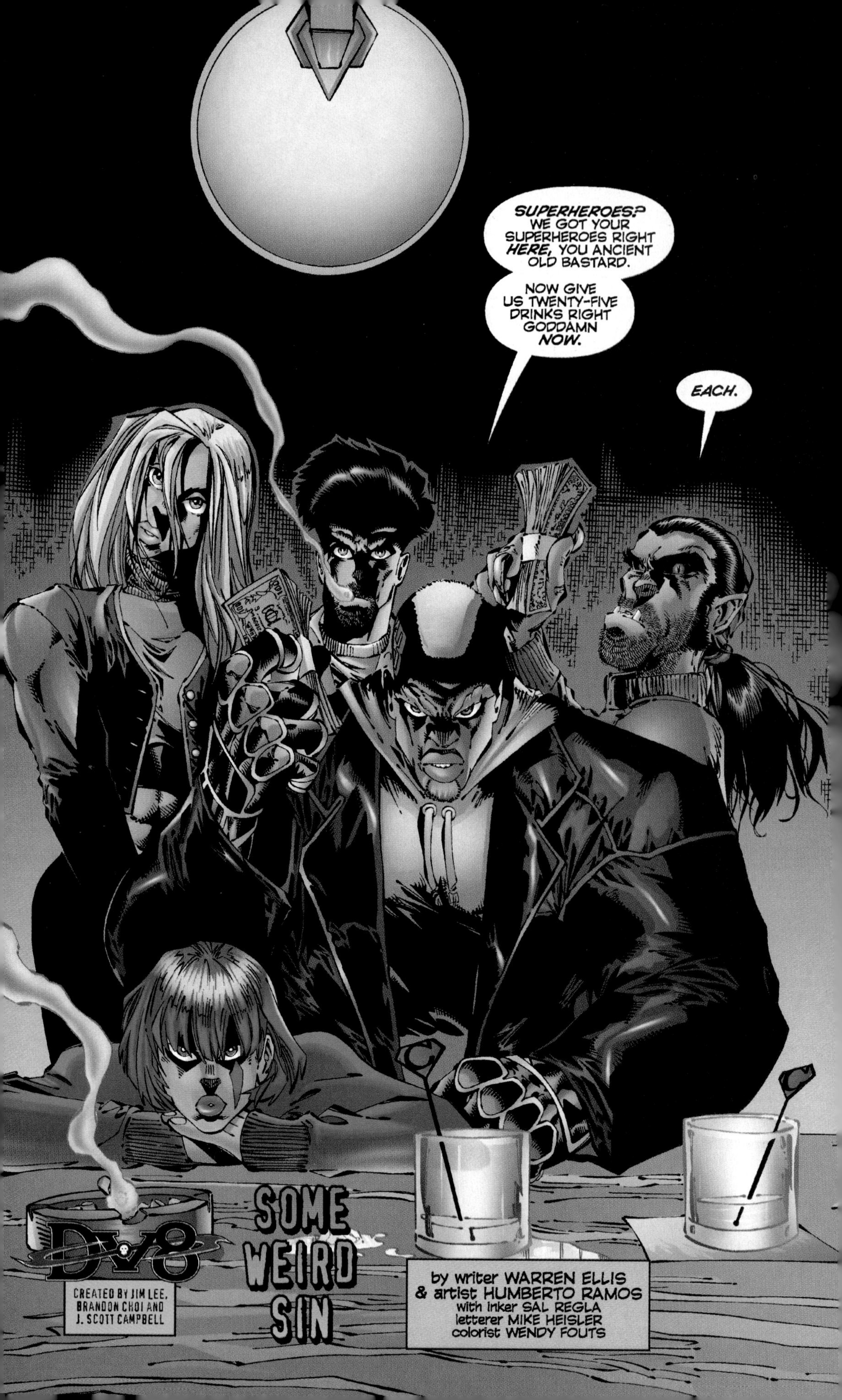

SUPERHEROES? WE GOT YOUR SUPERHEROES RIGHT HERE, YOU ANCIENT OLD BASTARD.
NOW GIVE US TWENTY-FIVE DRINKS RIGHT GODDAMN NOW.
EACH.
DV8
CREATED BY JIM LEE, BRANDON CHOI AND J. SCOTT CAMPBELL
SOME WEIRD SIN
by writer WARREN ELLIS & artist HUMBERTO RAMOS with inker SAL REGLA letterer MIKE HEISLER colorist WENDY FOUTS

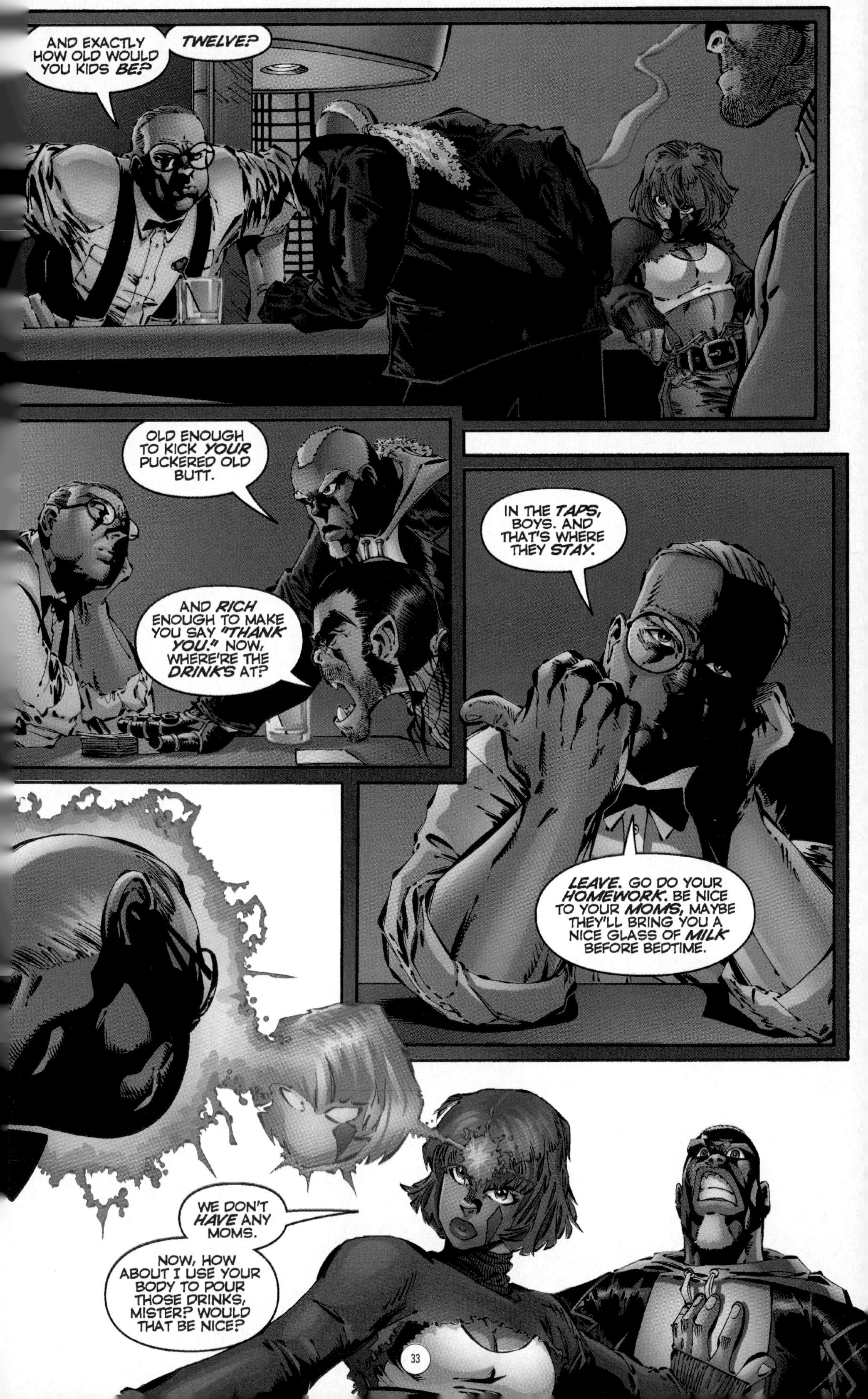
AND EXACTLY HOW OLD WOULD YOU KIDS BE?
TWELVE?
OLD ENOUGH TO KICK YOUR PUCKERED OLD BUTT.
AND RICH ENOUGH TO MAKE YOU SAY "THANK YOU." NOW, WHERE'RE THE DRINKS AT?
IN THE TAPS, BOYS. AND THAT'S WHERE THEY STAY.
LEAVE. GO DO YOUR HOMEWORK. BE NICE TO YOUR MOMS, MAYBE THEY'LL BRING YOU A NICE GLASS OF MILK BEFORE BEDTIME.
WE DON'T HAVE ANY MOMS.
NOW, HOW ABOUT I USE YOUR BODY TO POUR THOSE DRINKS, MISTER? WOULD THAT BE NICE?

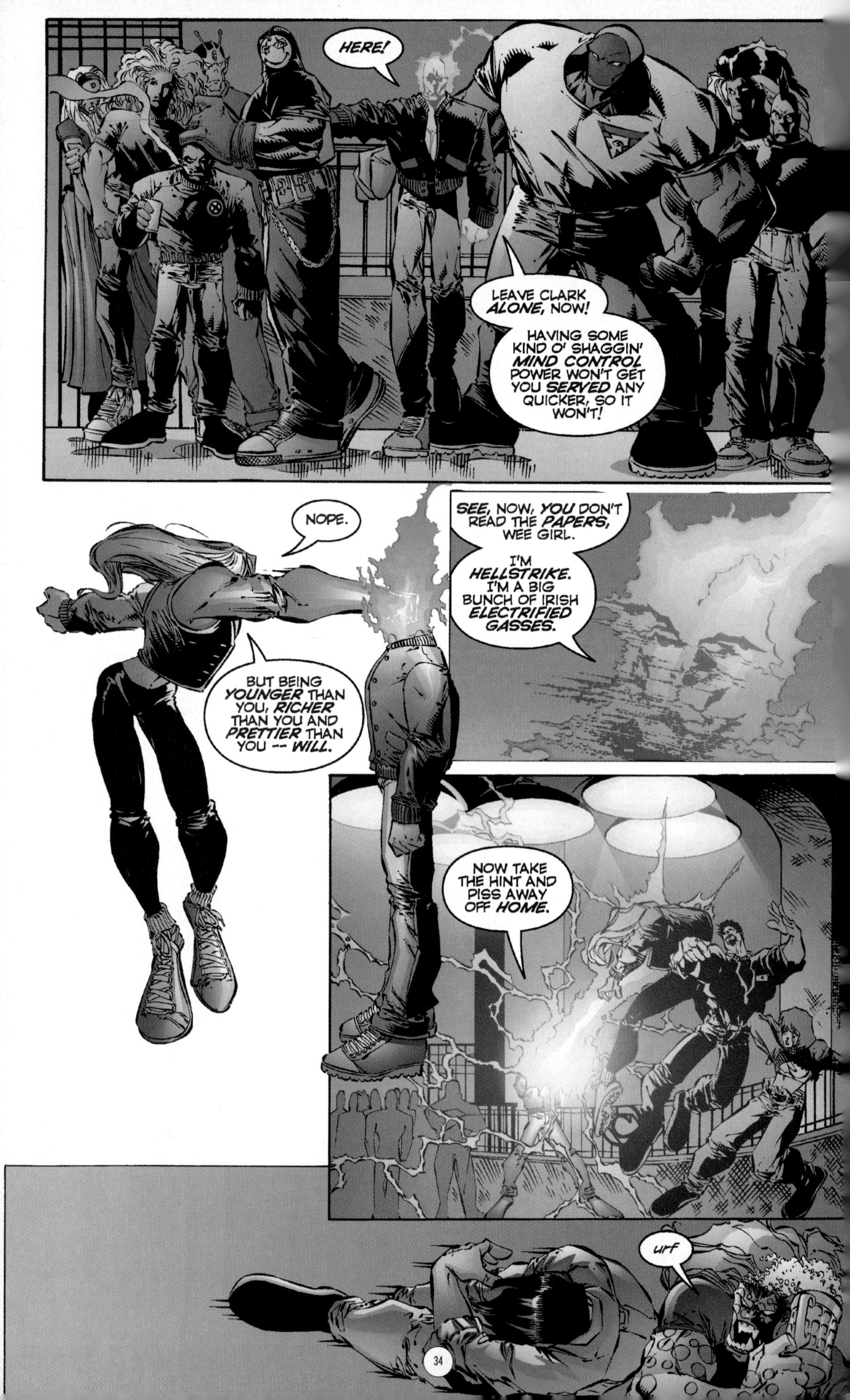
HERE!
LEAVE CLARK ALONE, NOW!
HAVING SOME KIND O' SHAGGIN' MIND CONTROL POWER WON'T GET YOU SERVED ANY QUICKER, SO IT WON'T!
NOPE.
BUT BEING YOUNGER THAN YOU, RICHER THAN YOU AND PRETTIER THAN YOU -- WILL.
SEE, NOW, YOU DON'T READ THE PAPERS, WEE GIRL.
I'M HELLSTRIKE. I'M A BIG BUNCH OF IRISH ELECTRIFIED GASSES.
NOW TAKE THE HINT AND PISS AWAY OFF HOME.
urf

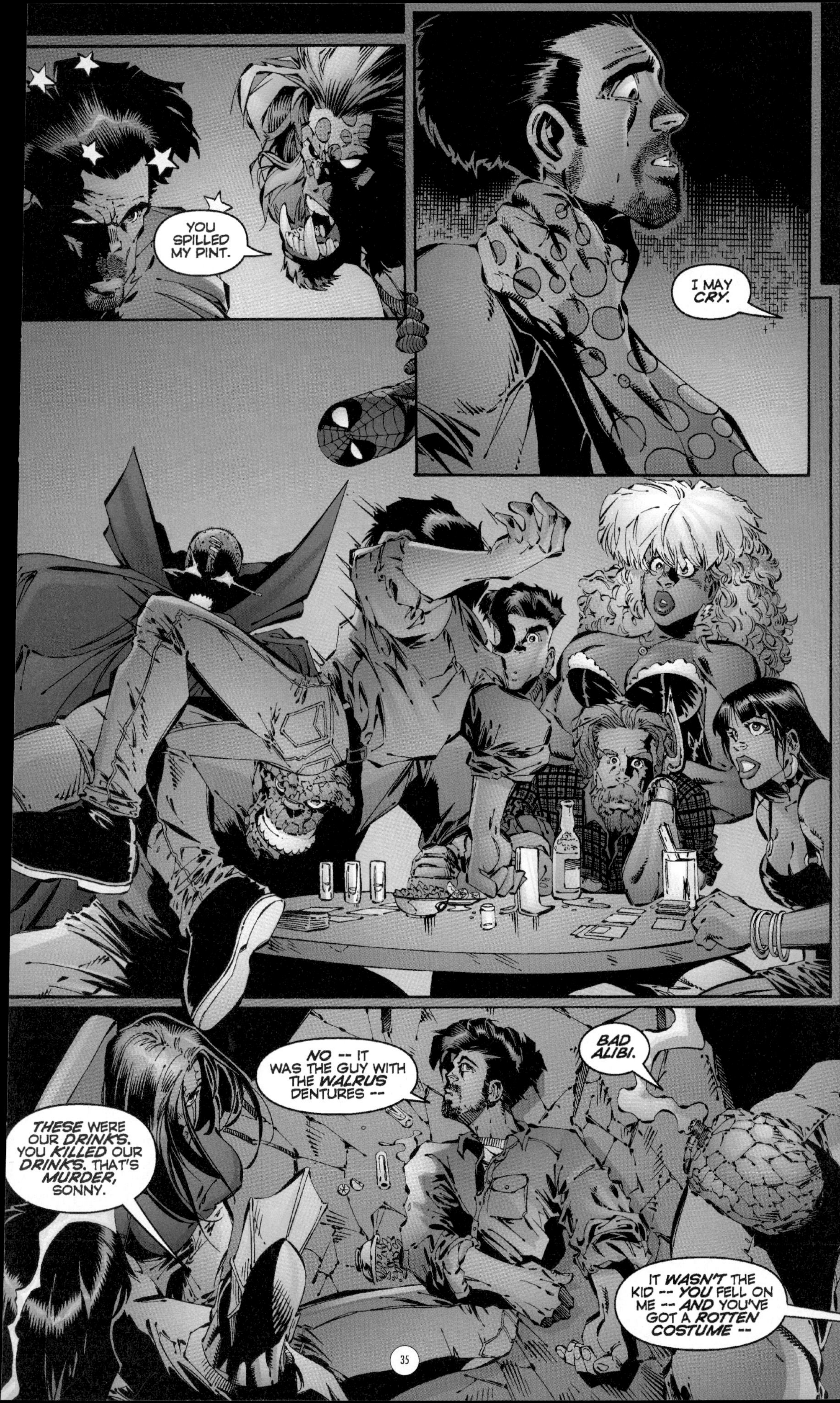
YOU SPILLED MY PINT.
I MAY CRY.
THESE WERE OUR DRINKS. YOU KILLED OUR DRINKS. THAT'S MURDER, SONNY.
NO -- IT WAS THE GUY WITH THE WALRUS DENTURES --
BAD ALIBI.
IT WASN'T THE KID -- YOU FELL ON ME -- AND YOU'VE GOT A ROTTEN COSTUME --

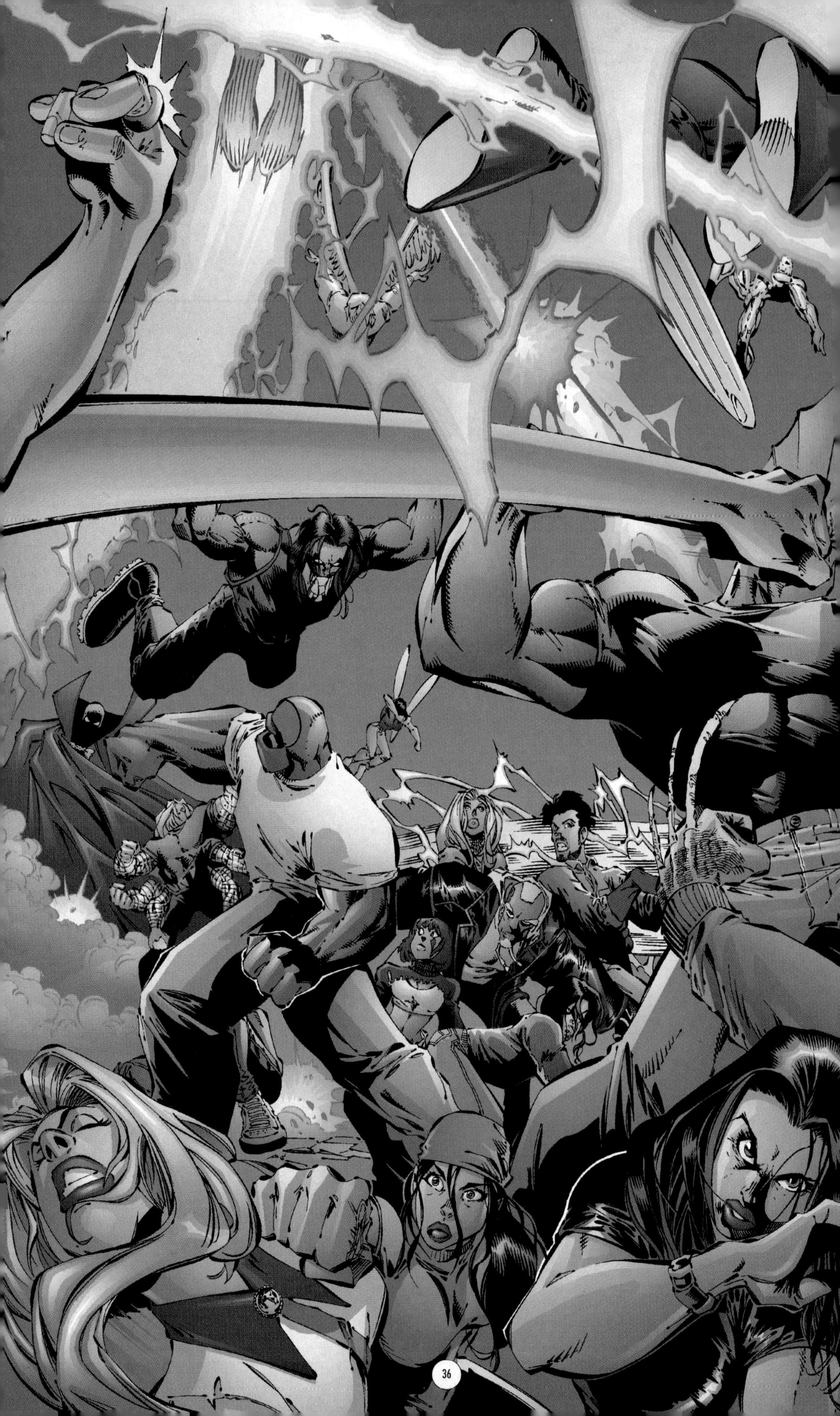

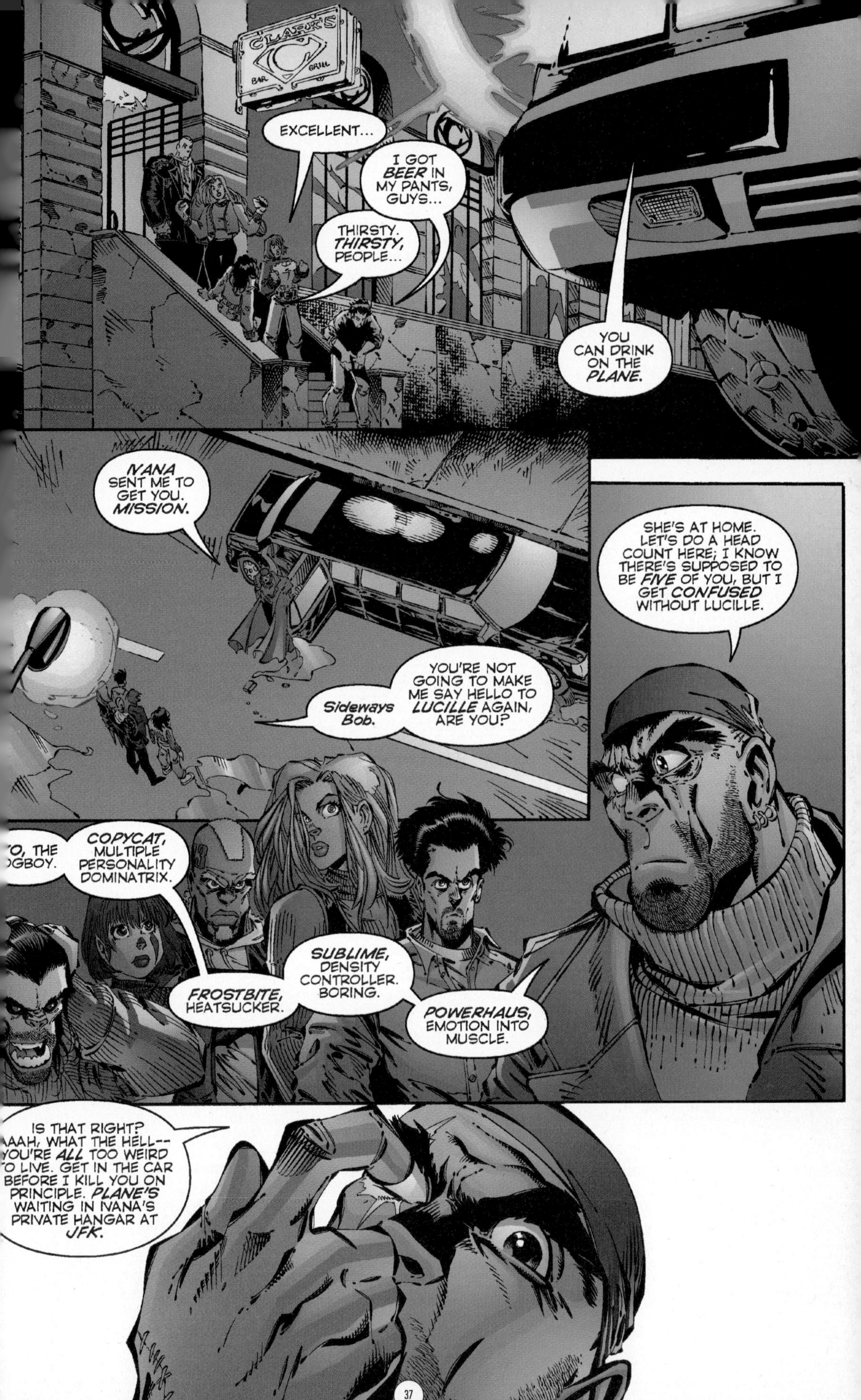

CLARK'S
BAR
GRILL
EXCELLENT...
I GOT *BEER* IN MY PANTS, GUYS...
THIRSTY. *THIRSTY,* PEOPLE...
YOU CAN DRINK ON THE *PLANE.*
IVANA SENT ME TO GET YOU. *MISSION.*
Sideways Bob.
YOU'RE NOT GOING TO MAKE ME SAY HELLO TO *LUCILLE* AGAIN, ARE YOU?
SHE'S AT HOME. LET'S DO A HEAD COUNT HERE; I KNOW THERE'S SUPPOSED TO BE *FIVE* OF YOU, BUT I GET *CONFUSED* WITHOUT LUCILLE.
O, THE OGBOY.
COPYCAT, MULTIPLE PERSONALITY DOMINATRIX.
FROSTBITE, HEATSUCKER.
SUBLIME, DENSITY CONTROLLER. BORING.
POWERHAUS, EMOTION INTO MUSCLE.
IS THAT RIGHT? AAH, WHAT THE HELL-- YOU'RE *ALL* TOO WEIRD TO LIVE. GET IN THE CAR BEFORE I KILL YOU ON PRINCIPLE. *PLANE'S* WAITING IN IVANA'S PRIVATE HANGAR AT *JFK.*

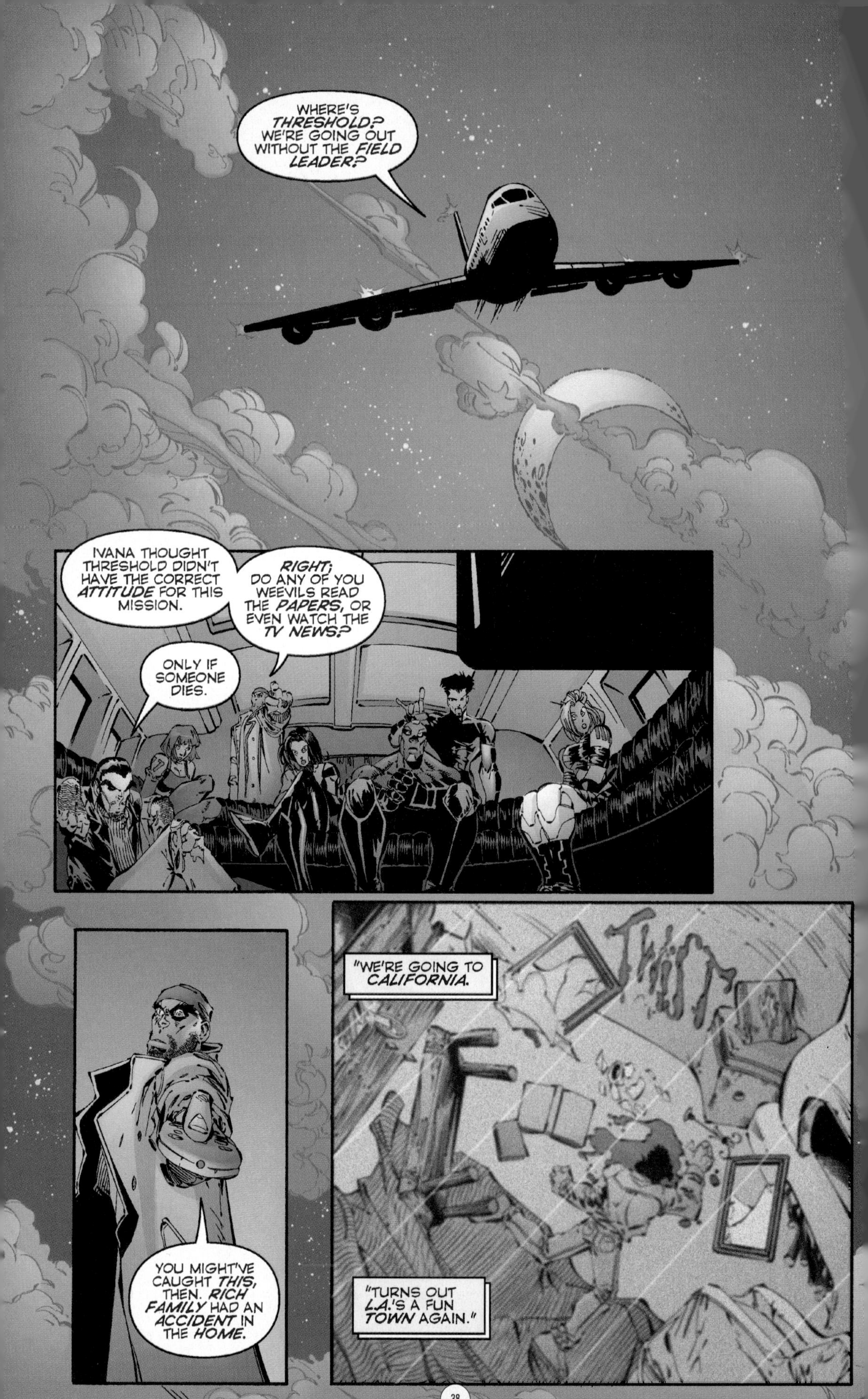
WHERE'S THRESHOLD? WE'RE GOING OUT WITHOUT THE FIELD LEADER?
IVANA THOUGHT THRESHOLD DIDN'T HAVE THE CORRECT ATTITUDE FOR THIS MISSION.
RIGHT; DO ANY OF YOU WEEVILS READ THE PAPERS, OR EVEN WATCH THE TV NEWS?
ONLY IF SOMEONE DIES.
YOU MIGHT'VE CAUGHT THIS, THEN. RICH FAMILY HAD AN ACCIDENT IN THE HOME.
"WE'RE GOING TO CALIFORNIA.
"TURNS OUT L.A.'S A FUN TOWN AGAIN."

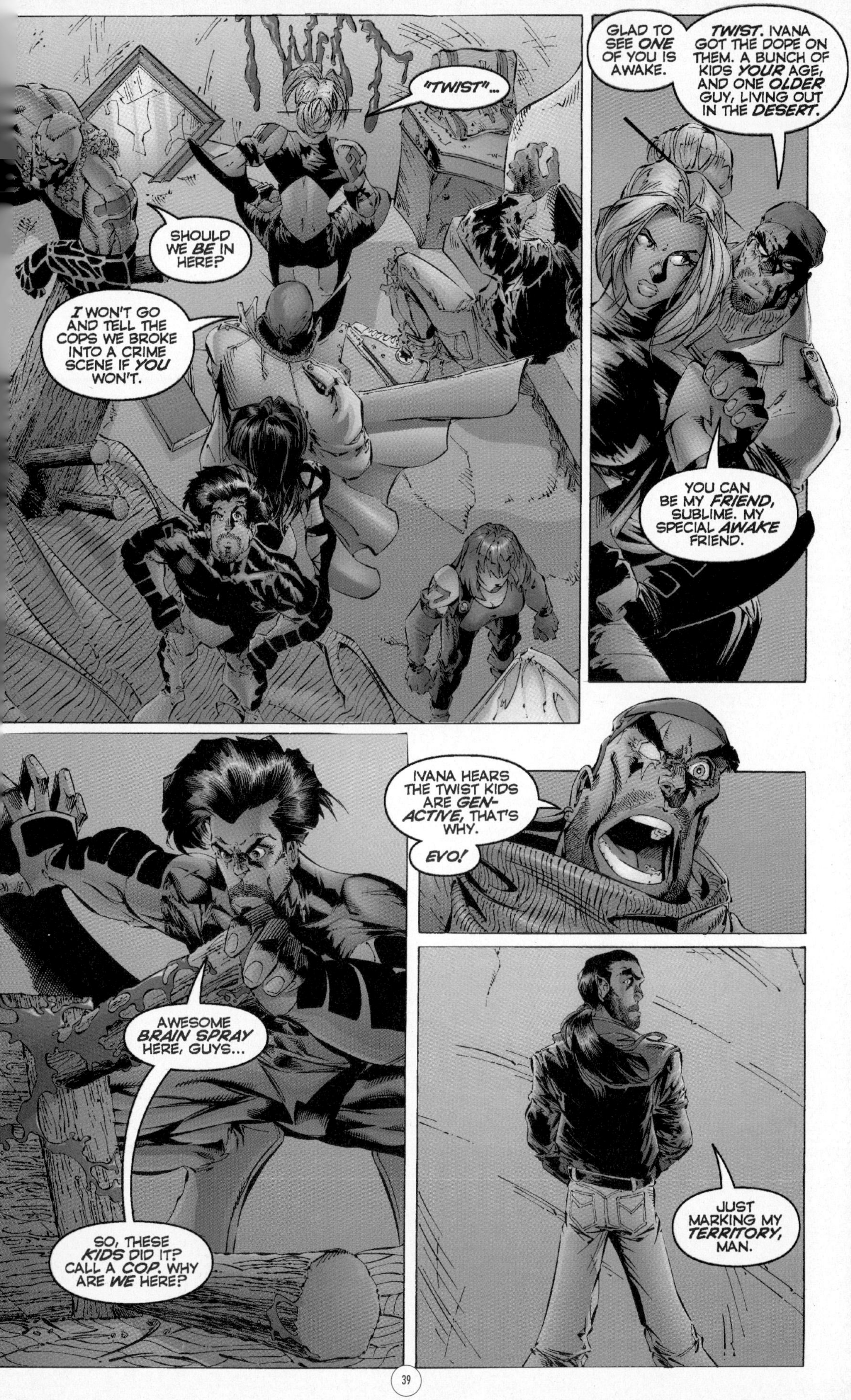
"TWIST"...
SHOULD WE BE IN HERE?
I WON'T GO AND TELL THE COPS WE BROKE INTO A CRIME SCENE IF YOU WON'T.
GLAD TO SEE ONE OF YOU IS AWAKE.
TWIST. IVANA GOT THE DOPE ON THEM. A BUNCH OF KIDS YOUR AGE, AND ONE OLDER GUY, LIVING OUT IN THE DESERT.
YOU CAN BE MY FRIEND, SUBLIME. MY SPECIAL AWAKE FRIEND.
AWESOME BRAIN SPRAY HERE, GUYS...
SO, THESE KIDS DID IT? CALL A COP. WHY ARE WE HERE?
IVANA HEARS THE TWIST KIDS ARE GEN-ACTIVE, THAT'S WHY.
EVO!
JUST MARKING MY TERRITORY, MAN.

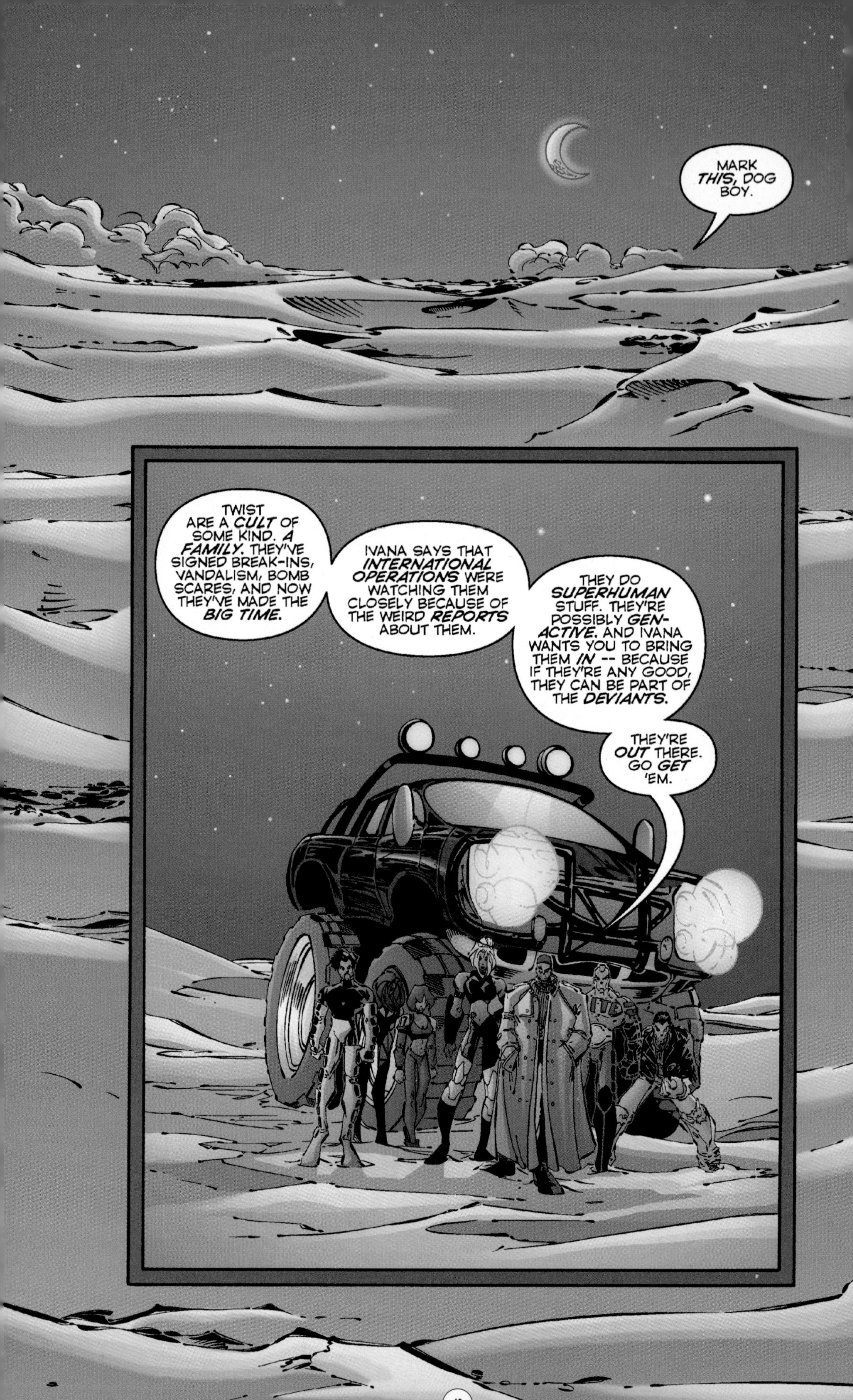
MARK THIS, DOG BOY.
TWIST ARE A CULT OF SOME KIND. A FAMILY. THEY'VE SIGNED BREAK-INS, VANDALISM, BOMB SCARES, AND NOW THEY'VE MADE THE BIG TIME.
IVANA SAYS THAT INTERNATIONAL OPERATIONS WERE WATCHING THEM CLOSELY BECAUSE OF THE WEIRD REPORTS ABOUT THEM.
THEY DO SUPERHUMAN STUFF. THEY'RE POSSIBLY GEN-ACTIVE. AND IVANA WANTS YOU TO BRING THEM IN -- BECAUSE IF THEY'RE ANY GOOD, THEY CAN BE PART OF THE DEVIANTS.
THEY'RE OUT THERE. GO GET 'EM.

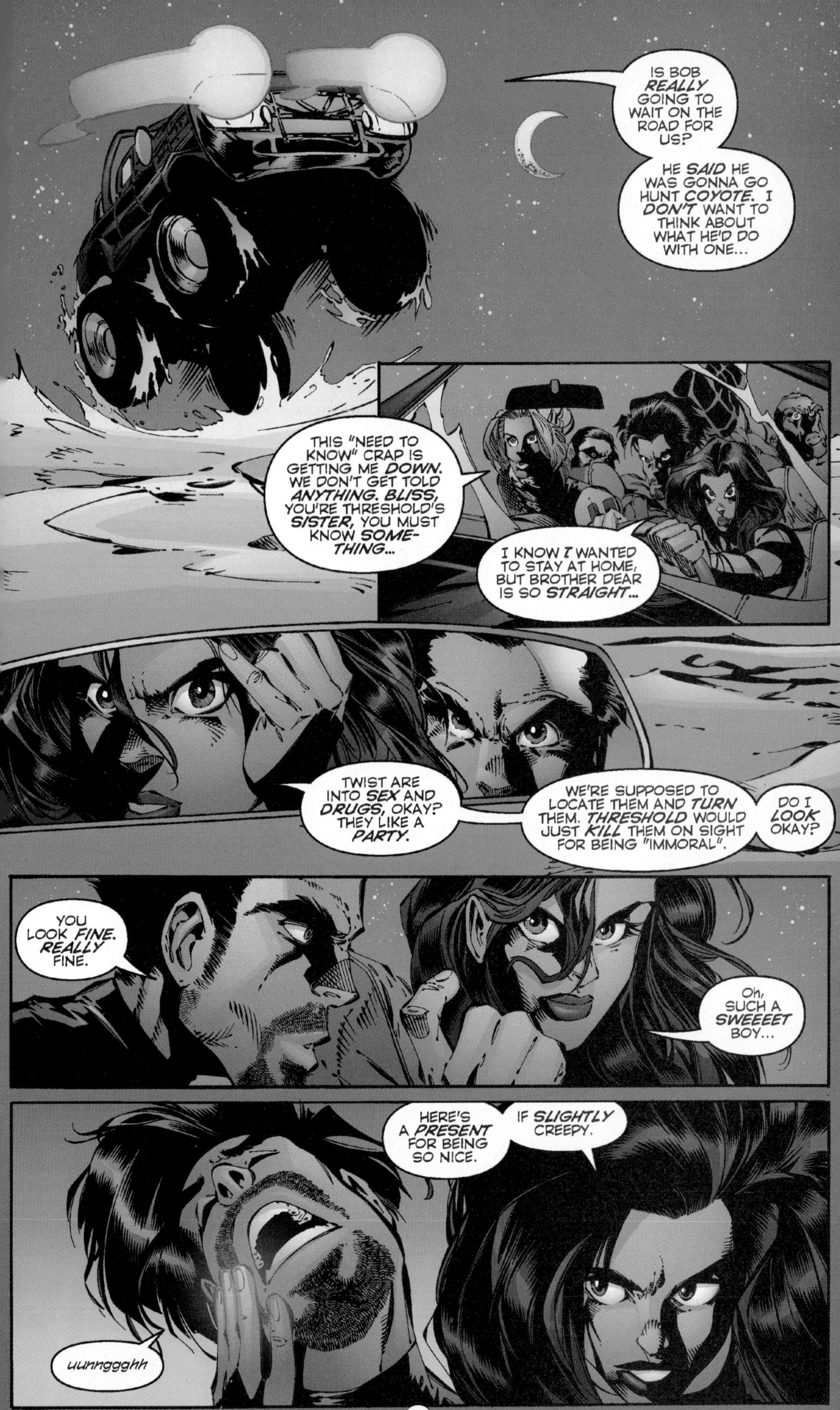

IS BOB REALLY GOING TO WAIT ON THE ROAD FOR US?
HE SAID HE WAS GONNA GO HUNT COYOTE. I DON'T WANT TO THINK ABOUT WHAT HE'D DO WITH ONE...
THIS "NEED TO KNOW" CRAP IS GETTING ME DOWN. WE DON'T GET TOLD ANYTHING. BLISS, YOU'RE THRESHOLD'S SISTER, YOU MUST KNOW SOME-THING...
I KNOW I WANTED TO STAY AT HOME, BUT BROTHER DEAR IS SO STRAIGHT...
TWIST ARE INTO SEX AND DRUGS, OKAY? THEY LIKE A PARTY.
WE'RE SUPPOSED TO LOCATE THEM AND TURN THEM. THRESHOLD WOULD JUST KILL THEM ON SIGHT FOR BEING "IMMORAL".
DO I LOOK OKAY?
YOU LOOK FINE. REALLY FINE.
Oh, SUCH A SWEEEET BOY...
HERE'S A PRESENT FOR BEING SO NICE.
IF SLIGHTLY CREEPY.
uunnggghh

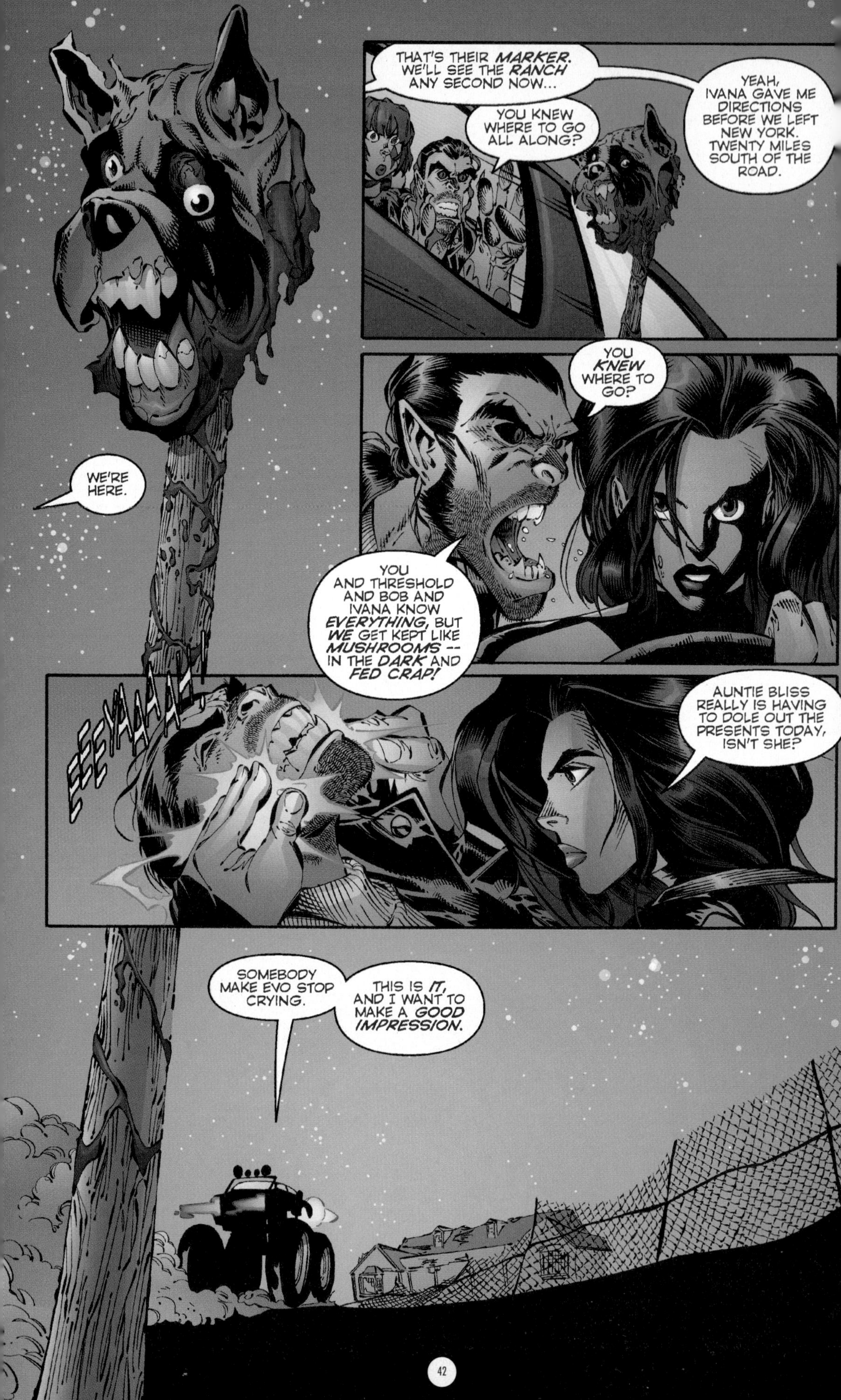
THAT'S THEIR MARKER. WE'LL SEE THE RANCH ANY SECOND NOW...
YOU KNEW WHERE TO GO ALL ALONG?
YEAH, IVANA GAVE ME DIRECTIONS BEFORE WE LEFT NEW YORK. TWENTY MILES SOUTH OF THE ROAD.
YOU KNEW WHERE TO GO?
YOU AND THRESHOLD AND BOB AND IVANA KNOW EVERYTHING, BUT WE GET KEPT LIKE MUSHROOMS -- IN THE DARK AND FED CRAP!
EEEYAAAAH!
AUNTIE BLISS REALLY IS HAVING TO DOLE OUT THE PRESENTS TODAY, ISN'T SHE?
WE'RE HERE.
SOMEBODY MAKE EVO STOP CRYING.
THIS IS IT, AND I WANT TO MAKE A GOOD IMPRESSION.

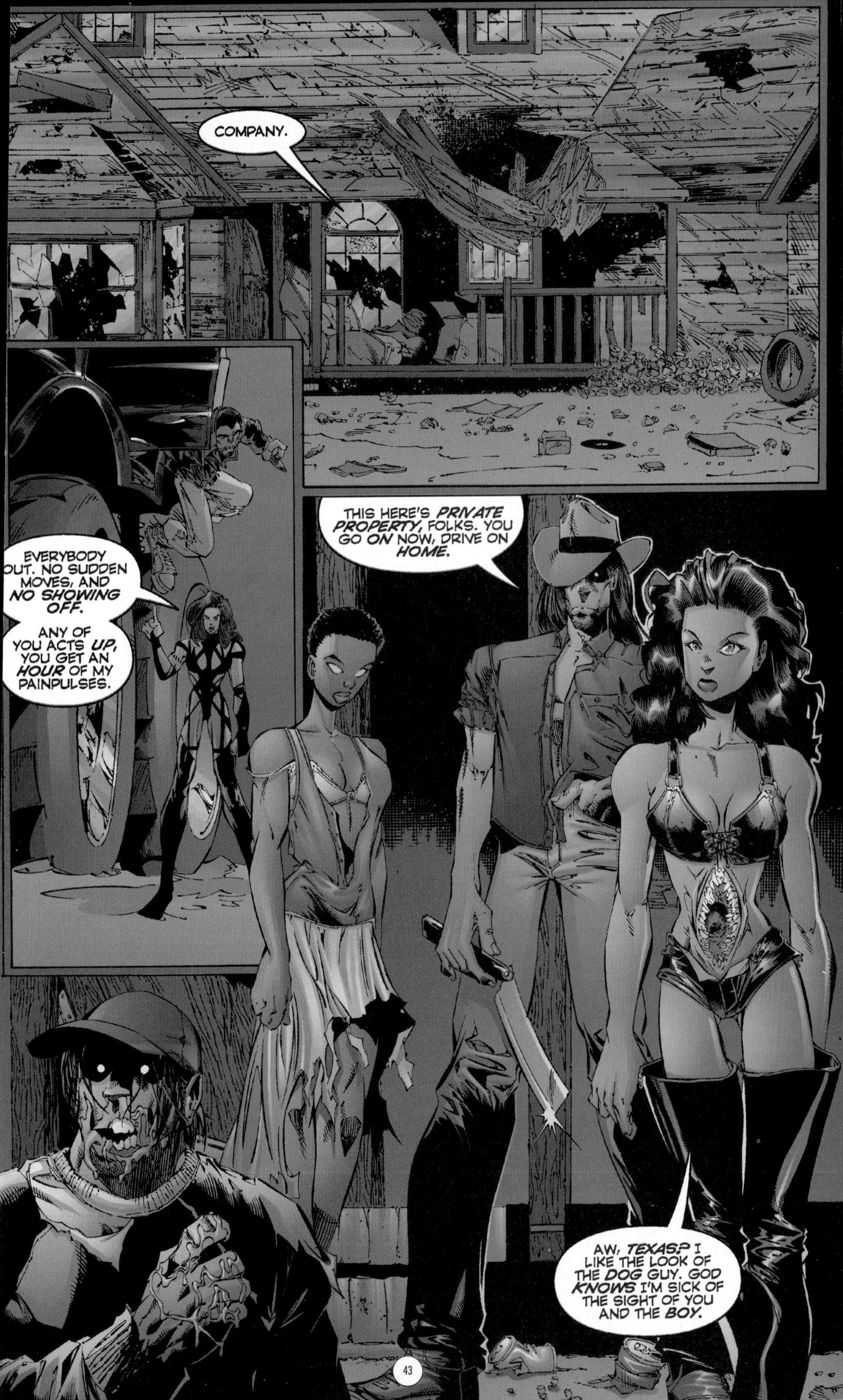
COMPANY.
EVERYBODY OUT. NO SUDDEN MOVES, AND NO SHOWING OFF.
ANY OF YOU ACTS UP, YOU GET AN HOUR OF MY PAINPULSES.
THIS HERE'S PRIVATE PROPERTY, FOLKS. YOU GO ON NOW, DRIVE ON HOME.
AW, TEXAS? I LIKE THE LOOK OF THE DOG GUY. GOD KNOWS I'M SICK OF THE SIGHT OF YOU AND THE BOY.

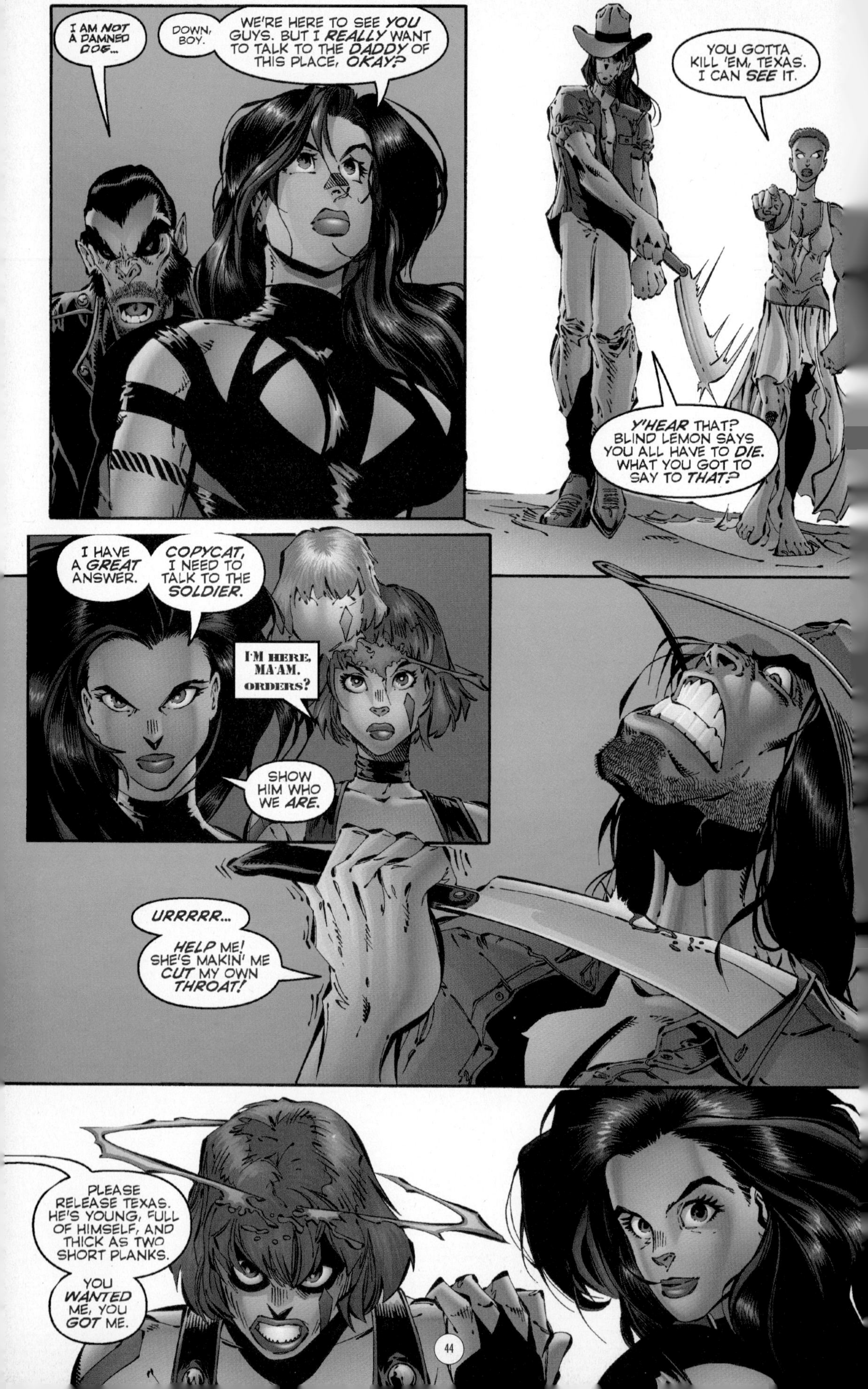
I AM NOT A DAMNED DOG...
DOWN, BOY.
WE'RE HERE TO SEE YOU GUYS. BUT I REALLY WANT TO TALK TO THE DADDY OF THIS PLACE, OKAY?
YOU GOTTA KILL 'EM, TEXAS. I CAN SEE IT.
Y'HEAR THAT? BLIND LEMON SAYS YOU ALL HAVE TO DIE. WHAT YOU GOT TO SAY TO THAT?
I HAVE A GREAT ANSWER.
COPYCAT, I NEED TO TALK TO THE SOLDIER.
I'M HERE, MA'AM. ORDERS?
SHOW HIM WHO WE ARE.
URRRRR...
HELP ME! SHE'S MAKIN' ME CUT MY OWN THROAT!
PLEASE RELEASE TEXAS. HE'S YOUNG, FULL OF HIMSELF, AND THICK AS TWO SHORT PLANKS.
YOU WANTED ME, YOU GOT ME.

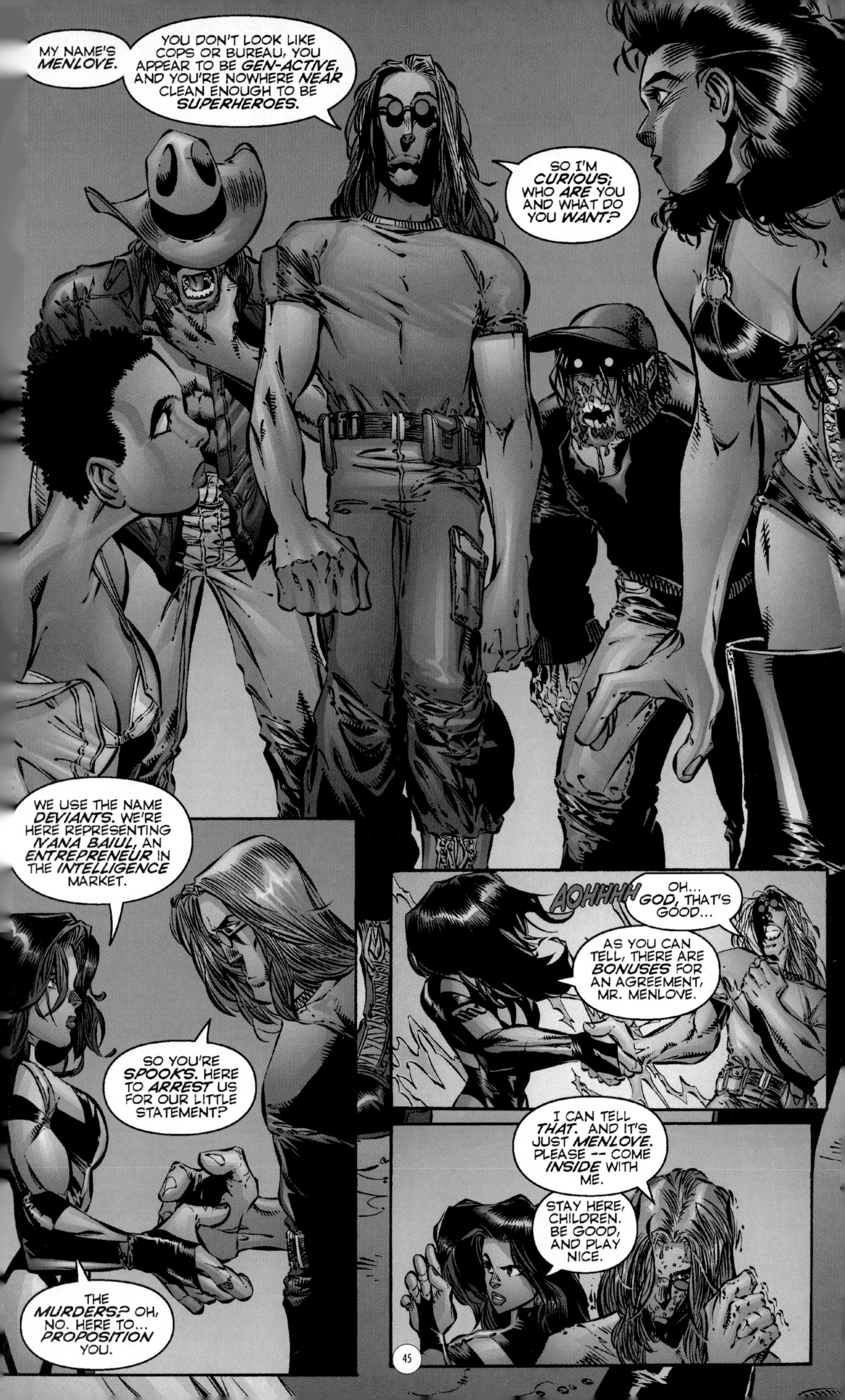
MY NAME'S MENLOVE.
YOU DON'T LOOK LIKE COPS OR BUREAU, YOU APPEAR TO BE GEN-ACTIVE, AND YOU'RE NOWHERE NEAR CLEAN ENOUGH TO BE SUPERHEROES.
SO I'M CURIOUS; WHO ARE YOU AND WHAT DO YOU WANT?
WE USE THE NAME DEVIANTS. WE'RE HERE REPRESENTING IVANA BAIUL, AN ENTREPRENEUR IN THE INTELLIGENCE MARKET.
SO YOU'RE SPOOKS. HERE TO ARREST US FOR OUR LITTLE STATEMENT?
THE MURDERS? OH, NO. HERE TO... PROPOSITION YOU.
AOHHHH
OH... GOD, THAT'S GOOD...
AS YOU CAN TELL, THERE ARE BONUSES FOR AN AGREEMENT, MR. MENLOVE.
I CAN TELL THAT. AND IT'S JUST MENLOVE. PLEASE -- COME INSIDE WITH ME.
STAY HERE, CHILDREN. BE GOOD, AND PLAY NICE.

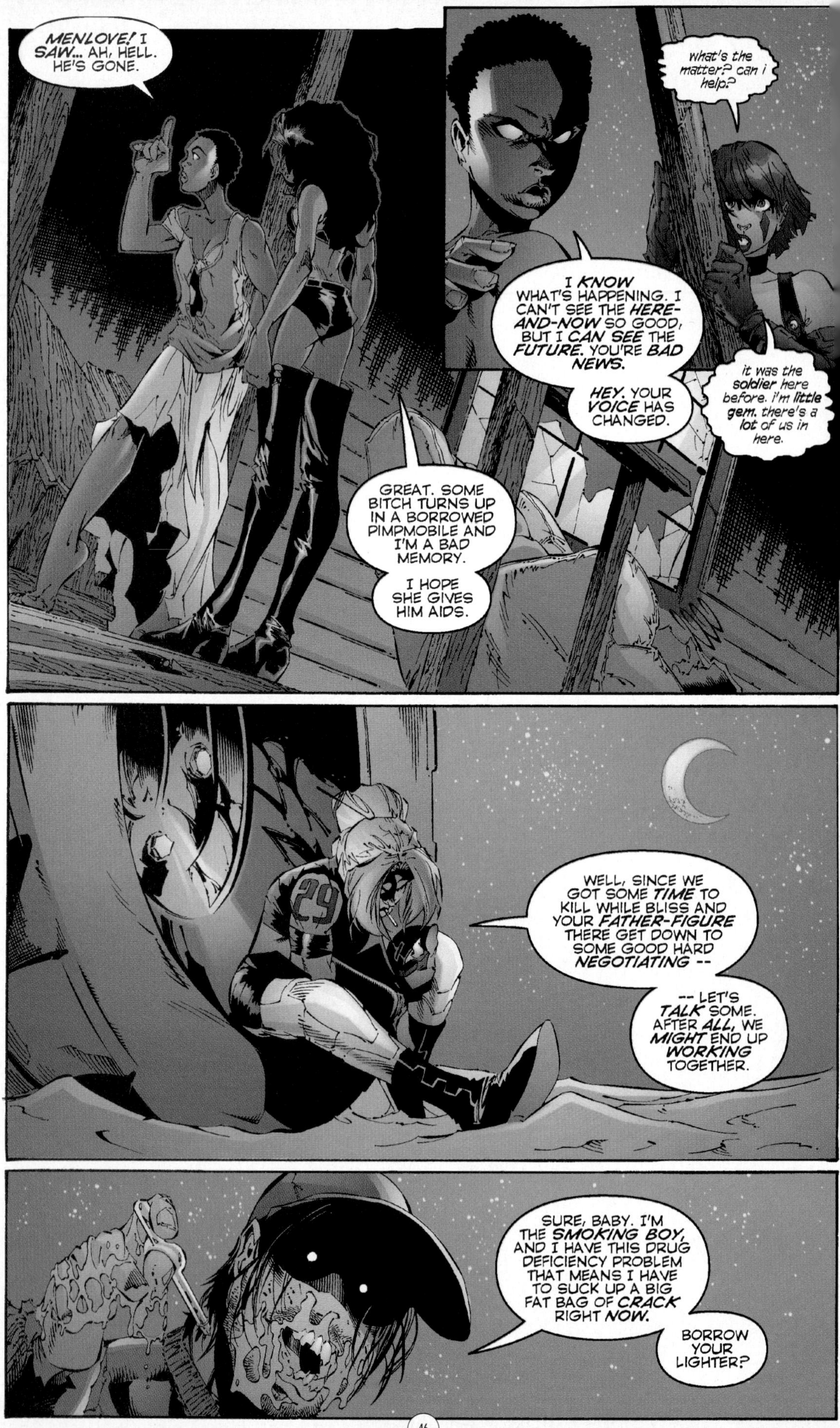
MENLOVE! I SAW... AH, HELL. HE'S GONE.
what's the matter? can i help?
I KNOW WHAT'S HAPPENING. I CAN'T SEE THE HERE-AND-NOW SO GOOD, BUT I CAN SEE THE FUTURE. YOU'RE BAD NEWS.
HEY. YOUR VOICE HAS CHANGED.
it was the soldier here before. i'm little gem. there's a lot of us in here.
GREAT. SOME BITCH TURNS UP IN A BORROWED PIMPMOBILE AND I'M A BAD MEMORY.
I HOPE SHE GIVES HIM AIDS.
WELL, SINCE WE GOT SOME TIME TO KILL WHILE BLISS AND YOUR FATHER-FIGURE THERE GET DOWN TO SOME GOOD HARD NEGOTIATING --
-- LET'S TALK SOME. AFTER ALL, WE MIGHT END UP WORKING TOGETHER.
SURE, BABY. I'M THE SMOKING BOY, AND I HAVE THIS DRUG DEFICIENCY PROBLEM THAT MEANS I HAVE TO SUCK UP A BIG FAT BAG OF CRACK RIGHT NOW.
BORROW YOUR LIGHTER?

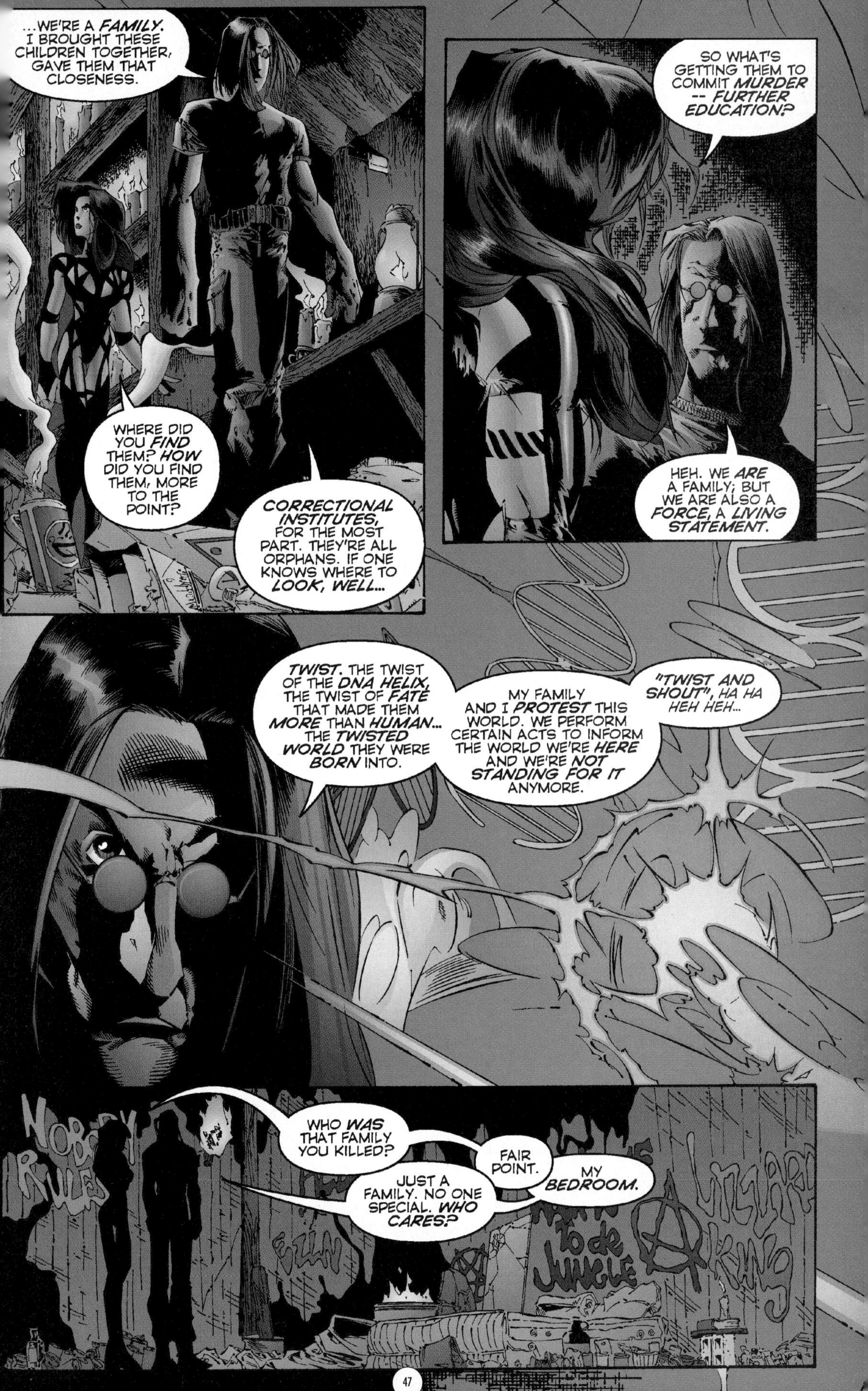
...WE'RE A FAMILY. I BROUGHT THESE CHILDREN TOGETHER, GAVE THEM THAT CLOSENESS.
WHERE DID YOU FIND THEM? HOW DID YOU FIND THEM, MORE TO THE POINT?
CORRECTIONAL INSTITUTES, FOR THE MOST PART. THEY'RE ALL ORPHANS. IF ONE KNOWS WHERE TO LOOK, WELL...
SO WHAT'S GETTING THEM TO COMMIT MURDER -- FURTHER EDUCATION?
HEH. WE ARE A FAMILY; BUT WE ARE ALSO A FORCE, A LIVING STATEMENT.
TWIST. THE TWIST OF THE DNA HELIX, THE TWIST OF FATE THAT MADE THEM MORE THAN HUMAN... THE TWISTED WORLD THEY WERE BORN INTO.
MY FAMILY AND I PROTEST THIS WORLD. WE PERFORM CERTAIN ACTS TO INFORM THE WORLD WE'RE HERE AND WE'RE NOT STANDING FOR IT ANYMORE.
"TWIST AND SHOUT", HA HA HEH HEH...
WHO WAS THAT FAMILY YOU KILLED?
JUST A FAMILY. NO ONE SPECIAL. WHO CARES?
FAIR POINT.
MY BEDROOM.
TO DE JUNGLE KING

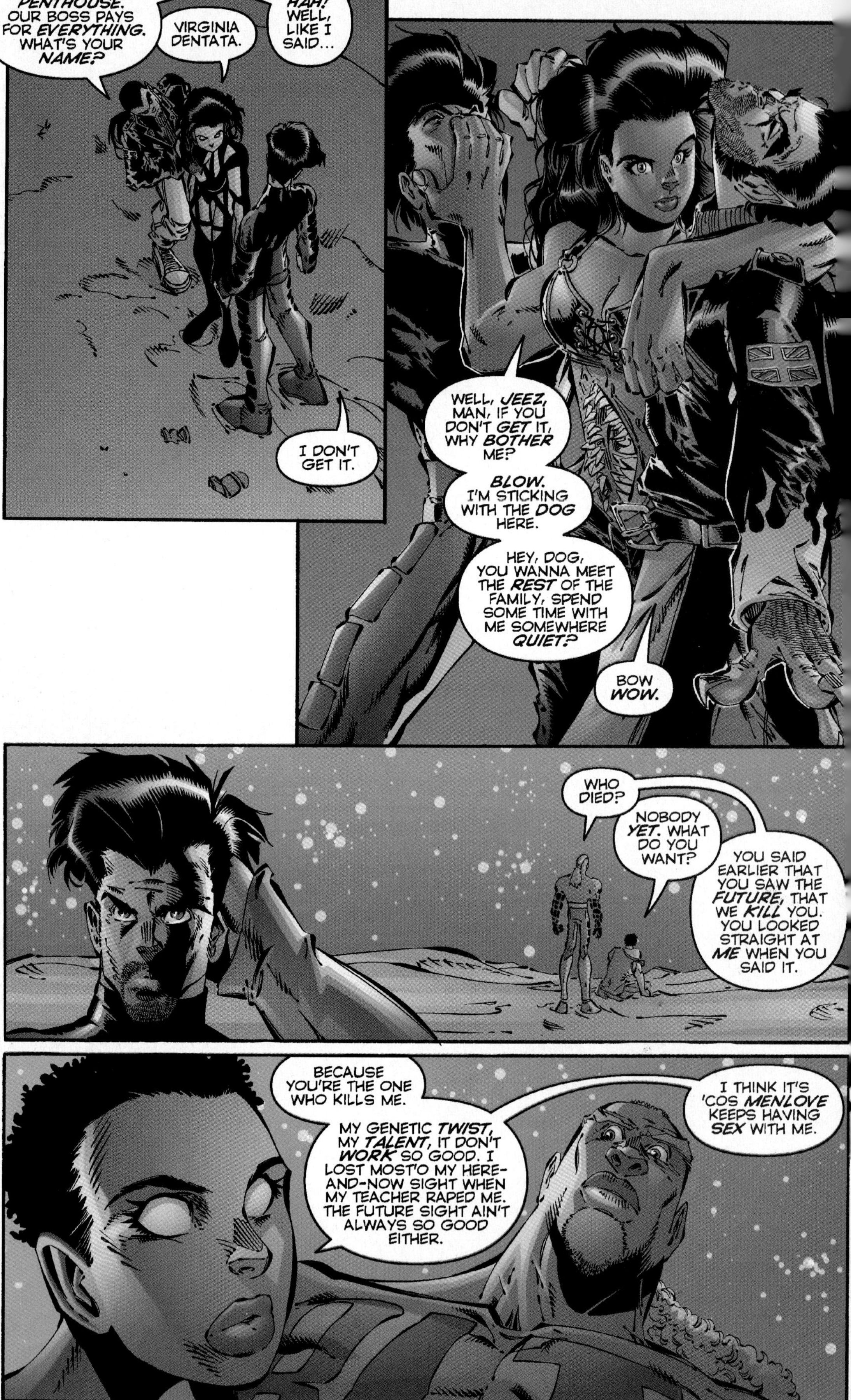
...YEAH, A PENTHOUSE. OUR BOSS PAYS FOR EVERYTHING. WHAT'S YOUR NAME?
VIRGINIA DENTATA.
HAH! WELL, LIKE I SAID...
I DON'T GET IT.
WELL, JEEZ, MAN, IF YOU DON'T GET IT, WHY BOTHER ME?
BLOW. I'M STICKING WITH THE DOG HERE.
HEY, DOG, YOU WANNA MEET THE REST OF THE FAMILY, SPEND SOME TIME WITH ME SOMEWHERE QUIET?
BOW WOW.
WHO DIED?
NOBODY YET. WHAT DO YOU WANT?
YOU SAID EARLIER THAT YOU SAW THE FUTURE, THAT WE KILL YOU. YOU LOOKED STRAIGHT AT ME WHEN YOU SAID IT.
BECAUSE YOU'RE THE ONE WHO KILLS ME.
MY GENETIC TWIST, MY TALENT, IT DON'T WORK SO GOOD. I LOST MOST'O MY HERE-AND-NOW SIGHT WHEN MY TEACHER RAPED ME. THE FUTURE SIGHT AIN'T ALWAYS SO GOOD EITHER.
I THINK IT'S 'COS MENLOVE KEEPS HAVING SEX WITH ME.

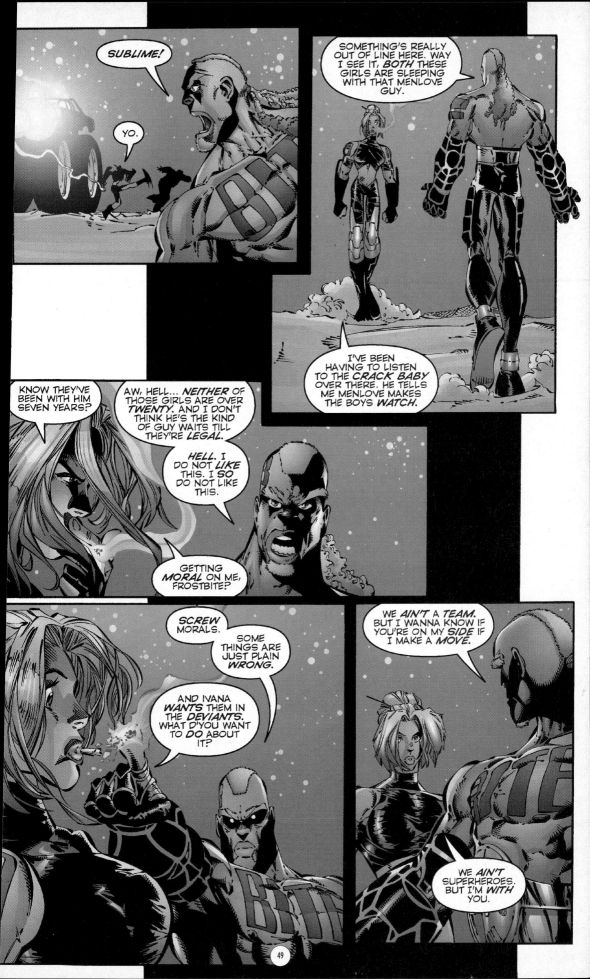

SUBLIME!

YO.

SOMETHING'S REALLY OUT OF LINE HERE. WAY I SEE IT, *BOTH* THESE GIRLS ARE SLEEPING WITH THAT MENLOVE GUY.

I'VE BEEN HAVING TO LISTEN TO THE *CRACK BABY* OVER THERE. HE TELLS ME MENLOVE MAKES THE BOYS *WATCH*.

KNOW THEY'VE BEEN WITH HIM SEVEN YEARS?

AW, HELL... *NEITHER* OF THOSE GIRLS ARE OVER *TWENTY*. AND I DON'T THINK HE'S THE KIND OF GUY WAITS TILL THEY'RE *LEGAL*.

HELL. I DO NOT *LIKE* THIS. I *SO* DO NOT LIKE THIS.

GETTING *MORAL* ON ME, FROSTBITE?

SCREW MORALS.

SOME THINGS ARE JUST PLAIN *WRONG*.

AND IVANA *WANTS* THEM IN THE *DEVIANTS*. WHAT D'YOU WANT TO *DO* ABOUT IT?

WE *AIN'T* A TEAM. BUT I WANNA KNOW IF YOU'RE ON MY *SIDE* IF I MAKE A *MOVE*.

WE *AIN'T* SUPERHEROES. BUT I'M *WITH* YOU.

49

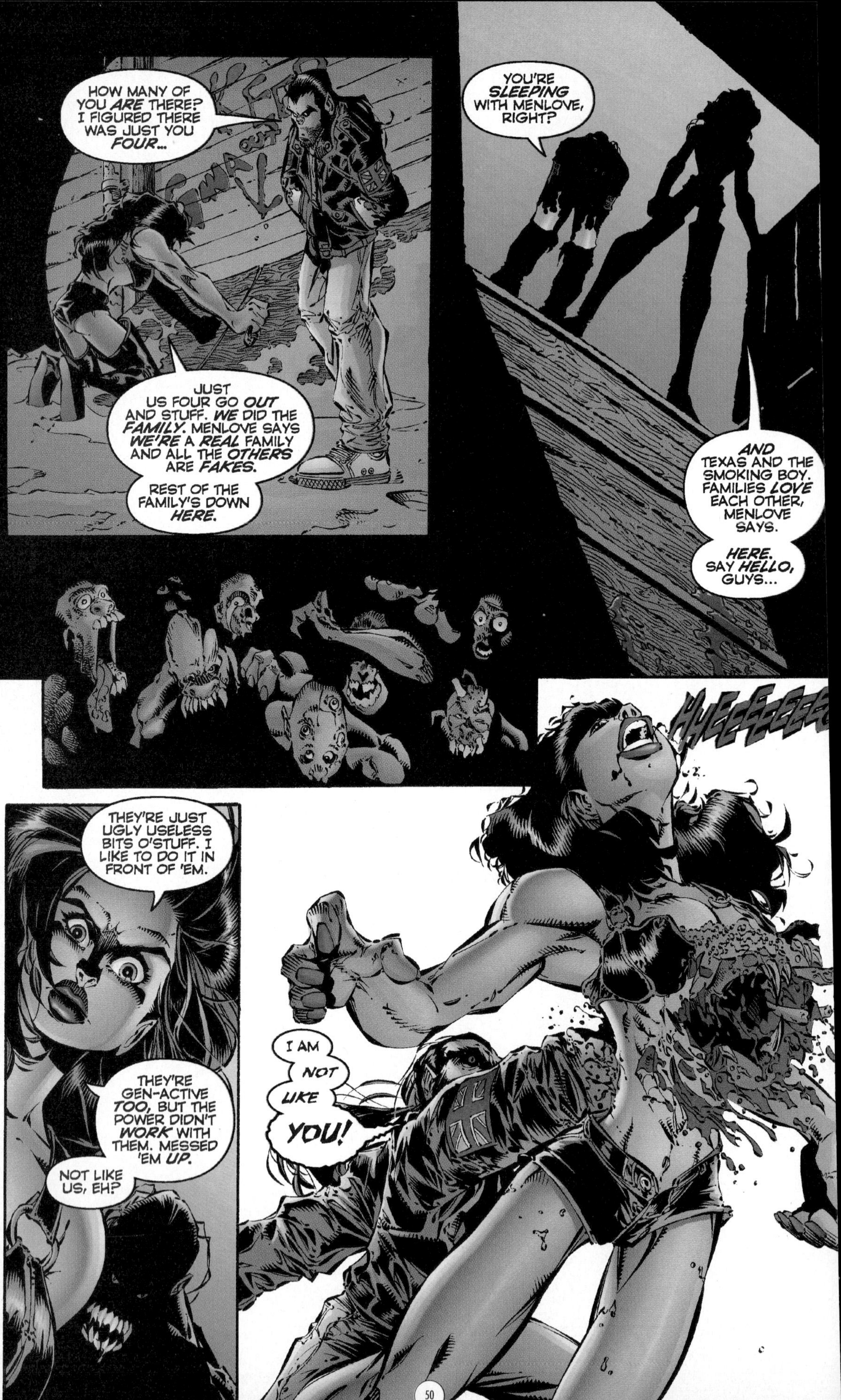

HOW MANY OF YOU *ARE* THERE? I FIGURED THERE WAS JUST YOU *FOUR*...
JUST US FOUR GO *OUT* AND STUFF. *WE* DID THE *FAMILY*. MENLOVE SAYS *WE'RE* A *REAL* FAMILY AND ALL THE *OTHERS* ARE *FAKES*.
REST OF THE FAMILY'S DOWN *HERE*.
YOU'RE *SLEEPING* WITH MENLOVE, RIGHT?
AND TEXAS AND THE SMOKING BOY. FAMILIES *LOVE* EACH OTHER, MENLOVE SAYS.
HERE. SAY *HELLO*, GUYS...
THEY'RE JUST UGLY USELESS BITS O'STUFF. I LIKE TO DO IT IN FRONT OF 'EM.
THEY'RE GEN-ACTIVE *TOO*, BUT THE POWER DIDN'T *WORK* WITH THEM. MESSED 'EM *UP*.
NOT LIKE US, EH?
HUEEEEEEE
I AM *NOT* *LIKE* *YOU!*

GOD, I LIKE THAT POWER...

I'LL TELL YOU THE TRUTH. I USED TO WORK FOR *INTERNATIONAL OPERATIONS*, JUST LIKE *IVANA BAIUL.*

I WAS A GRUNT ON *PROJECT GENESIS*, SEARCHING FOR *GEN-ACTIVE KIDS* LIKE YOURSELF.

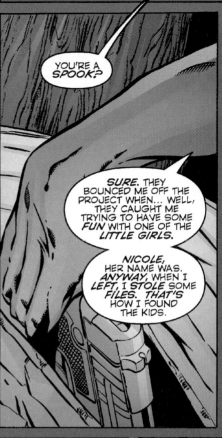

YOU'RE A *SPOOK?*

SURE. THEY BOUNCED ME OFF THE PROJECT WHEN... WELL, THEY CAUGHT ME TRYING TO HAVE SOME *FUN* WITH ONE OF THE *LITTLE GIRLS.*

NICOLE, HER NAME WAS. ANYWAY, WHEN I *LEFT*, I *STOLE* SOME *FILES. THAT'S* HOW I FOUND THE KIDS.

MY NAME'S NICOLE.

YOU WERE SWEET.

WEEEEEESH!

DIE! DIE! DIE!

EEEYAAAAAHH

51

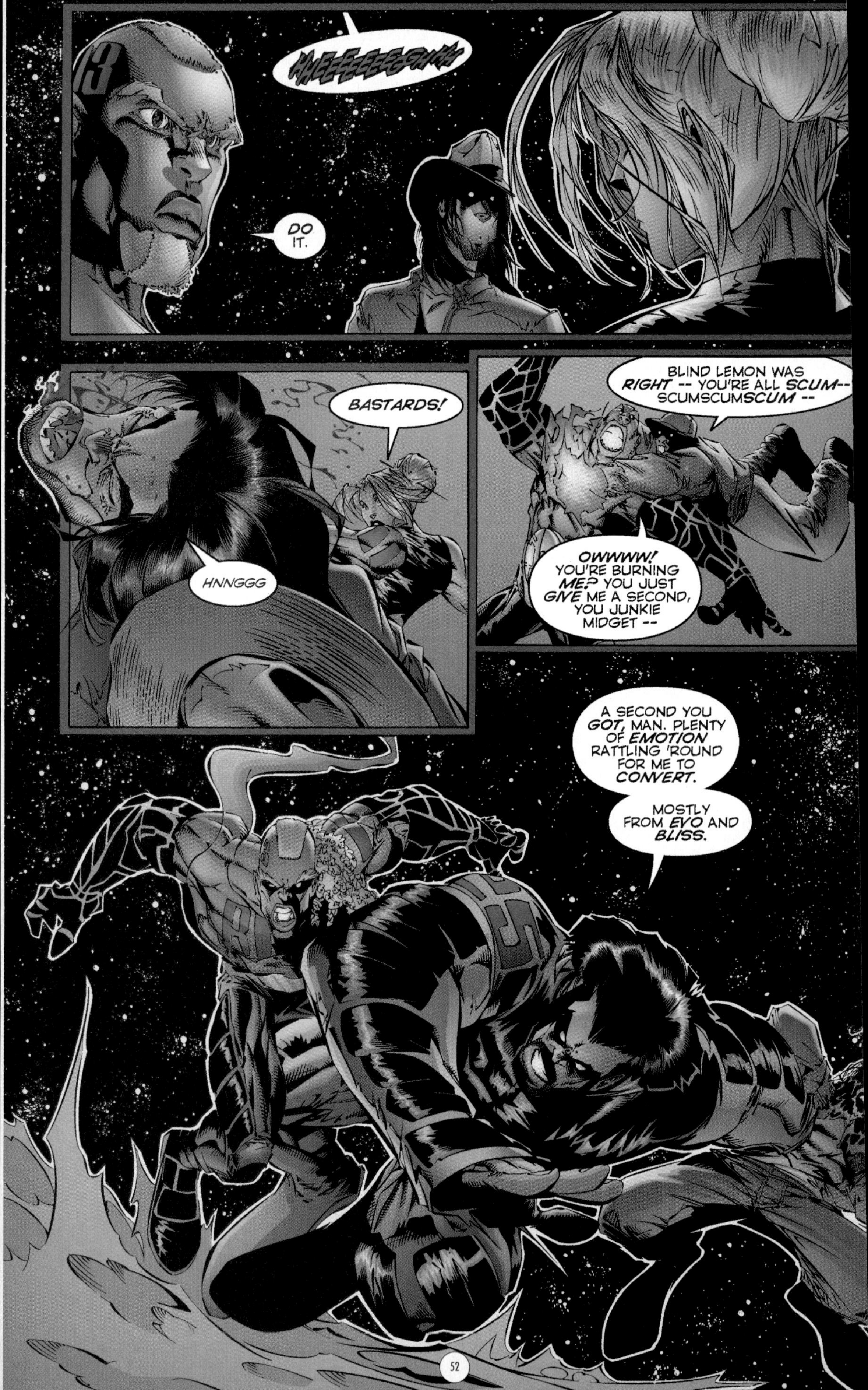
HAEEEEEEGHHH
DO IT.
BASTARDS!
HNNGGG
BLIND LEMON WAS *RIGHT* -- YOU'RE ALL *SCUM*-- SCUMSCUM*SCUM* --
OWWWW! YOU'RE BURNING *ME?* YOU JUST *GIVE* ME A SECOND, YOU JUNKIE MIDGET --
A SECOND YOU *GOT*, MAN. PLENTY OF *EMOTION* RATTLING 'ROUND FOR ME TO *CONVERT*.
MOSTLY FROM *EVO* AND *BLISS*.

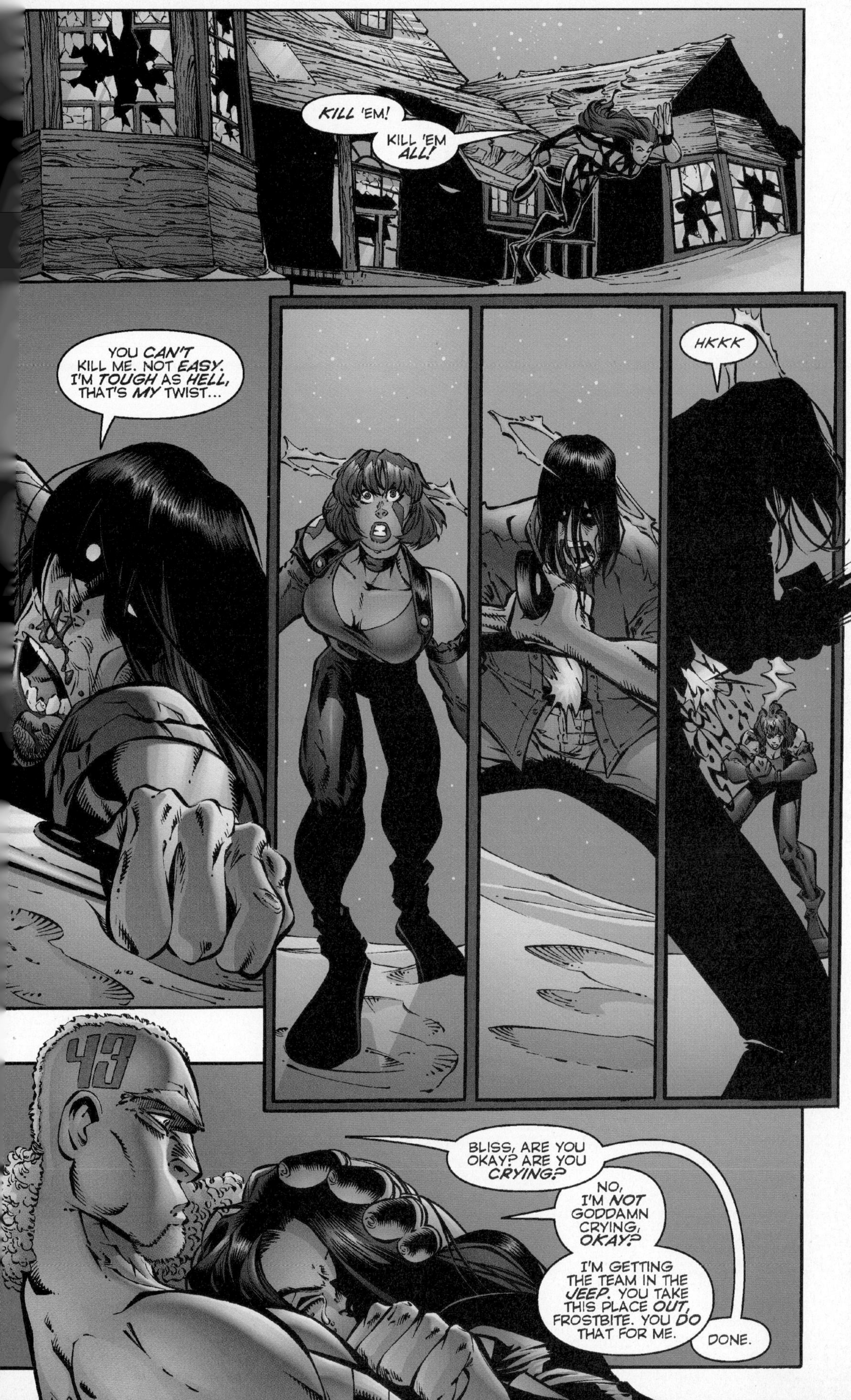
KILL 'EM!
KILL 'EM ALL!
YOU CAN'T KILL ME. NOT EASY. I'M TOUGH AS HELL, THAT'S MY TWIST...
HKKK
BLISS, ARE YOU OKAY? ARE YOU CRYING?
NO, I'M NOT GODDAMN CRYING, OKAY?
I'M GETTING THE TEAM IN THE JEEP. YOU TAKE THIS PLACE OUT, FROSTBITE. YOU DO THAT FOR ME.
DONE.

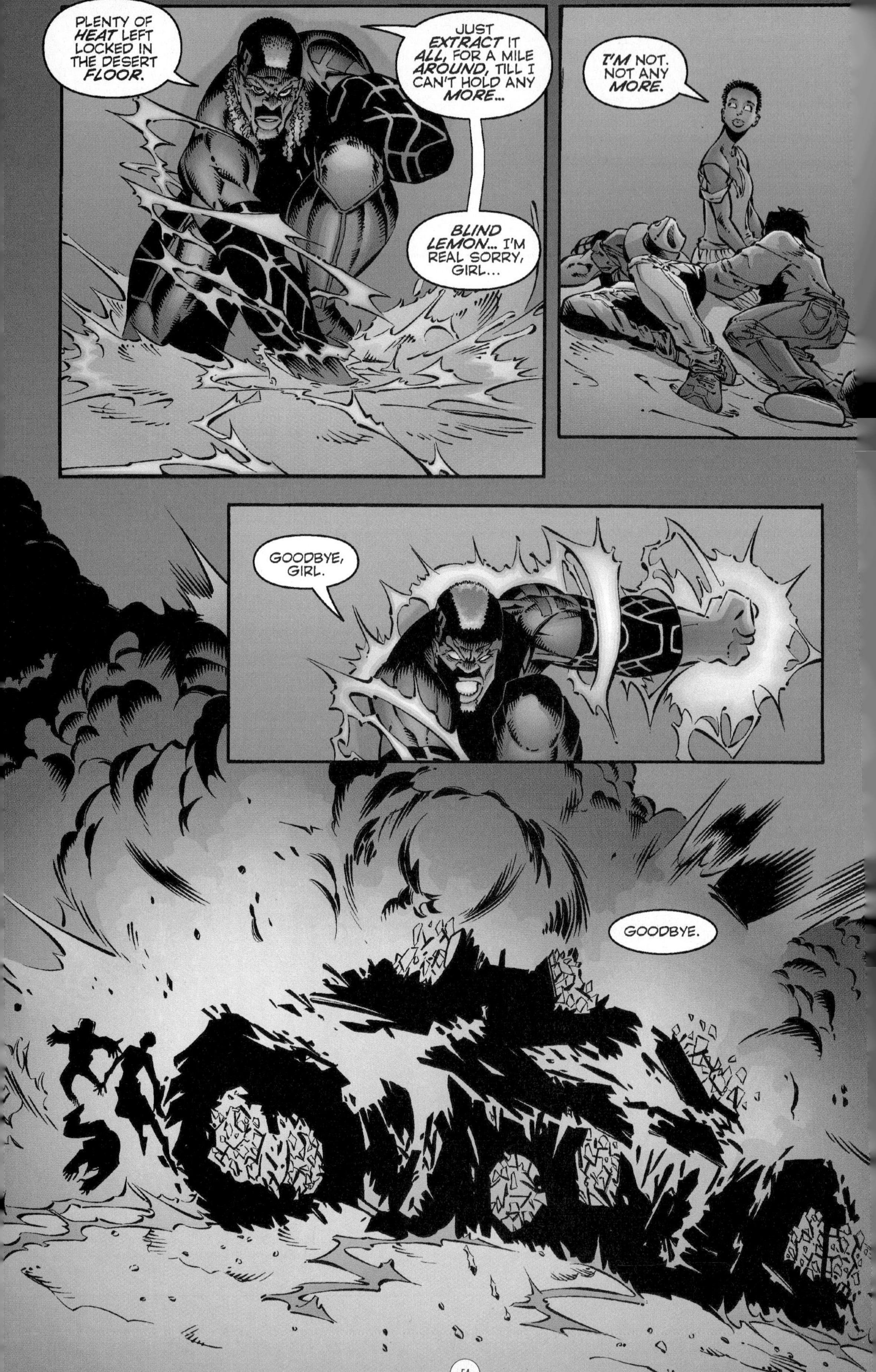
PLENTY OF *HEAT* LEFT LOCKED IN THE DESERT *FLOOR.*
JUST *EXTRACT* IT *ALL,* FOR A MILE *AROUND,* TILL I CAN'T HOLD ANY *MORE...*
BLIND LEMON... I'M REAL SORRY, GIRL...
I'M NOT. NOT ANY *MORE.*
GOODBYE, GIRL.
GOODBYE.

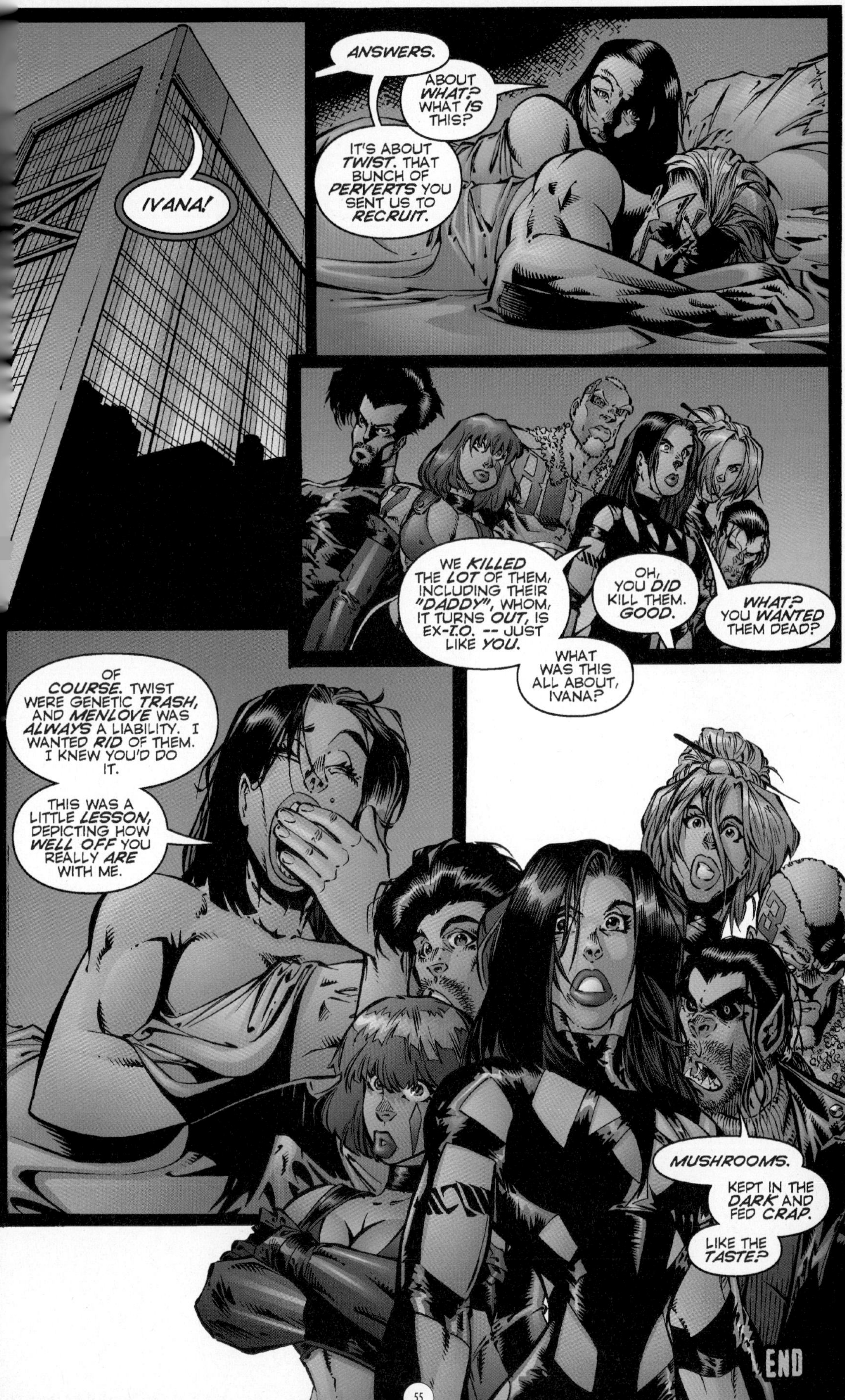
IVANA!
ANSWERS.
ABOUT WHAT? WHAT IS THIS?
IT'S ABOUT TWIST. THAT BUNCH OF PERVERTS YOU SENT US TO RECRUIT.
WE KILLED THE LOT OF THEM, INCLUDING THEIR "DADDY", WHOM, IT TURNS OUT, IS EX-I.O. -- JUST LIKE YOU.
OH, YOU DID KILL THEM. GOOD.
WHAT? YOU WANTED THEM DEAD?
WHAT WAS THIS ALL ABOUT, IVANA?
OF COURSE. TWIST WERE GENETIC TRASH, AND MENLOVE WAS ALWAYS A LIABILITY. I WANTED RID OF THEM. I KNEW YOU'D DO IT.
THIS WAS A LITTLE LESSON, DEPICTING HOW WELL OFF YOU REALLY ARE WITH ME.
MUSHROOMS.
KEPT IN THE DARK AND FED CRAP.
LIKE THE TASTE?
END

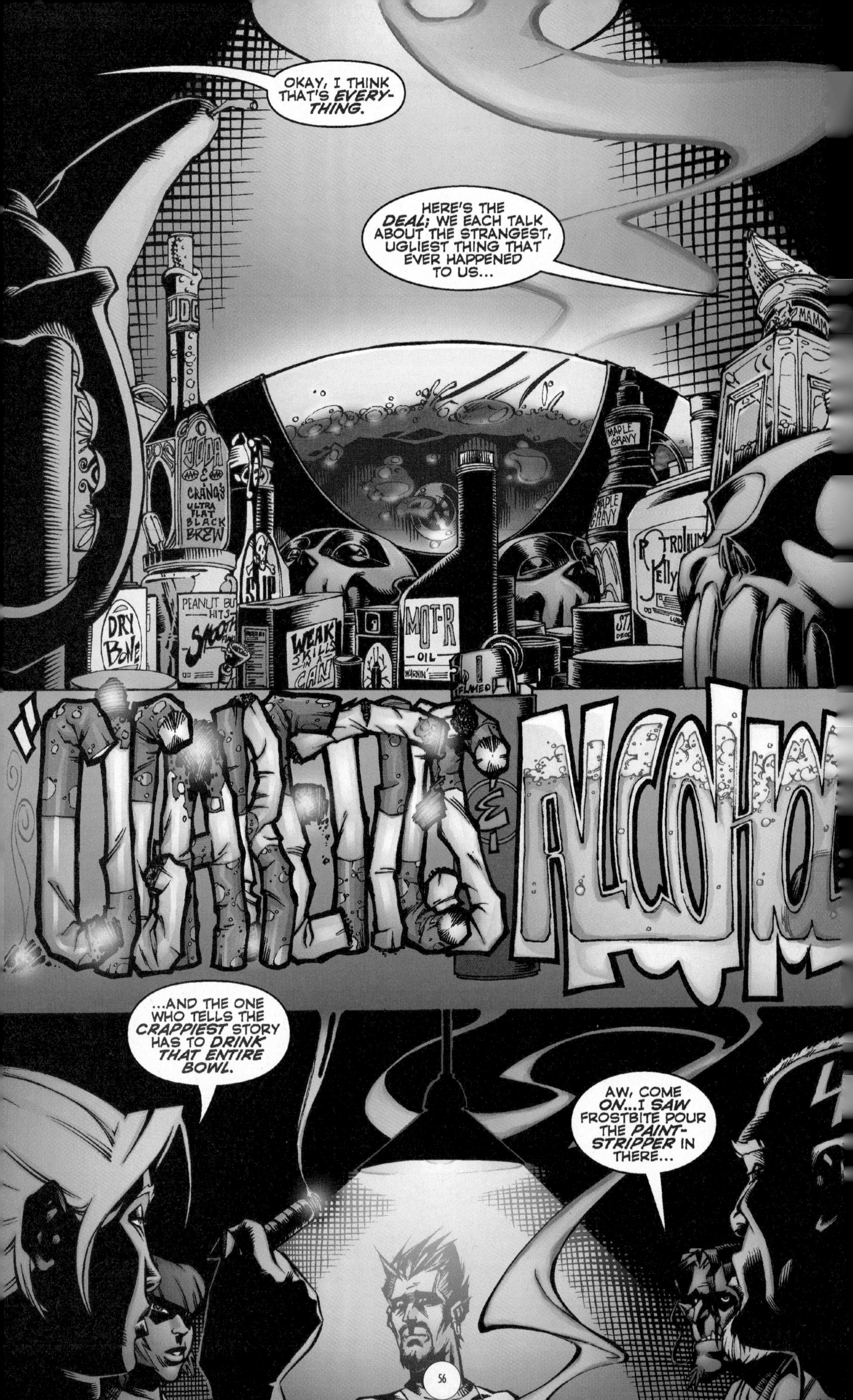
OKAY, I THINK THAT'S *EVERY-THING.*
HERE'S THE *DEAL;* WE EACH TALK ABOUT THE STRANGEST, UGLIEST THING THAT EVER HAPPENED TO US...
MAPLE GRAVY
DRY BONE
MOT-R OIL
...AND THE ONE WHO TELLS THE *CRAPPIEST* STORY HAS TO *DRINK THAT ENTIRE BOWL.*
AW, COME *ON*...I *SAW* FROSTBITE POUR THE *PAINT-STRIPPER* IN THERE...

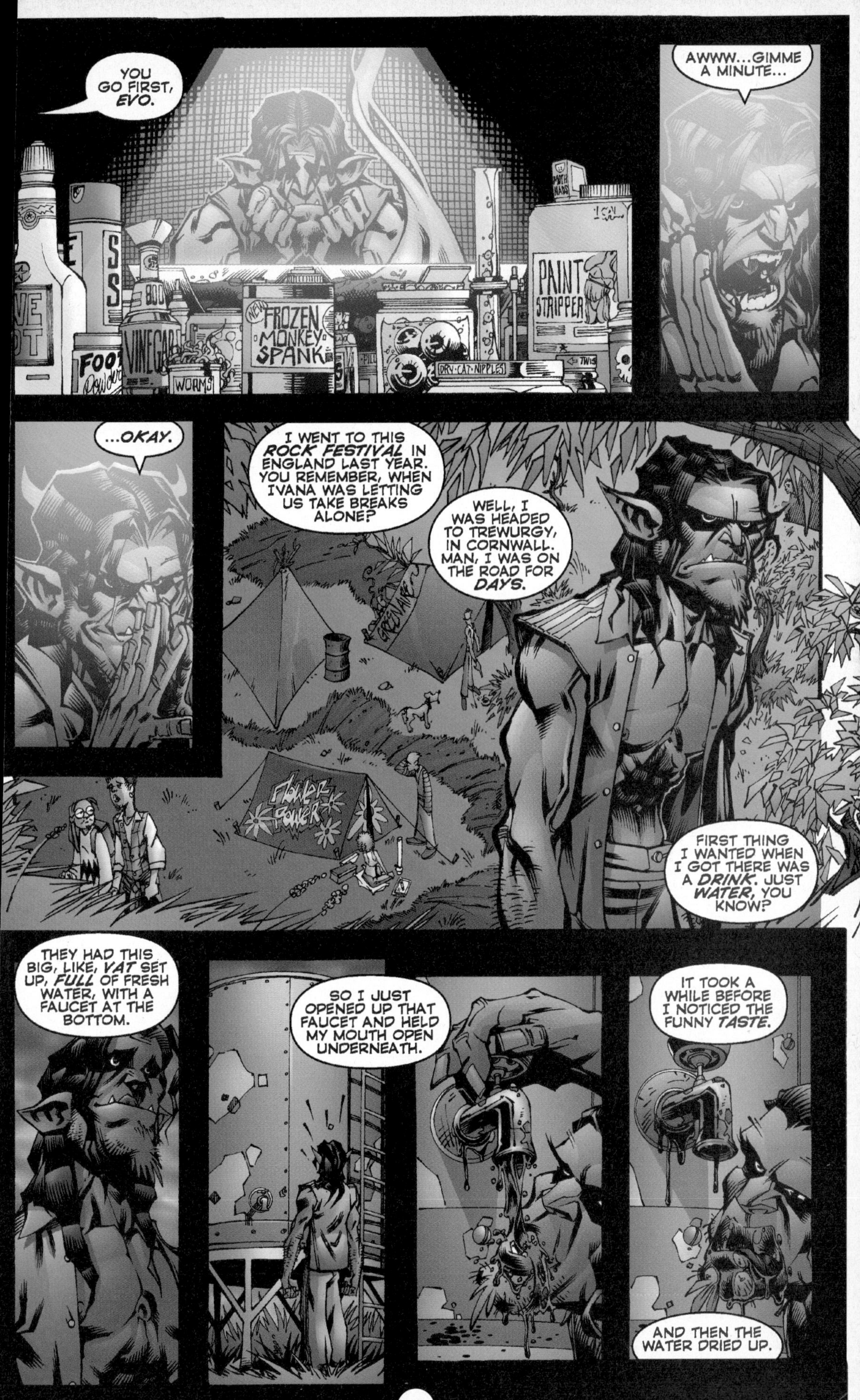
YOU GO FIRST, EVO.
NEW
FROZEN MONKEY SPANK
PAINT STRIPPER
VINEGAR
WORMS
DRY-CAT-NIPPLES
AWWW...GIMME A MINUTE...
...OKAY.
I WENT TO THIS ROCK FESTIVAL IN ENGLAND LAST YEAR. YOU REMEMBER, WHEN IVANA WAS LETTING US TAKE BREAKS ALONE?
WELL, I WAS HEADED TO TREWURGY, IN CORNWALL. MAN, I WAS ON THE ROAD FOR DAYS.
Flower Power
FIRST THING I WANTED WHEN I GOT THERE WAS A DRINK. JUST WATER, YOU KNOW?
THEY HAD THIS BIG, LIKE, VAT SET UP, FULL OF FRESH WATER, WITH A FAUCET AT THE BOTTOM.
SO I JUST OPENED UP THAT FAUCET AND HELD MY MOUTH OPEN UNDERNEATH.
IT TOOK A WHILE BEFORE I NOTICED THE FUNNY TASTE.
AND THEN THE WATER DRIED UP.

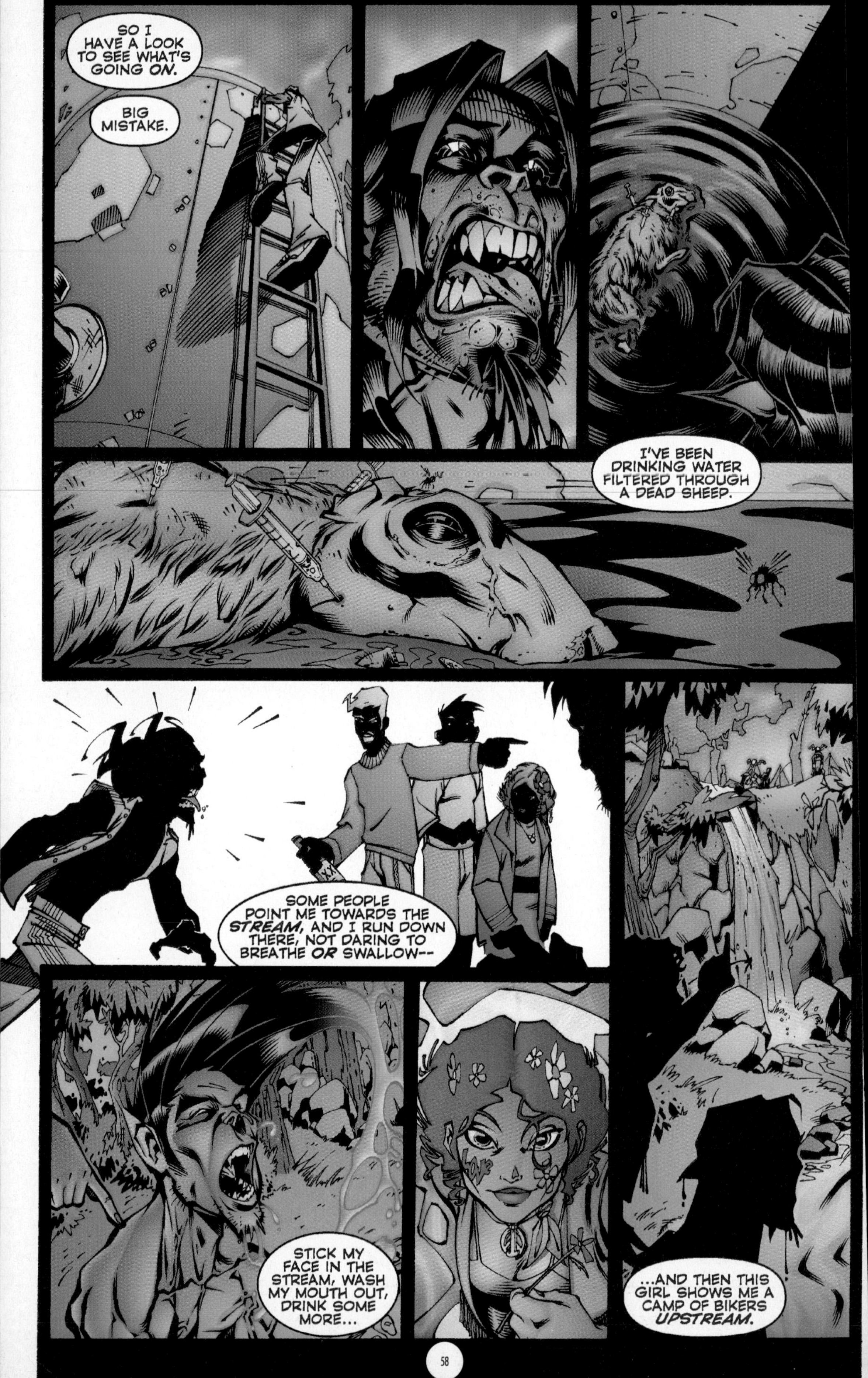
SO I HAVE A LOOK TO SEE WHAT'S GOING ON.
BIG MISTAKE.
I'VE BEEN DRINKING WATER FILTERED THROUGH A DEAD SHEEP.
SOME PEOPLE POINT ME TOWARDS THE STREAM, AND I RUN DOWN THERE, NOT DARING TO BREATHE OR SWALLOW--
STICK MY FACE IN THE STREAM, WASH MY MOUTH OUT, DRINK SOME MORE...
...AND THEN THIS GIRL SHOWS ME A CAMP OF BIKERS UPSTREAM.

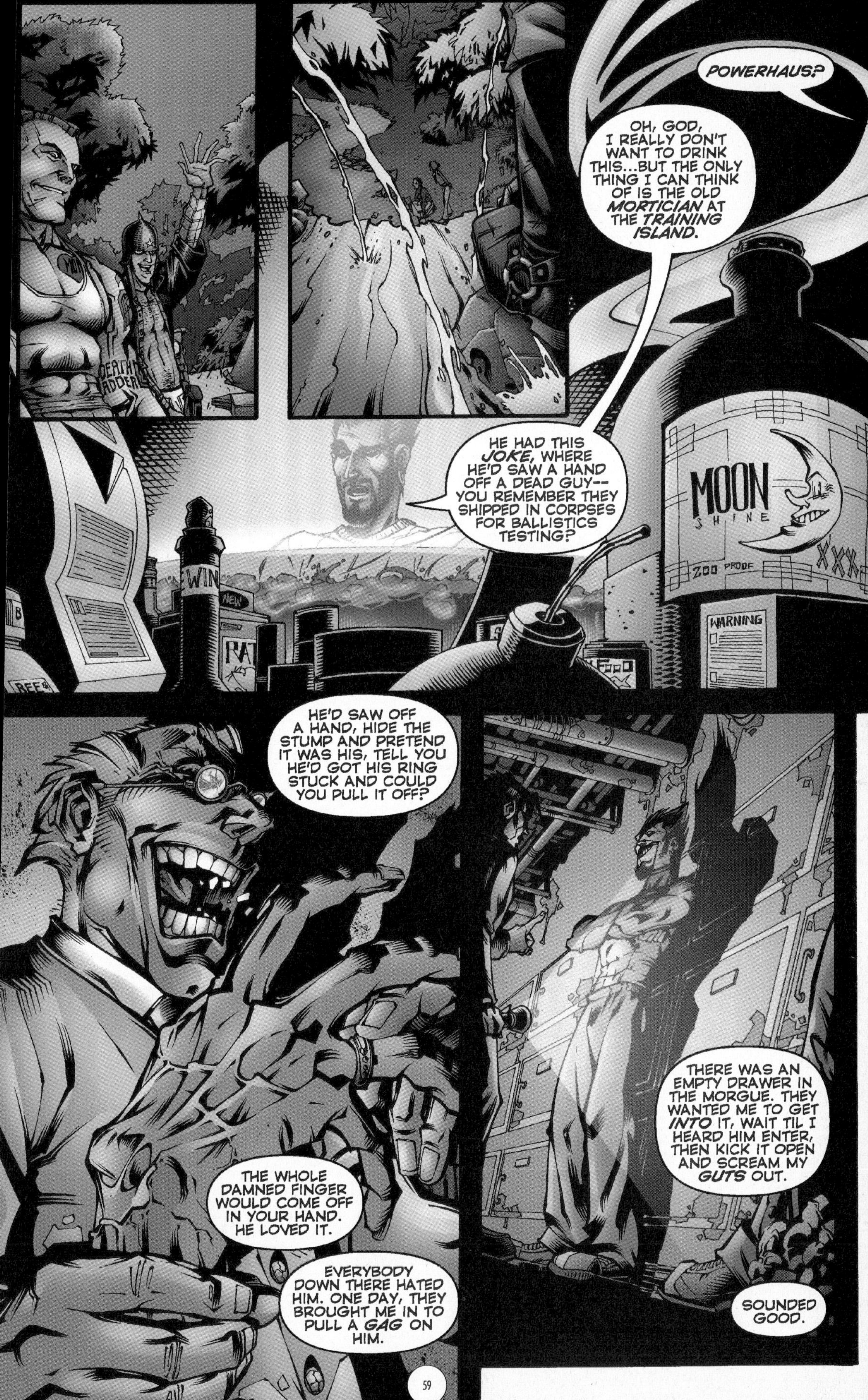
POWERHAUS?
OH, GOD, I REALLY DON'T WANT TO DRINK THIS...BUT THE ONLY THING I CAN THINK OF IS THE OLD *MORTICIAN* AT THE *TRAINING ISLAND.*
HE HAD THIS *JOKE,* WHERE HE'D SAW A HAND OFF A DEAD GUY-- YOU REMEMBER THEY SHIPPED IN CORPSES FOR BALLISTICS TESTING?
MOON SHINE
HE'D SAW OFF A HAND, HIDE THE STUMP AND PRETEND IT WAS HIS, TELL YOU HE'D GOT HIS RING STUCK AND COULD YOU PULL IT OFF?
THE WHOLE DAMNED FINGER WOULD COME OFF IN YOUR HAND. HE LOVED IT.
EVERYBODY DOWN THERE HATED HIM. ONE DAY, THEY BROUGHT ME IN TO PULL A *GAG* ON HIM.
THERE WAS AN EMPTY DRAWER IN THE MORGUE. THEY WANTED ME TO GET *INTO* IT, WAIT TIL I HEARD HIM ENTER, THEN KICK IT OPEN AND SCREAM MY *GUTS* OUT.
SOUNDED GOOD.

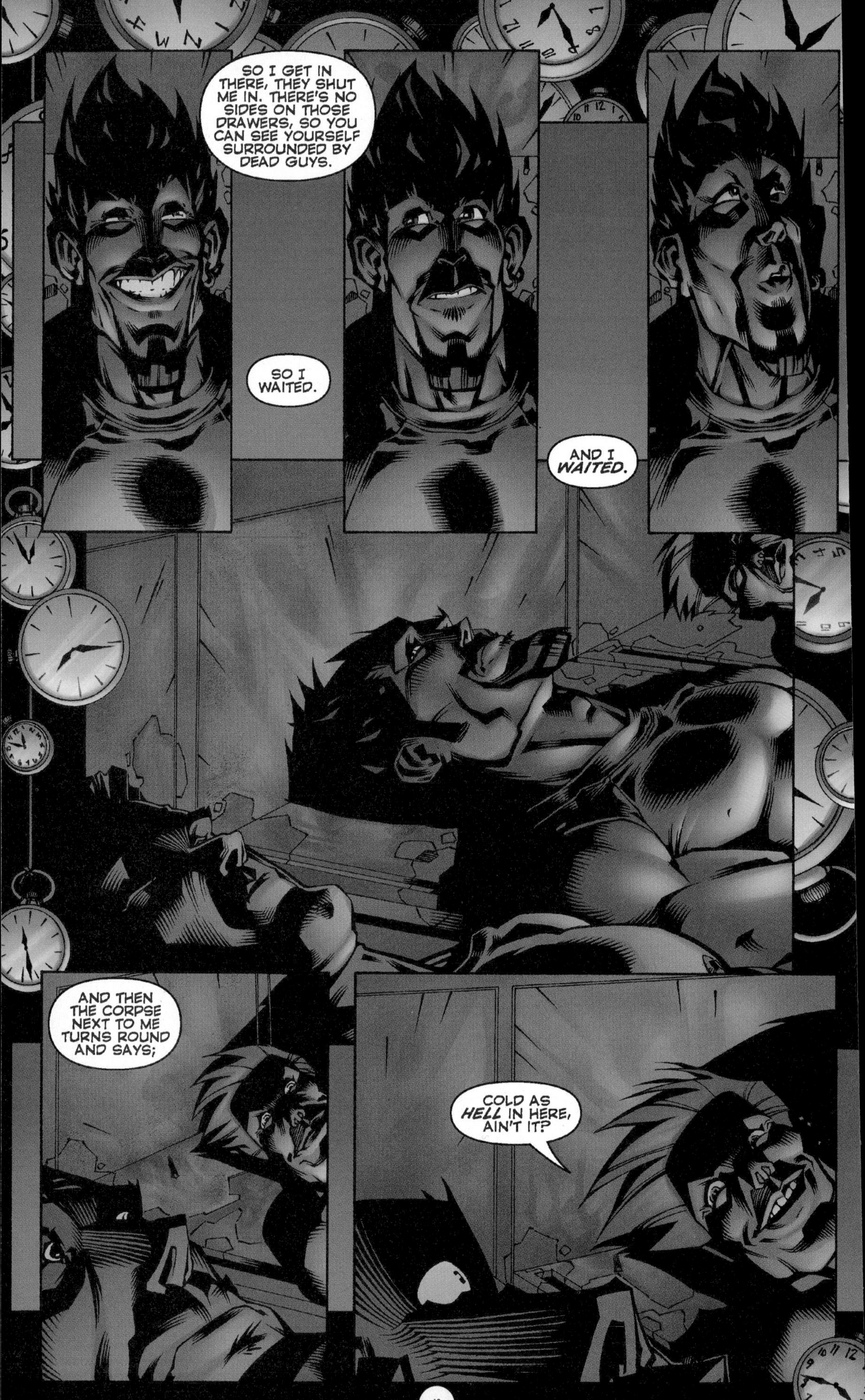
SO I GET IN THERE, THEY SHUT ME IN. THERE'S NO SIDES ON THOSE DRAWERS, SO YOU CAN SEE YOURSELF SURROUNDED BY DEAD GUYS.
SO I WAITED.
AND I *WAITED.*
AND THEN THE CORPSE NEXT TO ME TURNS ROUND AND SAYS;
COLD AS *HELL* IN HERE, AIN'T IT?

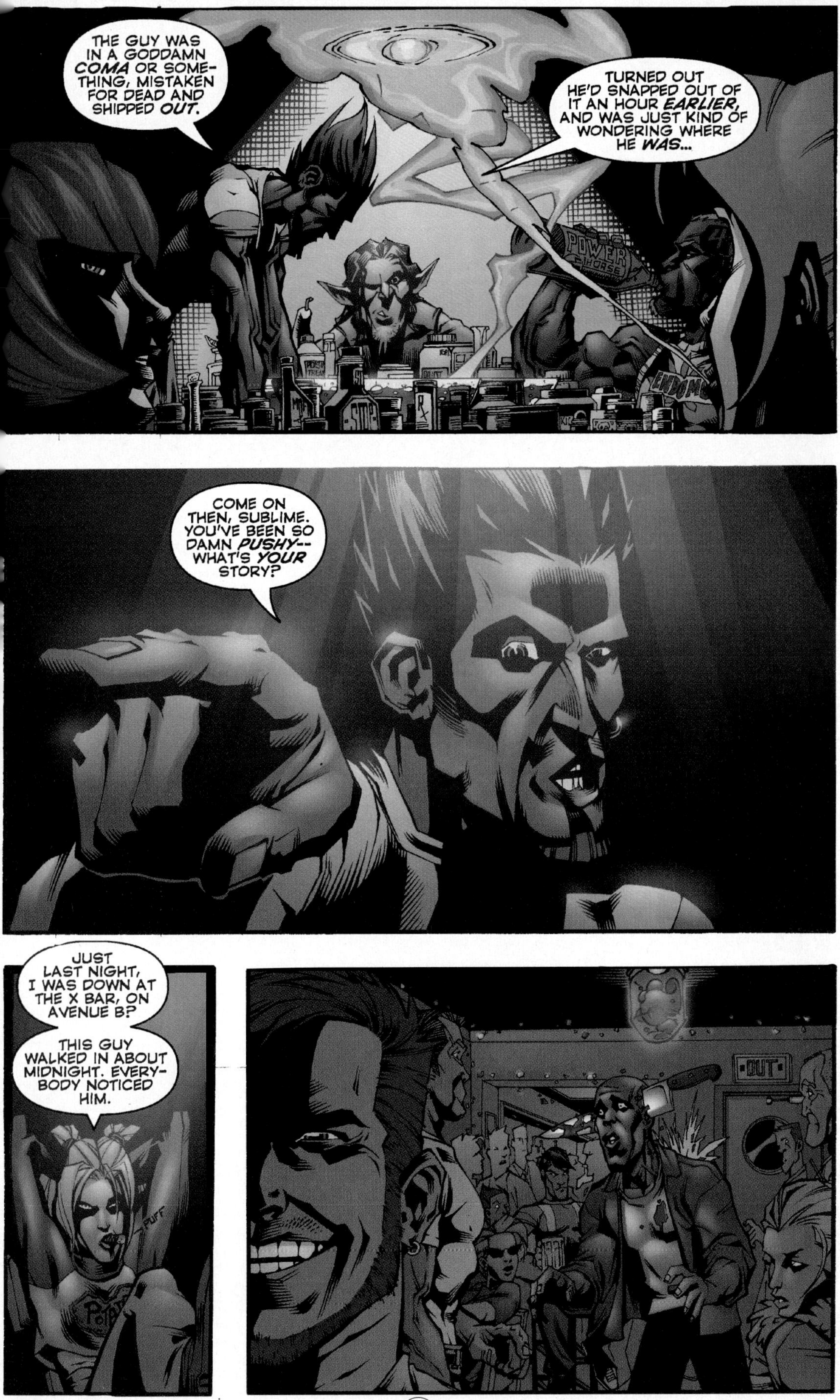
THE GUY WAS IN A GODDAMN *COMA* OR SOME-THING, MISTAKEN FOR DEAD AND SHIPPED *OUT*.
TURNED OUT HE'D SNAPPED OUT OF IT AN HOUR *EARLIER*, AND WAS JUST KIND OF WONDERING WHERE HE *WAS*...
POWER HORSE
COME ON THEN, SUBLIME. YOU'VE BEEN SO DAMN *PUSHY*-- WHAT'S *YOUR* STORY?
JUST LAST NIGHT, I WAS DOWN AT THE X BAR, ON AVENUE B?
THIS GUY WALKED IN ABOUT MIDNIGHT. EVERY-BODY NOTICED HIM.
PUFF
OUT

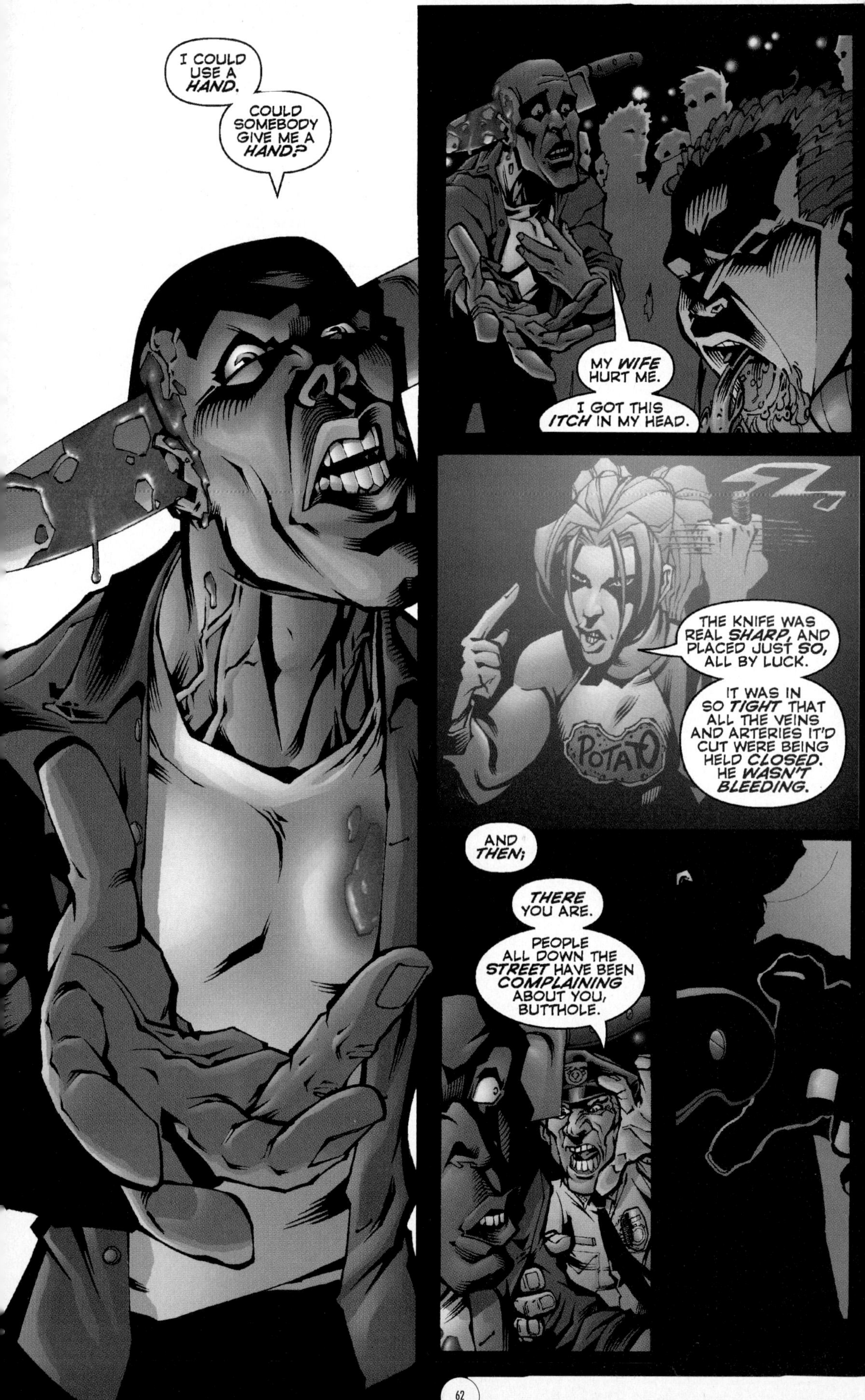
I COULD USE A *HAND*.
COULD SOMEBODY GIVE ME A *HAND?*
MY *WIFE* HURT ME.
I GOT THIS *ITCH* IN MY HEAD.
THE KNIFE WAS REAL *SHARP*, AND PLACED JUST *SO*, ALL BY LUCK.
IT WAS IN SO *TIGHT* THAT ALL THE VEINS AND ARTERIES IT'D CUT WERE BEING HELD *CLOSED*. HE *WASN'T BLEEDING*.
POTATO
AND *THEN*;
THERE YOU ARE.
PEOPLE ALL DOWN THE *STREET* HAVE BEEN *COMPLAINING* ABOUT YOU, BUTTHOLE.

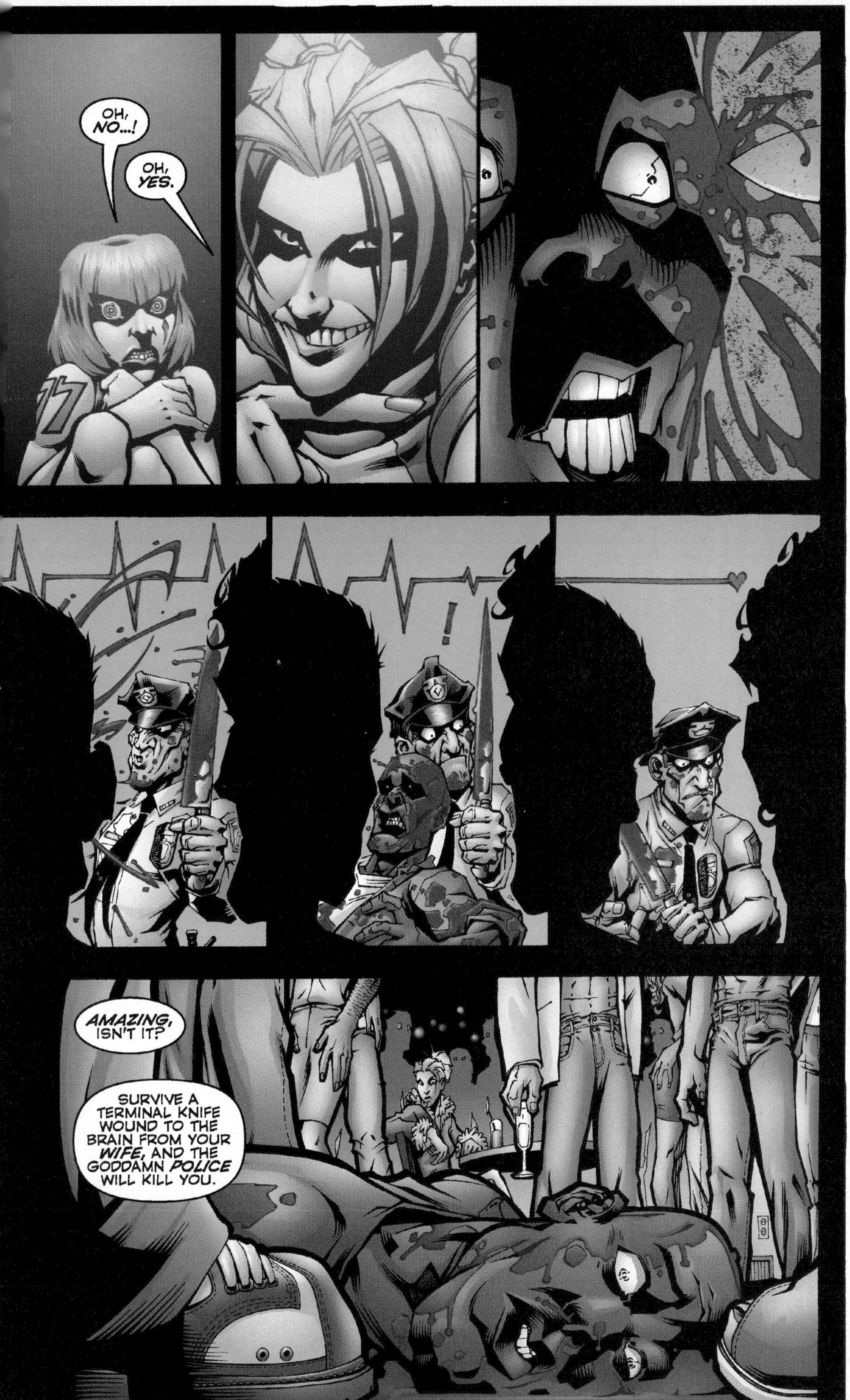
OH, NO...!
OH, YES.
AMAZING, ISN'T IT?
SURVIVE A TERMINAL KNIFE WOUND TO THE BRAIN FROM YOUR WIFE, AND THE GODDAMN POLICE WILL KILL YOU.

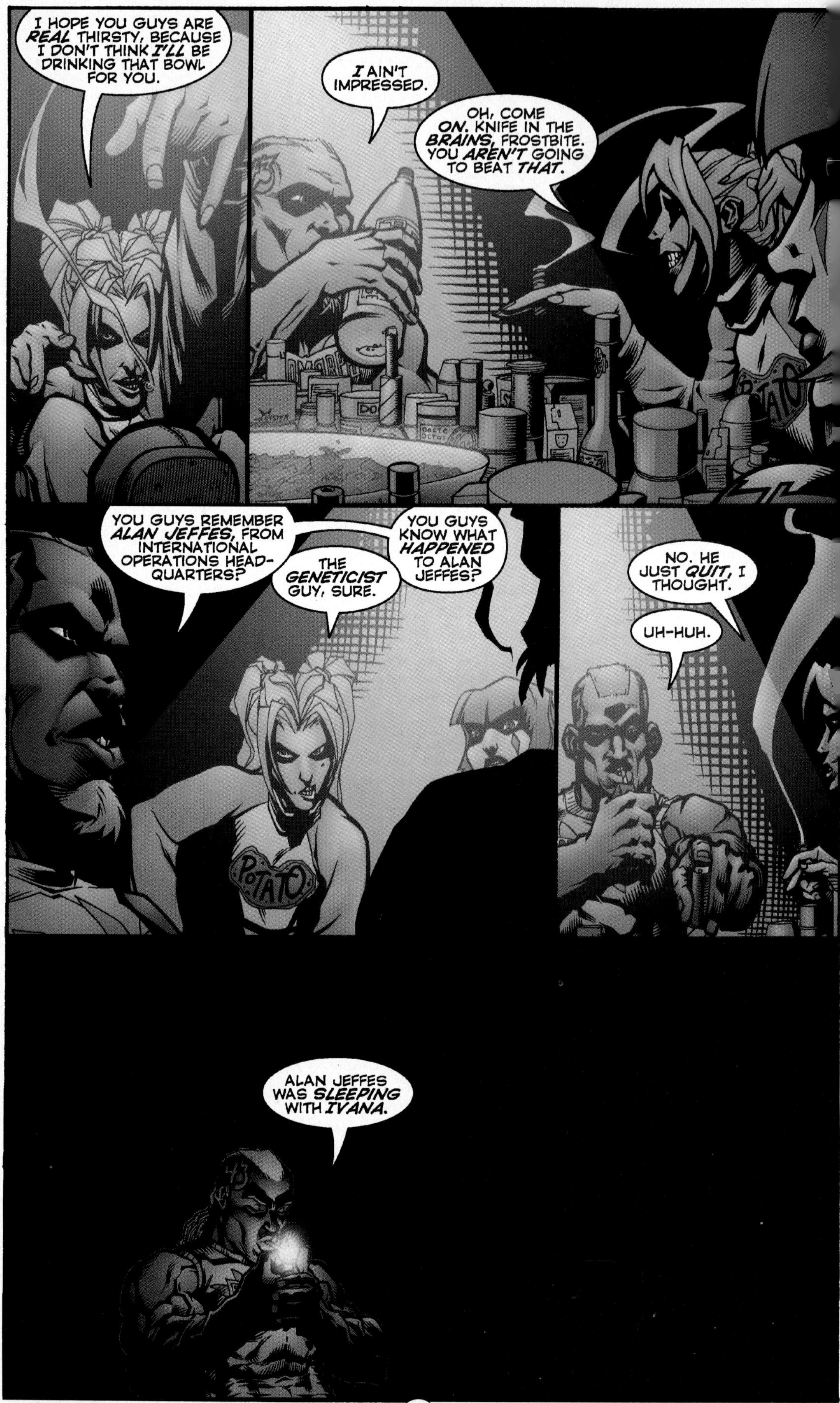
I HOPE YOU GUYS ARE REAL THIRSTY, BECAUSE I DON'T THINK I'LL BE DRINKING THAT BOWL FOR YOU.
I AIN'T IMPRESSED.
OH, COME ON. KNIFE IN THE BRAINS, FROSTBITE. YOU AREN'T GOING TO BEAT THAT.
YOU GUYS REMEMBER ALAN JEFFES, FROM INTERNATIONAL OPERATIONS HEAD-QUARTERS?
THE GENETICIST GUY, SURE.
YOU GUYS KNOW WHAT HAPPENED TO ALAN JEFFES?
NO. HE JUST QUIT, I THOUGHT.
UH-HUH.
ALAN JEFFES WAS SLEEPING WITH IVANA.

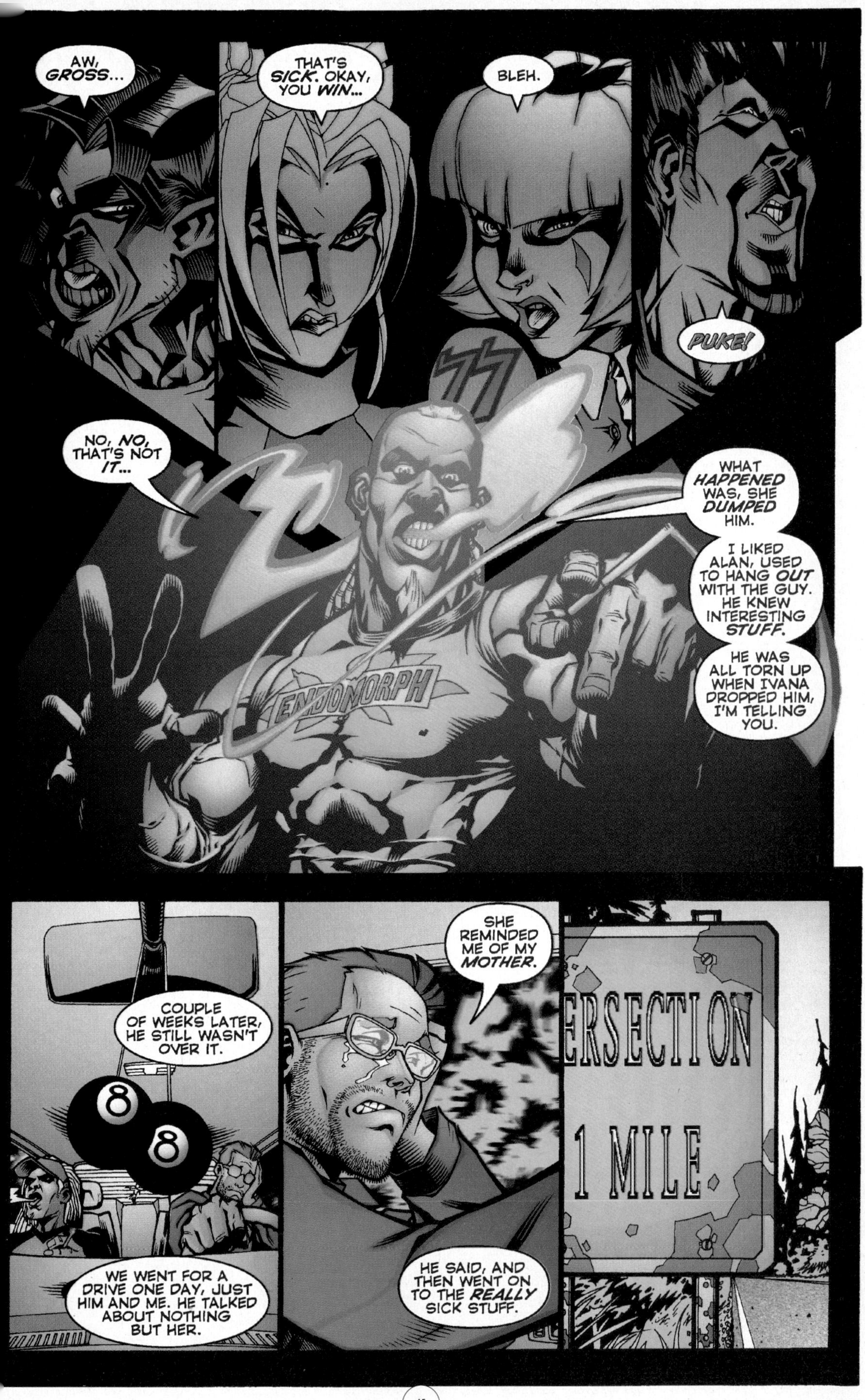

AW, GROSS...
THAT'S SICK. OKAY, YOU WIN...
BLEH.
PUKE!
NO, NO, THAT'S NOT IT...
ENDOMORPH
WHAT HAPPENED WAS, SHE DUMPED HIM.
I LIKED ALAN, USED TO HANG OUT WITH THE GUY. HE KNEW INTERESTING STUFF.
HE WAS ALL TORN UP WHEN IVANA DROPPED HIM, I'M TELLING YOU.
COUPLE OF WEEKS LATER, HE STILL WASN'T OVER IT.
WE WENT FOR A DRIVE ONE DAY, JUST HIM AND ME. HE TALKED ABOUT NOTHING BUT HER.
SHE REMINDED ME OF MY MOTHER.
HE SAID, AND THEN WENT ON TO THE REALLY SICK STUFF.
ERSECTION
1 MILE.

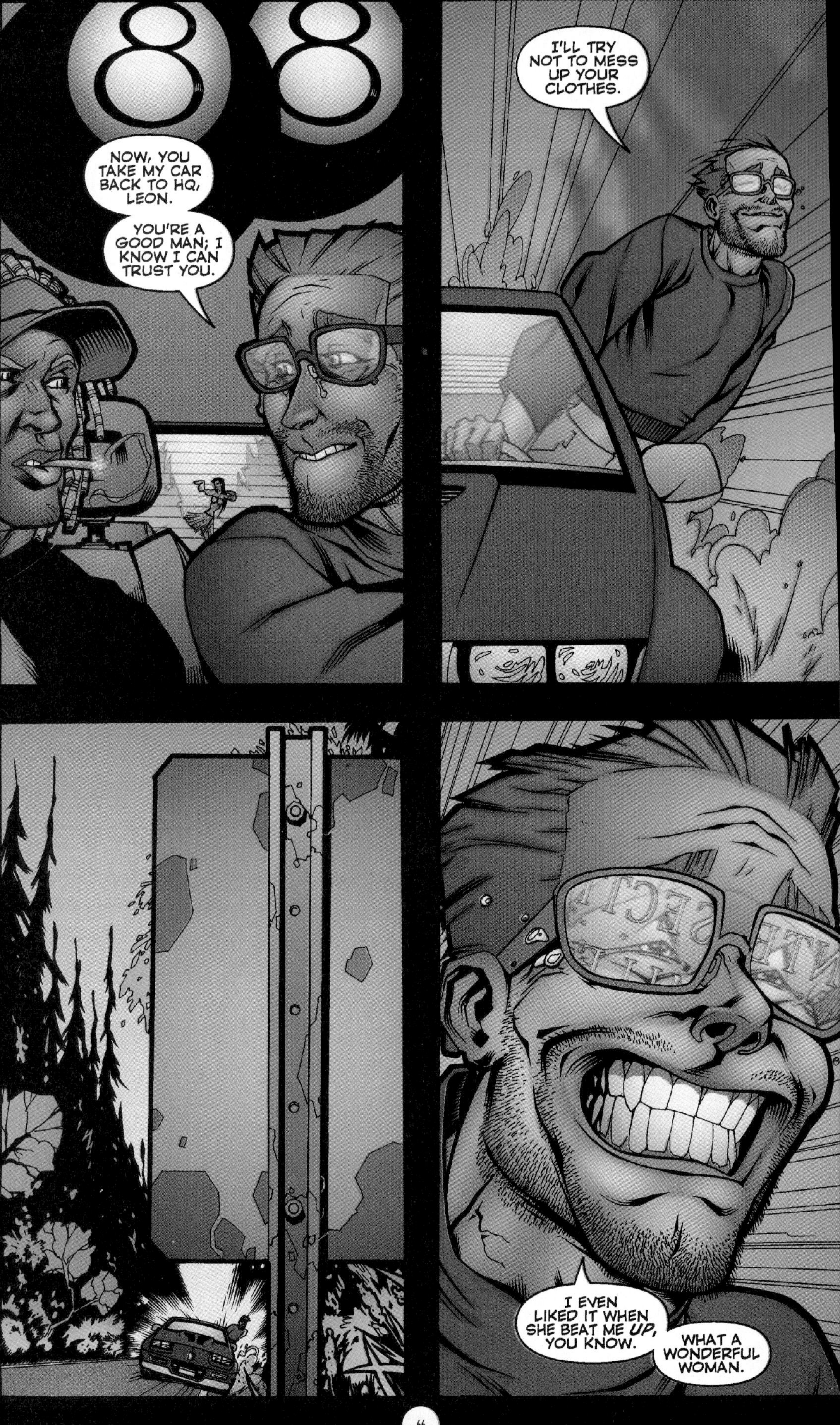

NOW, YOU TAKE MY CAR BACK TO HQ, LEON.
YOU'RE A GOOD MAN; I KNOW I CAN TRUST YOU.
I'LL TRY NOT TO MESS UP YOUR CLOTHES.
I EVEN LIKED IT WHEN SHE BEAT ME *UP*, YOU KNOW.
WHAT A WONDERFUL WOMAN.

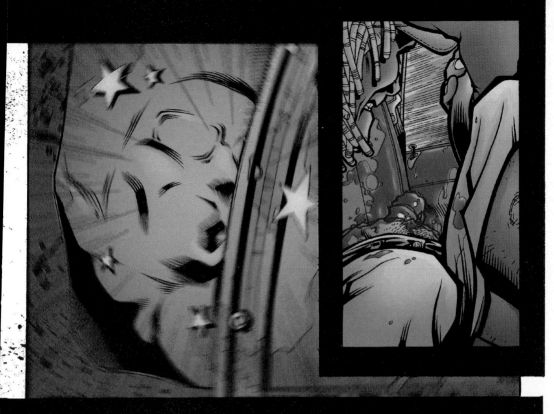

SO, UH...
WHAT DID
YOU *DO?*

WELL,
I COULDN'T
LEAVE THE GUY
LIKE *THAT,*
COULD I?

SO I, YOU
KNOW, REVERSED
THE CAR *UP,* AND
BALANCED THE *TOP*
OF ALAN ON THE
BOTTOM OF
ALAN, AND DROVE
HOME...

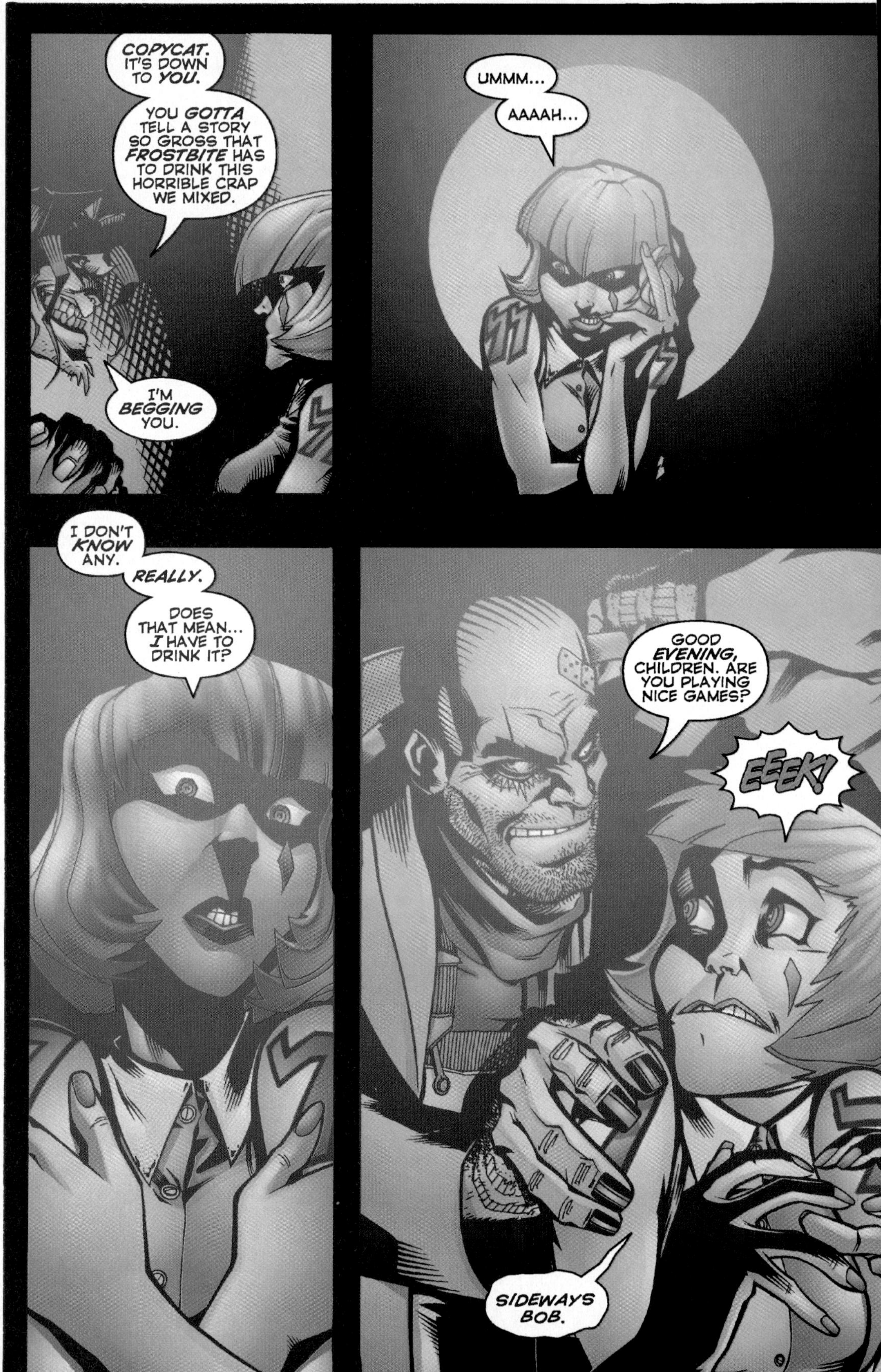
COPYCAT. IT'S DOWN TO YOU.
YOU GOTTA TELL A STORY SO GROSS THAT FROSTBITE HAS TO DRINK THIS HORRIBLE CRAP WE MIXED.
I'M BEGGING YOU.
UMMM...
AAAAH...
I DON'T KNOW ANY.
REALLY.
DOES THAT MEAN... I HAVE TO DRINK IT?
GOOD EVENING, CHILDREN. ARE YOU PLAYING NICE GAMES?
EEEK!
SIDEWAYS BOB.

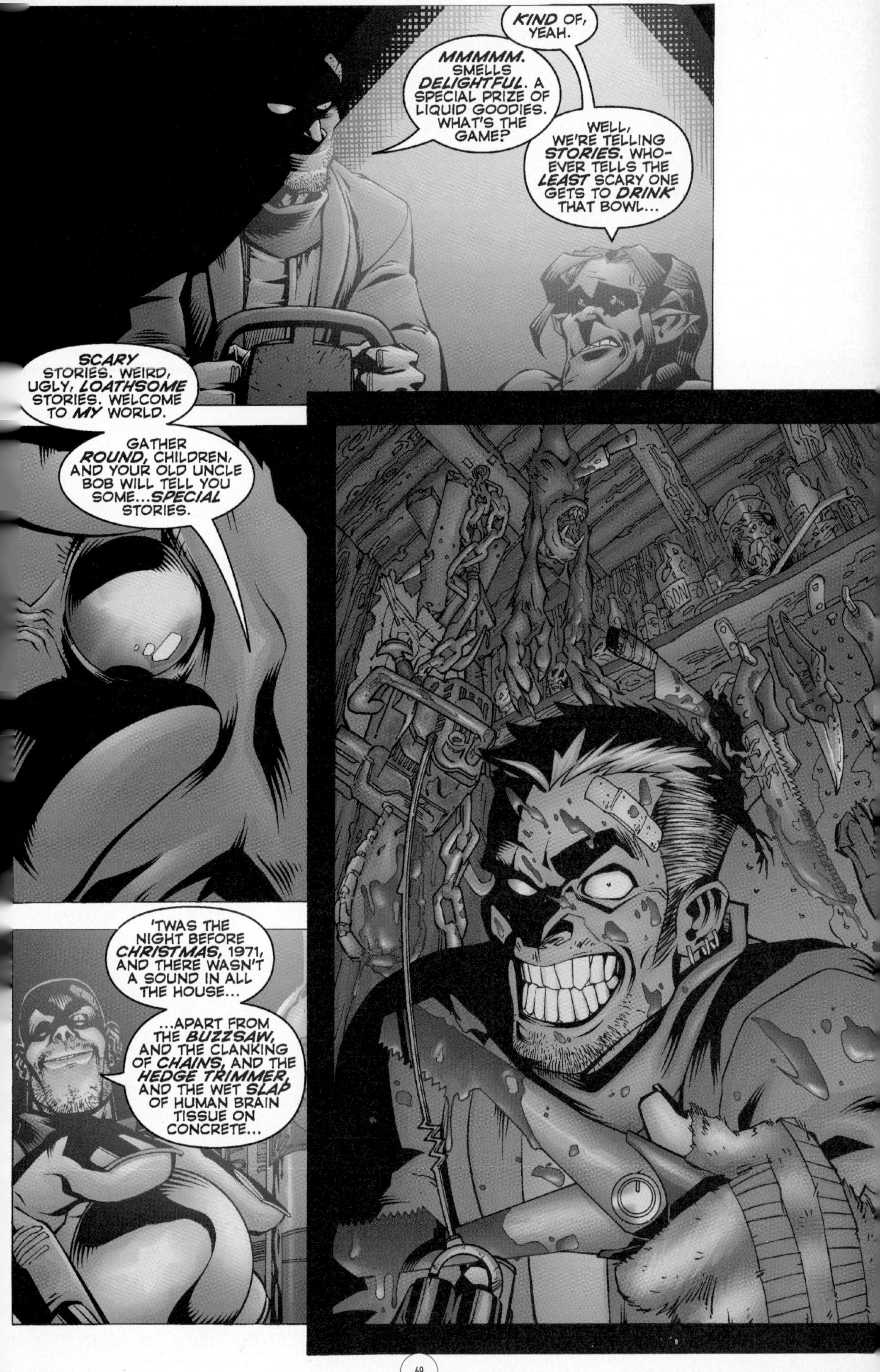
KIND OF, YEAH.
MMMMM. SMELLS DELIGHTFUL. A SPECIAL PRIZE OF LIQUID GOODIES. WHAT'S THE GAME?
WELL, WE'RE TELLING STORIES. WHO-EVER TELLS THE LEAST SCARY ONE GETS TO DRINK THAT BOWL...
SCARY STORIES. WEIRD, UGLY, LOATHSOME STORIES. WELCOME TO MY WORLD.
GATHER ROUND, CHILDREN, AND YOUR OLD UNCLE BOB WILL TELL YOU SOME...SPECIAL STORIES.
'TWAS THE NIGHT BEFORE CHRISTMAS, 1971, AND THERE WASN'T A SOUND IN ALL THE HOUSE...
...APART FROM THE BUZZSAW, AND THE CLANKING OF CHAINS, AND THE HEDGE TRIMMER, AND THE WET SLAP OF HUMAN BRAIN TISSUE ON CONCRETE...

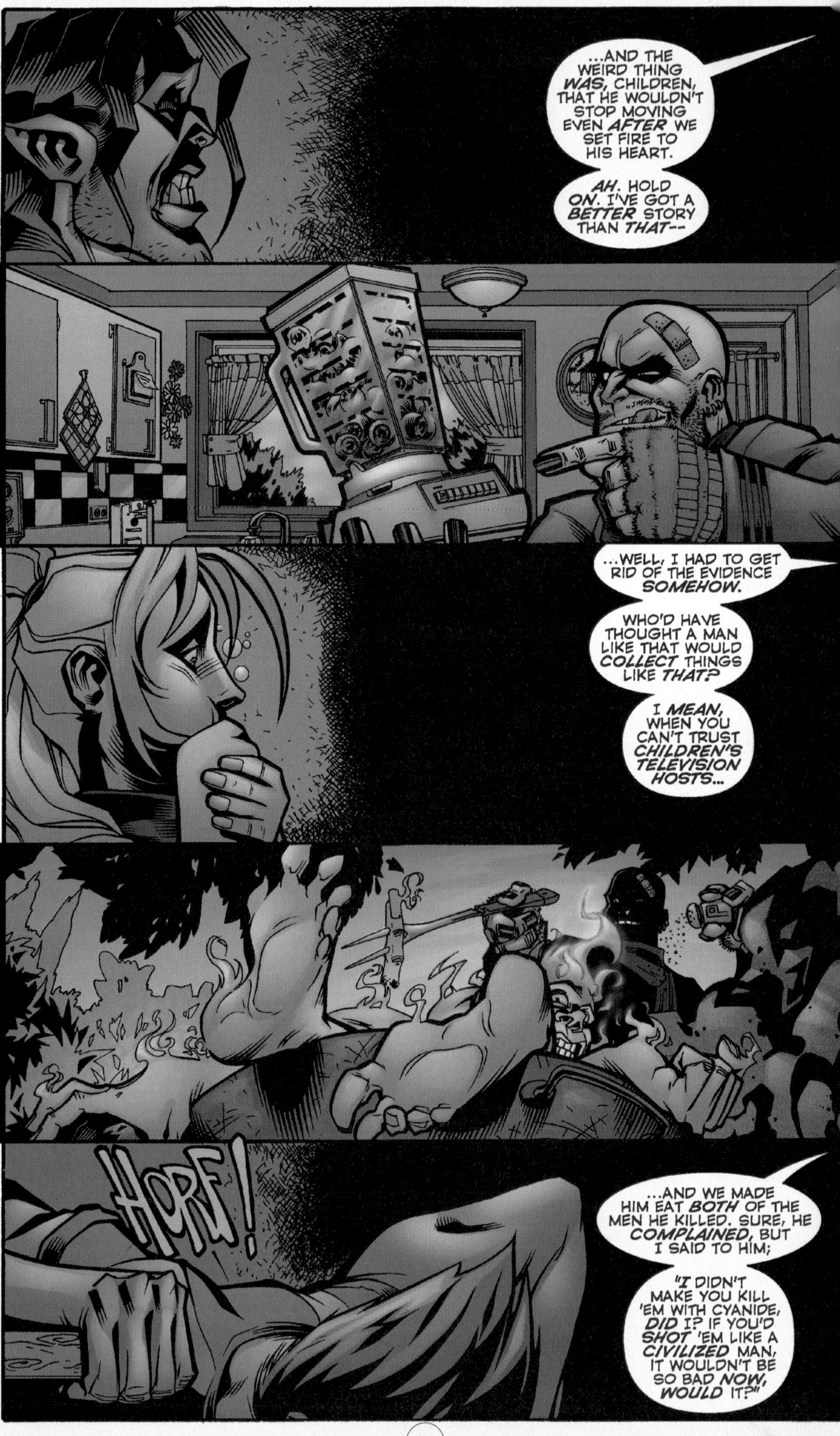
...AND THE WEIRD THING WAS, CHILDREN, THAT HE WOULDN'T STOP MOVING EVEN AFTER WE SET FIRE TO HIS HEART.
AH. HOLD ON. I'VE GOT A BETTER STORY THAN THAT--
...WELL, I HAD TO GET RID OF THE EVIDENCE SOMEHOW.
WHO'D HAVE THOUGHT A MAN LIKE THAT WOULD COLLECT THINGS LIKE THAT?
I MEAN, WHEN YOU CAN'T TRUST CHILDREN'S TELEVISION HOSTS...
HORF!
...AND WE MADE HIM EAT BOTH OF THE MEN HE KILLED. SURE, HE COMPLAINED, BUT I SAID TO HIM;
"I DIDN'T MAKE YOU KILL 'EM WITH CYANIDE, DID I? IF YOU'D SHOT 'EM LIKE A CIVILIZED MAN, IT WOULDN'T BE SO BAD NOW, WOULD IT?"

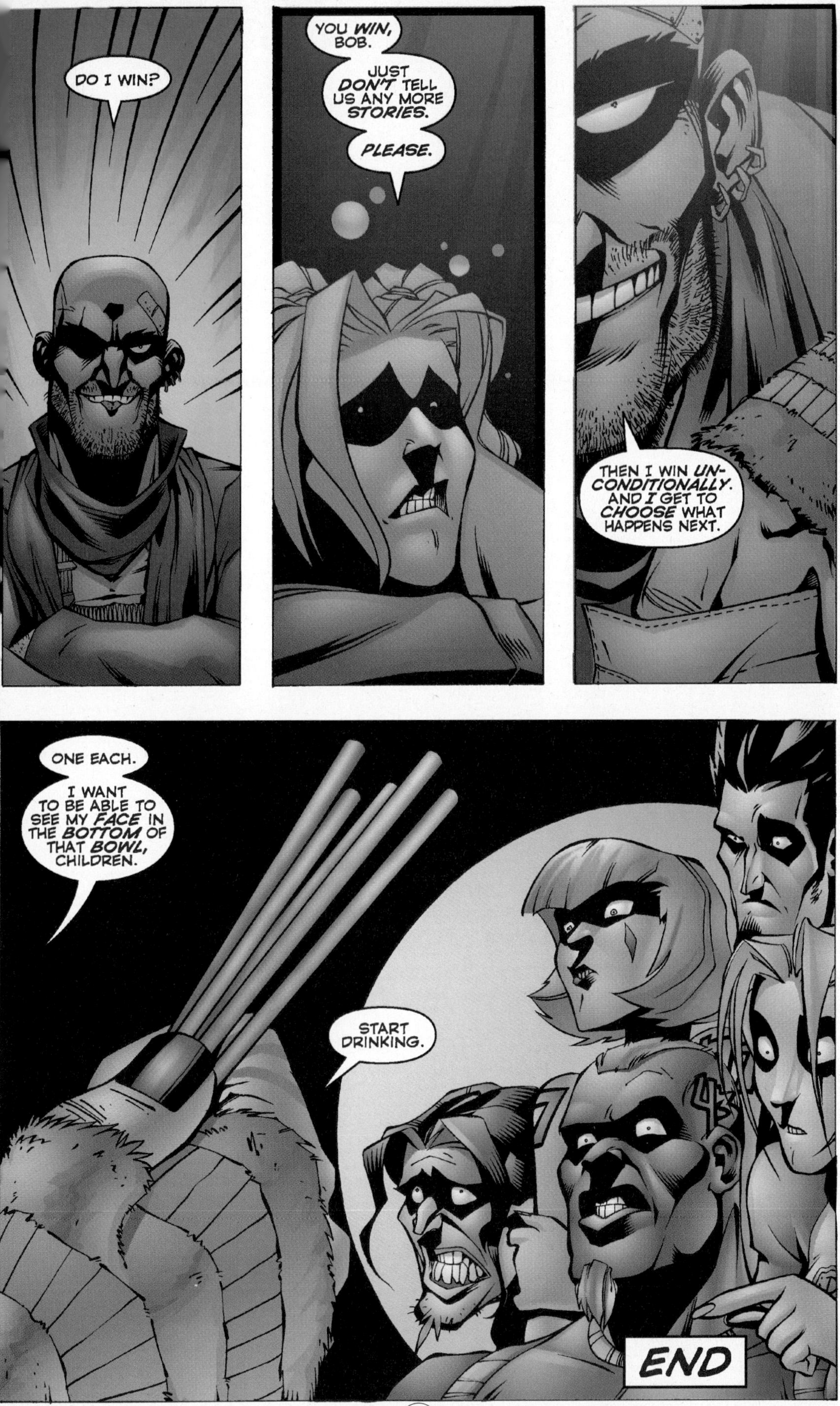
DO I WIN?
YOU WIN, BOB.
JUST DON'T TELL US ANY MORE STORIES.
PLEASE.
THEN I WIN UN-CONDITIONALLY. AND I GET TO CHOOSE WHAT HAPPENS NEXT.
ONE EACH.
I WANT TO BE ABLE TO SEE MY FACE IN THE BOTTOM OF THAT BOWL, CHILDREN.
START DRINKING.
END

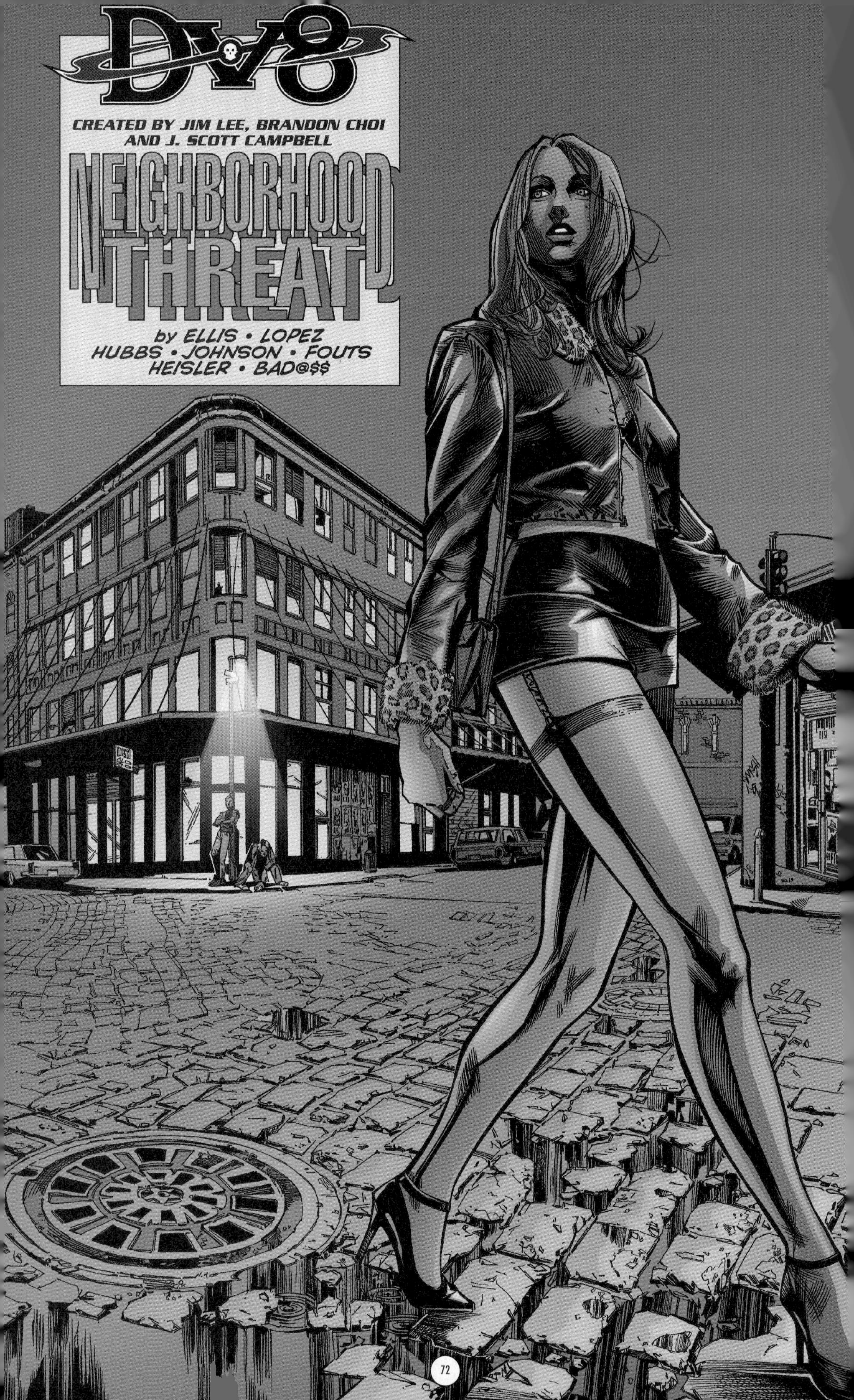
DV8
CREATED BY JIM LEE, BRANDON CHOI
AND J. SCOTT CAMPBELL
NEIGHBORHOOD THREAT
by ELLIS • LOPEZ
HUBBS • JOHNSON • FOUTS
HEISLER • BAD@$$

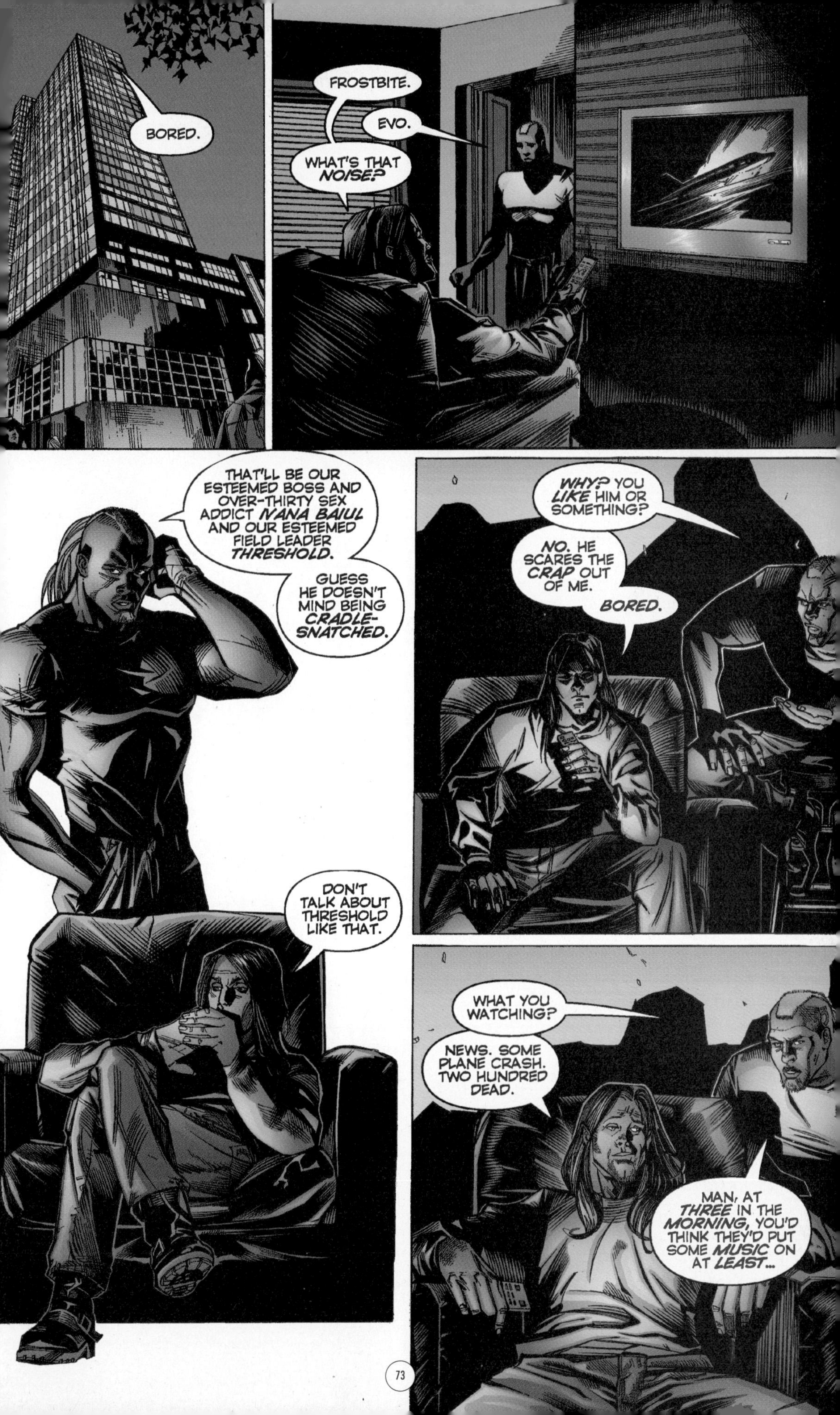
BORED.
FROSTBITE.
EVO.
WHAT'S THAT NOISE?
THAT'LL BE OUR ESTEEMED BOSS AND OVER-THIRTY SEX ADDICT IVANA BAIUL AND OUR ESTEEMED FIELD LEADER THRESHOLD.
GUESS HE DOESN'T MIND BEING CRADLE-SNATCHED.
DON'T TALK ABOUT THRESHOLD LIKE THAT.
WHY? YOU LIKE HIM OR SOMETHING?
NO. HE SCARES THE CRAP OUT OF ME.
BORED.
WHAT YOU WATCHING?
NEWS. SOME PLANE CRASH. TWO HUNDRED DEAD.
MAN, AT THREE IN THE MORNING, YOU'D THINK THEY'D PUT SOME MUSIC ON AT LEAST...

I'M GOING OUT FOR A WALK. BUY SOME DRUGS OR SOMETHING, I DUNNO...

I'LL COME WITH YOU.

WHAT'S UP?

AH, PROBABLY NOTHING.... COPYCAT'S BEEN LOOKING AT ME REAL STRANGELY LATELY, IS ALL. GIVES ME THE CREEPS, DUNNO WHY...

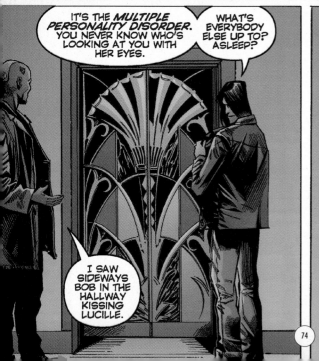

IT'S THE MULTIPLE PERSONALITY DISORDER. YOU NEVER KNOW WHO'S LOOKING AT YOU WITH HER EYES.

WHAT'S EVERYBODY ELSE UP TO? ASLEEP?

I SAW SIDEWAYS BOB IN THE HALLWAY KISSING LUCILLE.

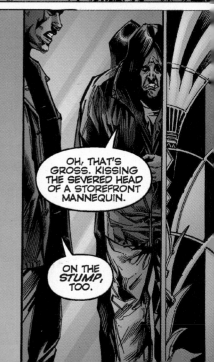

OH, THAT'S GROSS. KISSING THE SEVERED HEAD OF A STOREFRONT MANNEQUIN.

ON THE STUMP, TOO.

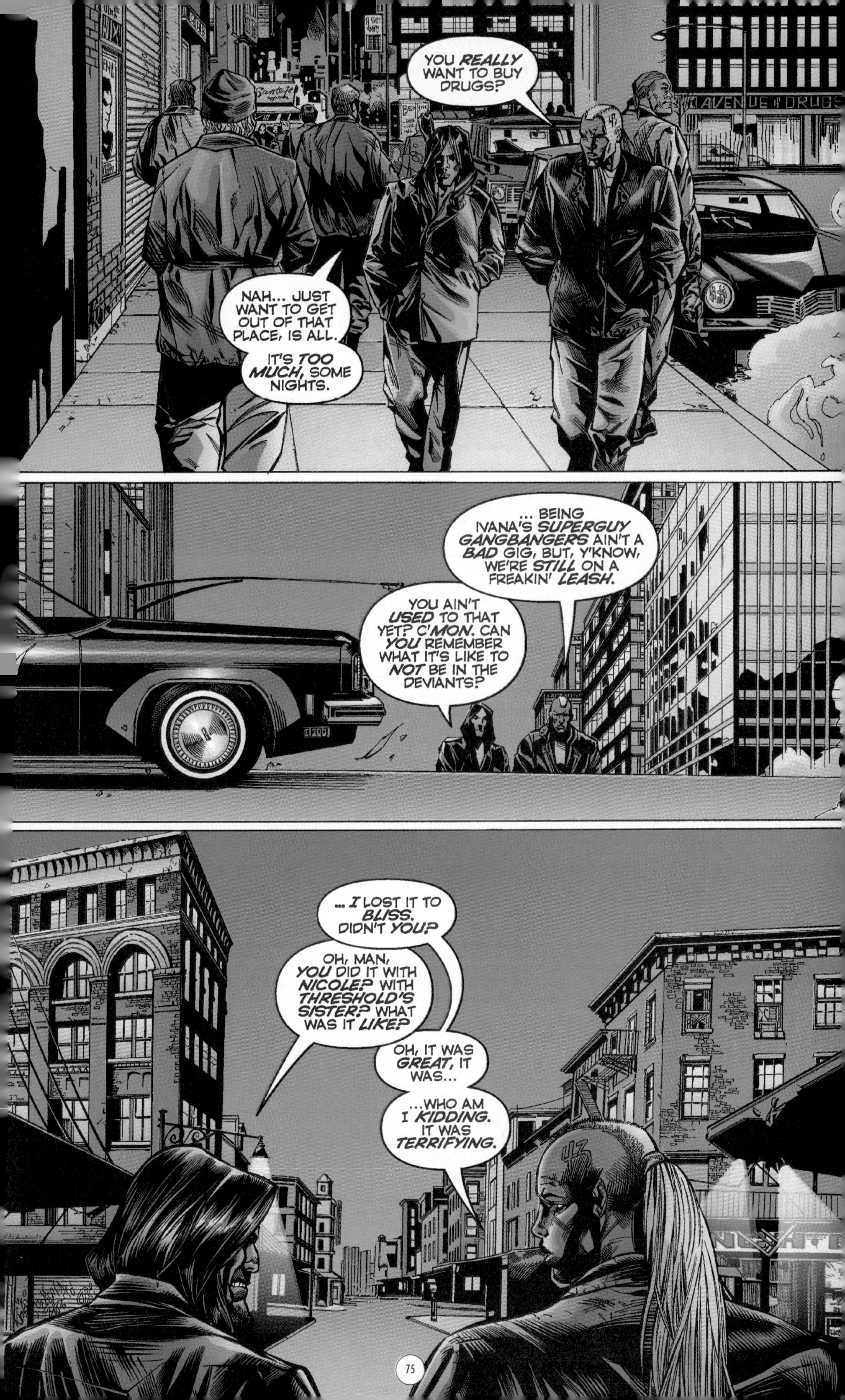
YOU *REALLY* WANT TO BUY DRUGS?
NAH... JUST WANT TO GET OUT OF THAT PLACE, IS ALL.
IT'S *TOO MUCH,* SOME NIGHTS.
... BEING IVANA'S *SUPERGUY GANGBANGERS* AIN'T A *BAD* GIG, BUT, Y'KNOW, WE'RE *STILL* ON A FREAKIN' *LEASH.*
YOU AIN'T *USED* TO THAT YET? C'*MON.* CAN *YOU* REMEMBER WHAT IT'S LIKE TO *NOT* BE IN THE DEVIANTS?
... *I* LOST IT TO *BLISS.* DIDN'T *YOU?*
OH, MAN, *YOU* DID IT WITH *NICOLE?* WITH *THRESHOLD'S SISTER?* WHAT WAS IT *LIKE?*
OH, IT WAS *GREAT,* IT WAS...
...WHO AM I *KIDDING.* IT WAS *TERRIFYING.*

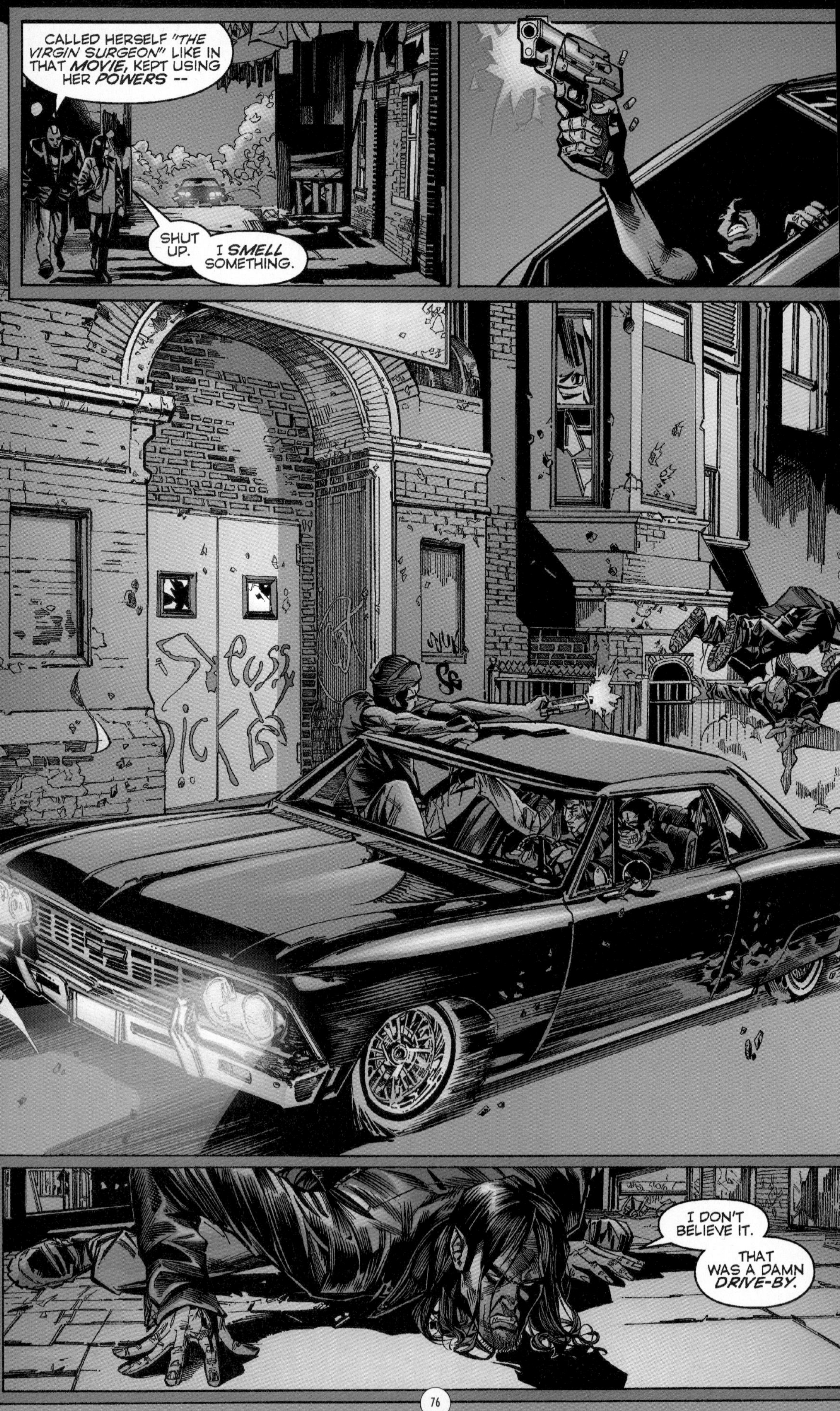
CALLED HERSELF "THE VIRGIN SURGEON" LIKE IN THAT MOVIE, KEPT USING HER POWERS --
SHUT UP.
I SMELL SOMETHING.
I DON'T BELIEVE IT.
THAT WAS A DAMN DRIVE-BY.

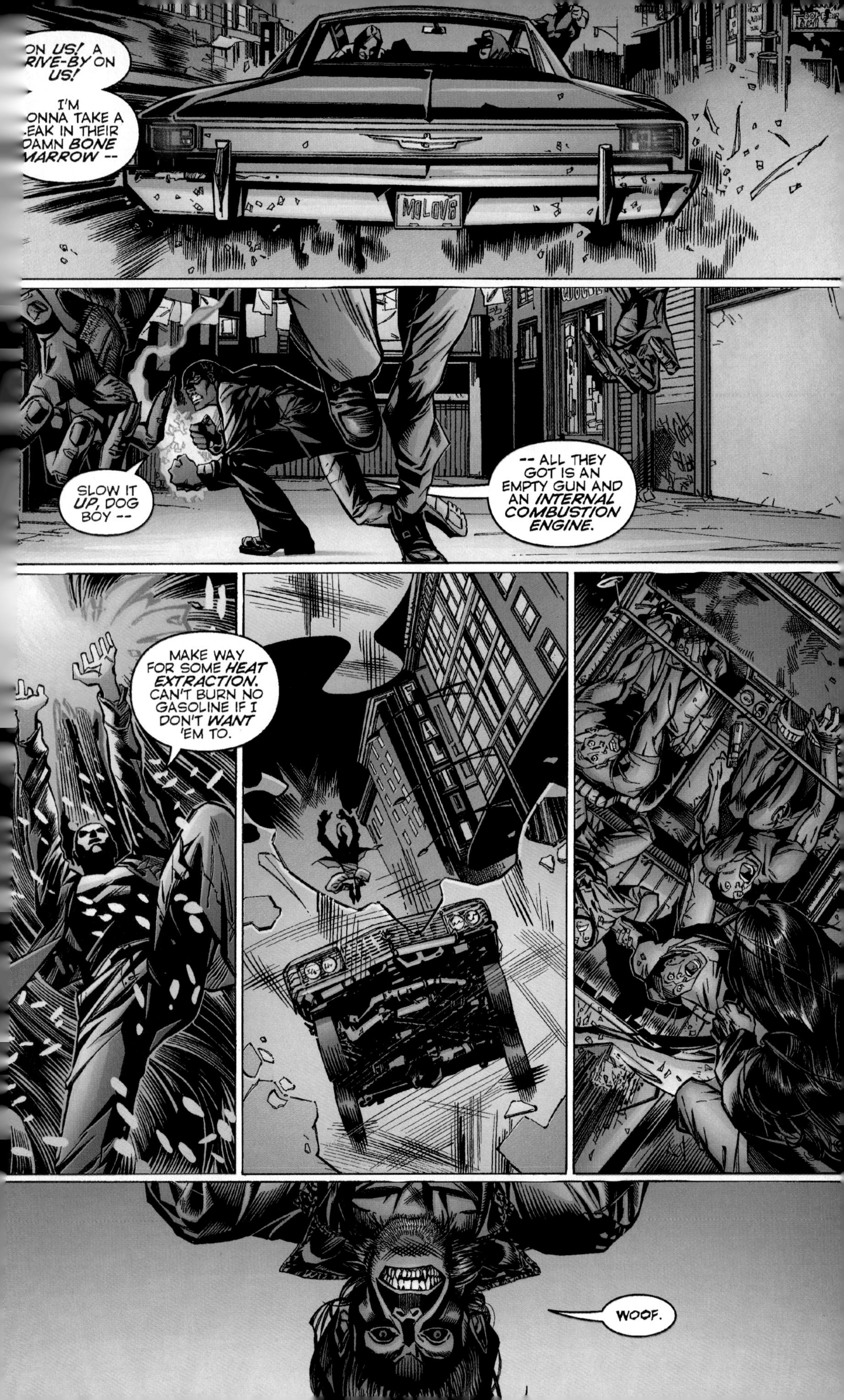
ON US! A RIVE-BY ON US!
I'M ONNA TAKE A EAK IN THEIR DAMN BONE MARROW --
SLOW IT UP, DOG BOY --
-- ALL THEY GOT IS AN EMPTY GUN AND AN INTERNAL COMBUSTION ENGINE.
MAKE WAY FOR SOME HEAT EXTRACTION. CAN'T BURN NO GASOLINE IF I DON'T WANT 'EM TO.
WOOF.

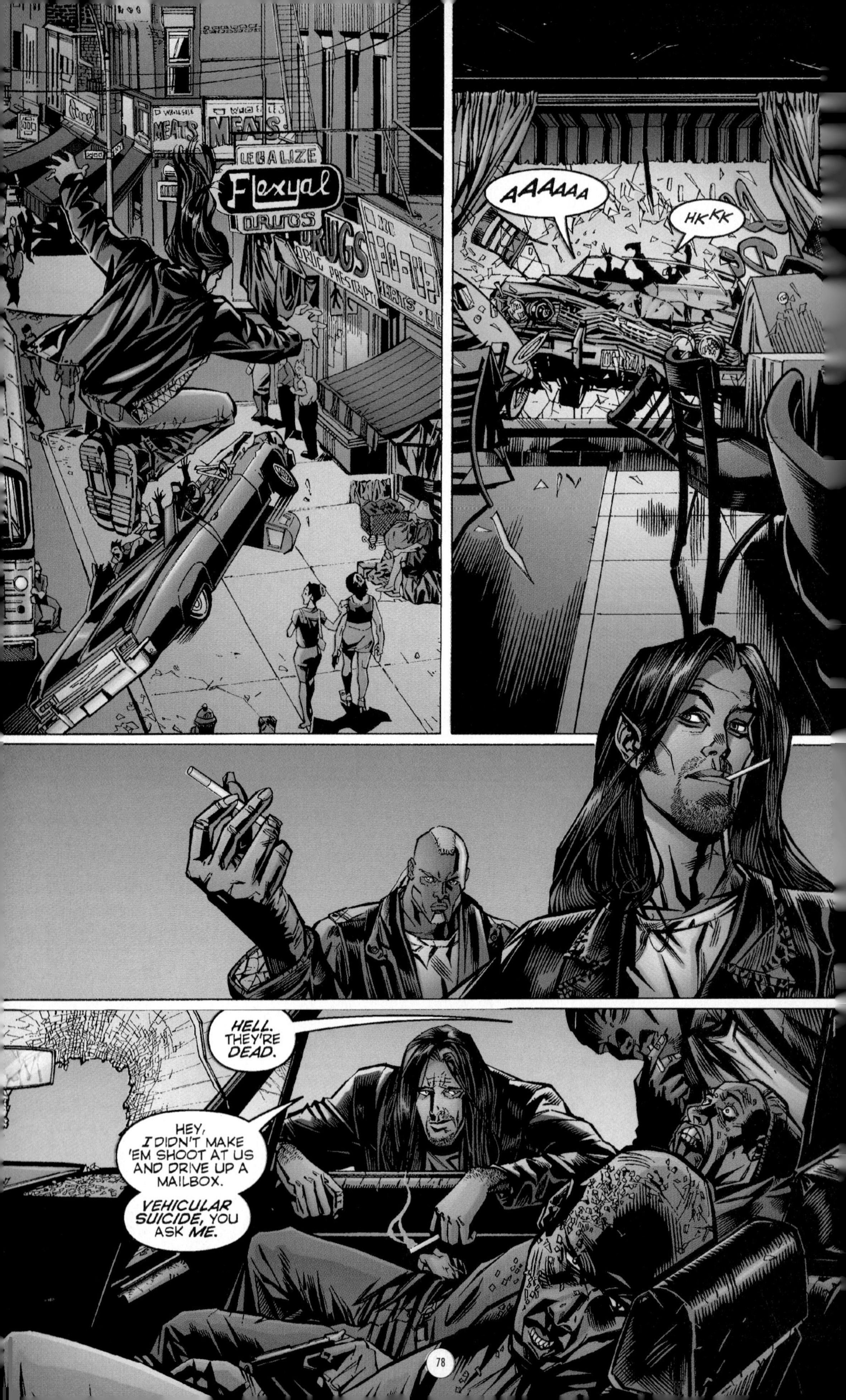

MEATS
MEATS
LEGALIZE
Flexyal
DRUGS
DRUGS
AAAAAA
HKKK
HELL. THEY'RE DEAD.
HEY, I DIDN'T MAKE 'EM SHOOT AT US AND DRIVE UP A MAILBOX.
VEHICULAR SUICIDE, YOU ASK ME.

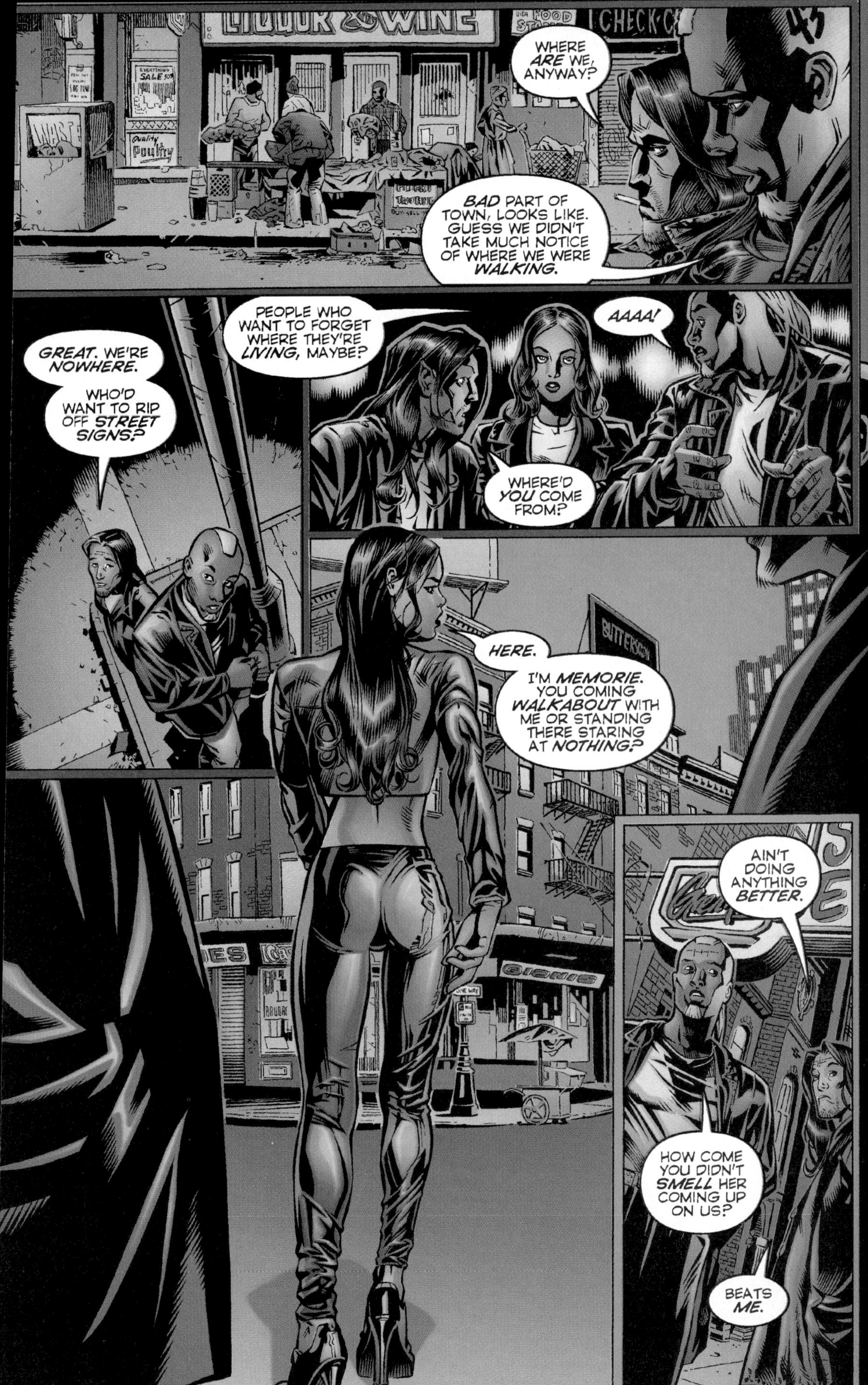
LIQUOR & WINE
Quality Poultry
WHERE ARE WE, ANYWAY?
BAD PART OF TOWN, LOOKS LIKE. GUESS WE DIDN'T TAKE MUCH NOTICE OF WHERE WE WERE WALKING.
GREAT. WE'RE NOWHERE.
WHO'D WANT TO RIP OFF STREET SIGNS?
PEOPLE WHO WANT TO FORGET WHERE THEY'RE LIVING, MAYBE?
AAAA!
WHERE'D YOU COME FROM?
HERE.
I'M MEMORIE. YOU COMING WALKABOUT WITH ME OR STANDING THERE STARING AT NOTHING?
AIN'T DOING ANYTHING BETTER.
HOW COME YOU DIDN'T SMELL HER COMING UP ON US?
BEATS ME.

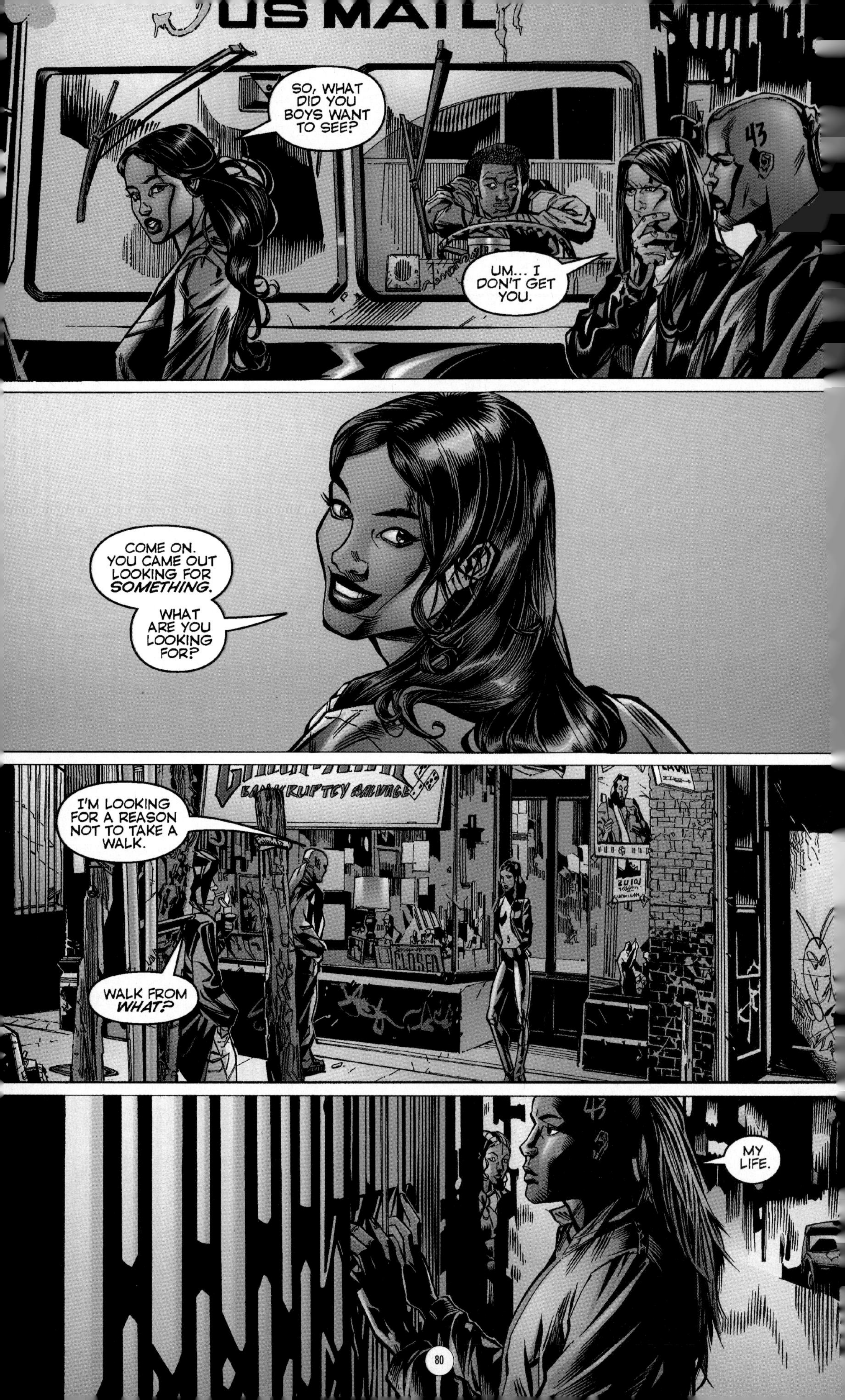
US MAIL
SO, WHAT DID YOU BOYS WANT TO SEE?
UM... I DON'T GET YOU.
COME ON. YOU CAME OUT LOOKING FOR *SOMETHING.*
WHAT ARE YOU LOOKING FOR?
I'M LOOKING FOR A REASON NOT TO TAKE A WALK.
WALK FROM *WHAT?*
CLOSED
MY LIFE.

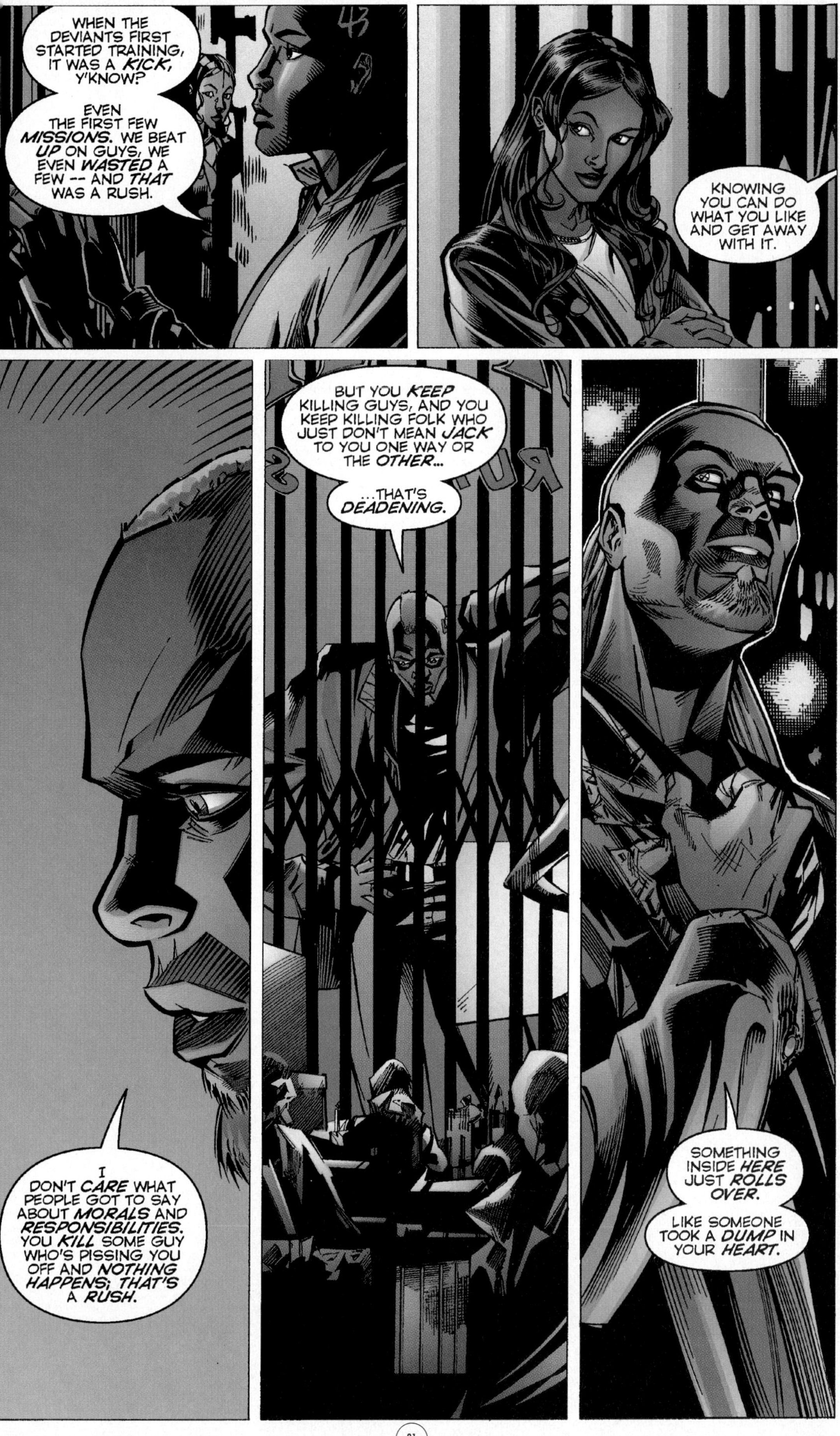
WHEN THE DEVIANTS FIRST STARTED TRAINING, IT WAS A KICK, Y'KNOW?
EVEN THE FIRST FEW MISSIONS. WE BEAT UP ON GUYS, WE EVEN WASTED A FEW -- AND THAT WAS A RUSH.
KNOWING YOU CAN DO WHAT YOU LIKE AND GET AWAY WITH IT.
I DON'T CARE WHAT PEOPLE GOT TO SAY ABOUT MORALS AND RESPONSIBILITIES. YOU KILL SOME GUY WHO'S PISSING YOU OFF AND NOTHING HAPPENS; THAT'S A RUSH.
BUT YOU KEEP KILLING GUYS, AND YOU KEEP KILLING FOLK WHO JUST DON'T MEAN JACK TO YOU ONE WAY OR THE OTHER...
...THAT'S DEADENING.
SOMETHING INSIDE HERE JUST ROLLS OVER.
LIKE SOMEONE TOOK A DUMP IN YOUR HEART.

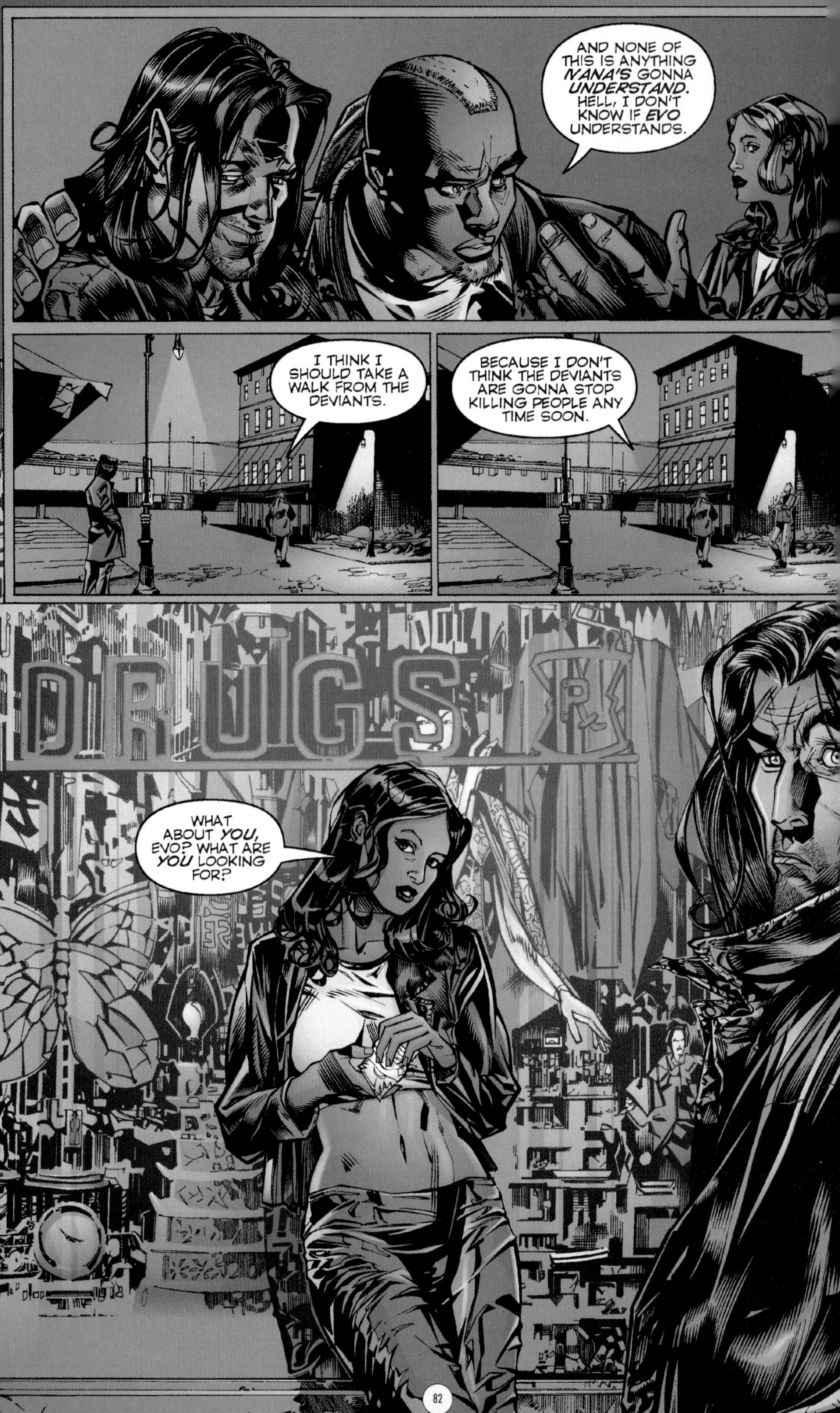

AND NONE OF THIS IS ANYTHING NANA'S GONNA UNDERSTAND. HELL, I DON'T KNOW IF EVO UNDERSTANDS.
I THINK I SHOULD TAKE A WALK FROM THE DEVIANTS.
BECAUSE I DON'T THINK THE DEVIANTS ARE GONNA STOP KILLING PEOPLE ANY TIME SOON.
DRUGS
WHAT ABOUT YOU, EVO? WHAT ARE YOU LOOKING FOR?

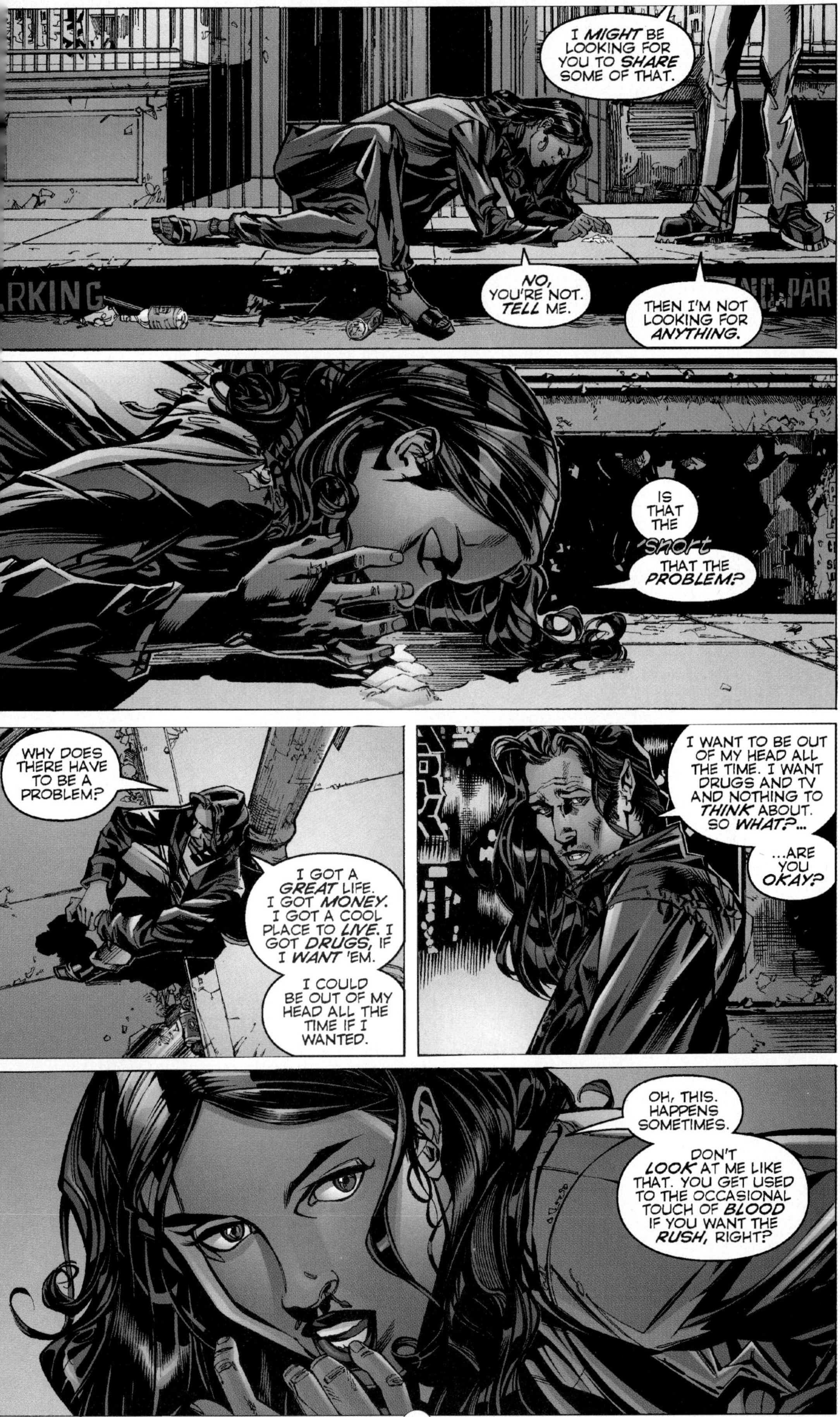
I MIGHT BE LOOKING FOR YOU TO SHARE SOME OF THAT.
RKING
NO, YOU'RE NOT. TELL ME.
THEN I'M NOT LOOKING FOR ANYTHING.
NO PAR
IS THAT THE snort THAT THE PROBLEM?
WHY DOES THERE HAVE TO BE A PROBLEM?
I GOT A GREAT LIFE. I GOT MONEY. I GOT A COOL PLACE TO LIVE. I GOT DRUGS, IF I WANT 'EM.
I COULD BE OUT OF MY HEAD ALL THE TIME IF I WANTED.
I WANT TO BE OUT OF MY HEAD ALL THE TIME. I WANT DRUGS AND TV AND NOTHING TO THINK ABOUT. SO WHAT?...
...ARE YOU OKAY?
OH, THIS. HAPPENS SOMETIMES.
DON'T LOOK AT ME LIKE THAT. YOU GET USED TO THE OCCASIONAL TOUCH OF BLOOD IF YOU WANT THE RUSH, RIGHT?

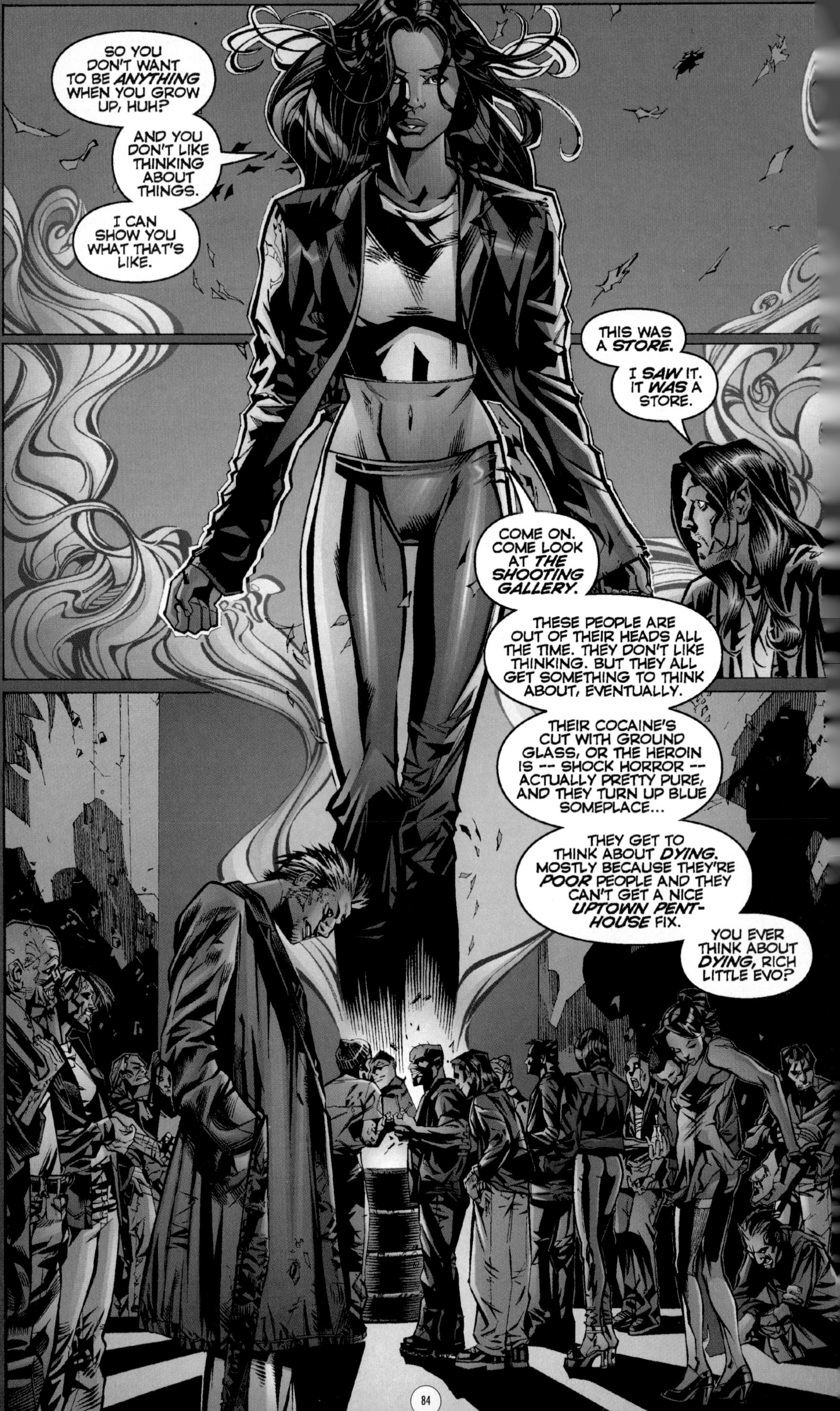
SO YOU DON'T WANT TO BE *ANYTHING* WHEN YOU GROW UP, HUH?
AND YOU DON'T LIKE THINKING ABOUT THINGS.
I CAN SHOW YOU WHAT THAT'S LIKE.
THIS WAS A *STORE.*
I *SAW* IT. IT *WAS* A STORE.
COME ON. COME LOOK AT *THE SHOOTING GALLERY.*
THESE PEOPLE ARE OUT OF THEIR HEADS ALL THE TIME. THEY DON'T LIKE THINKING. BUT THEY ALL GET SOMETHING TO THINK ABOUT, EVENTUALLY.
THEIR COCAINE'S CUT WITH GROUND GLASS, OR THE HEROIN IS -- SHOCK HORROR -- ACTUALLY PRETTY PURE, AND THEY TURN UP BLUE SOMEPLACE...
THEY GET TO THINK ABOUT *DYING.* MOSTLY BECAUSE THEY'RE *POOR* PEOPLE AND THEY CAN'T GET A NICE *UPTOWN PENT-HOUSE* FIX.
YOU EVER THINK ABOUT *DYING,* RICH LITTLE EVO?

I THINK ABOUT DYING FOR SOME DAMN THING OF IVANA'S THAT I DON'T UNDERSTAND.

I THINK ABOUT DYING WHEN I'VE NEVER HAD SEX.

I SIT ALONE IN MY DAMN ROOM, OR I GO TO A BAR OR A CLUB AND IT'S LIKE I'M *WEARING* THE DAMN ROOM, THE SPACE THAT CLEARS AROUND ME --

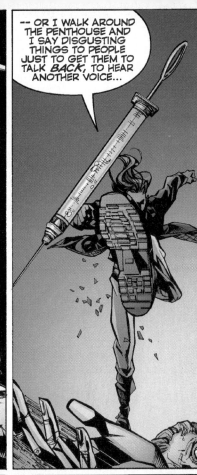

-- OR I WALK AROUND THE PENTHOUSE AND I SAY DISGUSTING THINGS TO PEOPLE JUST TO GET THEM TO TALK *BACK*, TO HEAR ANOTHER VOICE...

YOU KNOW I NEARLY DID IT WITH SOMEONE THE OTHER WEEK? A GIRL NAMED *VIRGINIA*.

BUT I *KILLED* HER *INSTEAD*. *HA!*

KNOW *WHY?*

BECAUSE SHE WANTED TO *DO* IT WITH ME IN FRONT OF *CHAINED, STARVING, CRIPPLED KIDS.*

AND YOU *WONDER* WHY I *DON'T* WANT TO *THINK?* WOULD *YOU* WANT TO THINK ABOUT *THAT?*

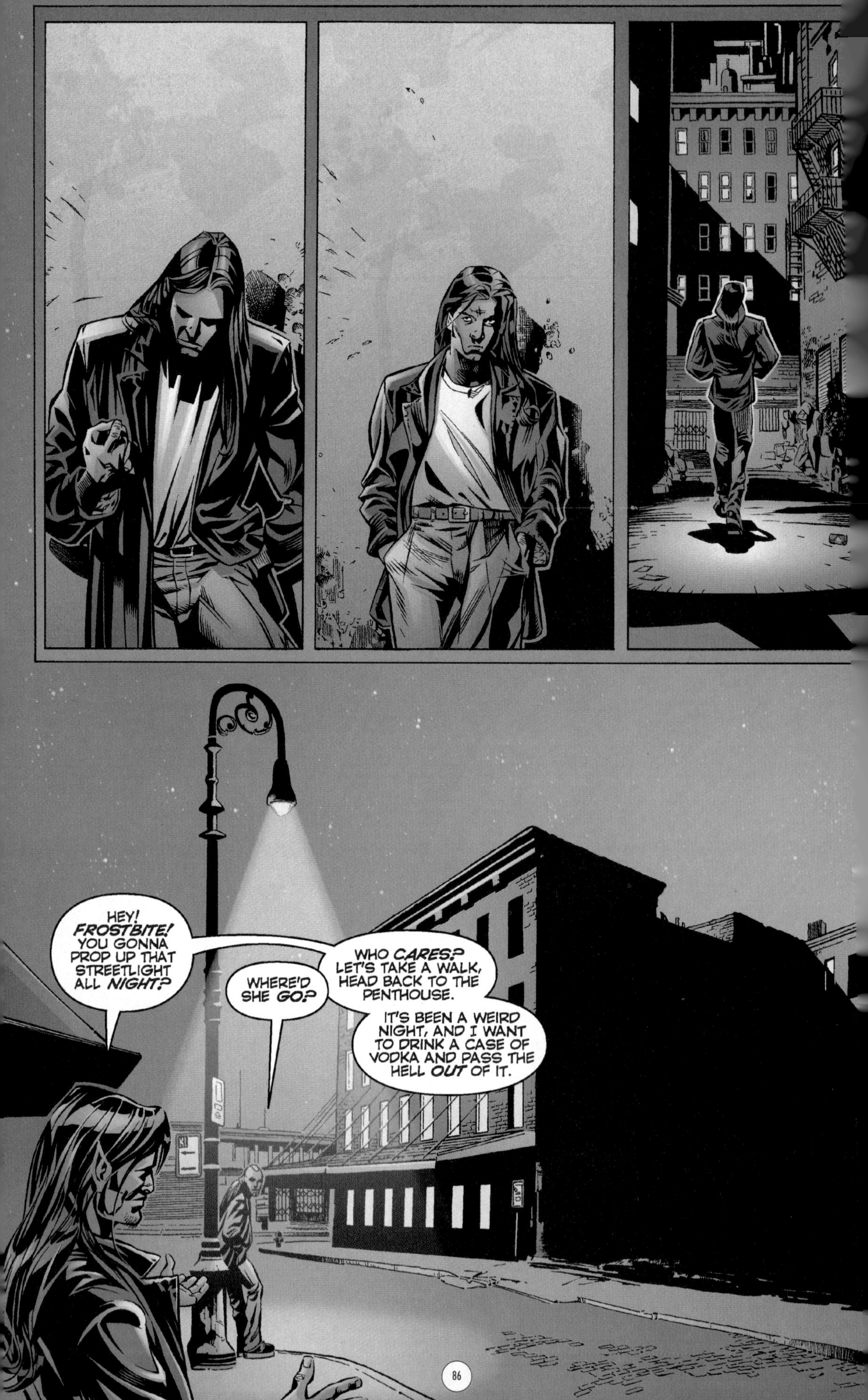
HEY! FROSTBITE! YOU GONNA PROP UP THAT STREETLIGHT ALL NIGHT?
WHERE'D SHE GO?
WHO CARES? LET'S TAKE A WALK, HEAD BACK TO THE PENTHOUSE.
IT'S BEEN A WEIRD NIGHT, AND I WANT TO DRINK A CASE OF VODKA AND PASS THE HELL OUT OF IT.

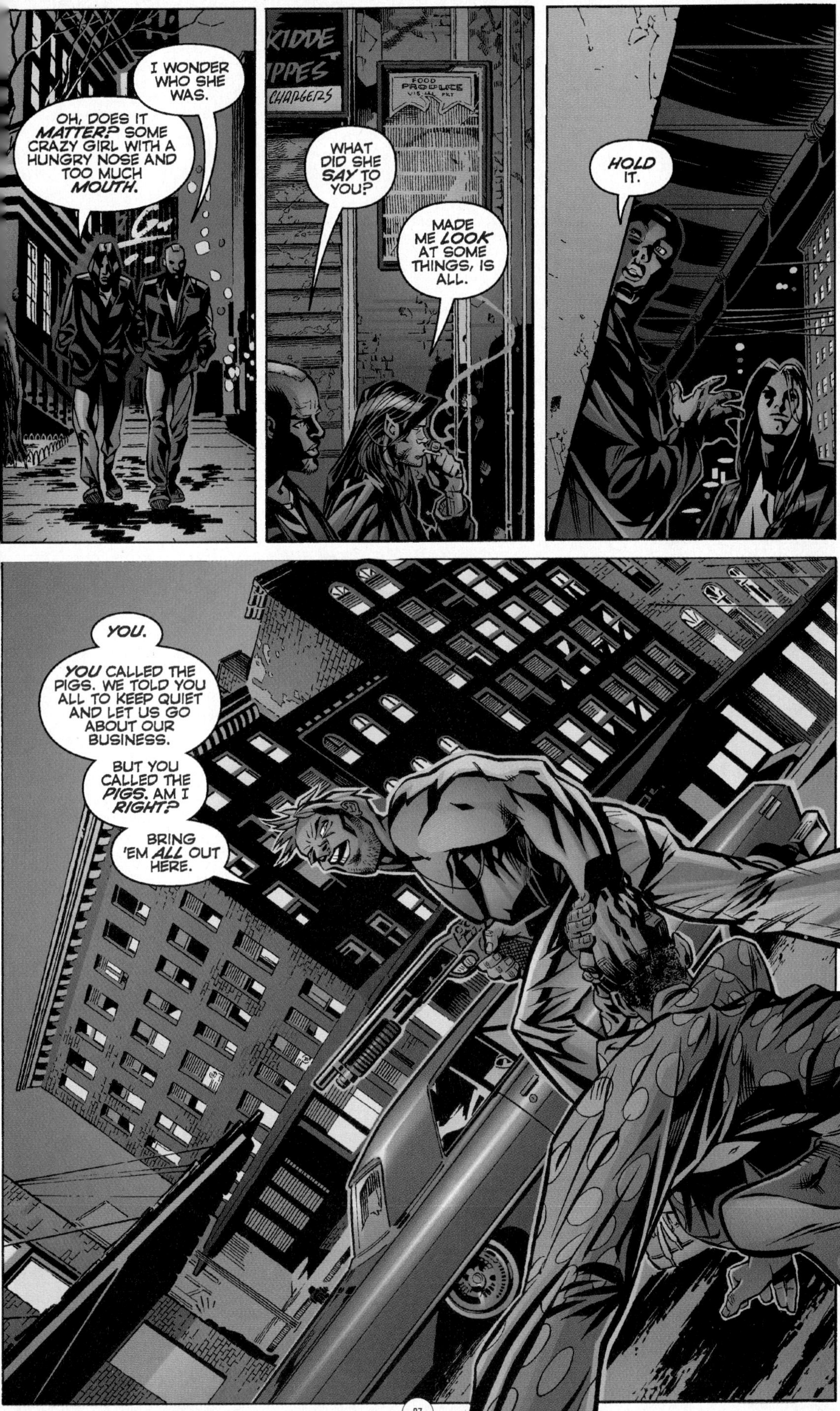
I WONDER WHO SHE WAS.
OH, DOES IT MATTER? SOME CRAZY GIRL WITH A HUNGRY NOSE AND TOO MUCH MOUTH.
KIDDE
IPPES
CHARGERS
FOOD PRODUCE
WHAT DID SHE SAY TO YOU?
MADE ME LOOK AT SOME THINGS, IS ALL.
HOLD IT.
YOU.
YOU CALLED THE PIGS. WE TOLD YOU ALL TO KEEP QUIET AND LET US GO ABOUT OUR BUSINESS.
BUT YOU CALLED THE PIGS. AM I RIGHT?
BRING 'EM ALL OUT HERE.

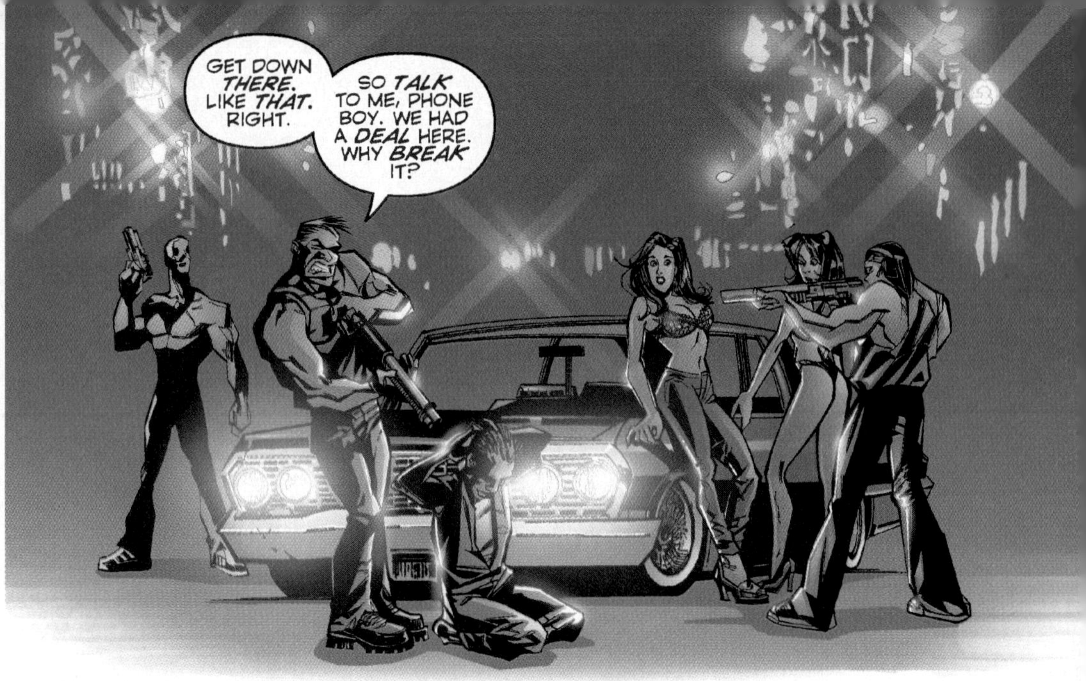
GET DOWN *THERE.* LIKE *THAT.* RIGHT.
SO *TALK* TO ME, PHONE BOY. WE HAD A *DEAL* HERE. WHY *BREAK* IT?

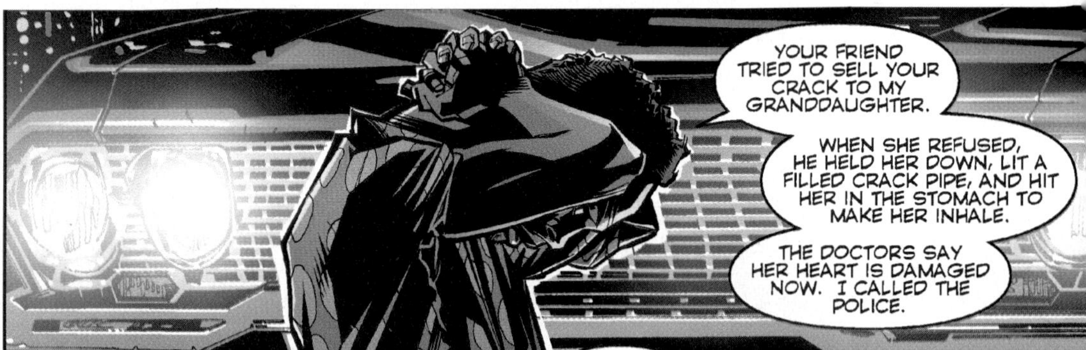
YOUR FRIEND TRIED TO SELL YOUR CRACK TO MY GRANDDAUGHTER.
WHEN SHE REFUSED, HE HELD HER DOWN, LIT A FILLED CRACK PIPE, AND HIT HER IN THE STOMACH TO MAKE HER INHALE.
THE DOCTORS SAY HER HEART IS DAMAGED NOW. I CALLED THE POLICE.

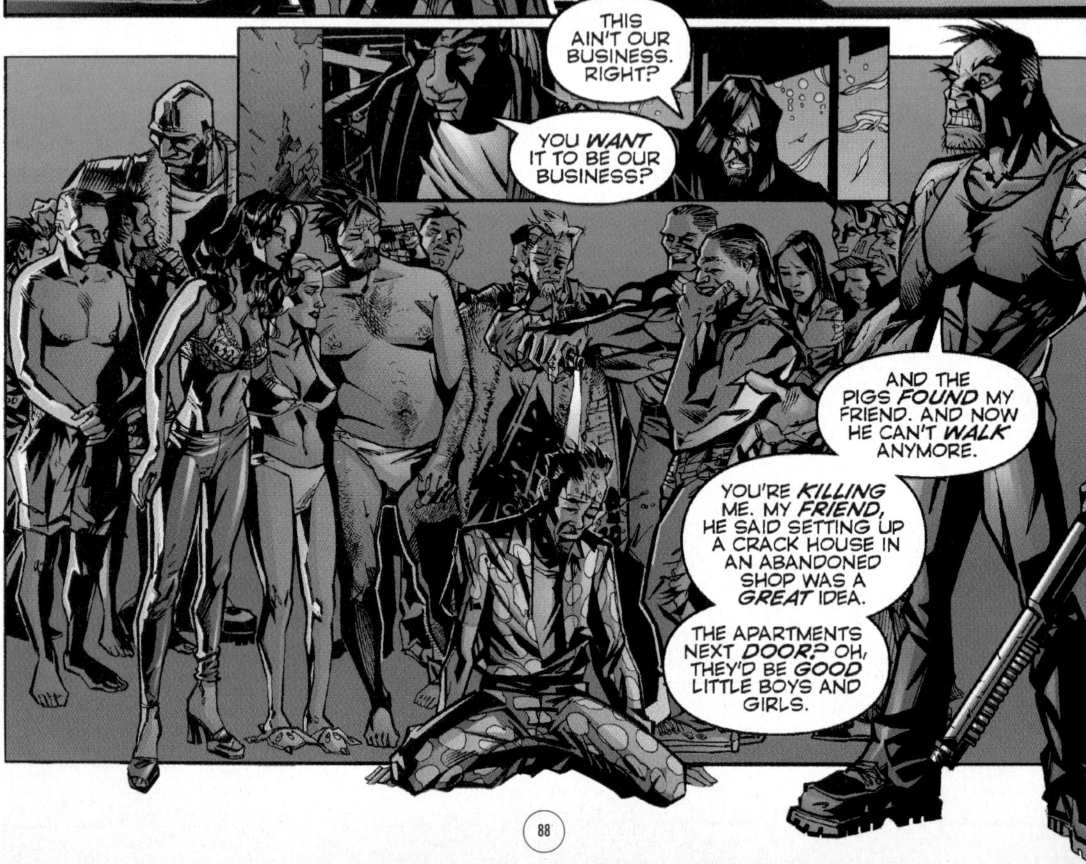
THIS AIN'T OUR BUSINESS. RIGHT?
YOU *WANT* IT TO BE OUR BUSINESS?
AND THE PIGS *FOUND* MY FRIEND. AND NOW HE CAN'T *WALK* ANYMORE.
YOU'RE *KILLING* ME. MY *FRIEND,* HE SAID SETTING UP A CRACK HOUSE IN AN ABANDONED SHOP WAS A *GREAT* IDEA.
THE APARTMENTS NEXT *DOOR?* OH, THEY'D BE *GOOD* LITTLE BOYS AND GIRLS.

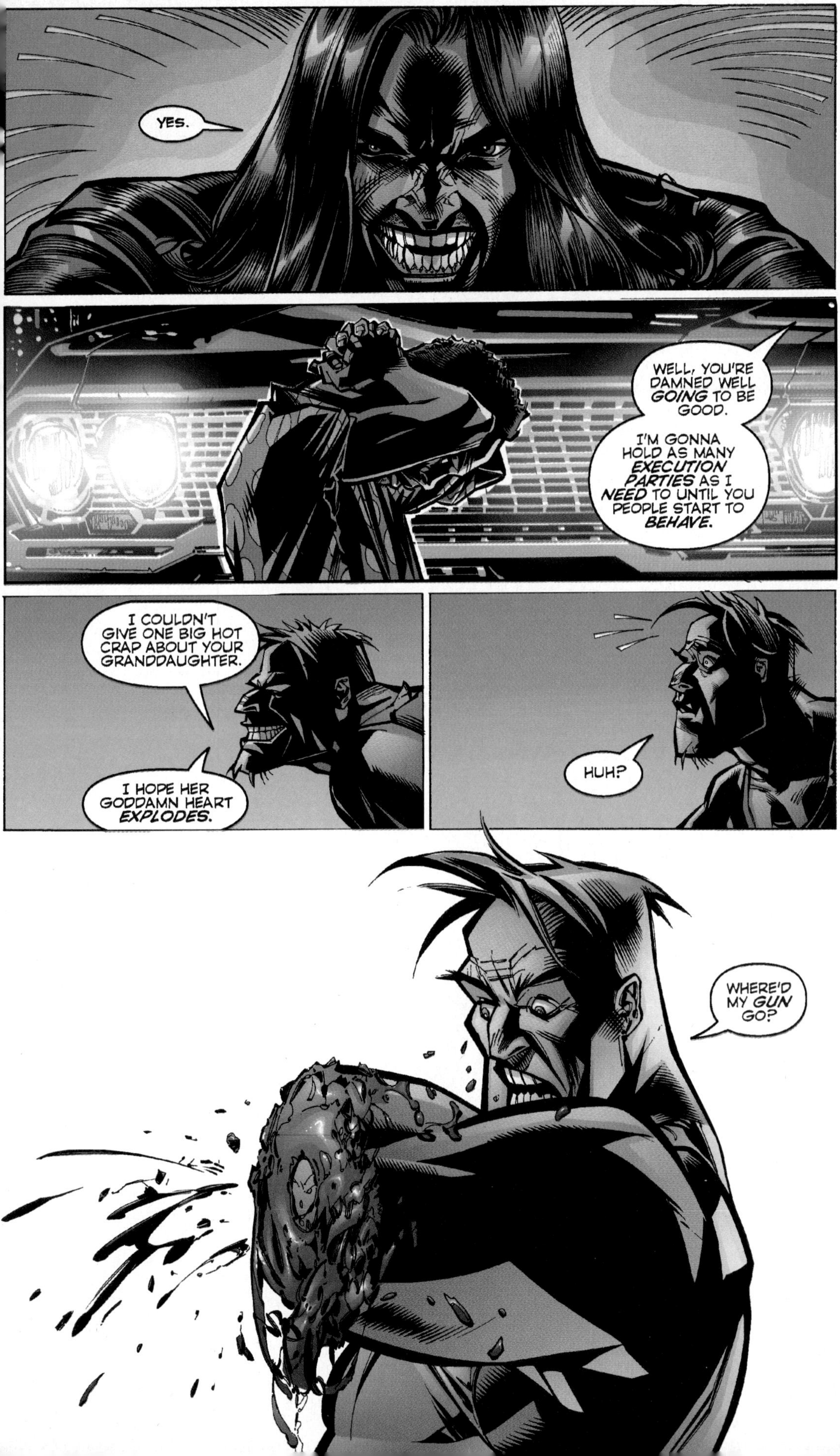
YES.
WELL, YOU'RE DAMNED WELL *GOING* TO BE GOOD.
I'M GONNA HOLD AS MANY *EXECUTION PARTIES* AS I *NEED* TO UNTIL YOU PEOPLE START TO *BEHAVE.*
I COULDN'T GIVE ONE BIG HOT CRAP ABOUT YOUR GRANDDAUGHTER.
I HOPE HER GODDAMN HEART *EXPLODES.*
HUH?
WHERE'D MY *GUN* GO?

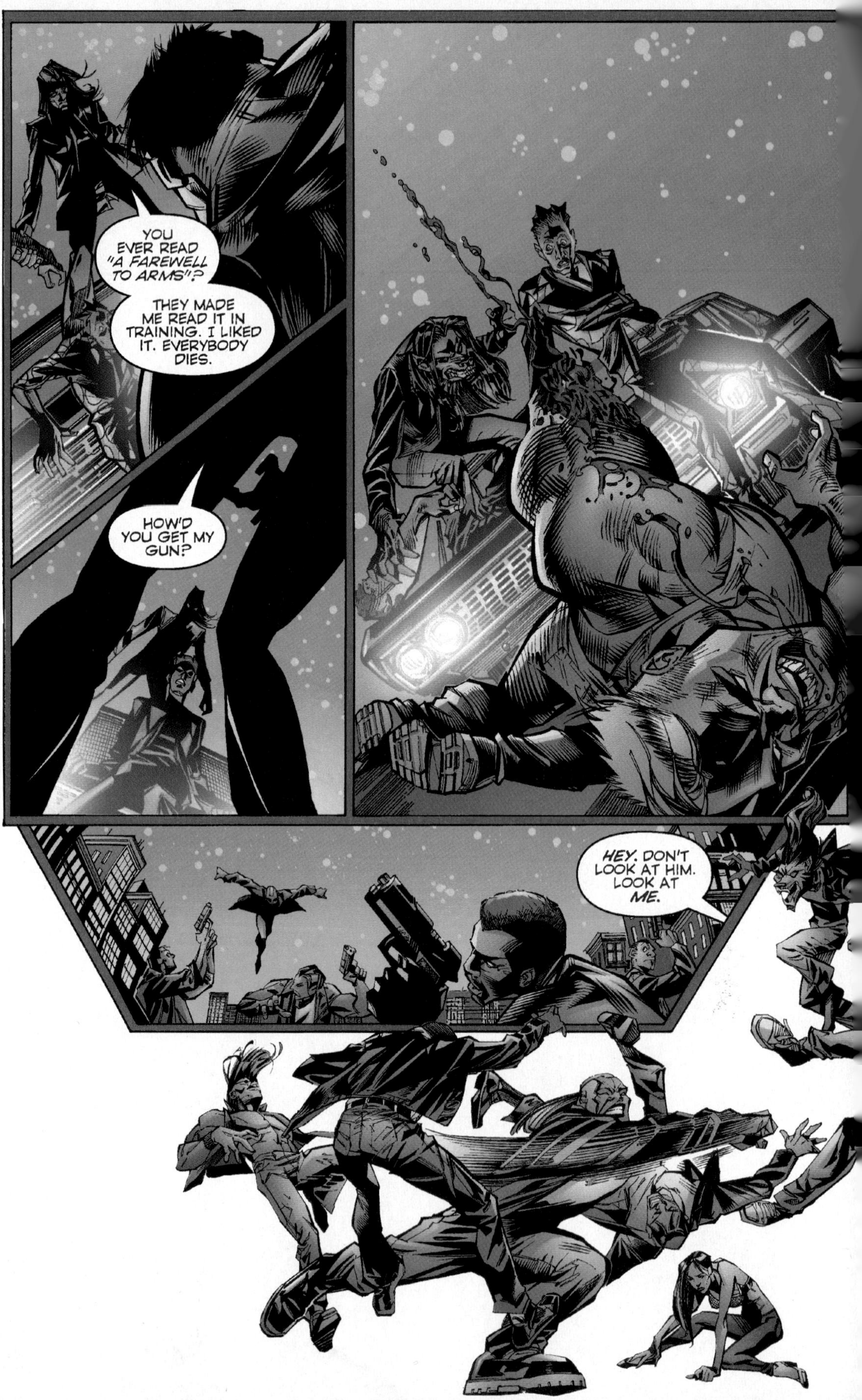
YOU EVER READ "A FAREWELL TO ARMS"?
THEY MADE ME READ IT IN TRAINING. I LIKED IT. EVERYBODY DIES.
HOW'D YOU GET MY GUN?
HEY. DON'T LOOK AT HIM. LOOK AT ME.

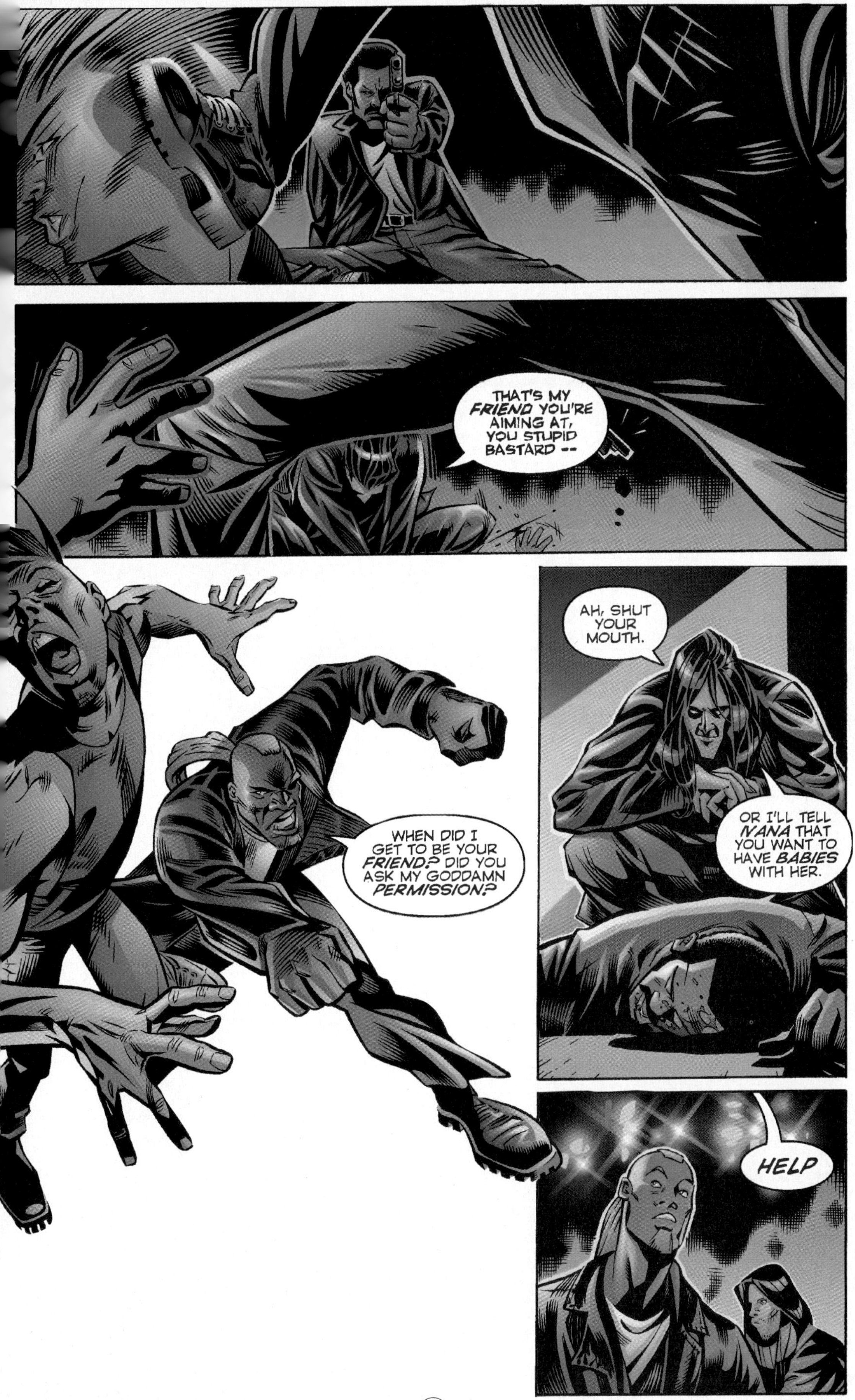
THAT'S MY FRIEND YOU'RE AIMING AT, YOU STUPID BASTARD --
WHEN DID I GET TO BE YOUR FRIEND? DID YOU ASK MY GODDAMN PERMISSION?
AH, SHUT YOUR MOUTH.
OR I'LL TELL IVANA THAT YOU WANT TO HAVE BABIES WITH HER.
HELP

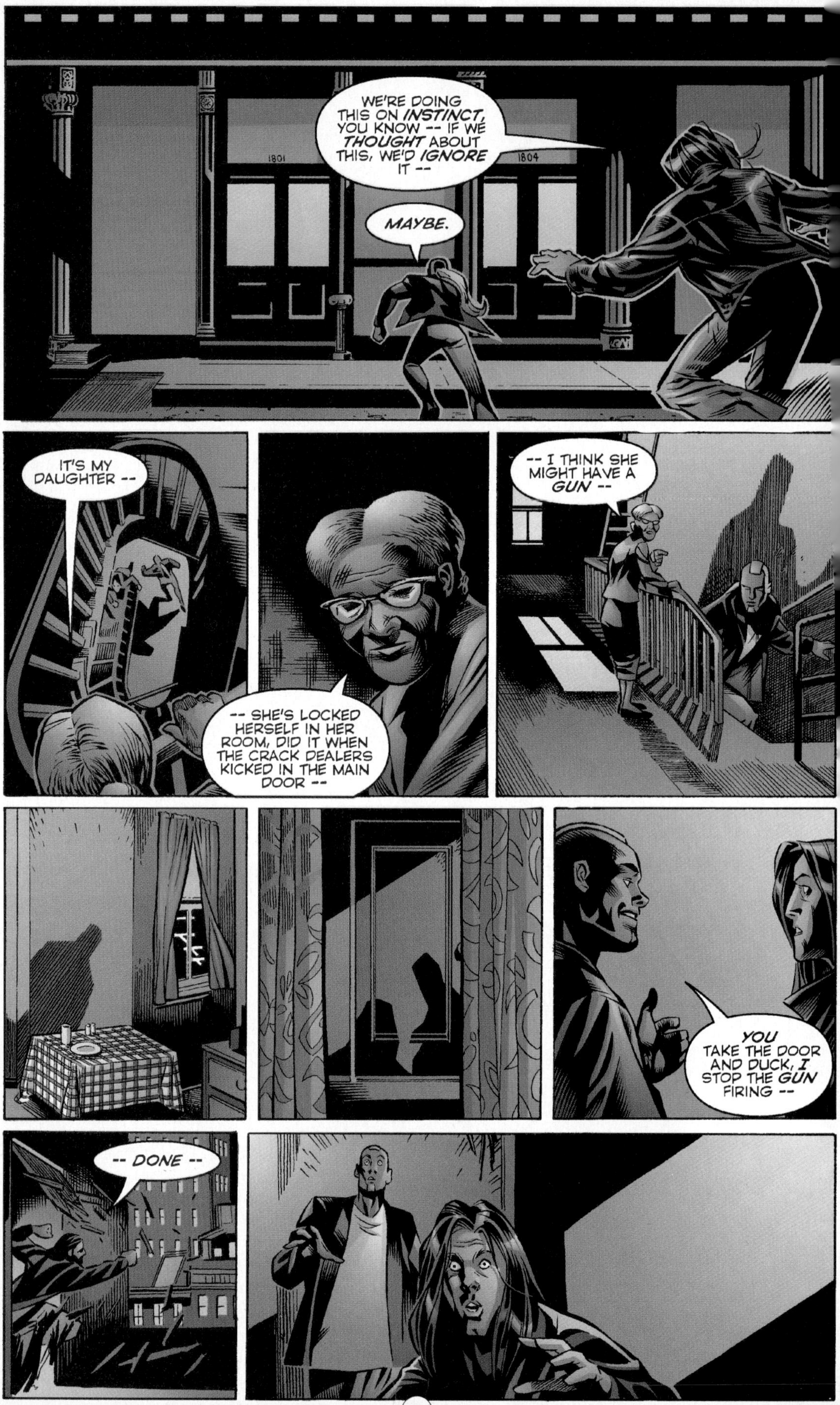
1801
1804
WE'RE DOING THIS ON *INSTINCT*, YOU KNOW -- IF WE *THOUGHT* ABOUT THIS, WE'D *IGNORE* IT --
MAYBE.
IT'S MY DAUGHTER --
-- SHE'S LOCKED HERSELF IN HER ROOM, DID IT WHEN THE CRACK DEALERS KICKED IN THE MAIN DOOR --
-- I THINK SHE MIGHT HAVE A *GUN* --
YOU TAKE THE DOOR AND DUCK, *I* STOP THE *GUN* FIRING --
-- *DONE* --

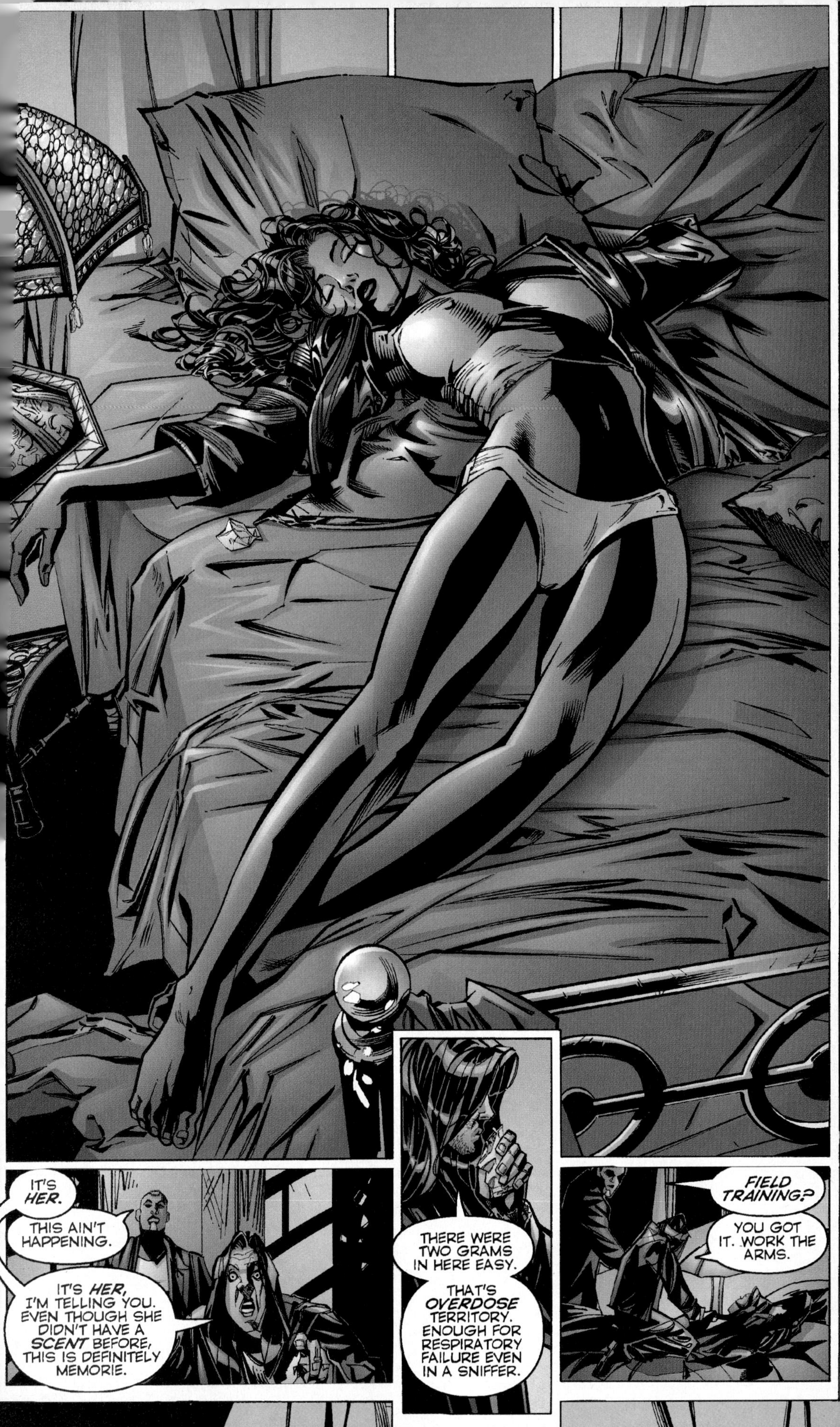
IT'S HER.
THIS AIN'T HAPPENING.
IT'S HER, I'M TELLING YOU. EVEN THOUGH SHE DIDN'T HAVE A SCENT BEFORE, THIS IS DEFINITELY MEMORIE.
THERE WERE TWO GRAMS IN HERE EASY.
THAT'S OVERDOSE TERRITORY. ENOUGH FOR RESPIRATORY FAILURE EVEN IN A SNIFFER.
FIELD TRAINING?
YOU GOT IT. WORK THE ARMS.

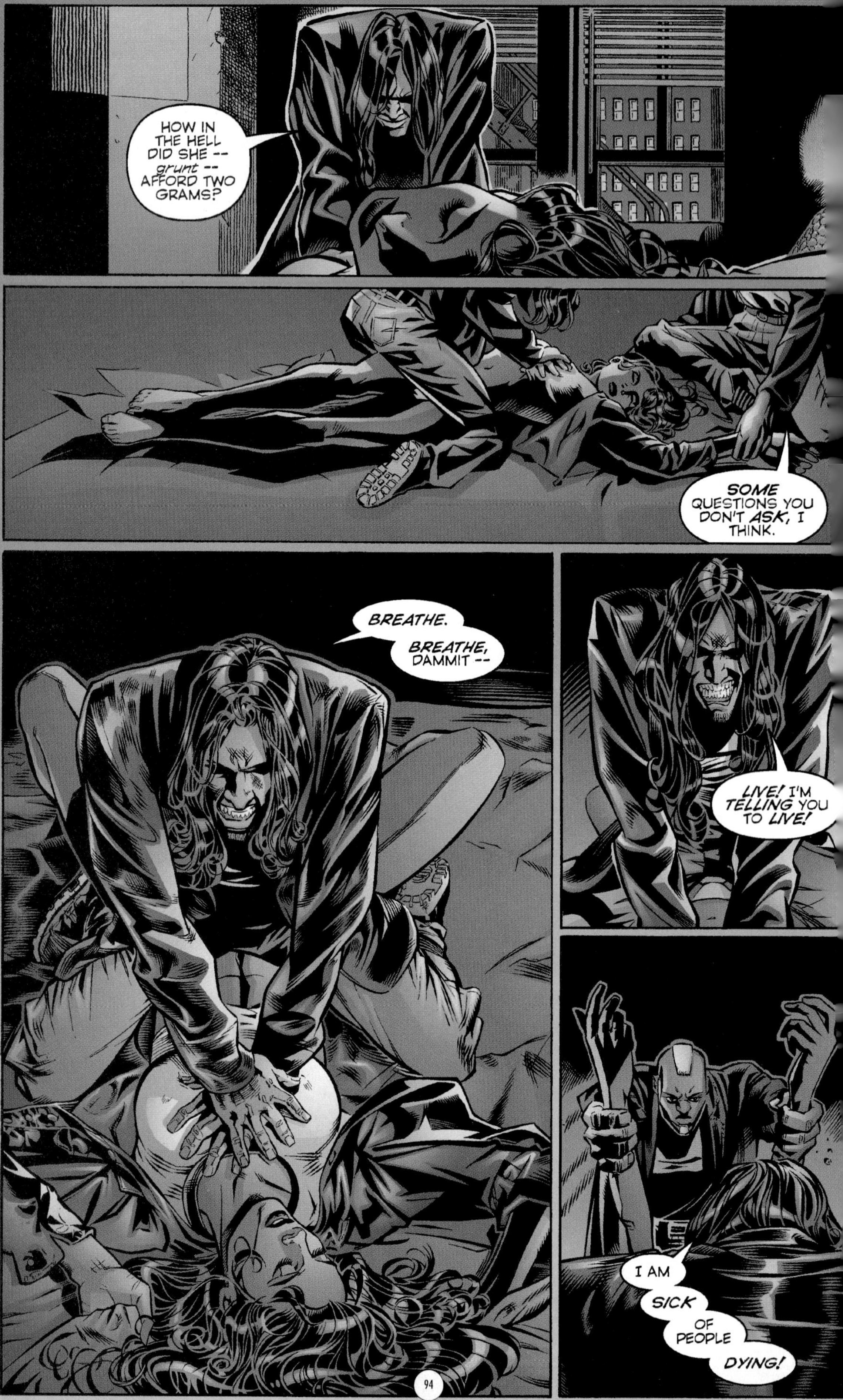
HOW IN THE HELL DID SHE -- *grunt* -- AFFORD TWO GRAMS?
SOME QUESTIONS YOU DON'T ***ASK***, I THINK.
BREATHE.
BREATHE, DAMMIT --
LIVE! I'M ***TELLING*** YOU TO ***LIVE!***
I AM ***SICK*** OF PEOPLE ***DYING!***

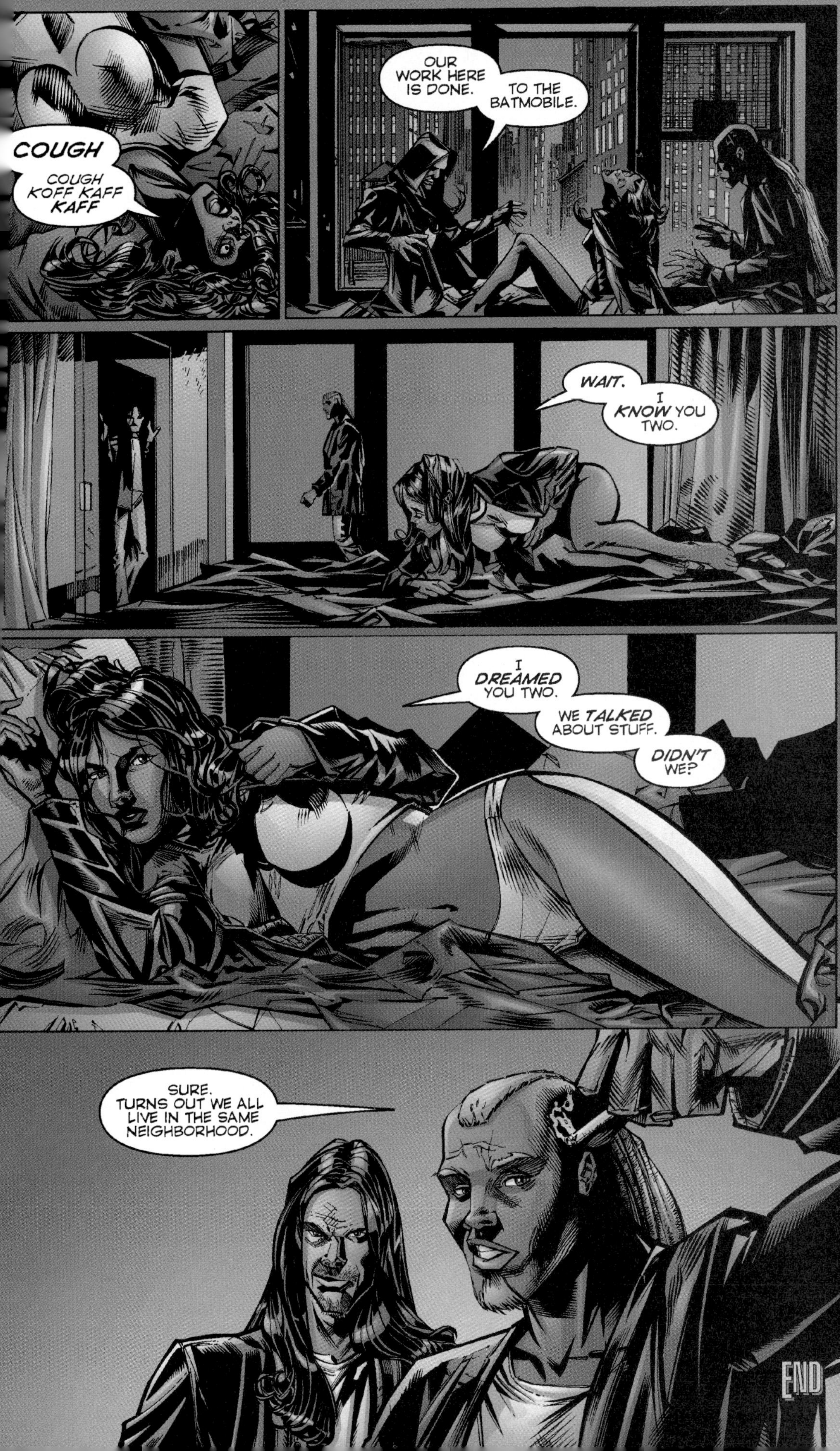
COUGH
COUGH KOFF KAFF KAFF
OUR WORK HERE IS DONE.
TO THE BATMOBILE.
WAIT.
I KNOW YOU TWO.
I DREAMED YOU TWO.
WE TALKED ABOUT STUFF.
DIDN'T WE?
SURE. TURNS OUT WE ALL LIVE IN THE SAME NEIGHBORHOOD.
END

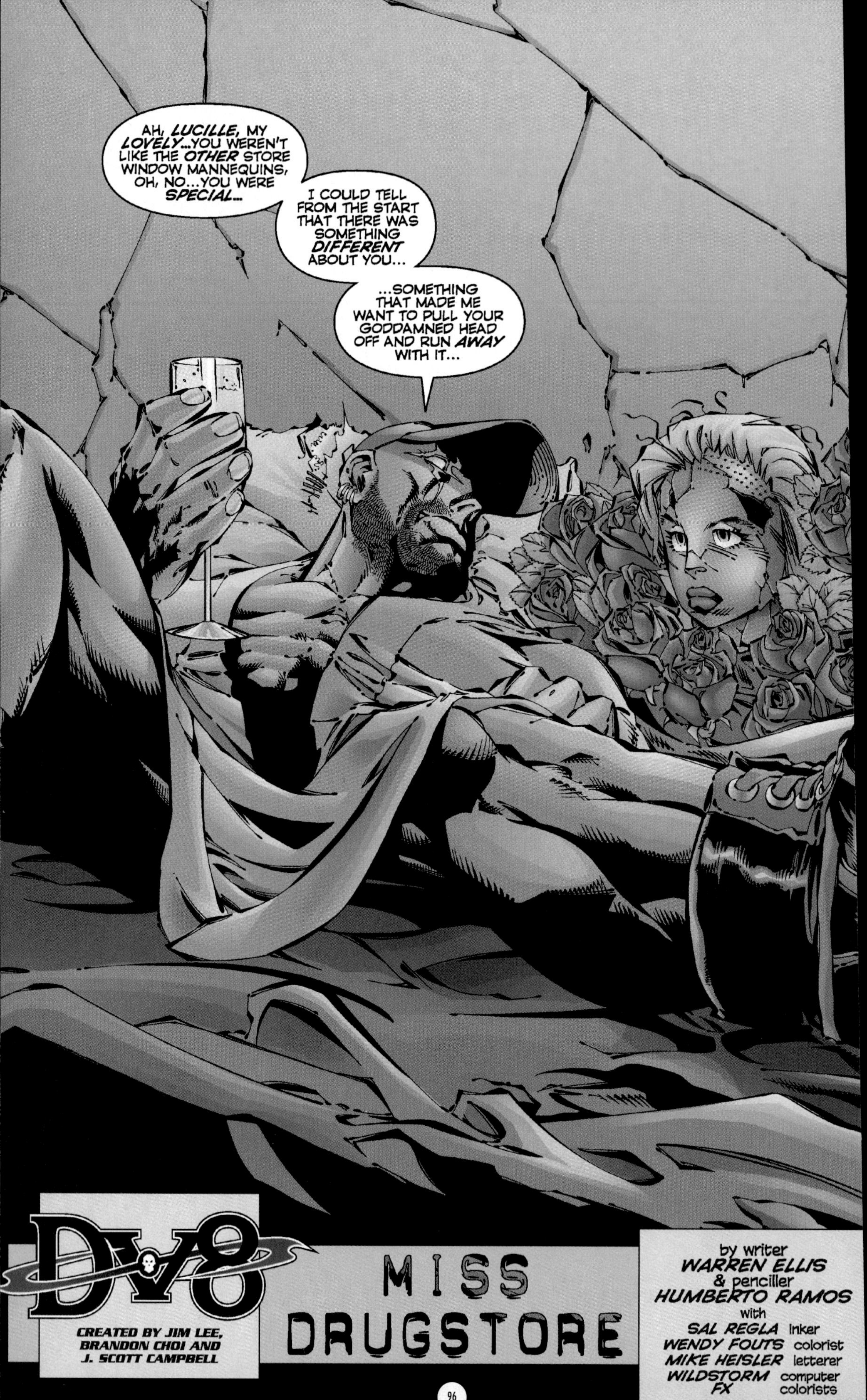
AH, LUCILLE, MY LOVELY...YOU WEREN'T LIKE THE OTHER STORE WINDOW MANNEQUINS, OH, NO...YOU WERE SPECIAL...
I COULD TELL FROM THE START THAT THERE WAS SOMETHING DIFFERENT ABOUT YOU...
...SOMETHING THAT MADE ME WANT TO PULL YOUR GODDAMNED HEAD OFF AND RUN AWAY WITH IT...
DV8
CREATED BY JIM LEE, BRANDON CHOI AND J. SCOTT CAMPBELL
MISS DRUGSTORE
by writer WARREN ELLIS & penciller HUMBERTO RAMOS with
SAL REGLA inker
WENDY FOUTS colorist
MIKE HEISLER letterer
WILDSTORM FX computer colorists

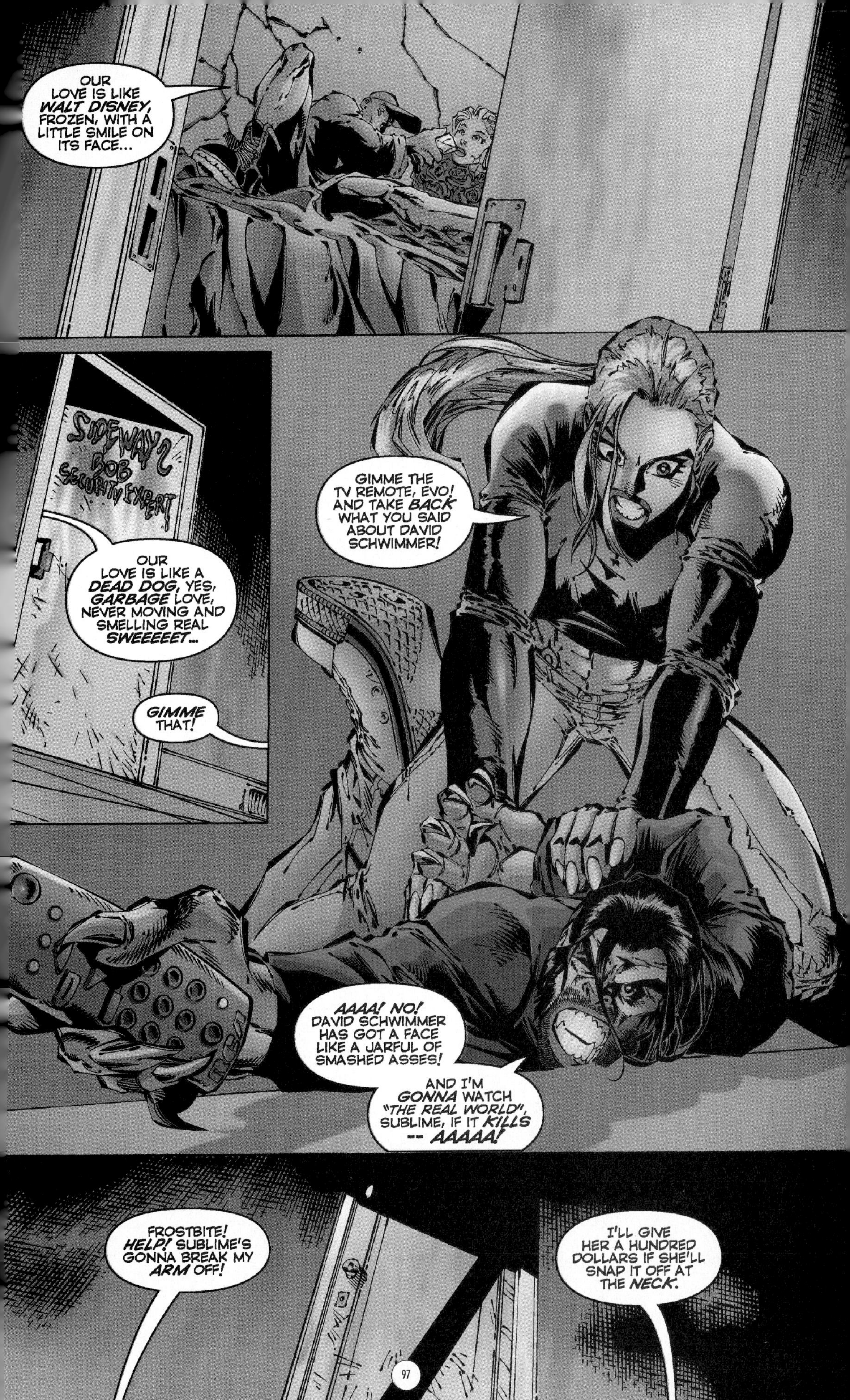
OUR LOVE IS LIKE WALT DISNEY, FROZEN, WITH A LITTLE SMILE ON ITS FACE...
SIDEWAYS BOB SECURITY EXPERT
GIMME THE TV REMOTE, EVO! AND TAKE BACK WHAT YOU SAID ABOUT DAVID SCHWIMMER!
OUR LOVE IS LIKE A DEAD DOG, YES, GARBAGE LOVE, NEVER MOVING AND SMELLING REAL SWEEEEET...
GIMME THAT!
AAAA! NO! DAVID SCHWIMMER HAS GOT A FACE LIKE A JARFUL OF SMASHED ASSES!
AND I'M GONNA WATCH "THE REAL WORLD", SUBLIME, IF IT KILLS -- AAAAA!
FROSTBITE! HELP! SUBLIME'S GONNA BREAK MY ARM OFF!
I'LL GIVE HER A HUNDRED DOLLARS IF SHE'LL SNAP IT OFF AT THE NECK.

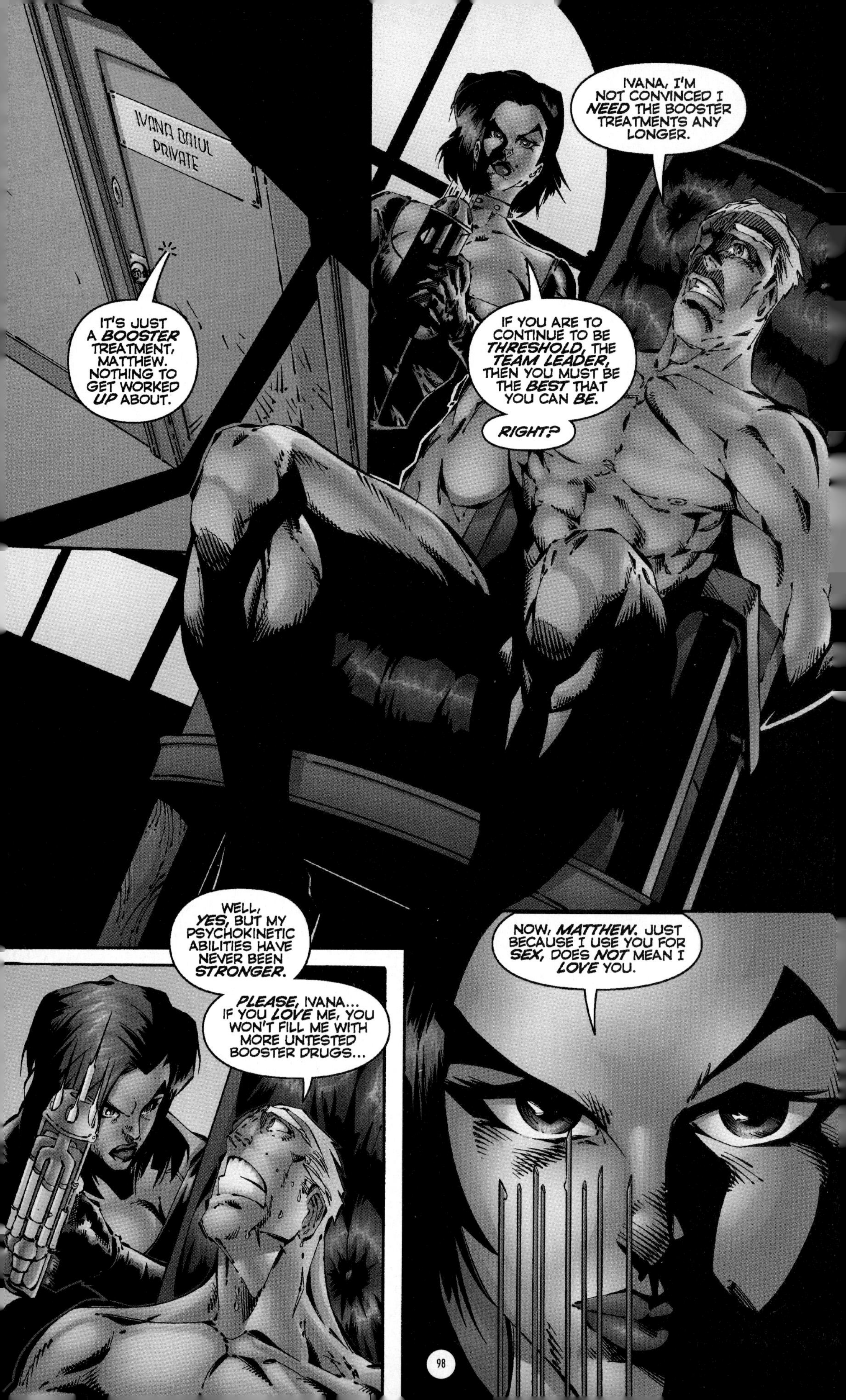
IVANA BAIUL PRIVATE
IT'S JUST A BOOSTER TREATMENT, MATTHEW. NOTHING TO GET WORKED UP ABOUT.
IVANA, I'M NOT CONVINCED I NEED THE BOOSTER TREATMENTS ANY LONGER.
IF YOU ARE TO CONTINUE TO BE THRESHOLD, THE TEAM LEADER, THEN YOU MUST BE THE BEST THAT YOU CAN BE.
RIGHT?
WELL, YES, BUT MY PSYCHOKINETIC ABILITIES HAVE NEVER BEEN STRONGER.
PLEASE, IVANA... IF YOU LOVE ME, YOU WON'T FILL ME WITH MORE UNTESTED BOOSTER DRUGS...
NOW, MATTHEW. JUST BECAUSE I USE YOU FOR SEX, DOES NOT MEAN I LOVE YOU.

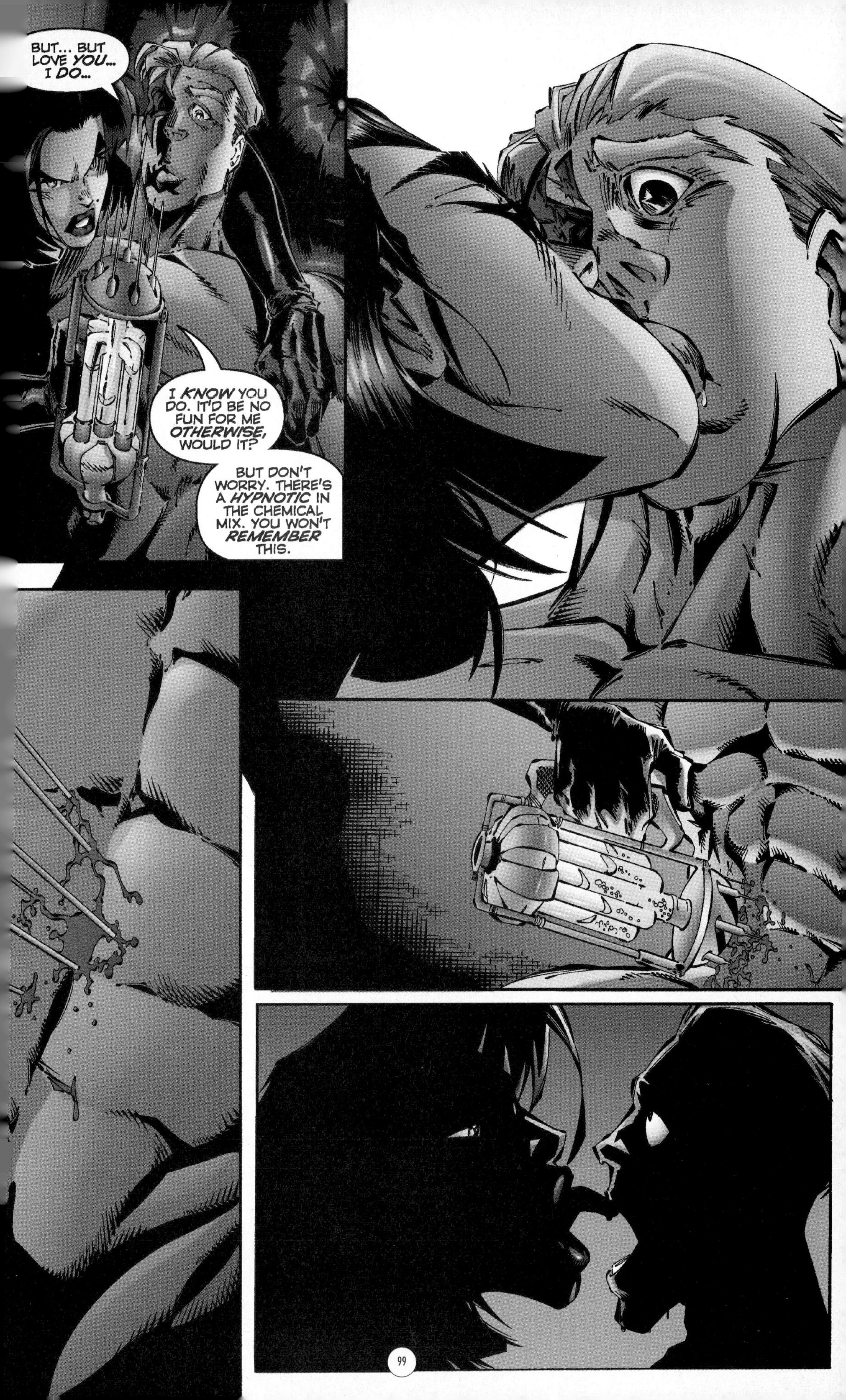
BUT... BUT LOVE YOU... I DO...
I KNOW YOU DO. IT'D BE NO FUN FOR ME OTHERWISE, WOULD IT?
BUT DON'T WORRY. THERE'S A HYPNOTIC IN THE CHEMICAL MIX. YOU WON'T REMEMBER THIS.

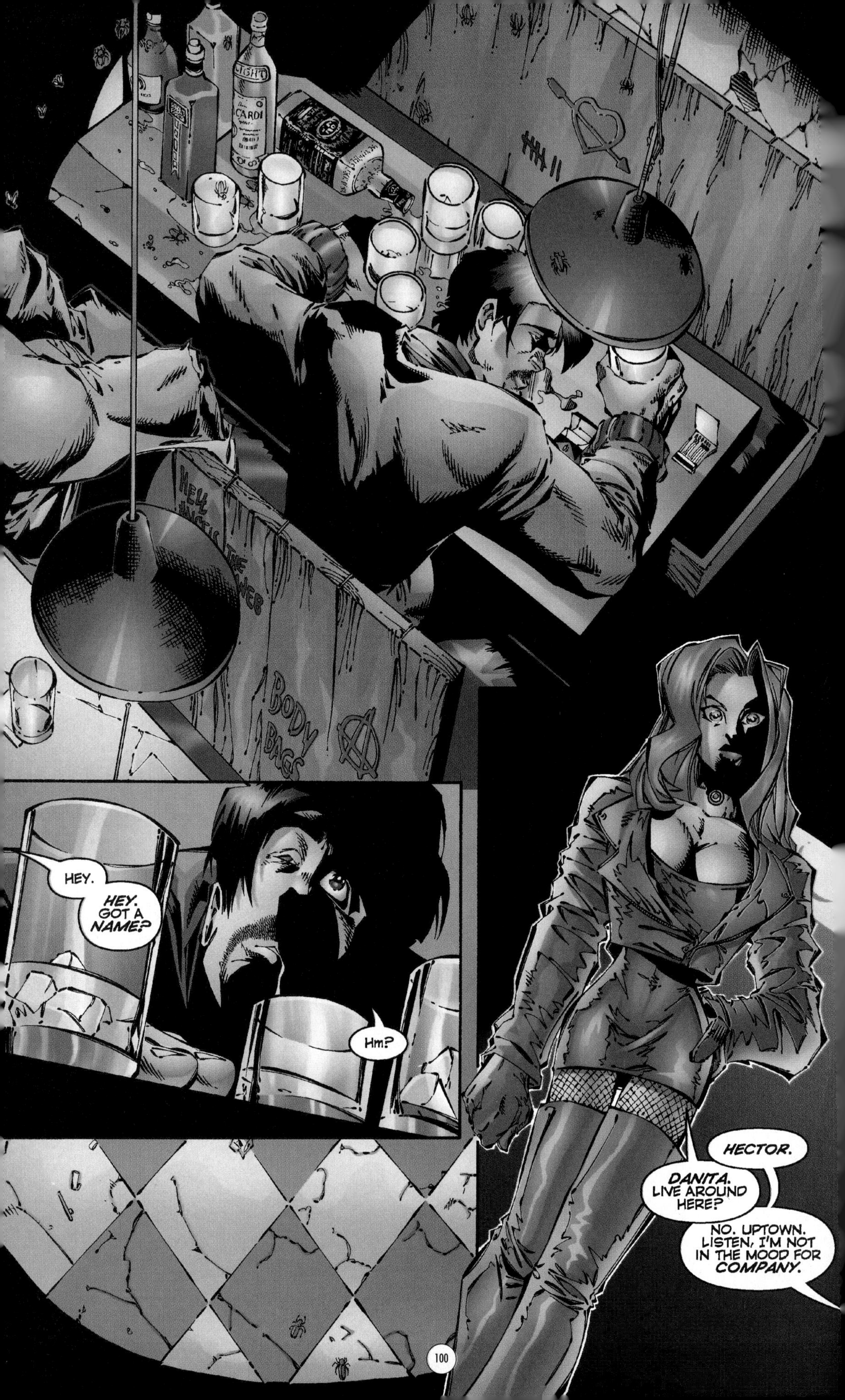
BODY BAGS
HEY.
HEY. GOT A NAME?
Hm?
HECTOR.
DANITA. LIVE AROUND HERE?
NO. UPTOWN. LISTEN, I'M NOT IN THE MOOD FOR COMPANY.

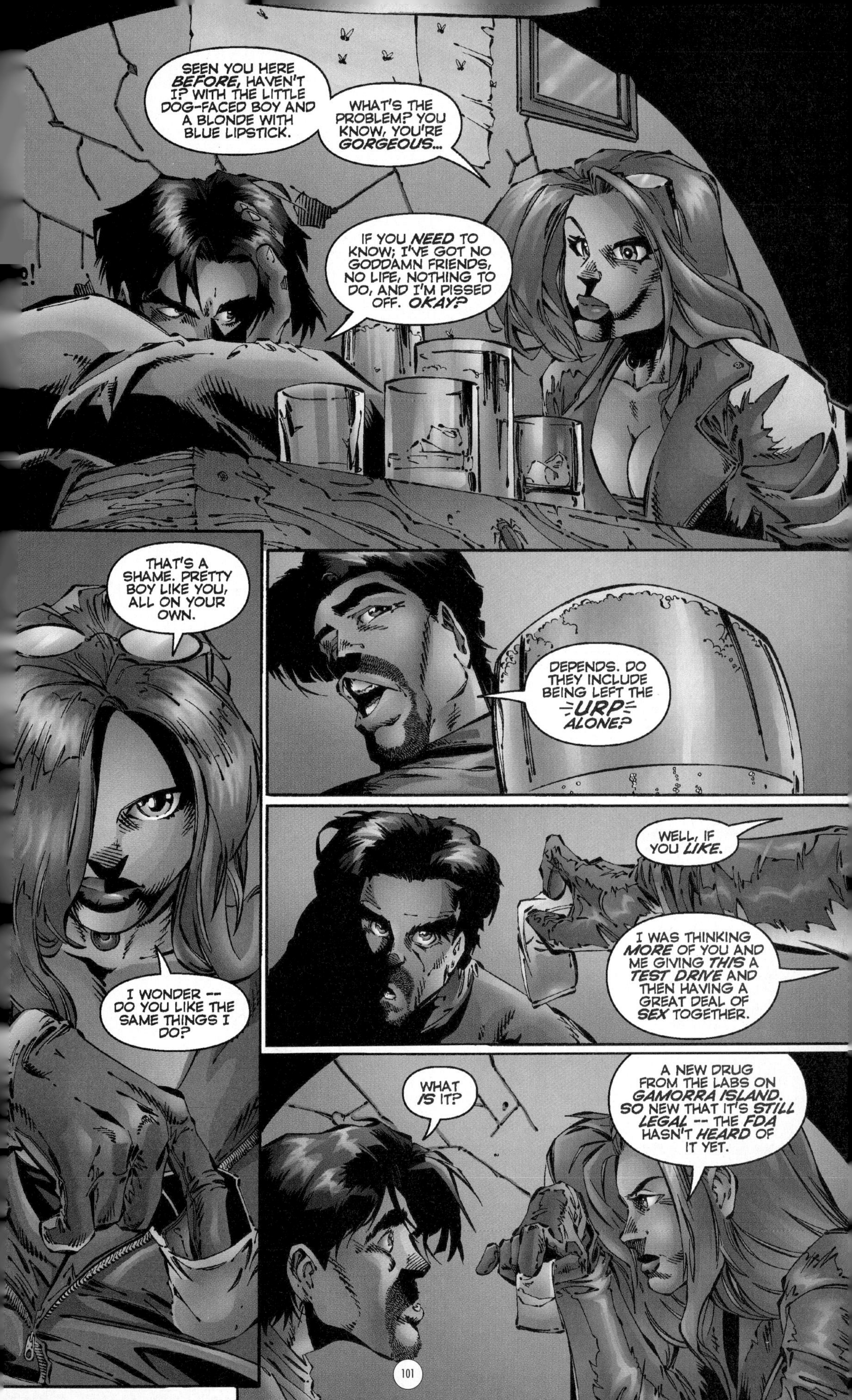
SEEN YOU HERE BEFORE, HAVEN'T I? WITH THE LITTLE DOG-FACED BOY AND A BLONDE WITH BLUE LIPSTICK.
WHAT'S THE PROBLEM? YOU KNOW, YOU'RE GORGEOUS...
IF YOU NEED TO KNOW; I'VE GOT NO GODDAMN FRIENDS, NO LIFE, NOTHING TO DO, AND I'M PISSED OFF. OKAY?
THAT'S A SHAME. PRETTY BOY LIKE YOU, ALL ON YOUR OWN.
I WONDER -- DO YOU LIKE THE SAME THINGS I DO?
DEPENDS. DO THEY INCLUDE BEING LEFT THE URP ALONE?
WELL, IF YOU LIKE.
I WAS THINKING MORE OF YOU AND ME GIVING THIS A TEST DRIVE AND THEN HAVING A GREAT DEAL OF SEX TOGETHER.
WHAT IS IT?
A NEW DRUG FROM THE LABS ON GAMORRA ISLAND. SO NEW THAT IT'S STILL LEGAL -- THE FDA HASN'T HEARD OF IT YET.

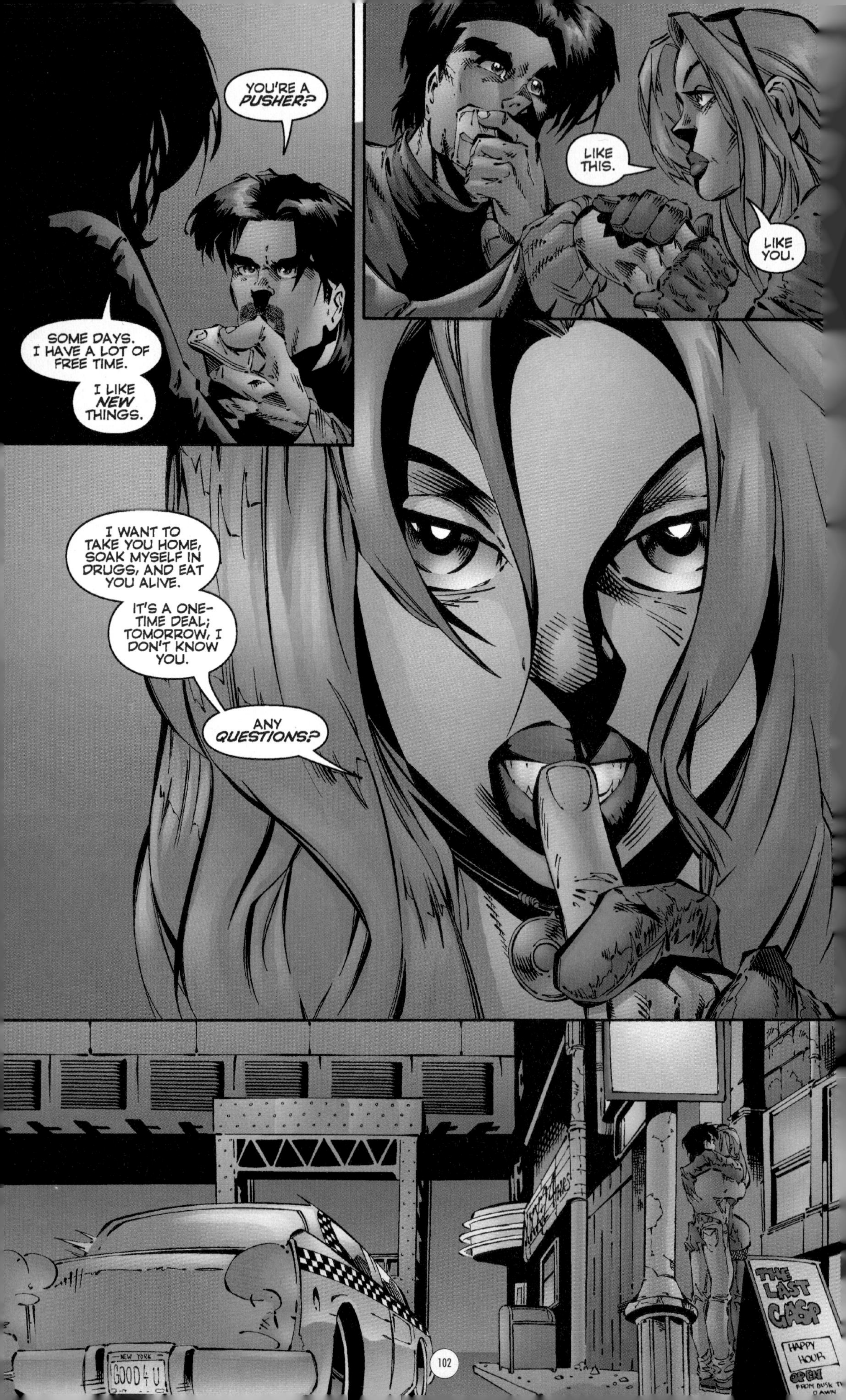
YOU'RE A *PUSHER?*
SOME DAYS. I HAVE A LOT OF FREE TIME.
I LIKE *NEW* THINGS.
LIKE THIS.
LIKE YOU.
I WANT TO TAKE YOU HOME, SOAK MYSELF IN DRUGS, AND EAT YOU ALIVE.
IT'S A ONE-TIME DEAL; TOMORROW, I DON'T KNOW YOU.
ANY *QUESTIONS?*
NEW YORK
GOOD 4 U
THE LAST GASP
HAPPY HOUR
OPEN

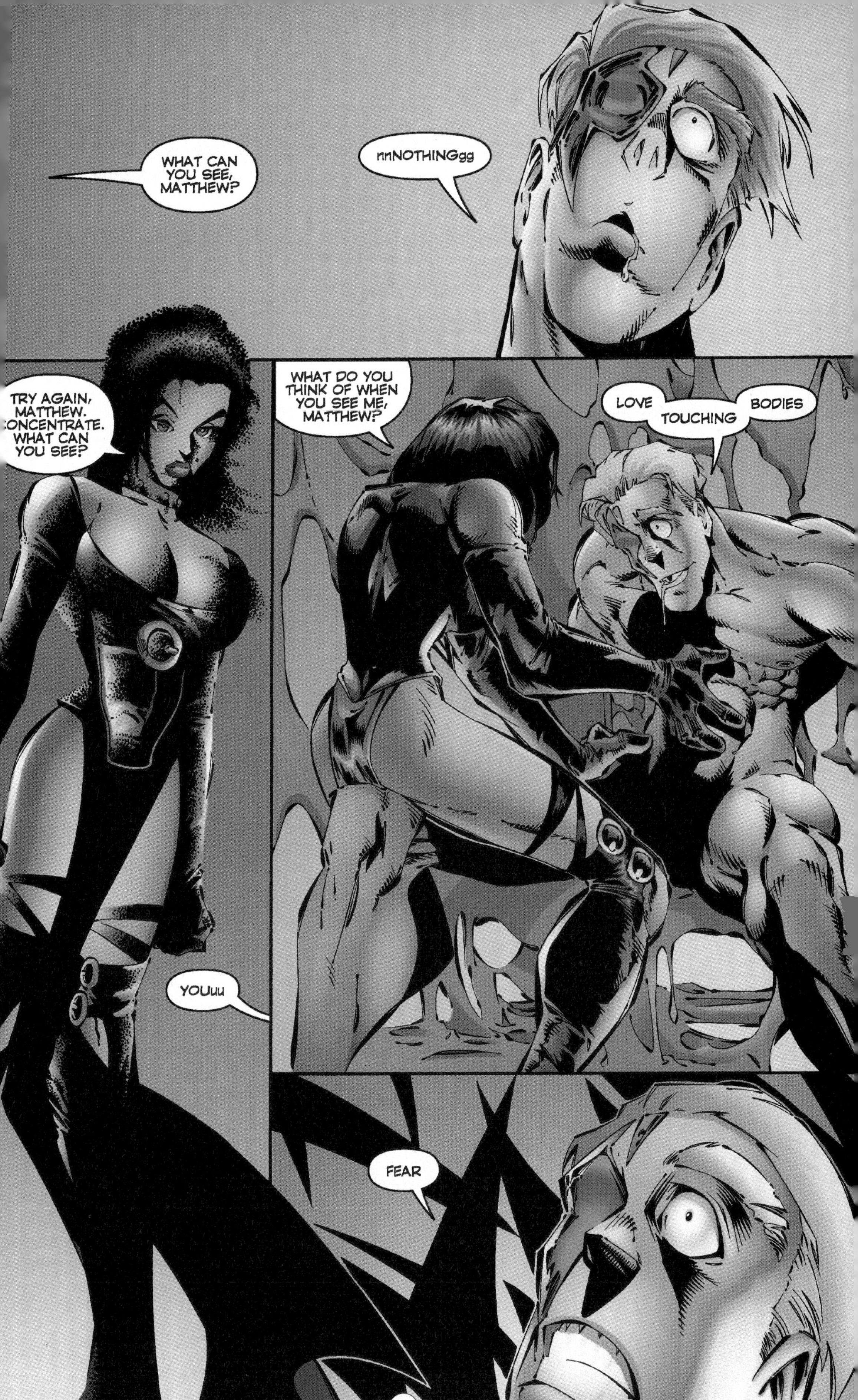
WHAT CAN YOU SEE, MATTHEW?
nnNOTHINGgg
TRY AGAIN, MATTHEW. CONCENTRATE. WHAT CAN YOU SEE?
WHAT DO YOU THINK OF WHEN YOU SEE ME, MATTHEW?
LOVE
TOUCHING
BODIES
YOUuu
FEAR

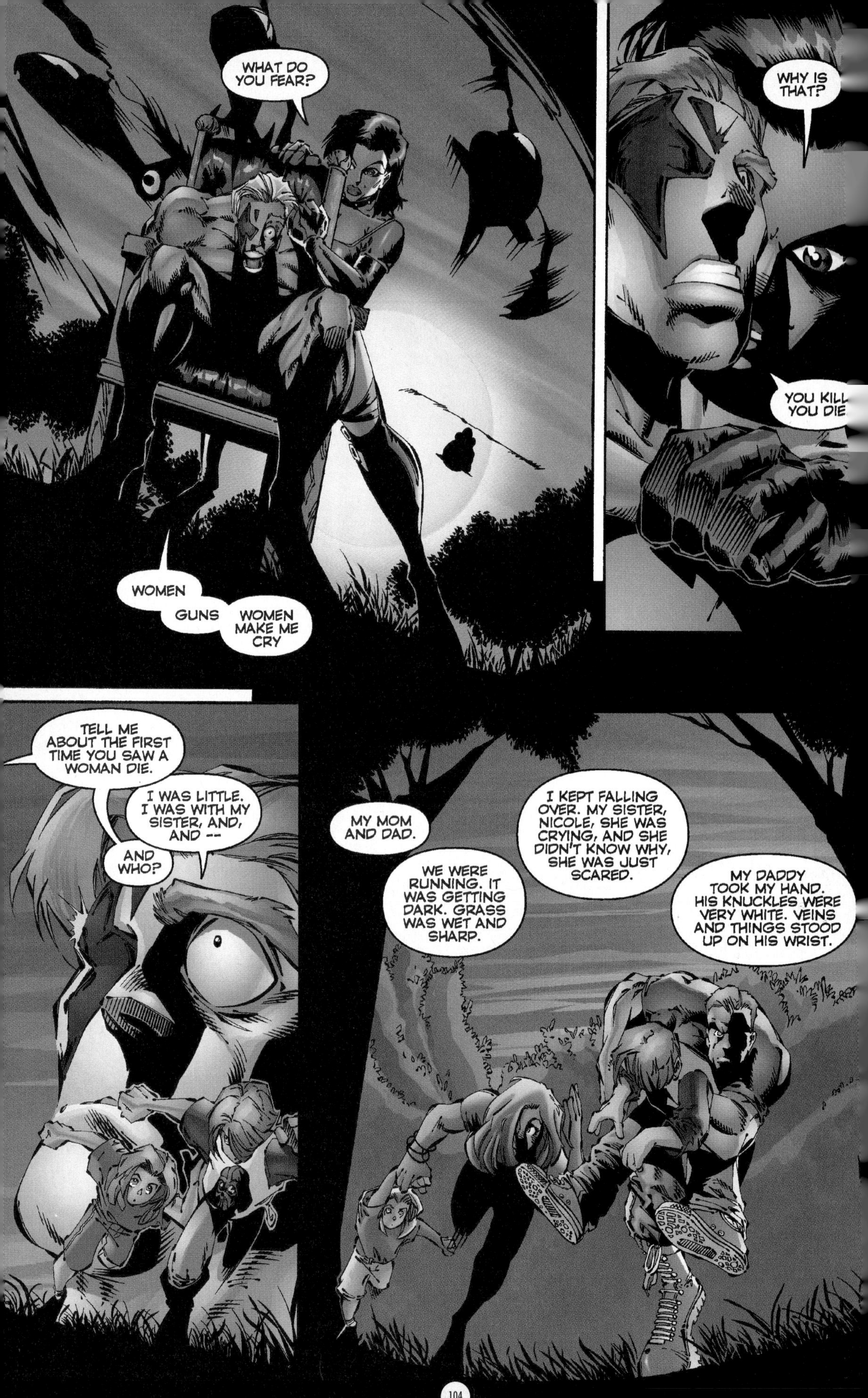
WHAT DO YOU FEAR?
WOMEN
GUNS
WOMEN MAKE ME CRY
WHY IS THAT?
YOU KILL YOU DIE
TELL ME ABOUT THE FIRST TIME YOU SAW A WOMAN DIE.
I WAS LITTLE. I WAS WITH MY SISTER, AND, AND --
AND WHO?
MY MOM AND DAD.
WE WERE RUNNING. IT WAS GETTING DARK. GRASS WAS WET AND SHARP.
I KEPT FALLING OVER. MY SISTER, NICOLE, SHE WAS CRYING, AND SHE DIDN'T KNOW WHY, SHE WAS JUST SCARED.
MY DADDY TOOK MY HAND. HIS KNUCKLES WERE VERY WHITE. VEINS AND THINGS STOOD UP ON HIS WRIST.

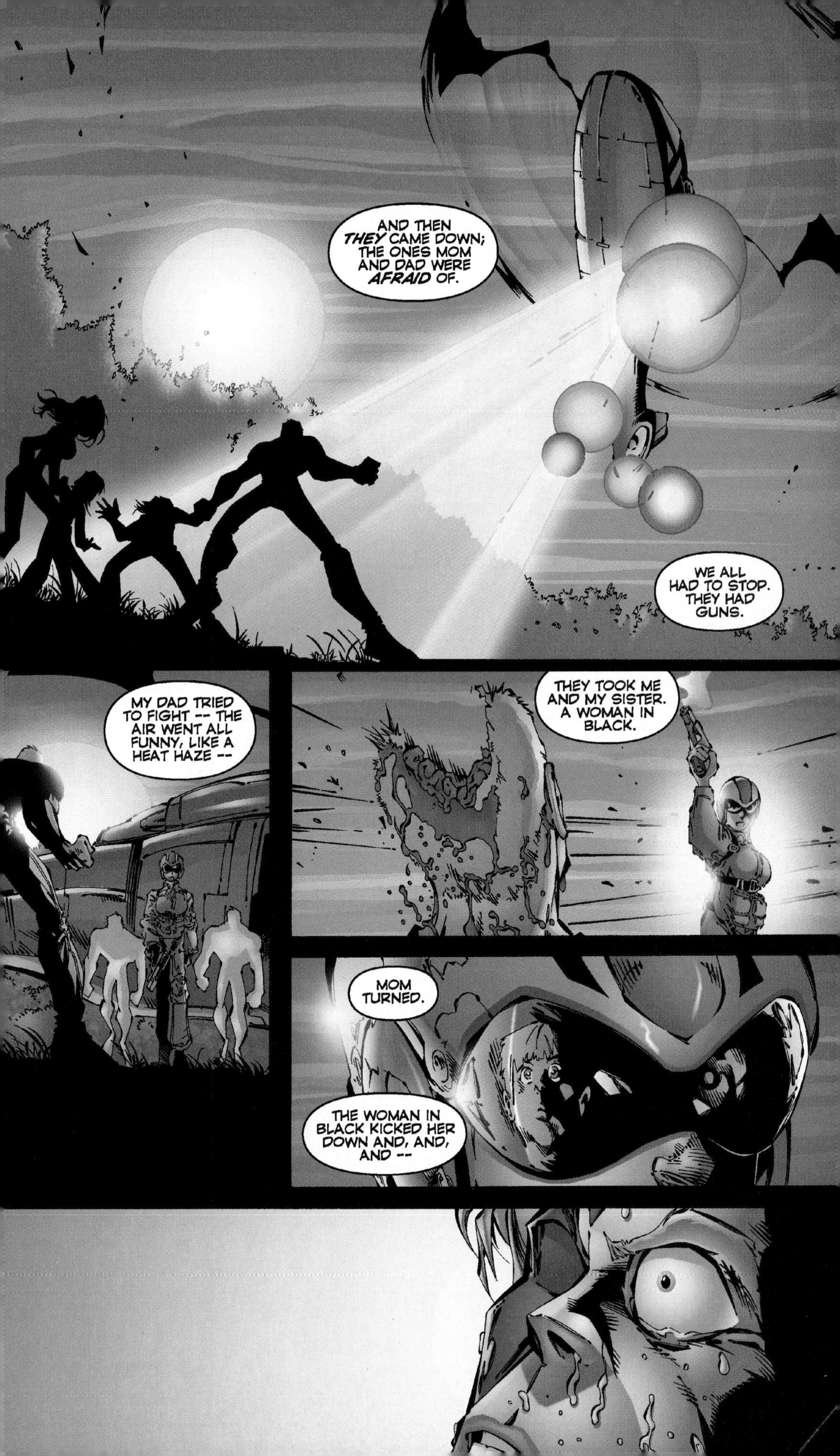
AND THEN THEY CAME DOWN; THE ONES MOM AND DAD WERE AFRAID OF.
WE ALL HAD TO STOP. THEY HAD GUNS.
MY DAD TRIED TO FIGHT -- THE AIR WENT ALL FUNNY, LIKE A HEAT HAZE --
THEY TOOK ME AND MY SISTER. A WOMAN IN BLACK.
MOM TURNED.
THE WOMAN IN BLACK KICKED HER DOWN AND, AND, AND --

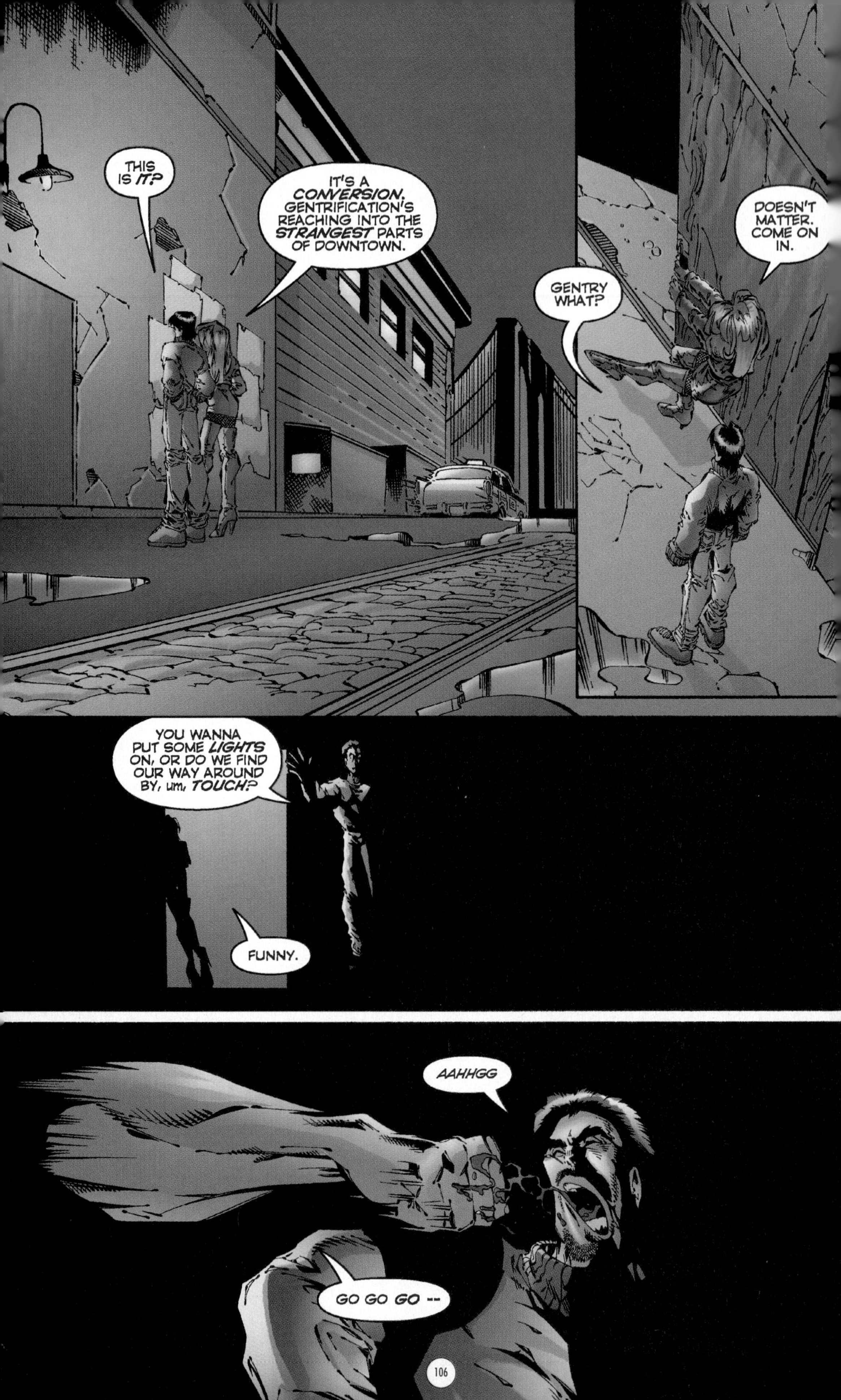
THIS IS IT?
IT'S A CONVERSION. GENTRIFICATION'S REACHING INTO THE STRANGEST PARTS OF DOWNTOWN.
GENTRY WHAT?
DOESN'T MATTER. COME ON IN.
YOU WANNA PUT SOME LIGHTS ON, OR DO WE FIND OUR WAY AROUND BY, um, TOUCH?
FUNNY.
AAHHGG
GO GO GO --

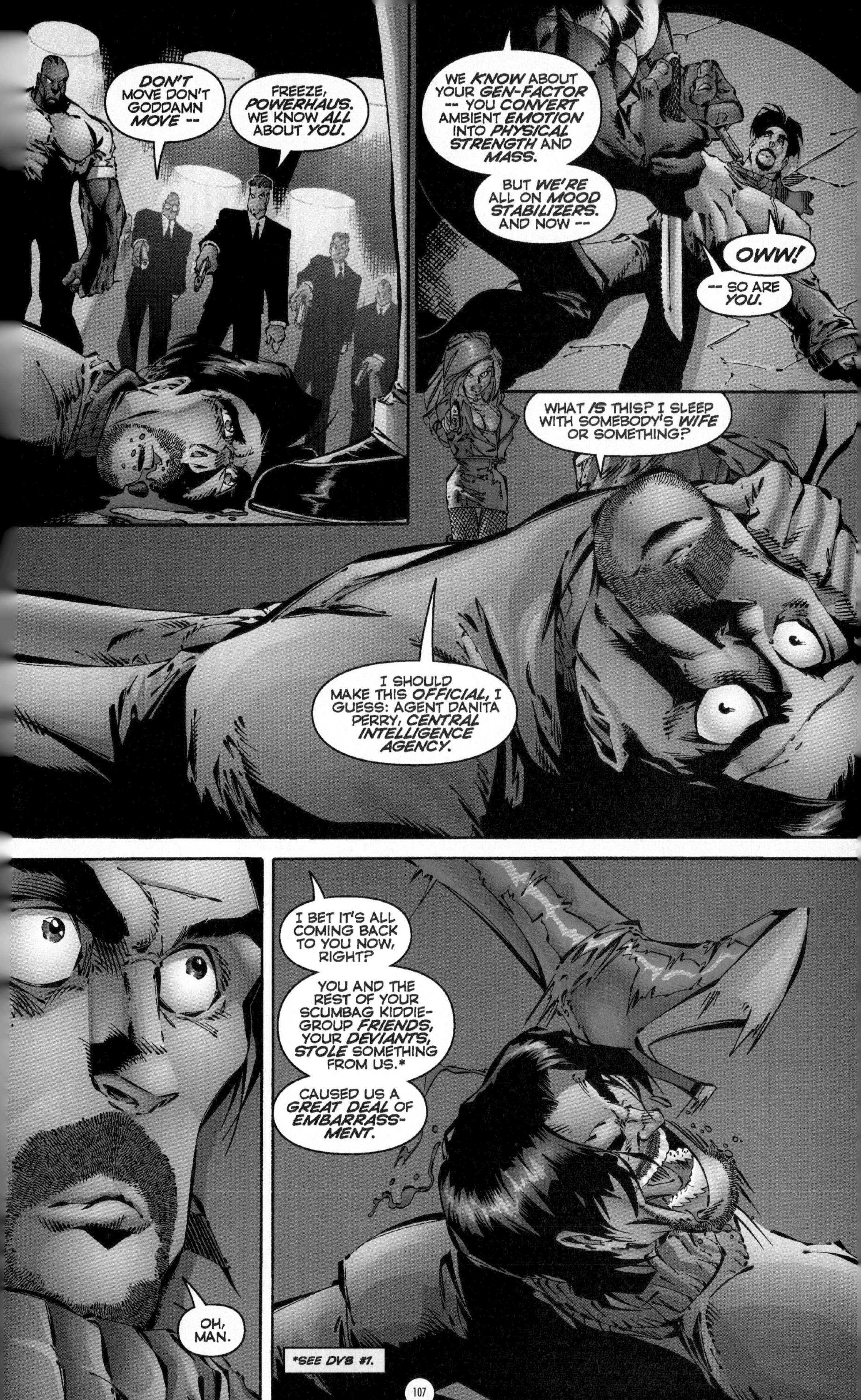
DON'T MOVE DON'T GODDAMN MOVE --
FREEZE, POWERHAUS. WE KNOW ALL ABOUT YOU.
WE KNOW ABOUT YOUR GEN-FACTOR -- YOU CONVERT AMBIENT EMOTION INTO PHYSICAL STRENGTH AND MASS.
BUT WE'RE ALL ON MOOD STABILIZERS. AND NOW --
OWW!
-- SO ARE YOU.
WHAT IS THIS? I SLEEP WITH SOMEBODY'S WIFE OR SOMETHING?
I SHOULD MAKE THIS OFFICIAL, I GUESS: AGENT DANITA PERRY, CENTRAL INTELLIGENCE AGENCY.
OH, MAN.
I BET IT'S ALL COMING BACK TO YOU NOW, RIGHT?
YOU AND THE REST OF YOUR SCUMBAG KIDDIE-GROUP FRIENDS, YOUR DEVIANTS, STOLE SOMETHING FROM US.*
CAUSED US A GREAT DEAL OF EMBARRASS-MENT.
*SEE DV8 #1.

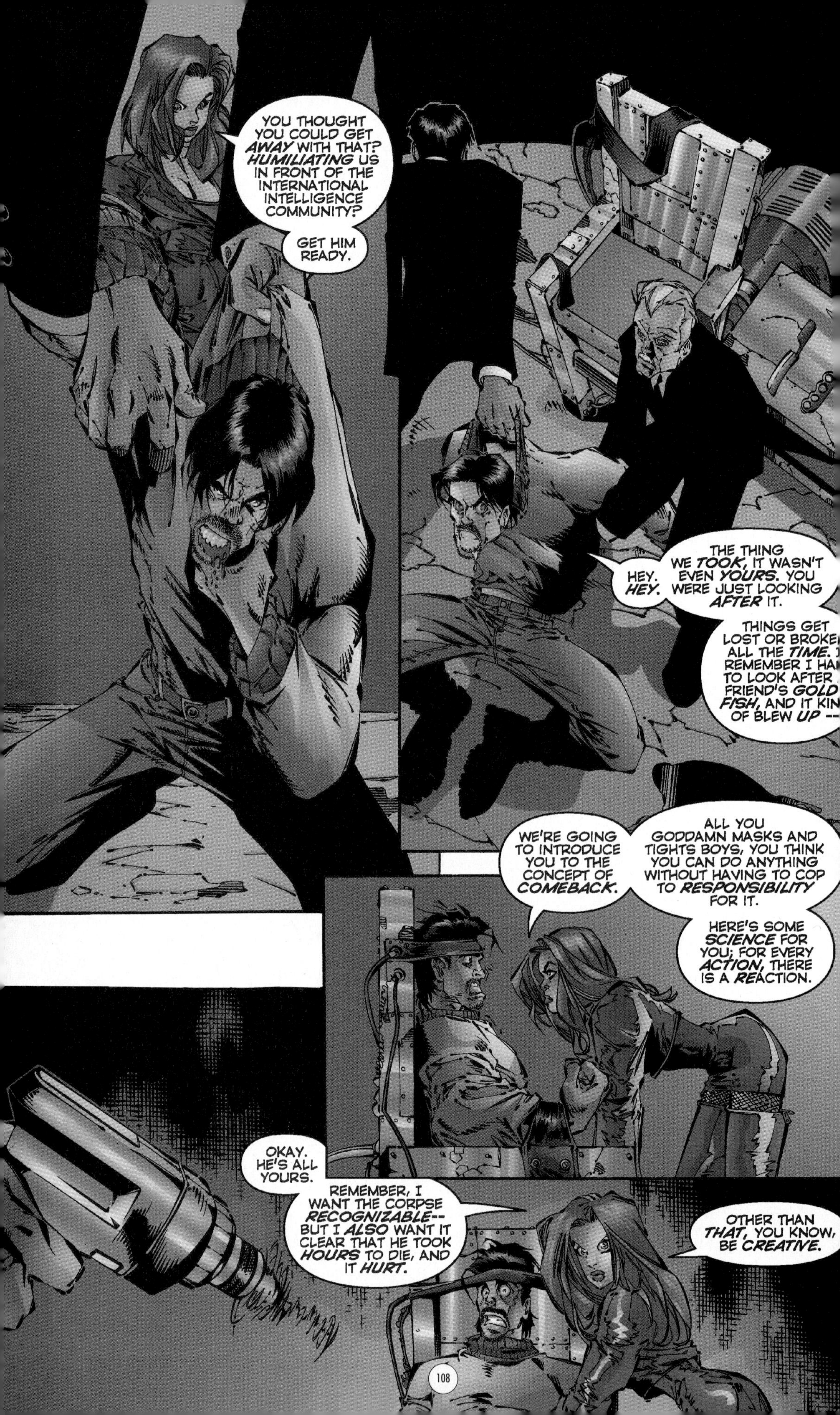
YOU THOUGHT YOU COULD GET AWAY WITH THAT? HUMILIATING US IN FRONT OF THE INTERNATIONAL INTELLIGENCE COMMUNITY?
GET HIM READY.
HEY. HEY.
THE THING WE TOOK, IT WASN'T EVEN YOURS. YOU WERE JUST LOOKING AFTER IT.
THINGS GET LOST OR BROKE ALL THE TIME. REMEMBER I HA TO LOOK AFTER FRIEND'S GOLD FISH, AND IT KIN OF BLEW UP --
WE'RE GOING TO INTRODUCE YOU TO THE CONCEPT OF COMEBACK.
ALL YOU GODDAMN MASKS AND TIGHTS BOYS, YOU THINK YOU CAN DO ANYTHING WITHOUT HAVING TO COP TO RESPONSIBILITY FOR IT.
HERE'S SOME SCIENCE FOR YOU; FOR EVERY ACTION, THERE IS A REACTION.
OKAY. HE'S ALL YOURS.
REMEMBER, I WANT THE CORPSE RECOGNIZABLE-- BUT I ALSO WANT IT CLEAR THAT HE TOOK HOURS TO DIE, AND IT HURT.
OTHER THAN THAT, YOU KNOW, BE CREATIVE.

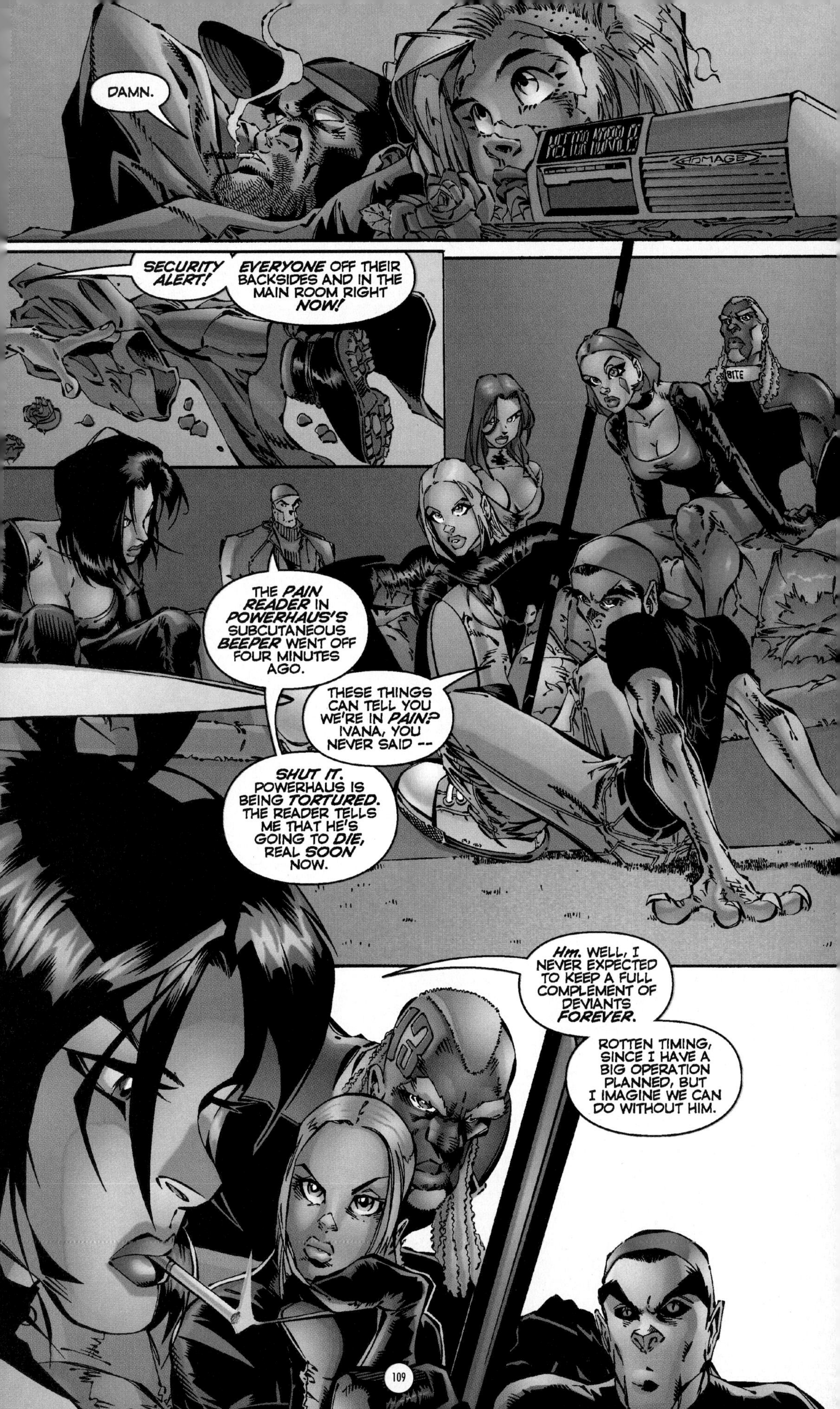
DAMN.
SECURITY ALERT!
EVERYONE OFF THEIR BACKSIDES AND IN THE MAIN ROOM RIGHT NOW!
THE PAIN READER IN POWERHAUS'S SUBCUTANEOUS BEEPER WENT OFF FOUR MINUTES AGO.
THESE THINGS CAN TELL YOU WE'RE IN PAIN? IVANA, YOU NEVER SAID --
SHUT IT. POWERHAUS IS BEING TORTURED. THE READER TELLS ME THAT HE'S GOING TO DIE, REAL SOON NOW.
BITE
Hm. WELL, I NEVER EXPECTED TO KEEP A FULL COMPLEMENT OF DEVIANTS FOREVER.
ROTTEN TIMING, SINCE I HAVE A BIG OPERATION PLANNED, BUT I IMAGINE WE CAN DO WITHOUT HIM.

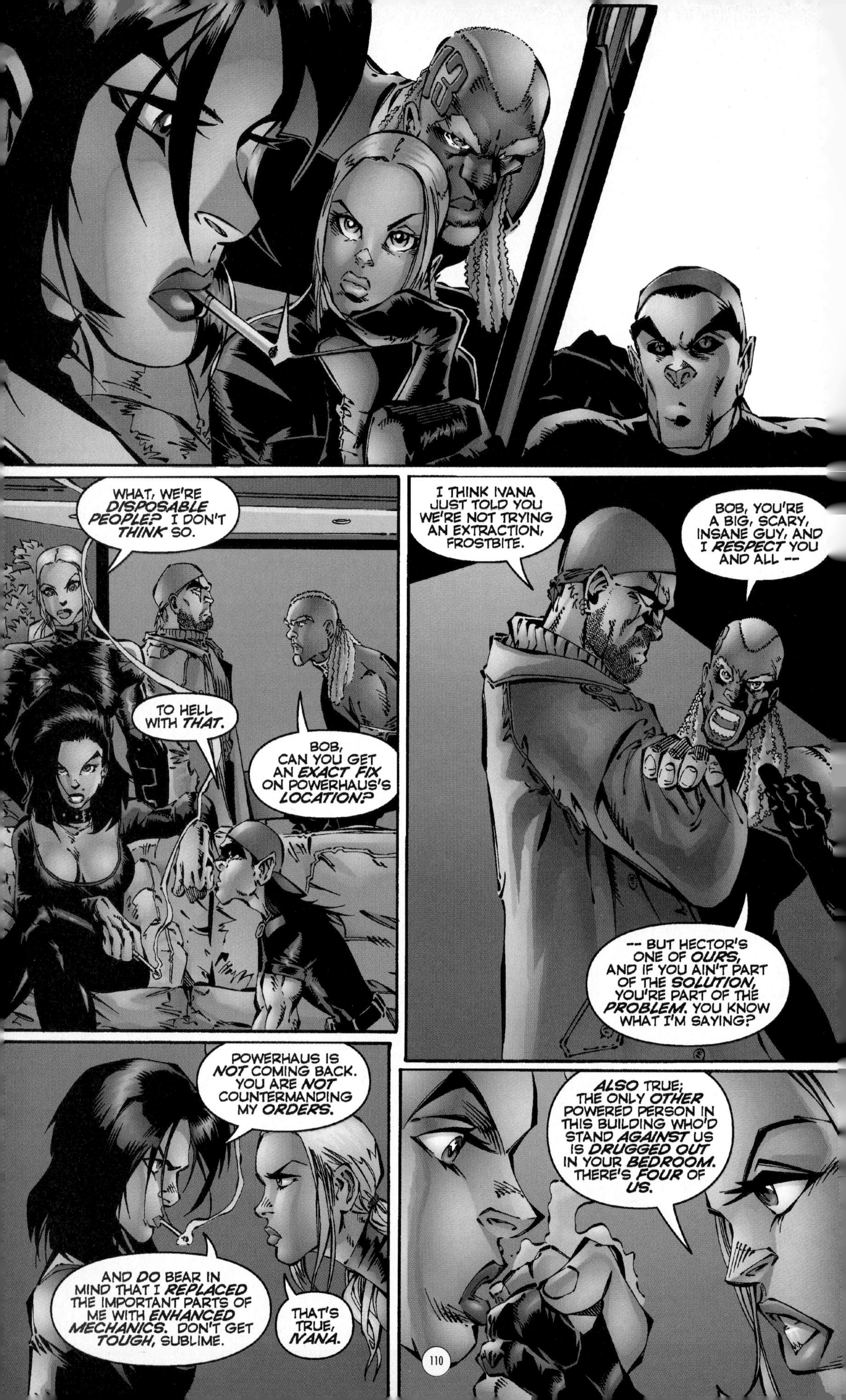

WHAT, WE'RE DISPOSABLE PEOPLE? I DON'T THINK SO.
TO HELL WITH THAT.
BOB, CAN YOU GET AN EXACT FIX ON POWERHAUS'S LOCATION?
I THINK IVANA JUST TOLD YOU WE'RE NOT TRYING AN EXTRACTION, FROSTBITE.
BOB, YOU'RE A BIG, SCARY, INSANE GUY, AND I RESPECT YOU AND ALL --
-- BUT HECTOR'S ONE OF OURS, AND IF YOU AIN'T PART OF THE SOLUTION, YOU'RE PART OF THE PROBLEM. YOU KNOW WHAT I'M SAYING?
POWERHAUS IS NOT COMING BACK. YOU ARE NOT COUNTERMANDING MY ORDERS.
AND DO BEAR IN MIND THAT I REPLACED THE IMPORTANT PARTS OF ME WITH ENHANCED MECHANICS. DON'T GET TOUGH, SUBLIME.
THAT'S TRUE, IVANA.
ALSO TRUE; THE ONLY OTHER POWERED PERSON IN THIS BUILDING WHO'D STAND AGAINST US IS DRUGGED OUT IN YOUR BEDROOM. THERE'S FOUR OF US.

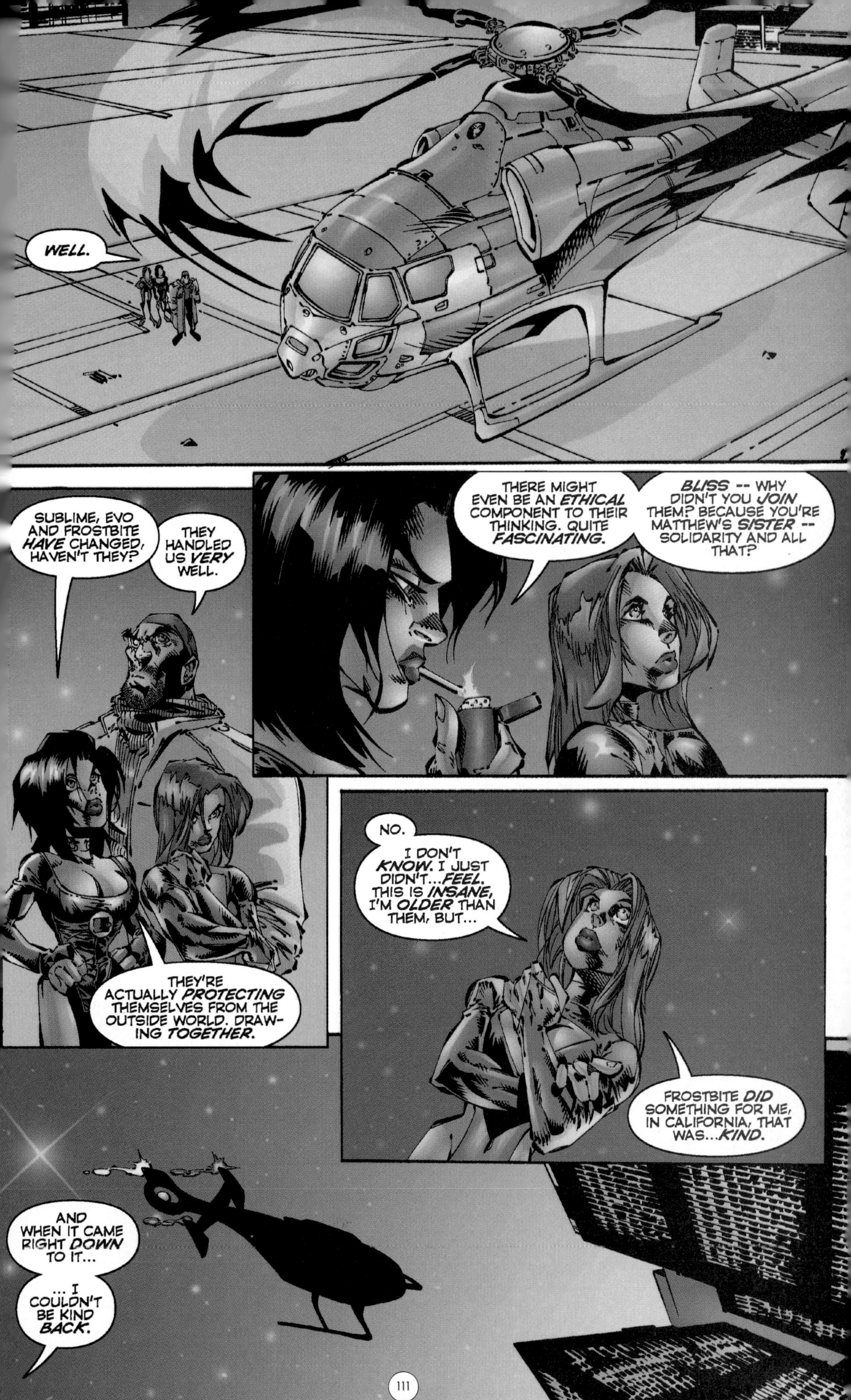
WELL.
SUBLIME, EVO AND FROSTBITE HAVE CHANGED, HAVEN'T THEY?
THEY HANDLED US VERY WELL.
THEY'RE ACTUALLY PROTECTING THEMSELVES FROM THE OUTSIDE WORLD. DRAWING TOGETHER.
THERE MIGHT EVEN BE AN ETHICAL COMPONENT TO THEIR THINKING. QUITE FASCINATING.
BLISS -- WHY DIDN'T YOU JOIN THEM? BECAUSE YOU'RE MATTHEW'S SISTER -- SOLIDARITY AND ALL THAT?
NO.
I DON'T KNOW. I JUST DIDN'T...FEEL. THIS IS INSANE, I'M OLDER THAN THEM, BUT...
FROSTBITE DID SOMETHING FOR ME, IN CALIFORNIA, THAT WAS...KIND.
AND WHEN IT CAME RIGHT DOWN TO IT...
... I COULDN'T BE KIND BACK.

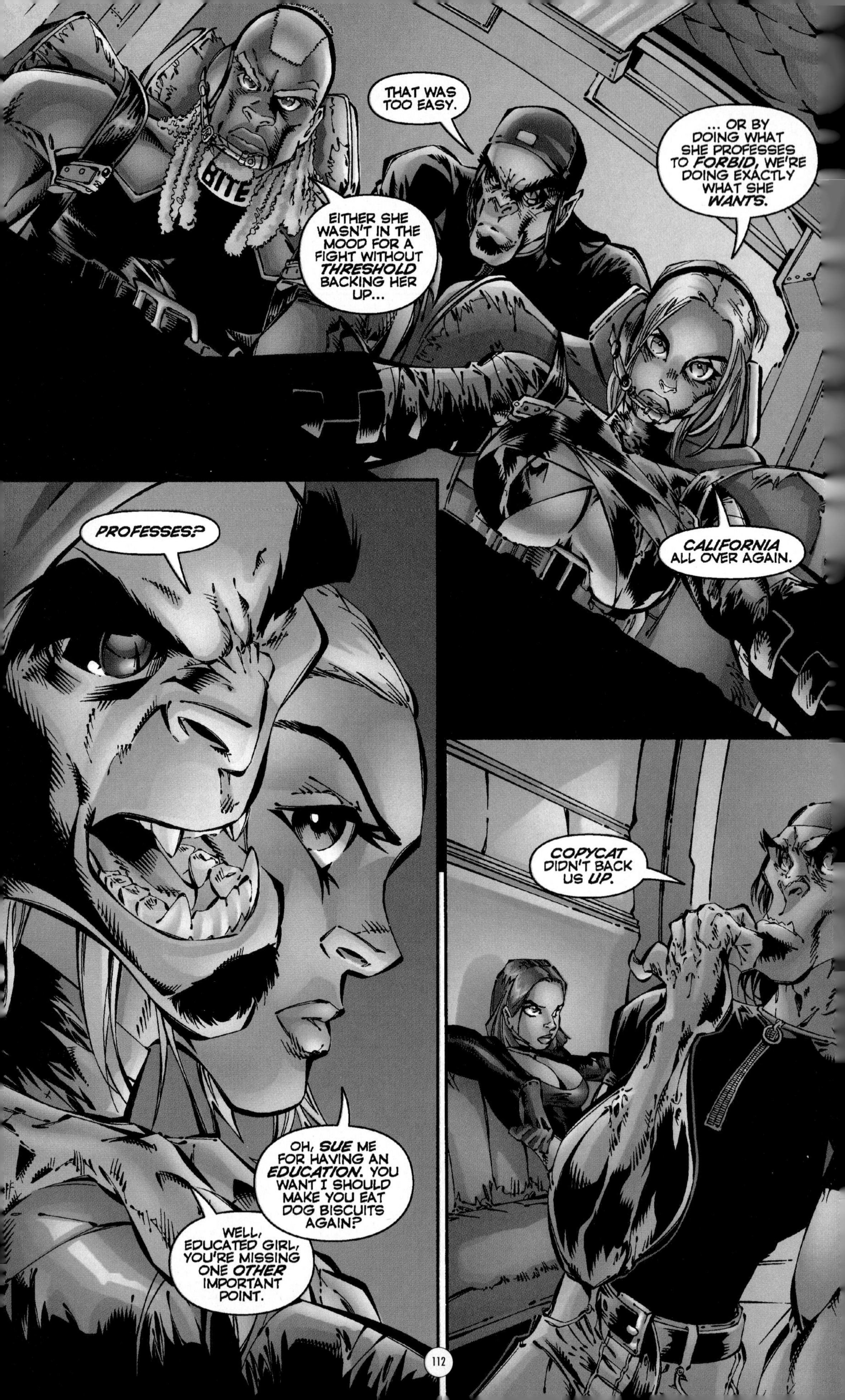
THAT WAS TOO EASY.
EITHER SHE WASN'T IN THE MOOD FOR A FIGHT WITHOUT *THRESHOLD* BACKING HER UP...
... OR BY DOING WHAT SHE PROFESSES TO *FORBID*, WE'RE DOING EXACTLY WHAT SHE *WANTS*.
CALIFORNIA ALL OVER AGAIN.
PROFESSES?
OH, *SUE* ME FOR HAVING AN *EDUCATION*. YOU WANT I SHOULD MAKE YOU EAT DOG BISCUITS AGAIN?
WELL, EDUCATED GIRL, YOU'RE MISSING ONE *OTHER* IMPORTANT POINT.
COPYCAT DIDN'T BACK US *UP*.

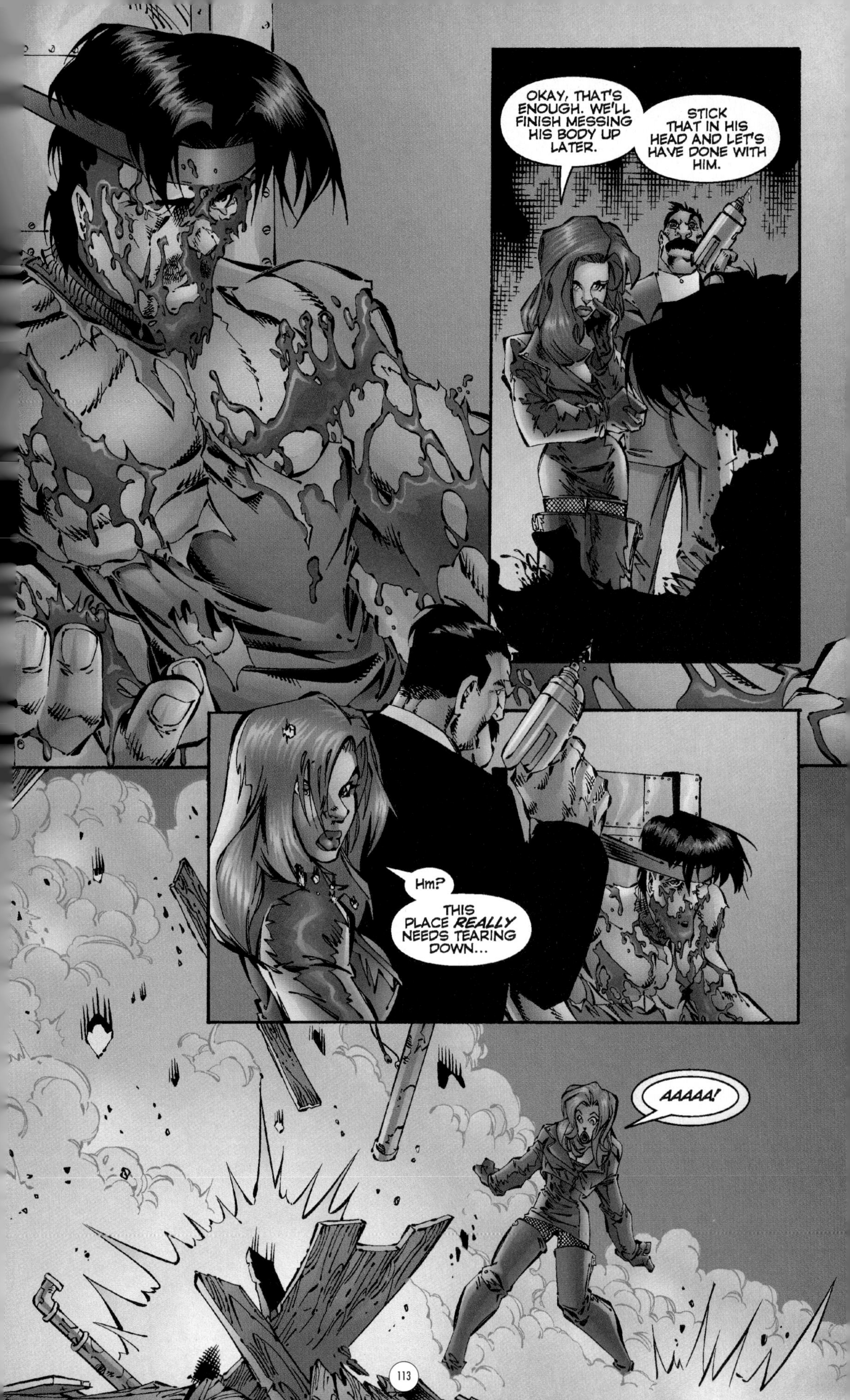
OKAY, THAT'S ENOUGH. WE'LL FINISH MESSING HIS BODY UP LATER.
STICK THAT IN HIS HEAD AND LET'S HAVE DONE WITH HIM.
Hm?
THIS PLACE *REALLY* NEEDS TEARING DOWN...
AAAAA!

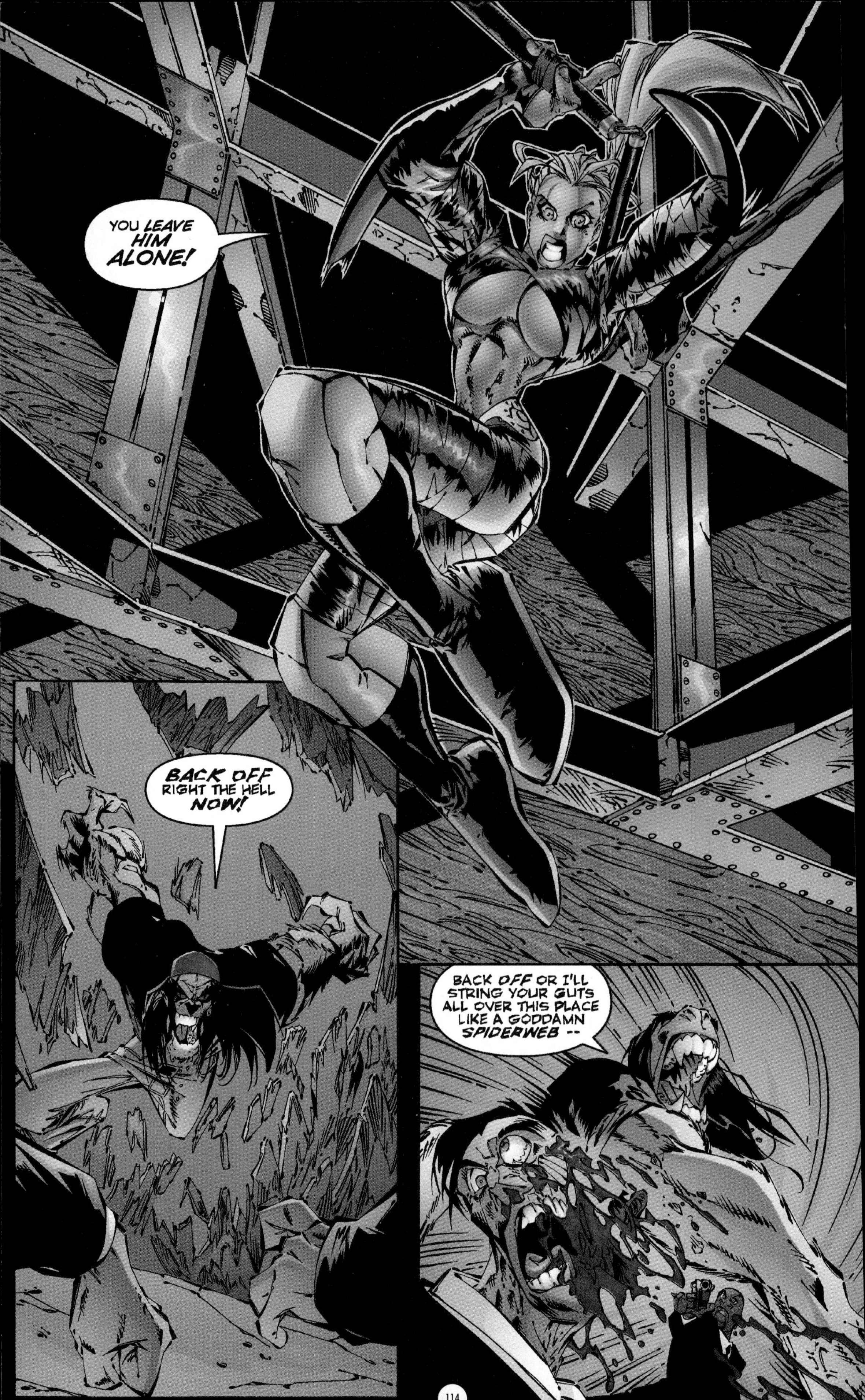
YOU LEAVE HIM ALONE!
BACK OFF RIGHT THE HELL NOW!
BACK OFF OR I'LL STRING YOUR GUTS ALL OVER THIS PLACE LIKE A GODDAMN SPIDERWEB --

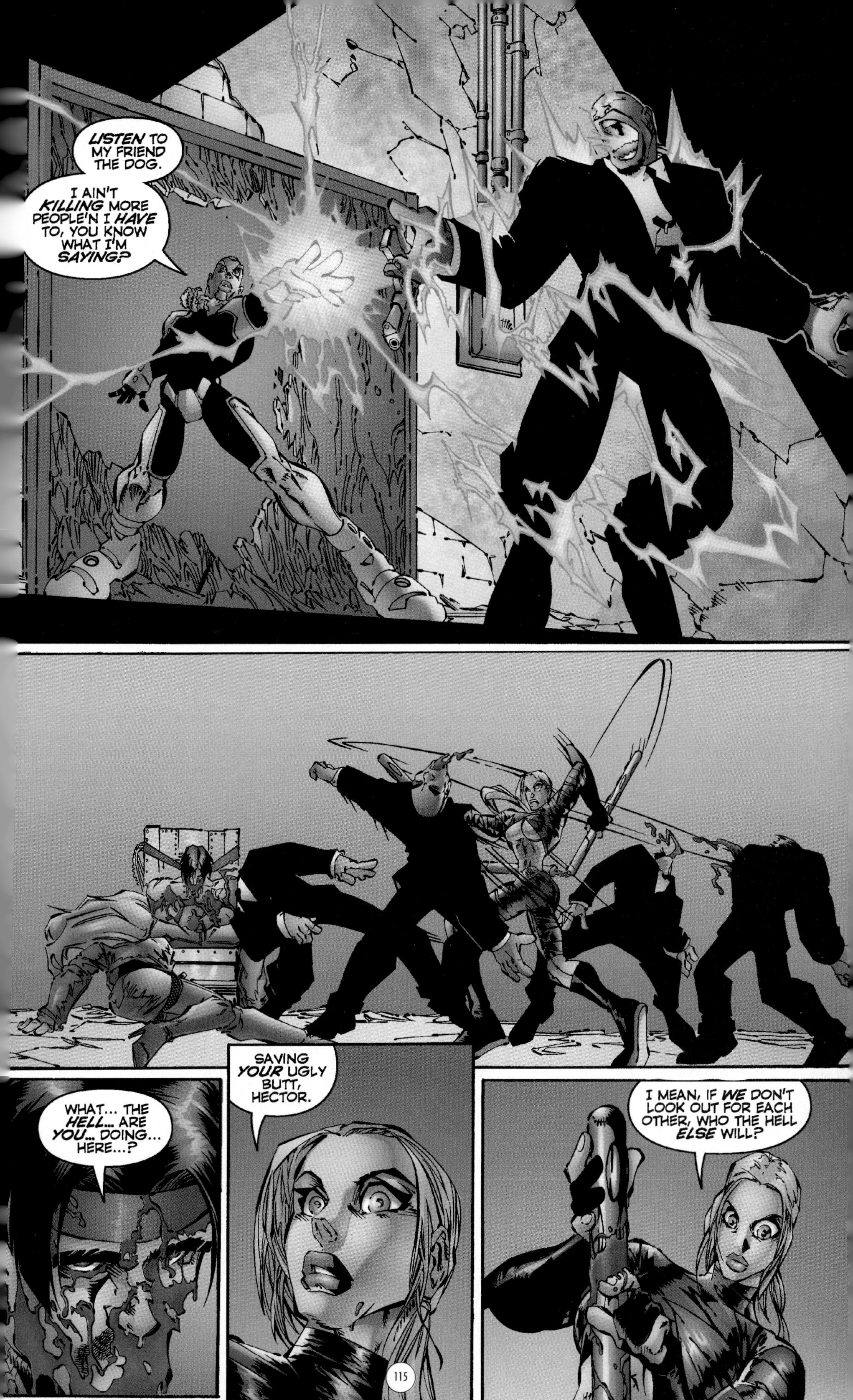
LISTEN TO MY FRIEND THE DOG.
I AIN'T KILLING MORE PEOPLE'N I HAVE TO, YOU KNOW WHAT I'M SAYING?
WHAT... THE HELL... ARE YOU... DOING... HERE...?
SAVING YOUR UGLY BUTT, HECTOR.
I MEAN, IF WE DON'T LOOK OUT FOR EACH OTHER, WHO THE HELL ELSE WILL?

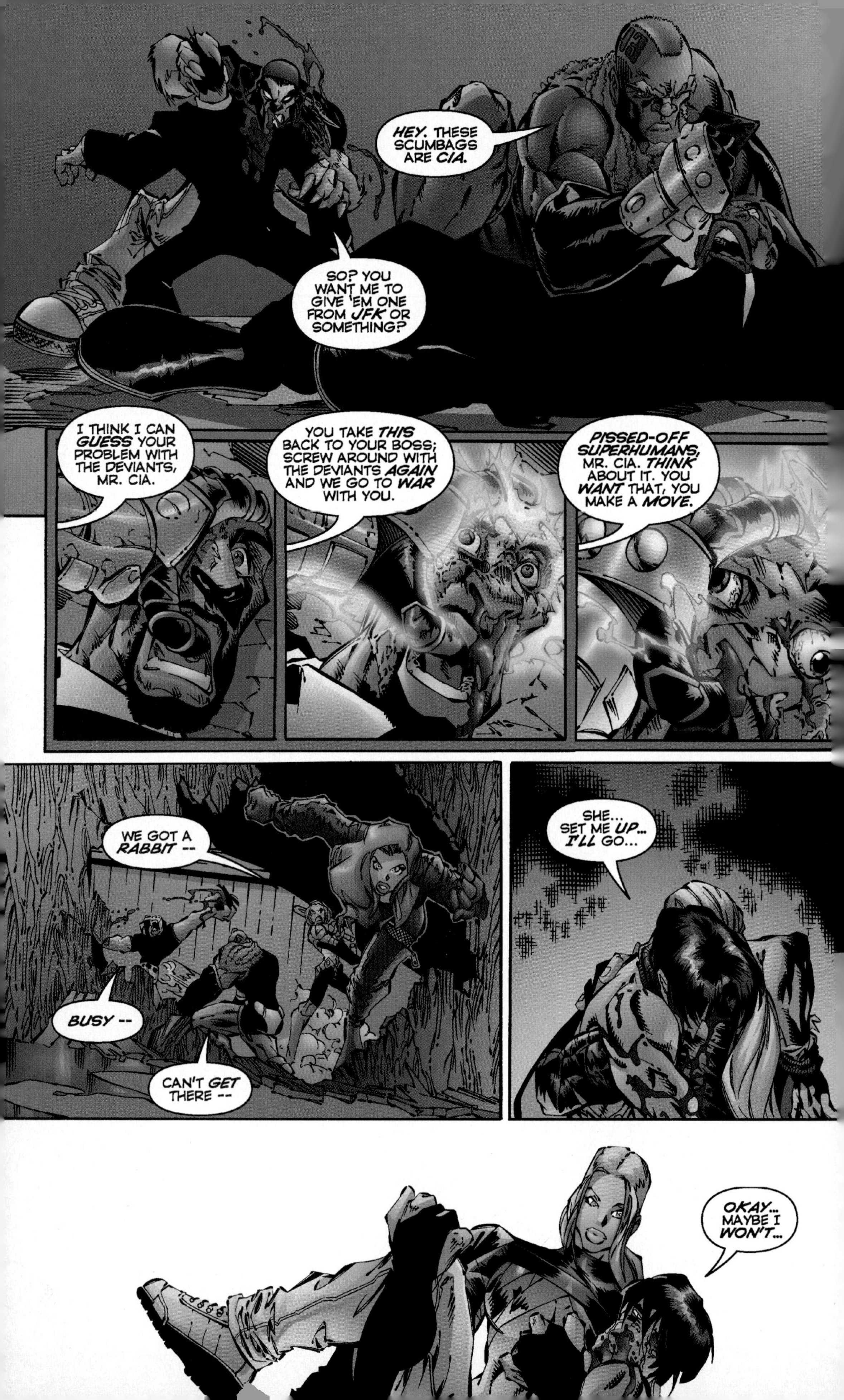
HEY. THESE SCUMBAGS ARE CIA.
SO? YOU WANT ME TO GIVE 'EM ONE FROM JFK OR SOMETHING?
I THINK I CAN GUESS YOUR PROBLEM WITH THE DEVIANTS, MR. CIA.
YOU TAKE THIS BACK TO YOUR BOSS; SCREW AROUND WITH THE DEVIANTS AGAIN AND WE GO TO WAR WITH YOU.
PISSED-OFF SUPERHUMANS, MR. CIA. THINK ABOUT IT. YOU WANT THAT, YOU MAKE A MOVE.
WE GOT A RABBIT --
BUSY --
CAN'T GET THERE --
SHE... SET ME UP... I'LL GO...
OKAY... MAYBE I WON'T...

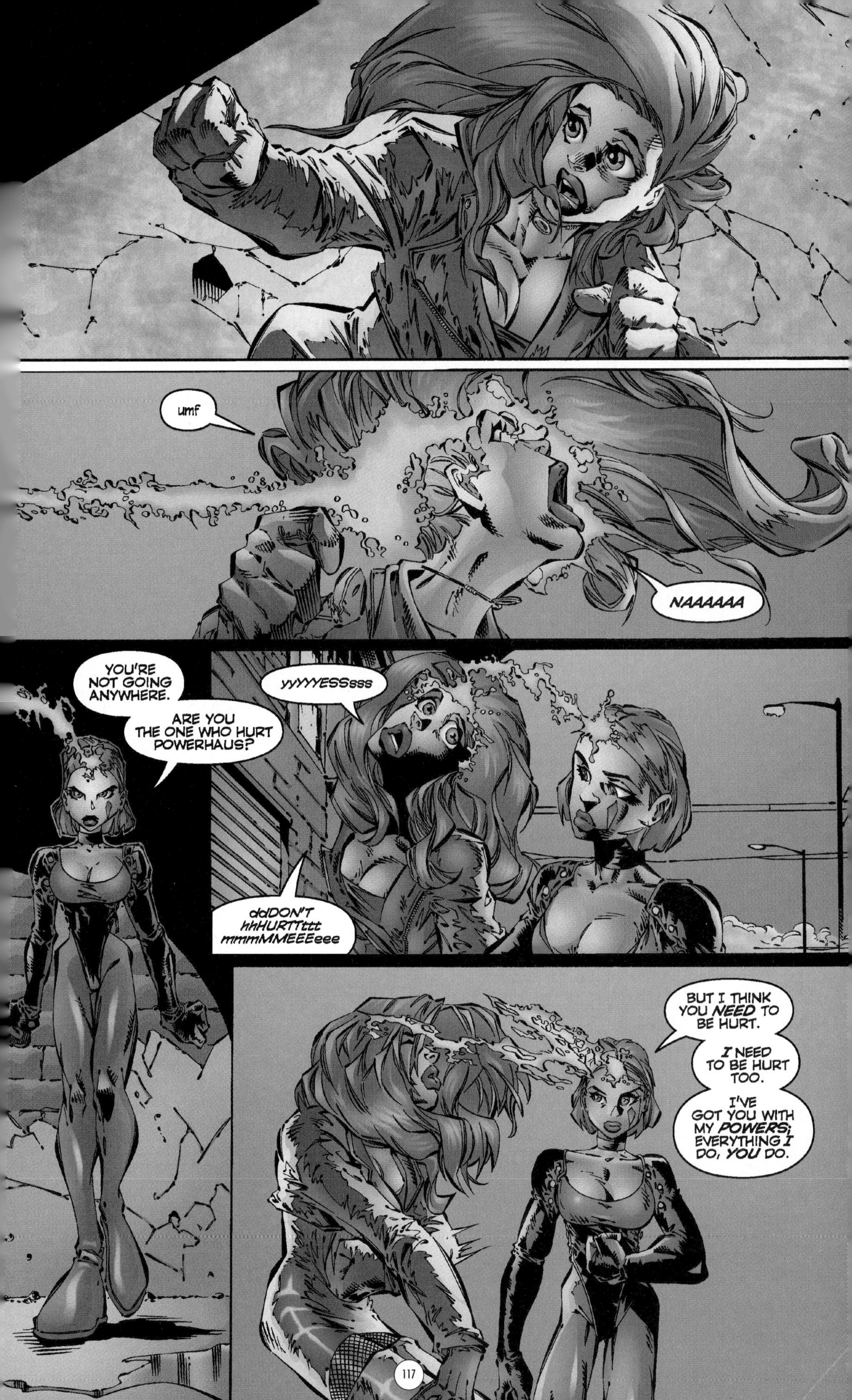
umf
NAAAAAA
YOU'RE NOT GOING ANYWHERE.
ARE YOU THE ONE WHO HURT POWERHAUS?
yyYYYESSsss
ddDON'T hhHURTTttt mmmmMMEEEeee
BUT I THINK YOU NEED TO BE HURT.
I NEED TO BE HURT TOO.
I'VE GOT YOU WITH MY POWERS; EVERYTHING I DO, YOU DO.

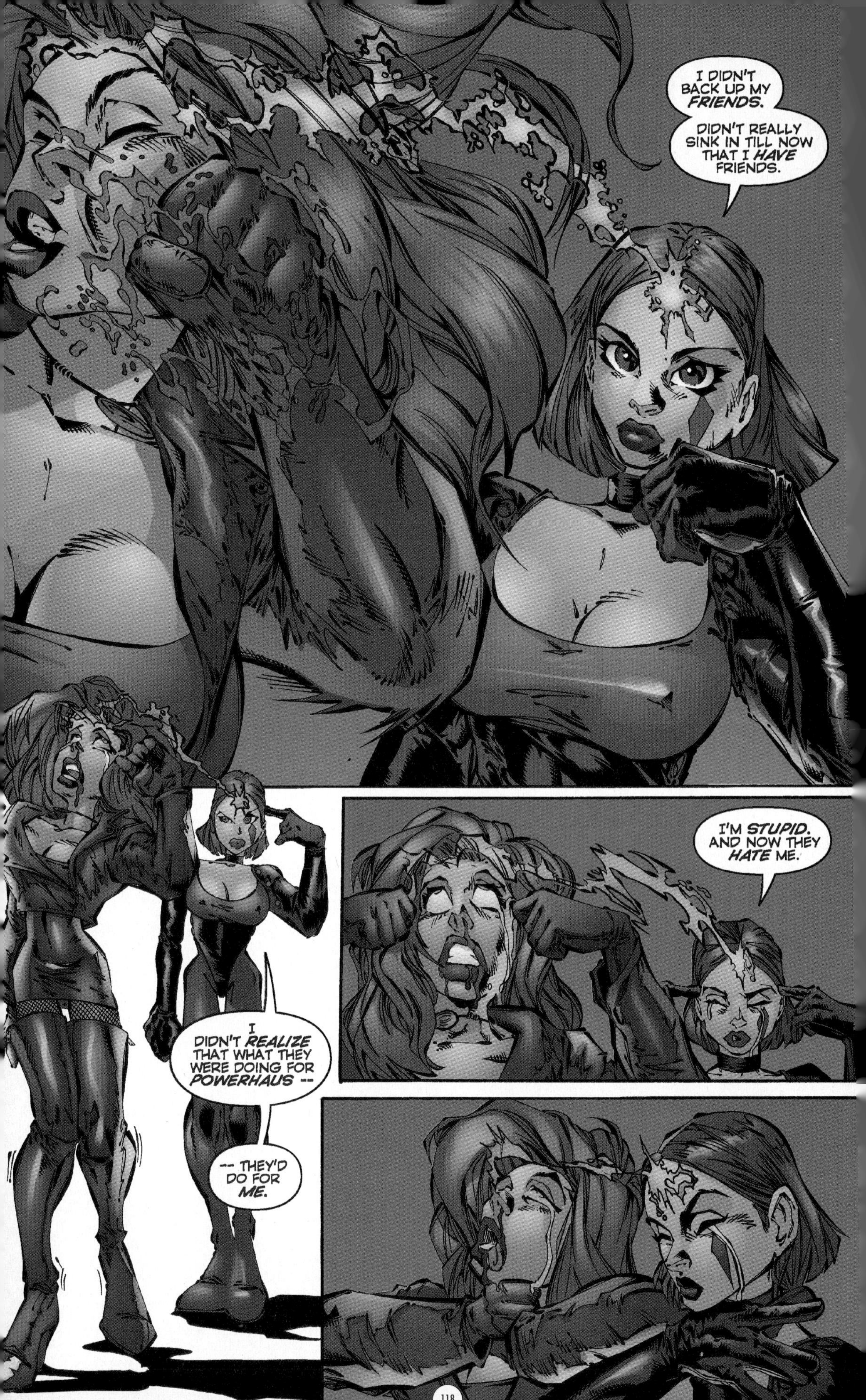
I DIDN'T BACK UP MY ***FRIENDS***.
DIDN'T REALLY SINK IN TILL NOW THAT I ***HAVE*** FRIENDS.
I DIDN'T ***REALIZE*** THAT WHAT THEY WERE DOING FOR ***POWERHAUS*** --
-- THEY'D DO FOR ***ME***.
I'M ***STUPID***. AND NOW THEY ***HATE*** ME.

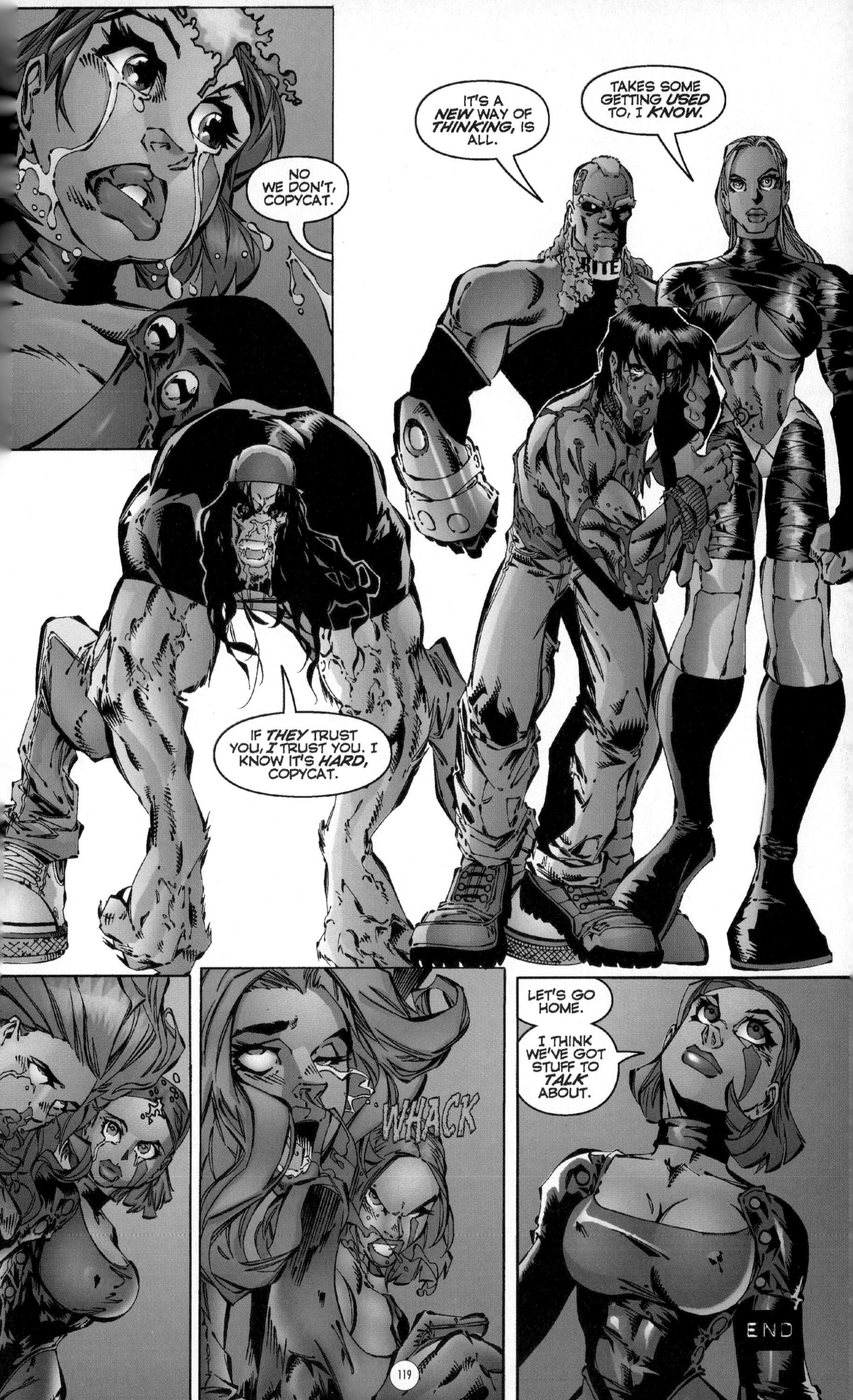
NO WE DON'T, COPYCAT.
IT'S A NEW WAY OF THINKING, IS ALL.
TAKES SOME GETTING USED TO, I KNOW.
IF THEY TRUST YOU, I TRUST YOU. I KNOW IT'S HARD, COPYCAT.
WHACK
LET'S GO HOME.
I THINK WE'VE GOT STUFF TO TALK ABOUT.
END

DV8

CREATED BY JIM LEE,
BRANDON CHOI AND
J. SCOTT CAMPBELL

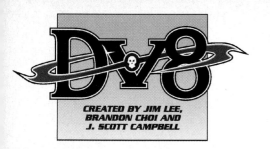

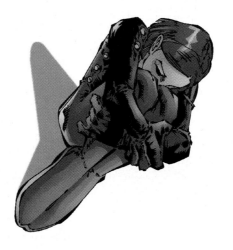

ISOLATION

BY

WARREN ELLIS & HUMBERTO RAMOS
WRITER ARTIST

SAL REGLA
INKS

WENDY FOUTS
COLORS

JIM-BOB O'NEIL
LETTERS

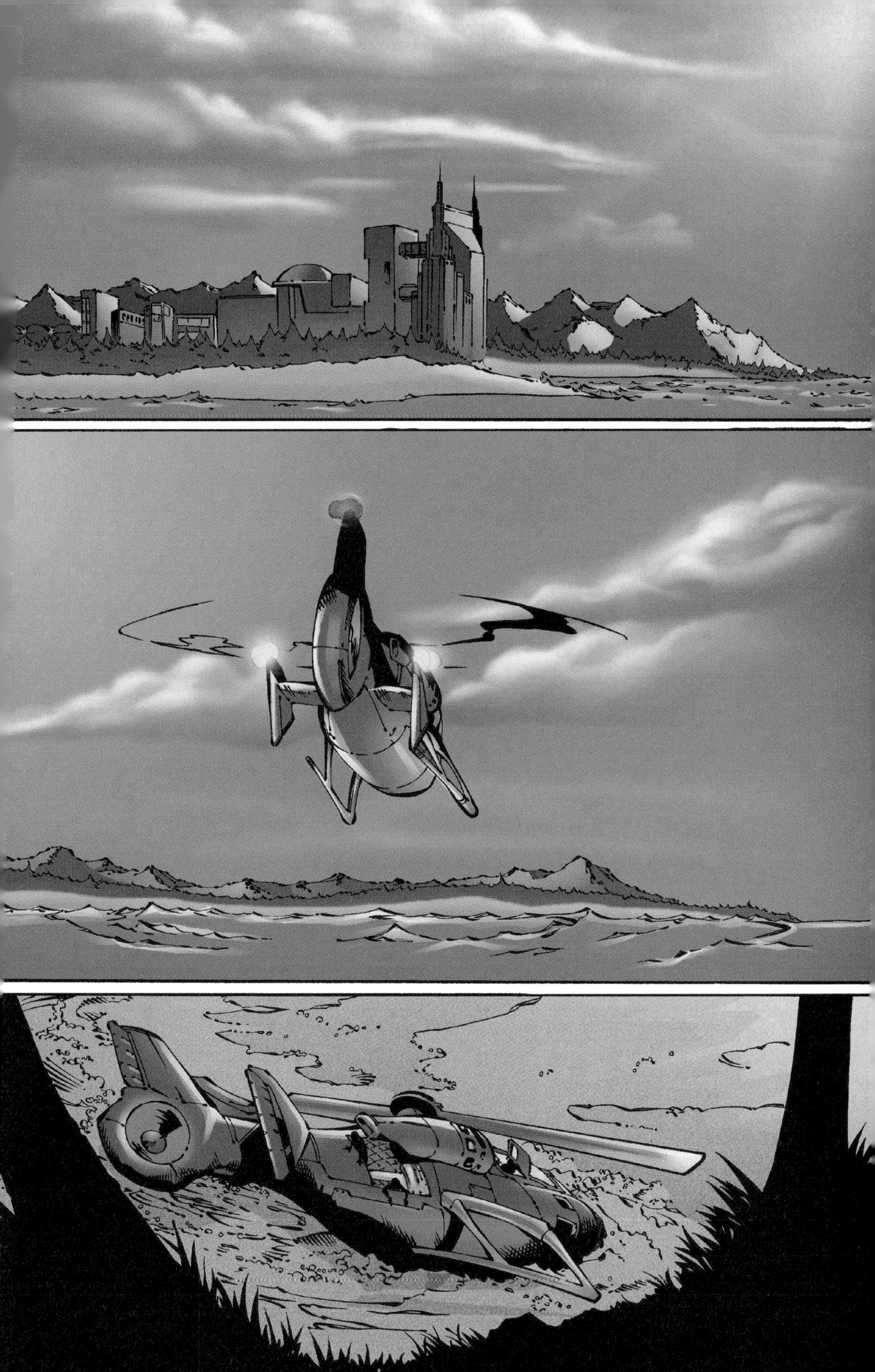

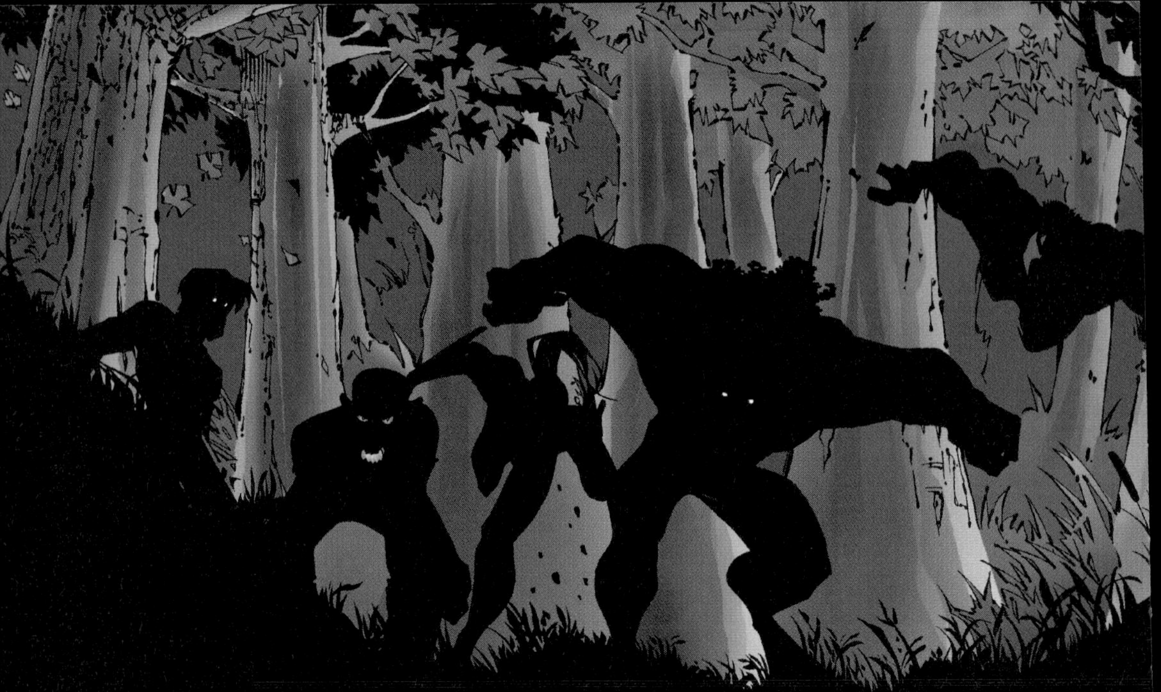

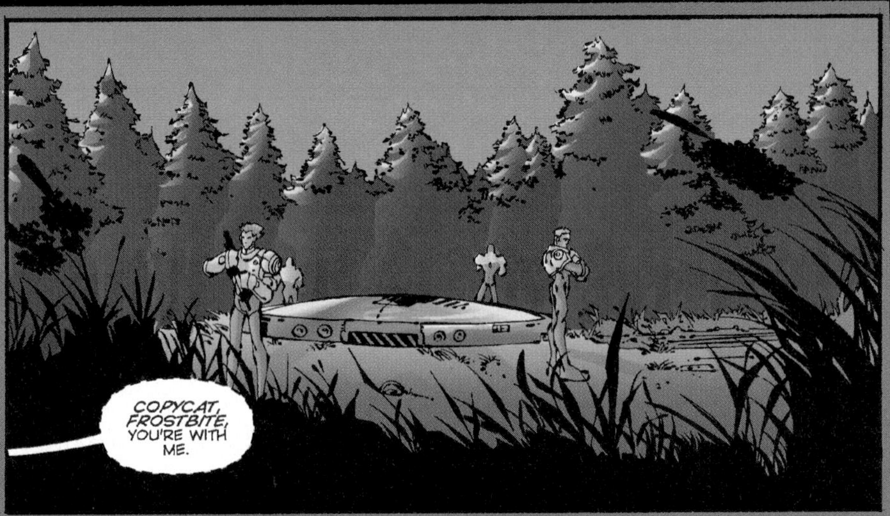
COPYCAT, FROSTBITE, YOU'RE WITH ME.

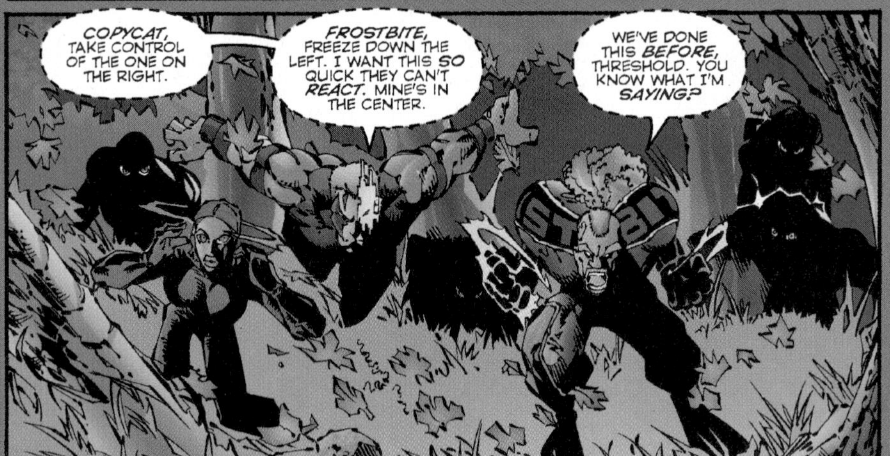
COPYCAT, TAKE CONTROL OF THE ONE ON THE RIGHT.
FROSTBITE, FREEZE DOWN THE LEFT. I WANT THIS SO QUICK THEY CAN'T REACT. MINE'S IN THE CENTER.
WE'VE DONE THIS BEFORE, THRESHOLD. YOU KNOW WHAT I'M SAYING?

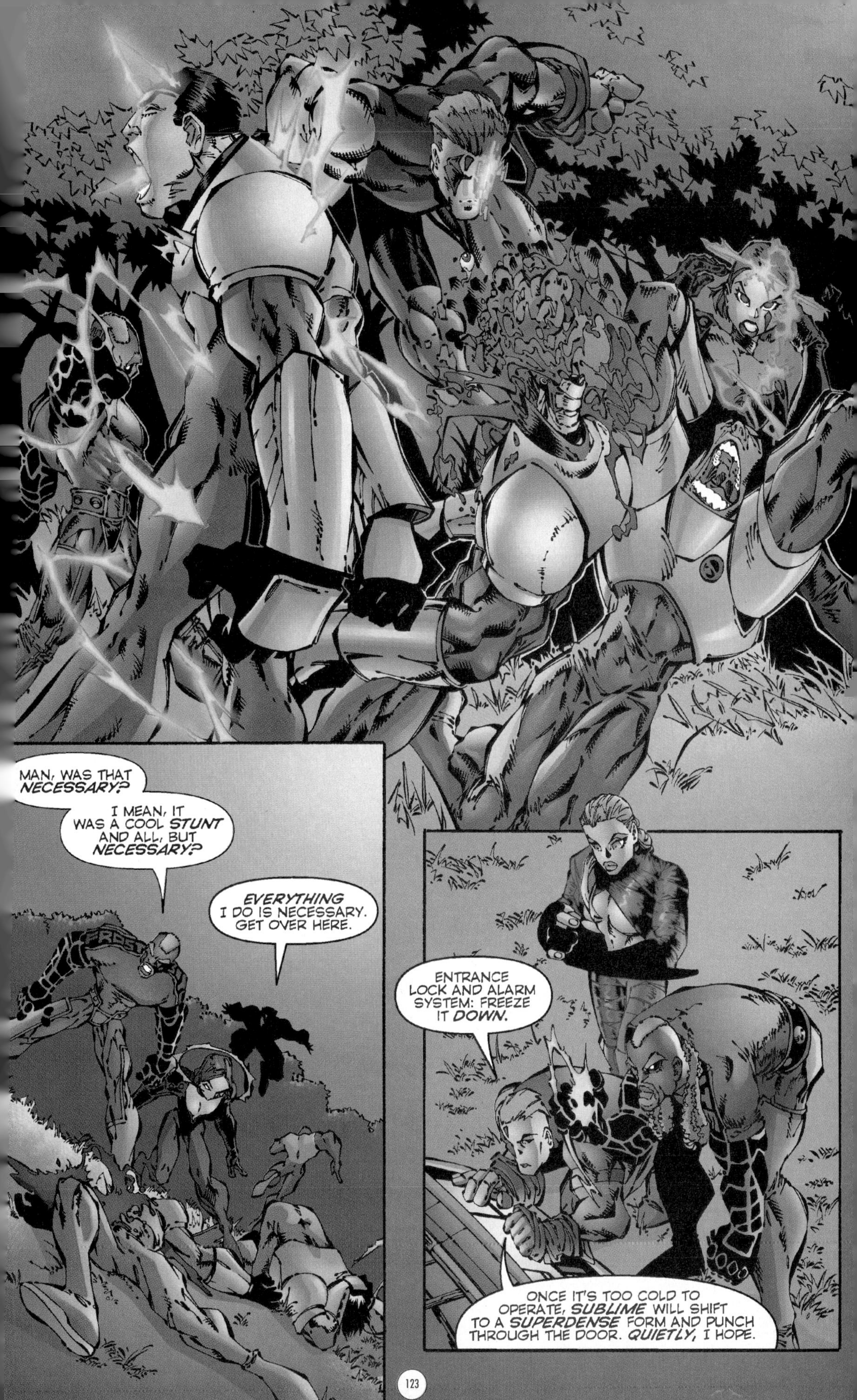
MAN, WAS THAT *NECESSARY?*
I MEAN, IT WAS A COOL *STUNT* AND ALL, BUT *NECESSARY?*
EVERYTHING I DO IS NECESSARY. GET OVER HERE.
ENTRANCE LOCK AND ALARM SYSTEM: FREEZE IT *DOWN.*
ONCE IT'S TOO COLD TO OPERATE, *SUBLIME* WILL SHIFT TO A *SUPERDENSE* FORM AND PUNCH THROUGH THE DOOR. *QUIETLY,* I HOPE.

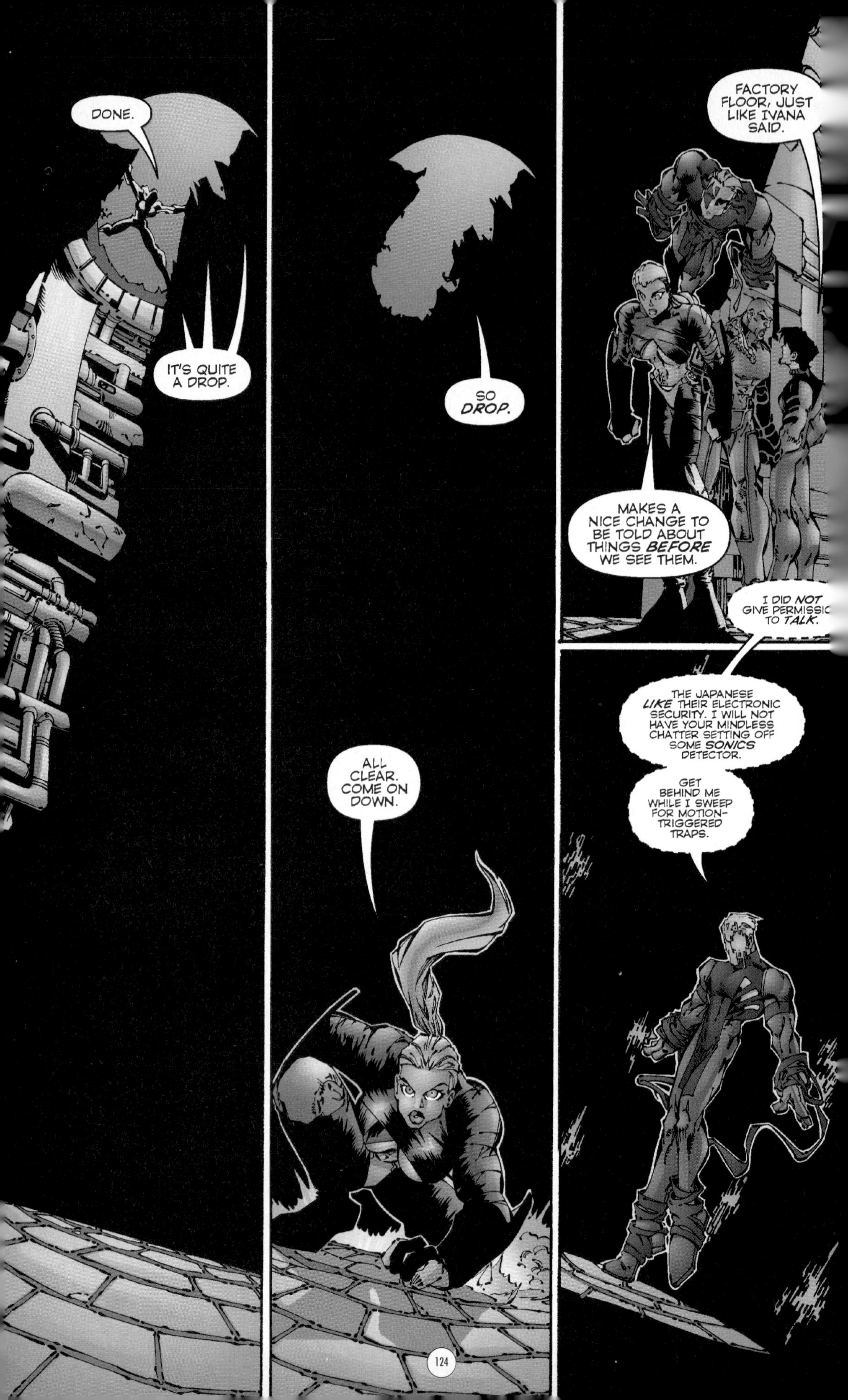
DONE.
IT'S QUITE A DROP.
SO *DROP*.
ALL CLEAR. COME ON DOWN.
FACTORY FLOOR, JUST LIKE IVANA SAID.
MAKES A NICE CHANGE TO BE TOLD ABOUT THINGS *BEFORE* WE SEE THEM.
I DID *NOT* GIVE PERMISSIC TO *TALK*.
THE JAPANESE *LIKE* THEIR ELECTRONIC SECURITY. I WILL NOT HAVE YOUR MINDLESS CHATTER SETTING OFF SOME *SONICS* DETECTOR.
GET BEHIND ME WHILE I SWEEP FOR MOTION-TRIGGERED TRAPS.

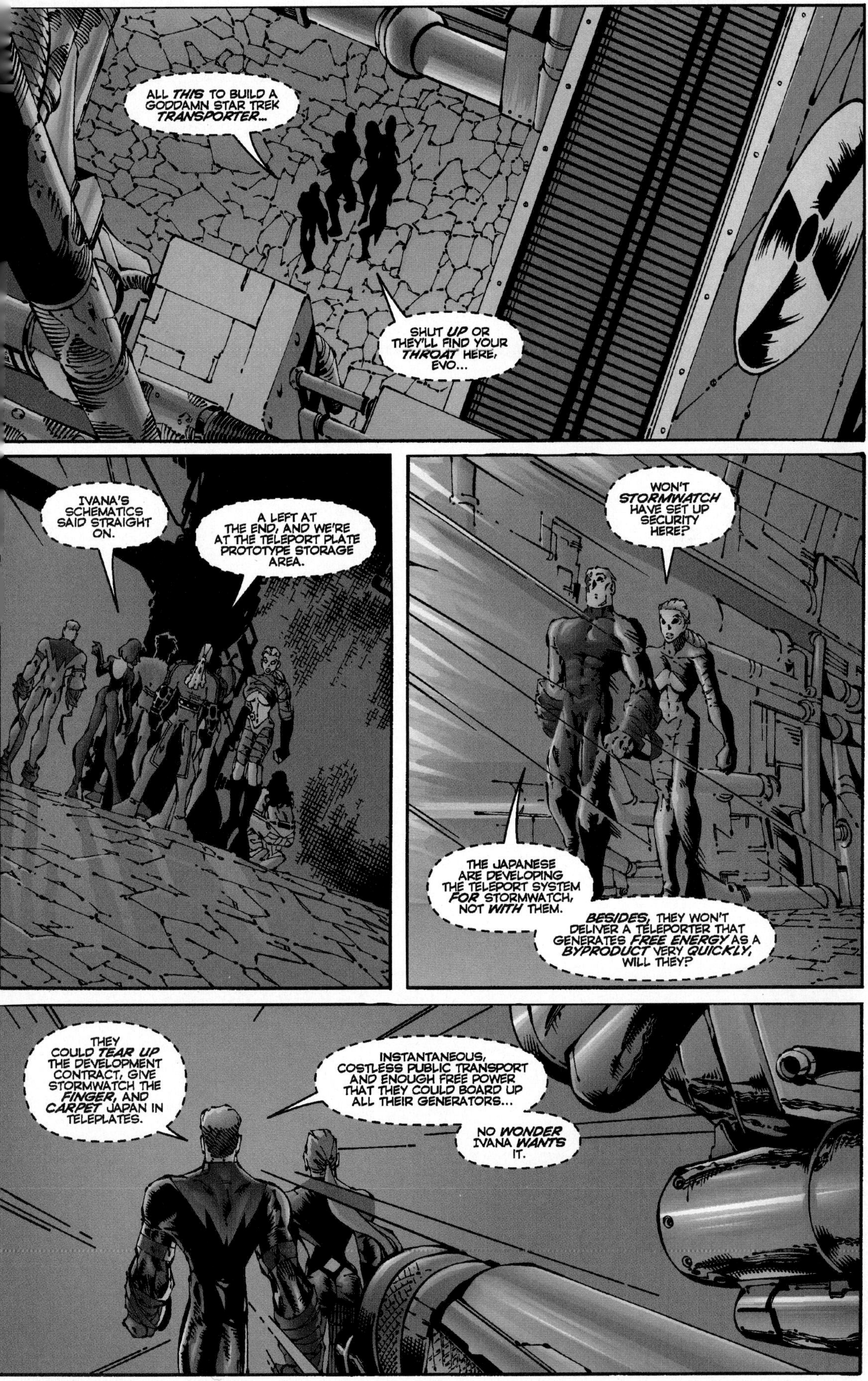
ALL *THIS* TO BUILD A GODDAMN STAR TREK *TRANSPORTER*...
SHUT *UP* OR THEY'LL FIND YOUR *THROAT* HERE, EVO...
IVANA'S SCHEMATICS SAID STRAIGHT ON.
A LEFT AT THE END, AND WE'RE AT THE TELEPORT PLATE PROTOTYPE STORAGE AREA.
WON'T *STORMWATCH* HAVE SET UP SECURITY HERE?
THE JAPANESE ARE DEVELOPING THE TELEPORT SYSTEM *FOR* STORMWATCH, NOT *WITH* THEM.
BESIDES, THEY WON'T DELIVER A TELEPORTER THAT GENERATES *FREE ENERGY* AS A *BYPRODUCT* VERY *QUICKLY,* WILL THEY?
THEY COULD *TEAR UP* THE DEVELOPMENT CONTRACT, GIVE STORMWATCH THE *FINGER,* AND *CARPET* JAPAN IN TELEPLATES.
INSTANTANEOUS, COSTLESS PUBLIC TRANSPORT AND ENOUGH FREE POWER THAT THEY COULD BOARD UP ALL THEIR GENERATORS...
NO *WONDER* IVANA *WANTS* IT.

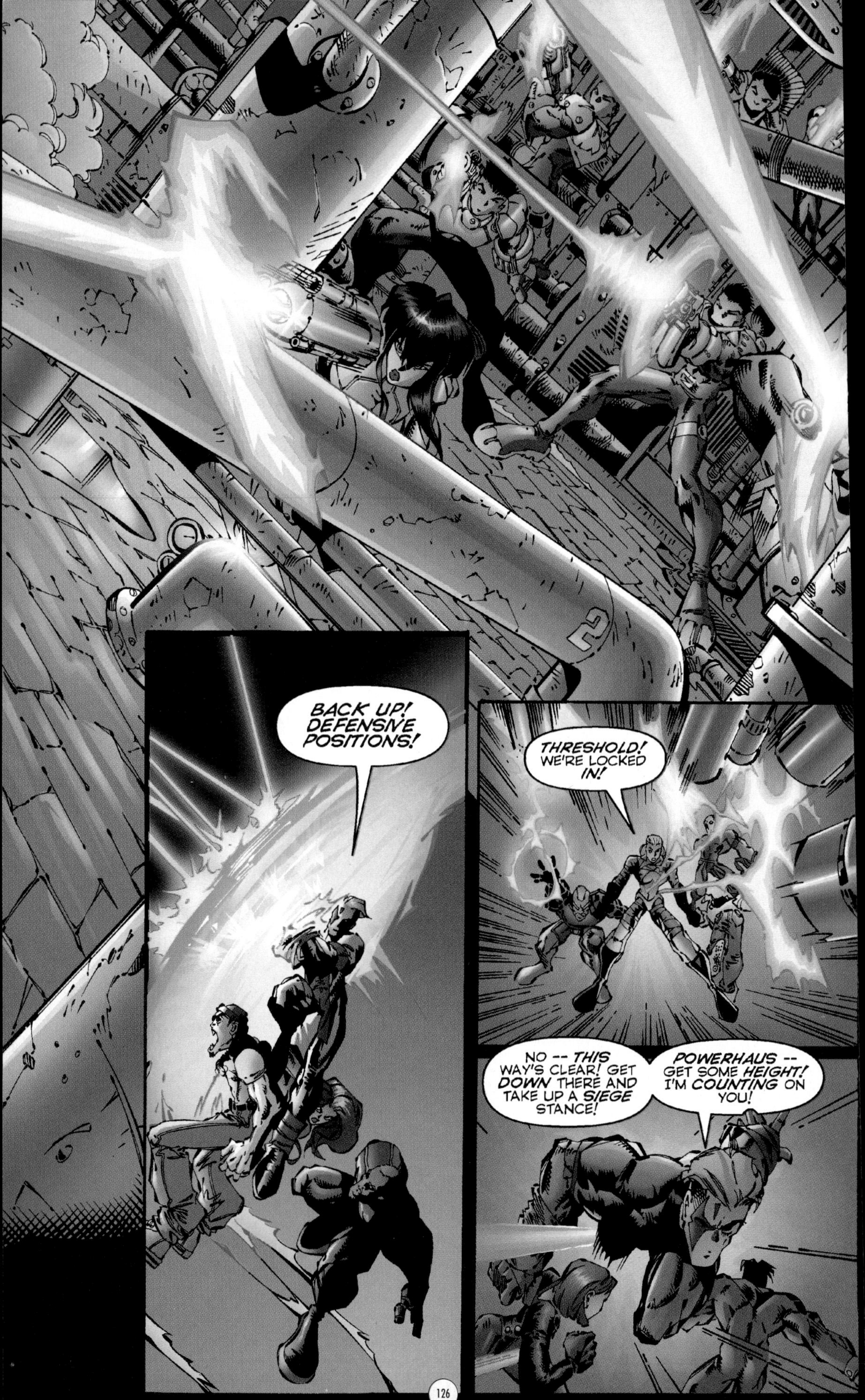
BACK UP! DEFENSIVE POSITIONS!
THRESHOLD! WE'RE LOCKED IN!
NO -- THIS WAY'S CLEAR! GET DOWN THERE AND TAKE UP A SIEGE STANCE!
POWERHAUS -- GET SOME HEIGHT! I'M COUNTING ON YOU!

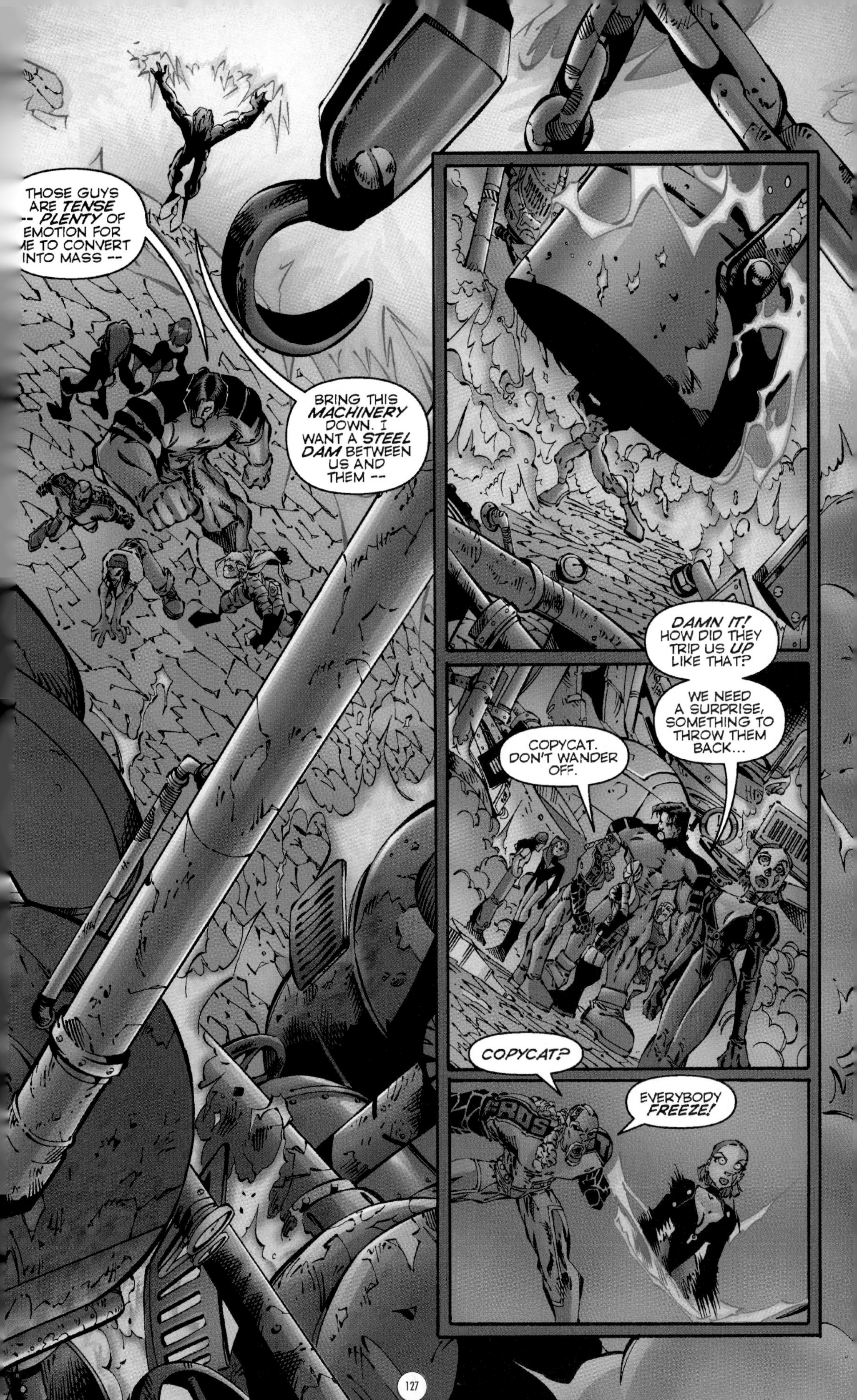
THOSE GUYS ARE TENSE -- PLENTY OF EMOTION FOR ME TO CONVERT INTO MASS --
BRING THIS MACHINERY DOWN. I WANT A STEEL DAM BETWEEN US AND THEM --
DAMN IT! HOW DID THEY TRIP US UP LIKE THAT?
WE NEED A SURPRISE, SOMETHING TO THROW THEM BACK...
COPYCAT. DON'T WANDER OFF.
COPYCAT?
EVERYBODY FREEZE!

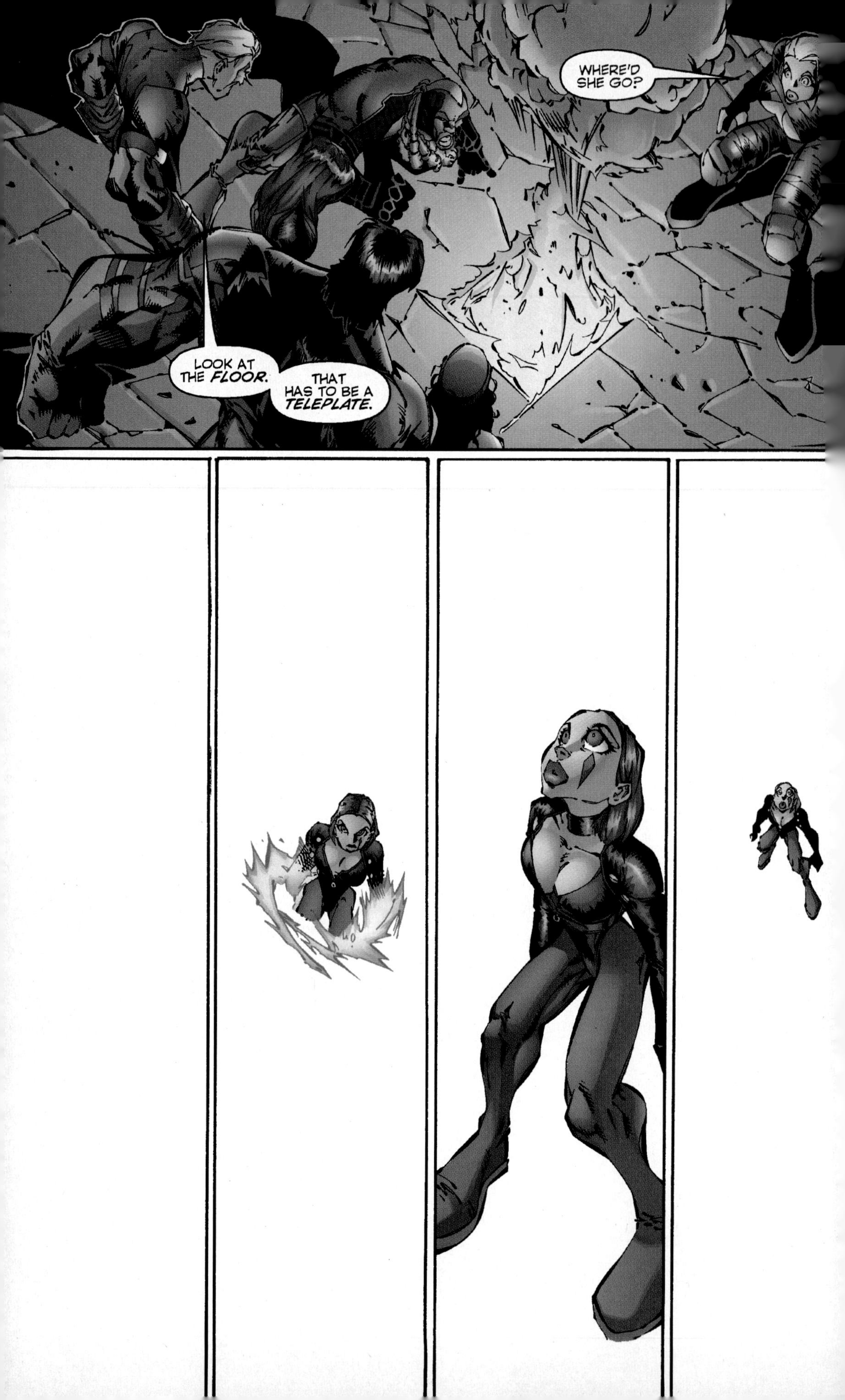
WHERE'D SHE GO?
LOOK AT THE *FLOOR*.
THAT HAS TO BE A *TELEPLATE*.

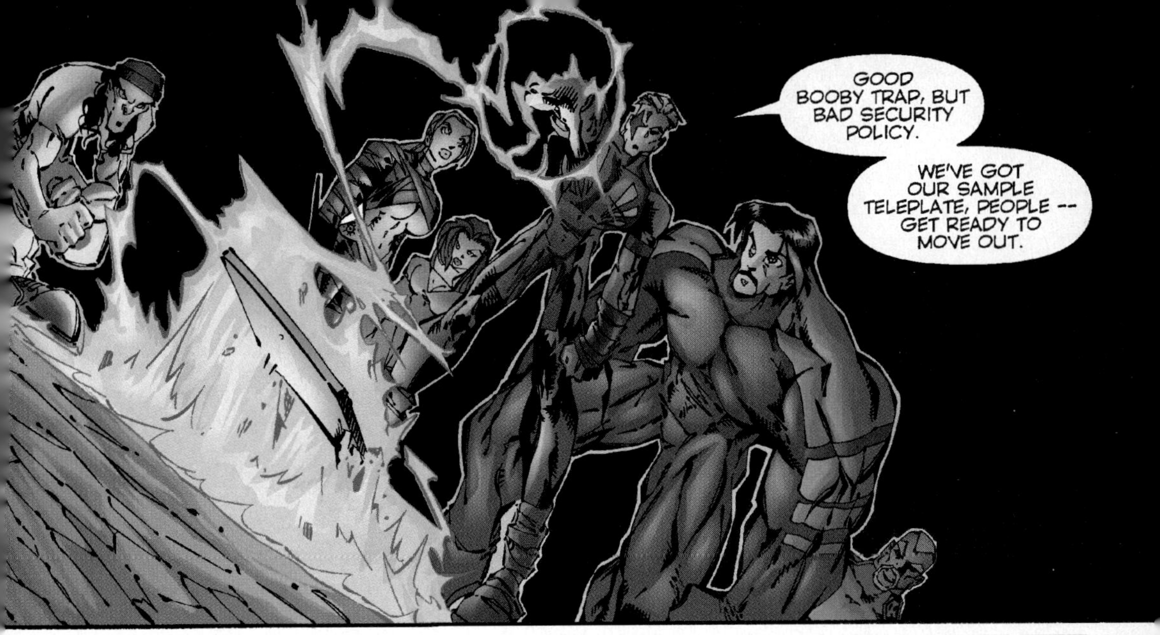
GOOD BOOBY TRAP, BUT BAD SECURITY POLICY.
WE'VE GOT OUR SAMPLE TELEPLATE, PEOPLE -- GET READY TO MOVE OUT.

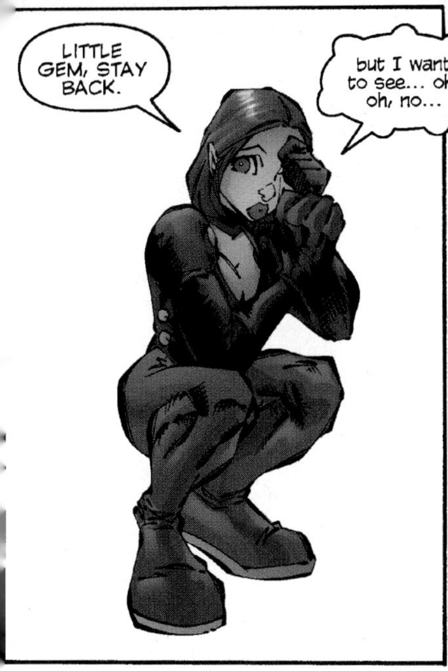
LITTLE GEM, STAY BACK.
but I want to see... oh. oh, no...

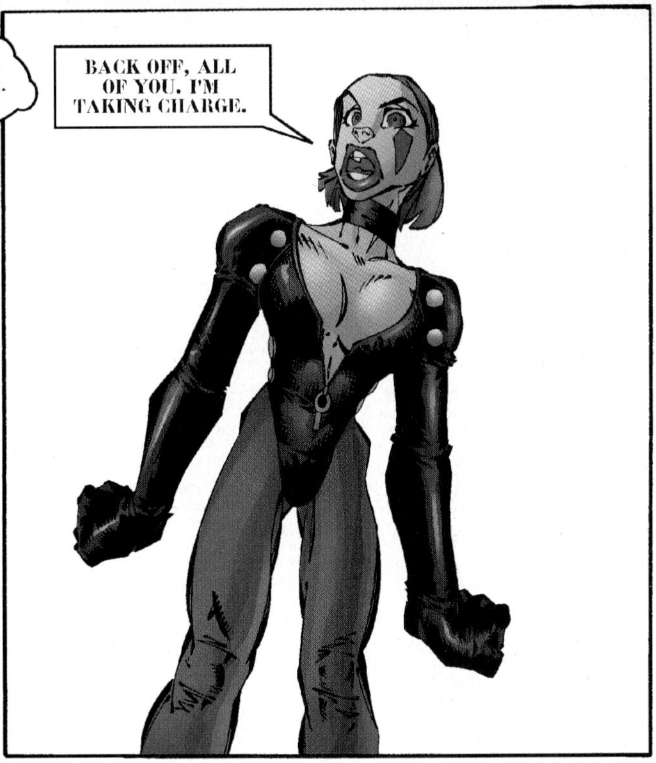
BACK OFF, ALL OF YOU. I'M TAKING CHARGE.

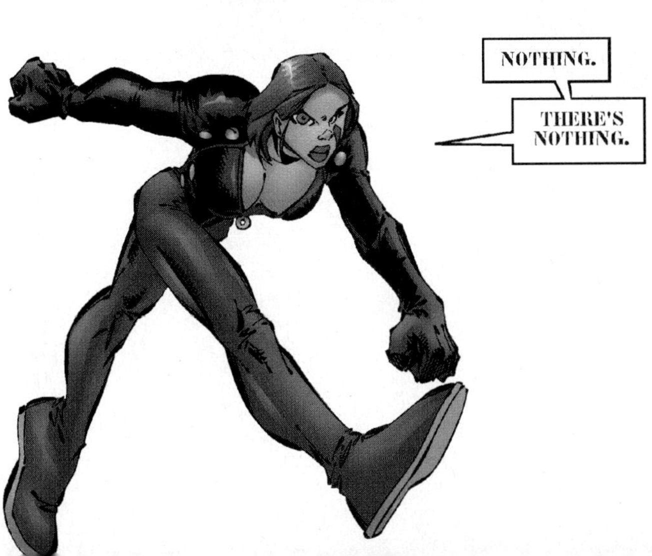
NOTHING.
THERE'S NOTHING.

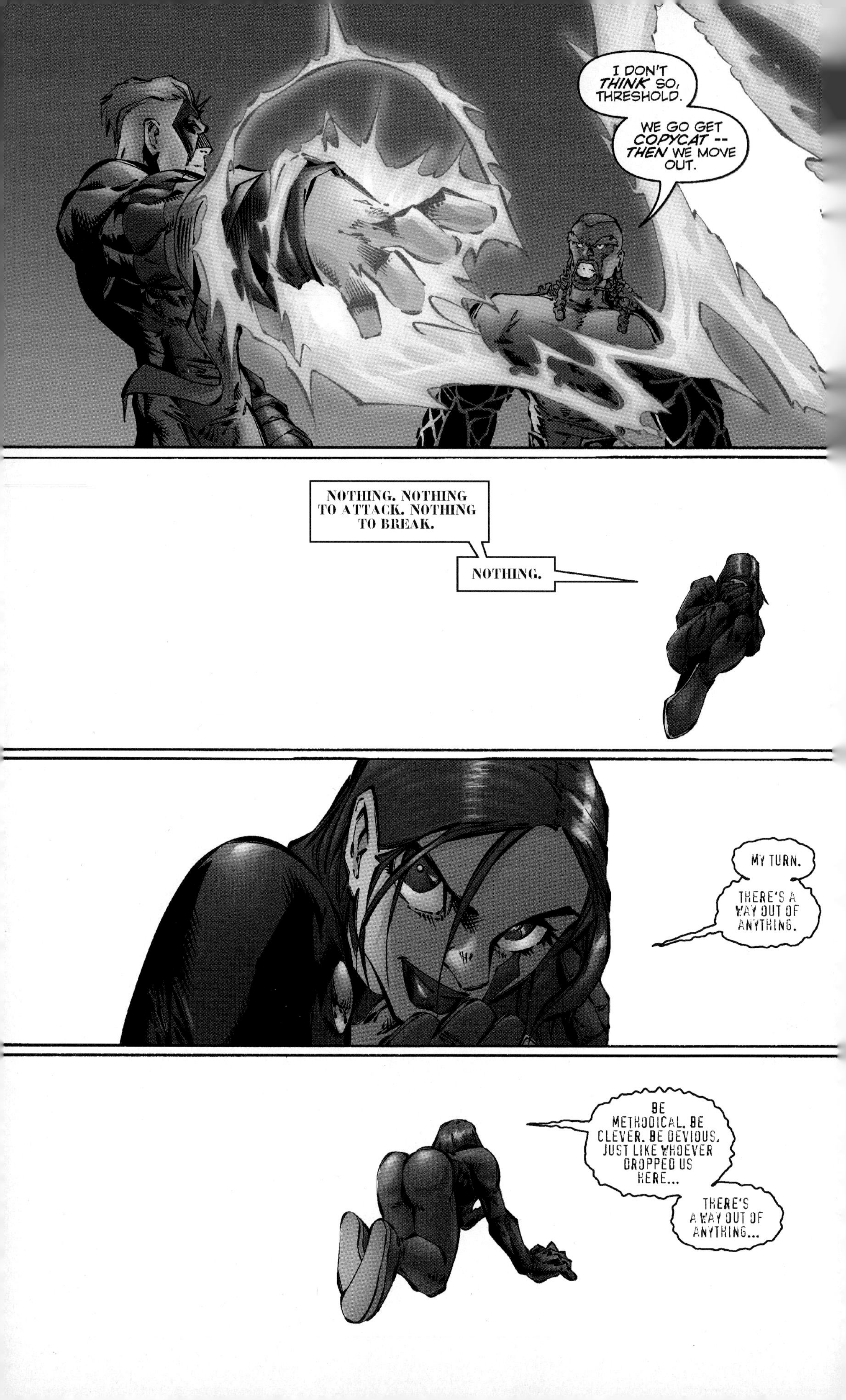

I DON'T THINK SO, THRESHOLD.
WE GO GET COPYCAT -- THEN WE MOVE OUT.
NOTHING. NOTHING TO ATTACK. NOTHING TO BREAK.
NOTHING.
MY TURN.
THERE'S A WAY OUT OF ANYTHING.
BE METHODICAL. BE CLEVER. BE DEVIOUS. JUST LIKE WHOEVER DROPPED US HERE...
THERE'S A WAY OUT OF ANYTHING...

COPYCAT'S GOT *MULTIPLE PERSONALITY DISORDER,* THRESHOLD -- AND HER PERSONALITY STRUCTURE *FRAGMENTS* EVEN *MORE* UNDER *STRESS!*

WE HAVE TO *FIND* HER BEFORE SHE BECOMES A *COMPLETE* BASKET CASE!

WE DON'T LEAVE WITHOUT HER. END OF STORY.

...WAY ...UT.

NO DOORS. NO WALLS. NO JOINS. NO CRACKS.

BUT MAYBE THERE ARE PEOPLE NEARBY.

REACH OUT WITH OUR POWER. FIND BODIES TO CONTROL. BRING THEM TOWARDS US.

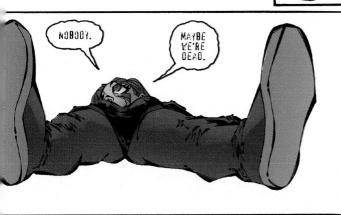

NOBODY.

MAYBE WE'RE DEAD.

DEAD

DEAD

dead

DEAD.

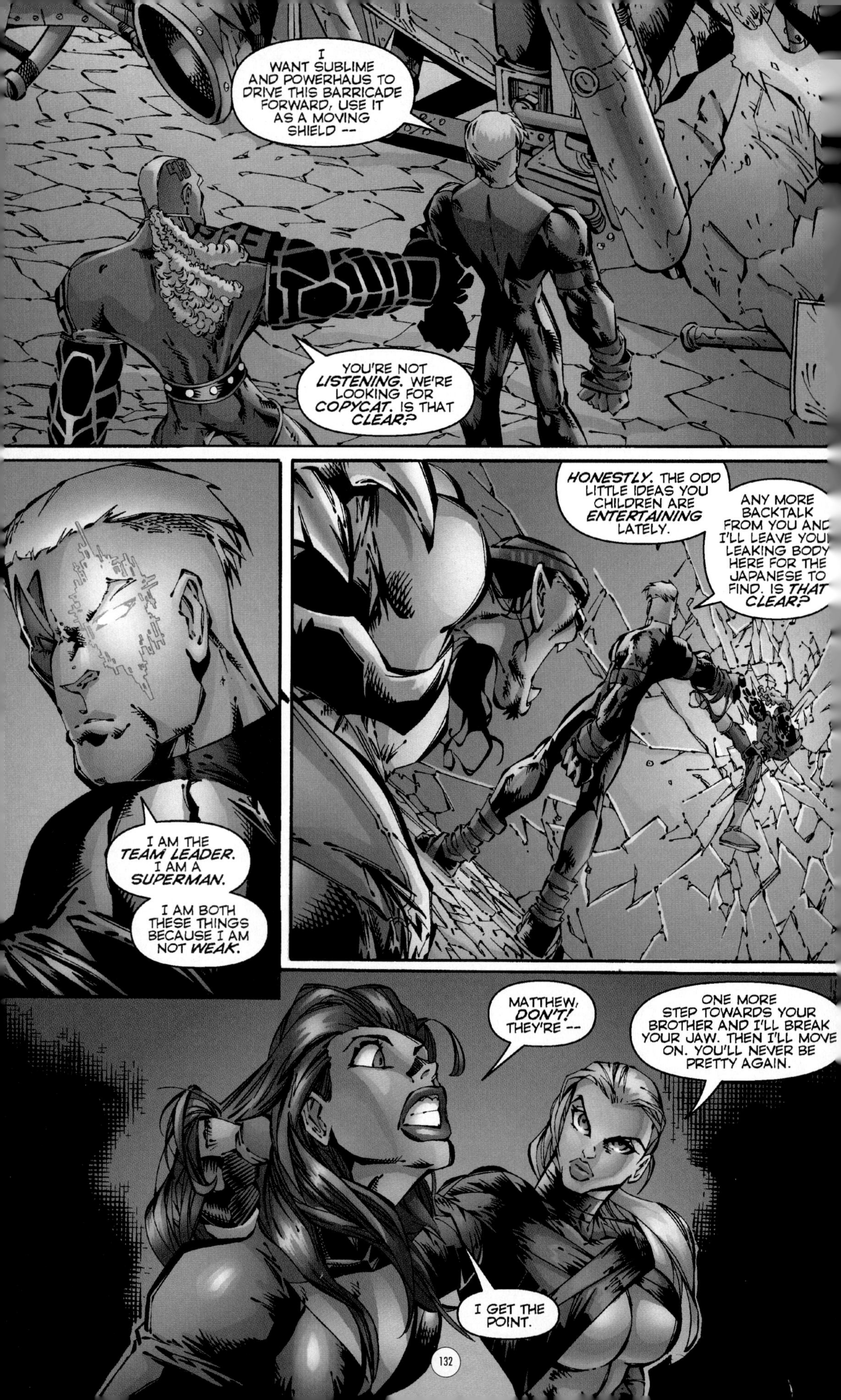
I WANT SUBLIME AND POWERHAUS TO DRIVE THIS BARRICADE FORWARD, USE IT AS A MOVING SHIELD --
YOU'RE NOT *LISTENING*. WE'RE LOOKING FOR *COPYCAT*. IS THAT *CLEAR?*
I AM THE *TEAM LEADER*. I AM A *SUPERMAN*.
I AM BOTH THESE THINGS BECAUSE I AM NOT *WEAK*.
HONESTLY. THE ODD LITTLE IDEAS YOU CHILDREN ARE *ENTERTAINING* LATELY.
ANY MORE BACKTALK FROM YOU AND I'LL LEAVE YOUR LEAKING BODY HERE FOR THE JAPANESE TO FIND. IS *THAT CLEAR?*
MATTHEW, *DON'T!* THEY'RE --
ONE MORE STEP TOWARDS YOUR BROTHER AND I'LL BREAK YOUR JAW. THEN I'LL MOVE ON. YOU'LL NEVER BE PRETTY AGAIN.
I GET THE POINT.

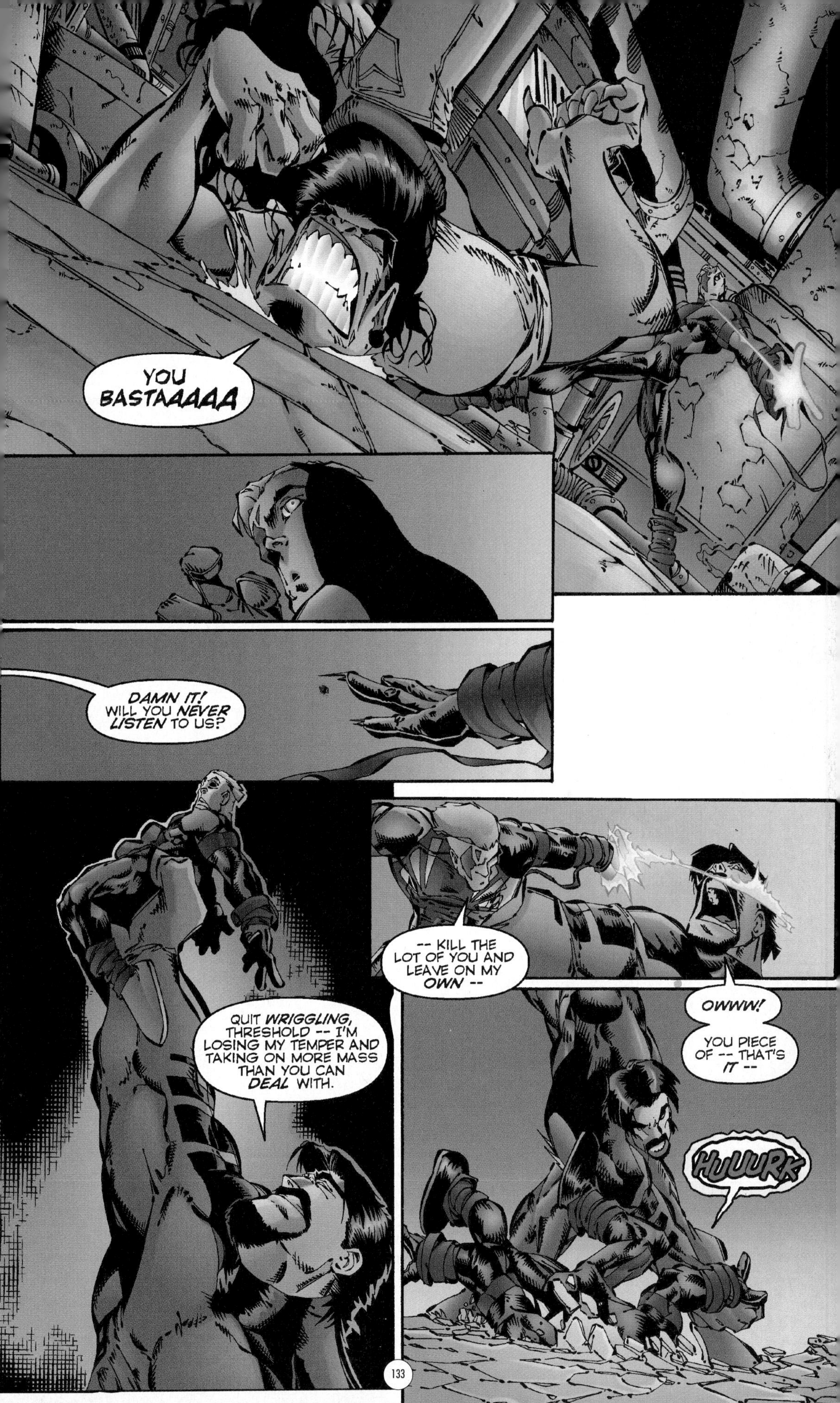
YOU BASTAAAAA
DAMN IT! WILL YOU NEVER LISTEN TO US?
QUIT WRIGGLING, THRESHOLD -- I'M LOSING MY TEMPER AND TAKING ON MORE MASS THAN YOU CAN DEAL WITH.
-- KILL THE LOT OF YOU AND LEAVE ON MY OWN --
OWWW!
YOU PIECE OF -- THAT'S IT --
HUUURK

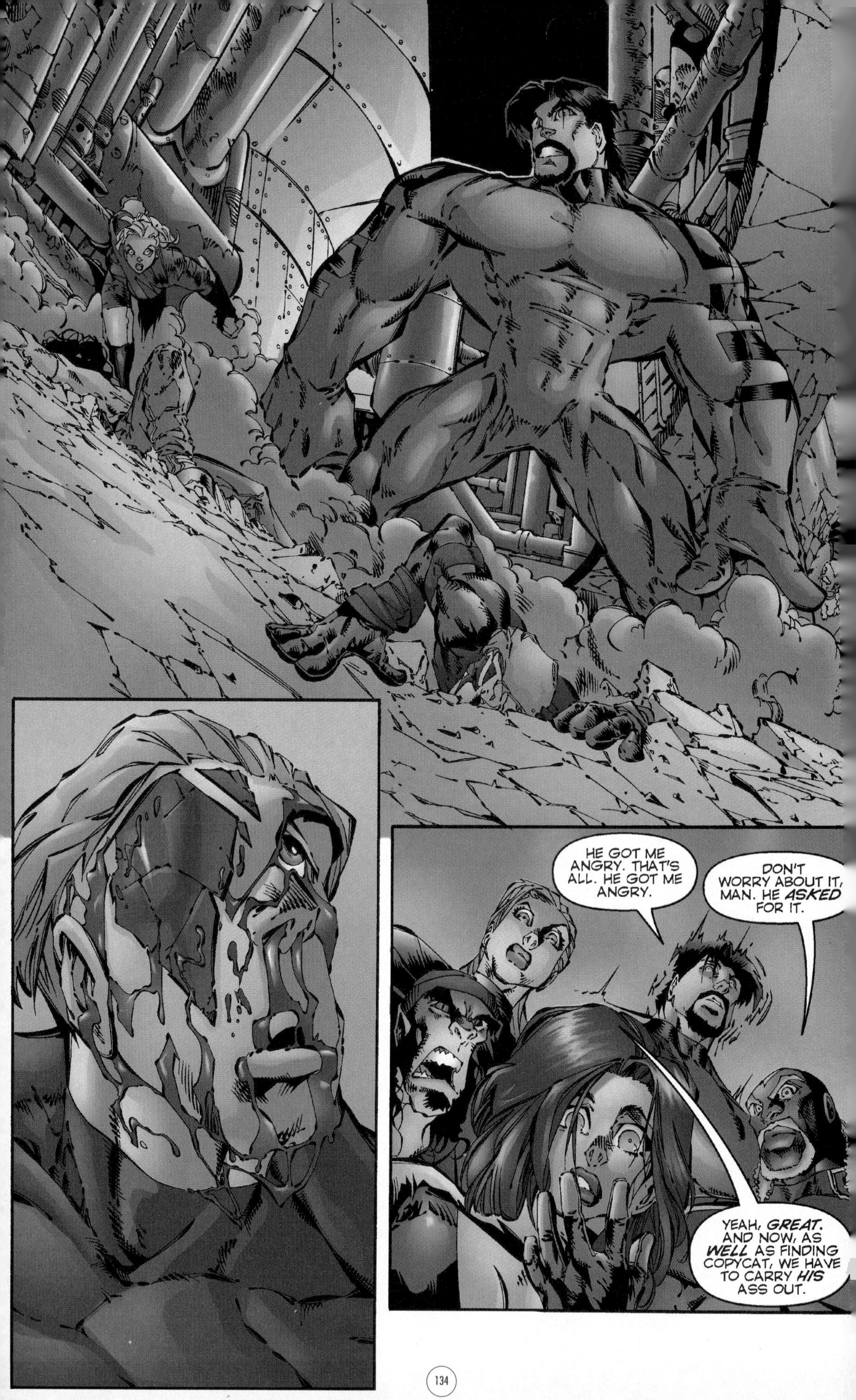
HE GOT ME ANGRY. THAT'S ALL. HE GOT ME ANGRY.
DON'T WORRY ABOUT IT, MAN. HE *ASKED* FOR IT.
YEAH, *GREAT.* AND NOW, AS *WELL* AS FINDING COPYCAT, WE HAVE TO CARRY *HIS* ASS OUT.

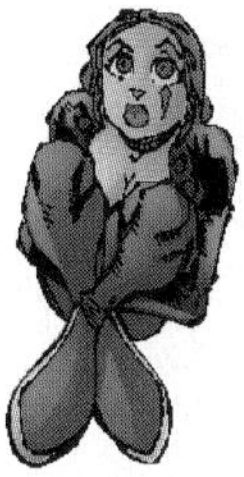

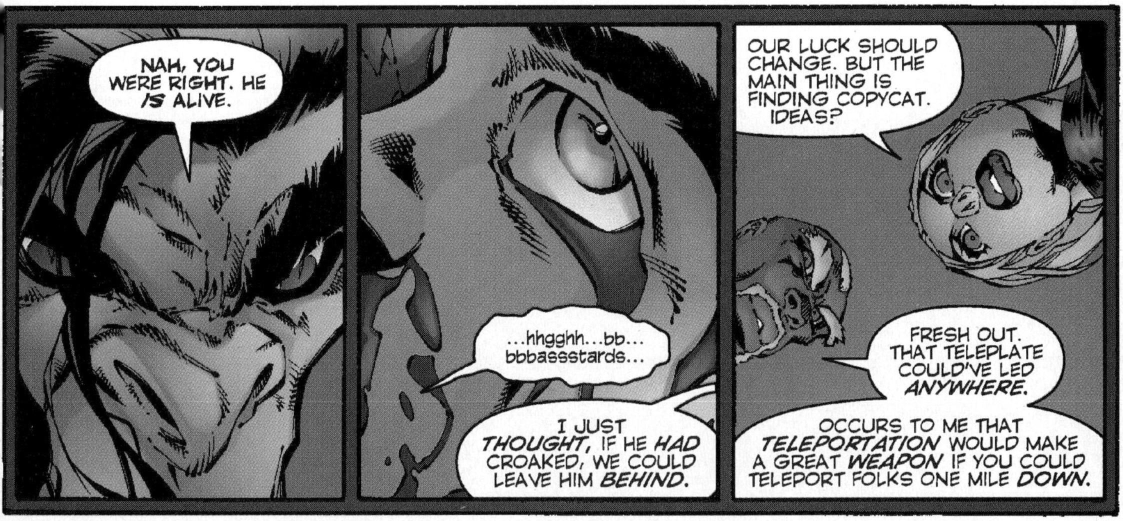

NAH, YOU WERE RIGHT. HE *IS* ALIVE.
...hhgghh...bb... bbbassstards...
I JUST *THOUGHT*, IF HE *HAD* CROAKED, WE COULD LEAVE HIM *BEHIND*.
OUR LUCK SHOULD CHANGE. BUT THE MAIN THING IS FINDING COPYCAT. IDEAS?
FRESH OUT. THAT TELEPLATE COULD'VE LED *ANYWHERE*.
OCCURS TO ME THAT *TELEPORTATION* WOULD MAKE A GREAT *WEAPON* IF YOU COULD TELEPORT FOLKS ONE MILE *DOWN*.

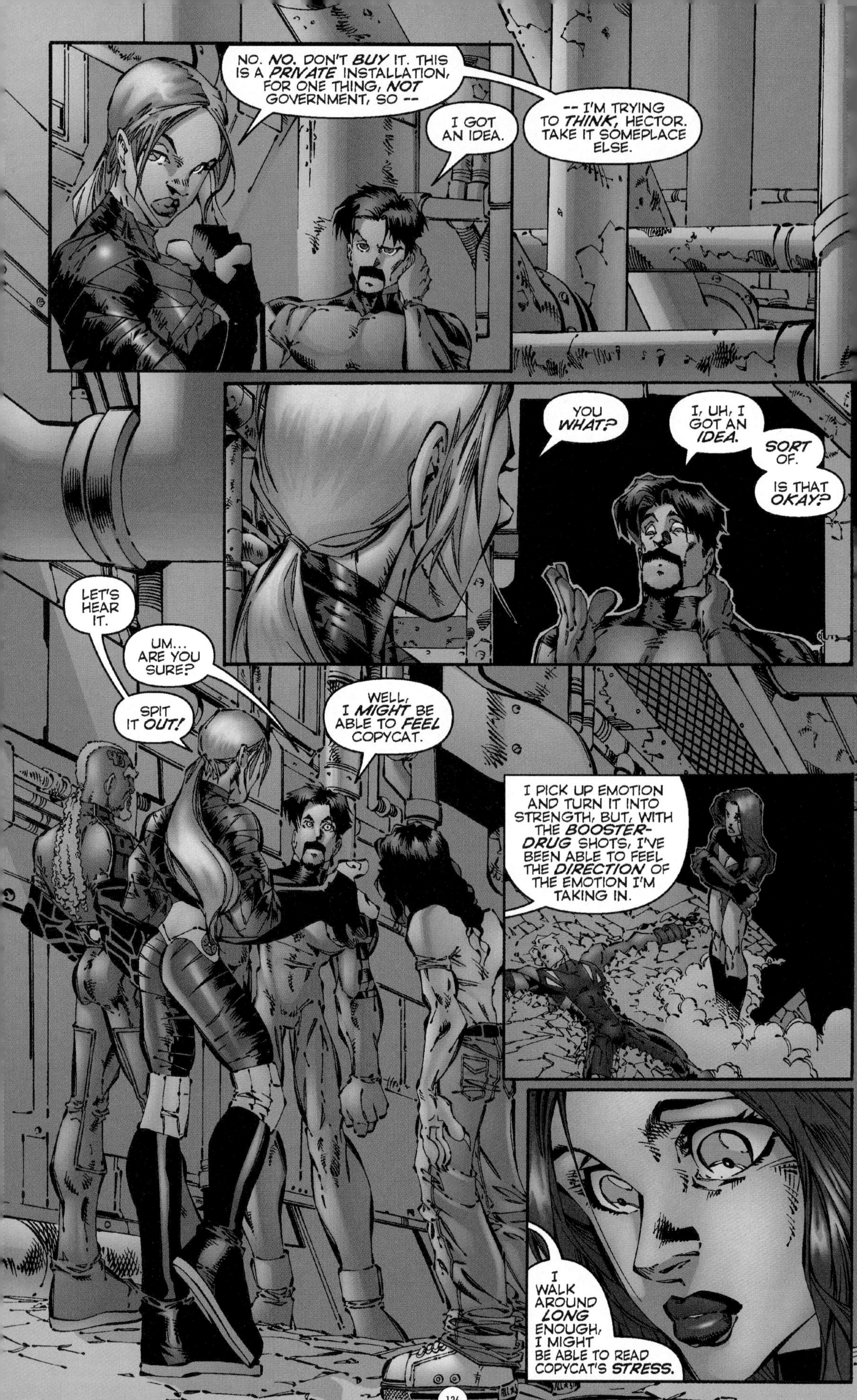

NO. NO. DON'T BUY IT. THIS IS A PRIVATE INSTALLATION, FOR ONE THING, NOT GOVERNMENT, SO --
I GOT AN IDEA.
-- I'M TRYING TO THINK, HECTOR. TAKE IT SOMEPLACE ELSE.
YOU WHAT?
I, UH, I GOT AN IDEA.
SORT OF.
IS THAT OKAY?
LET'S HEAR IT.
UM... ARE YOU SURE?
SPIT IT OUT!
WELL, I MIGHT BE ABLE TO FEEL COPYCAT.
I PICK UP EMOTION AND TURN IT INTO STRENGTH, BUT, WITH THE BOOSTER-DRUG SHOTS, I'VE BEEN ABLE TO FEEL THE DIRECTION OF THE EMOTION I'M TAKING IN.
I WALK AROUND LONG ENOUGH, I MIGHT BE ABLE TO READ COPYCAT'S STRESS.

I DON'T KNOW,

OH, I BELIEVE YOU COULD *DO* IT, BUT GOING OUT THERE...LISTEN, COULD YOU FIND HER FROM *HERE?*

UMM... WHAT?

SURE YOU COULD. BECAUSE SOMEWHERE IN THIS PLACE IS A CHICK THROWING OUT A *DOZEN* DIFFERENT STRONG EMOTIONS ALL AT *ONCE.*

SHE'S A *MULTIPLE PERSONALITY*, HECTOR -- AND HER PERSONALITIES GO *WILD* UNDER *STRESS.* EMOTIONALLY, SHE'S THE WEIRDEST THING IN THIS *HEMISPHERE.*

YEAH, I CAN *SEE* IT NOW. EVERYONE KEEP *QUIET*, I DON'T WANNA LOSE IT TO *DISTRACTION...*

WHAT I GOTTA DO IS *SCREEN OUT* YOU GUYS...

GIMME A MINUTE.

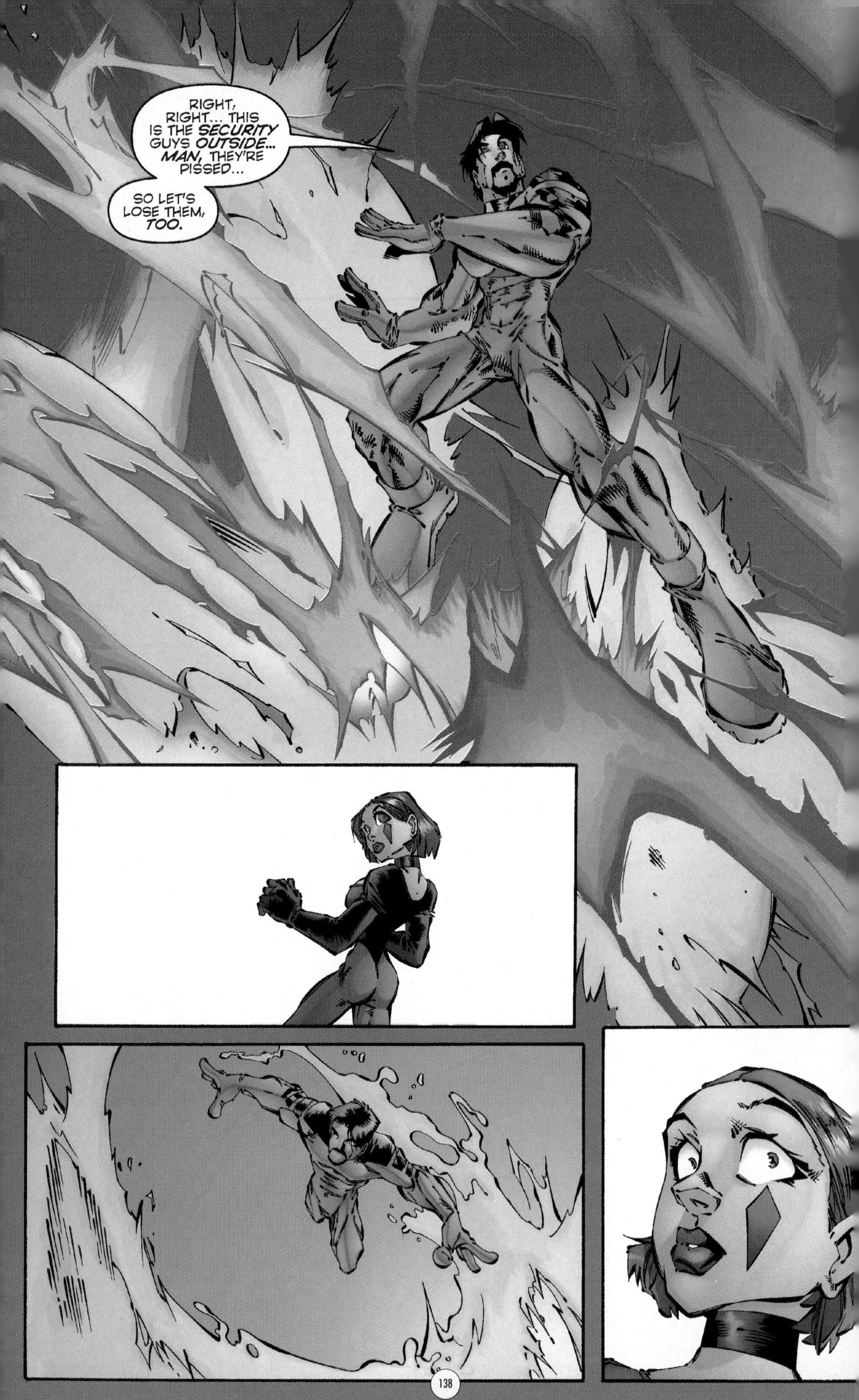
RIGHT, RIGHT... THIS IS THE SECURITY GUYS OUTSIDE... MAN, THEY'RE PISSED...
SO LET'S LOSE THEM, TOO.

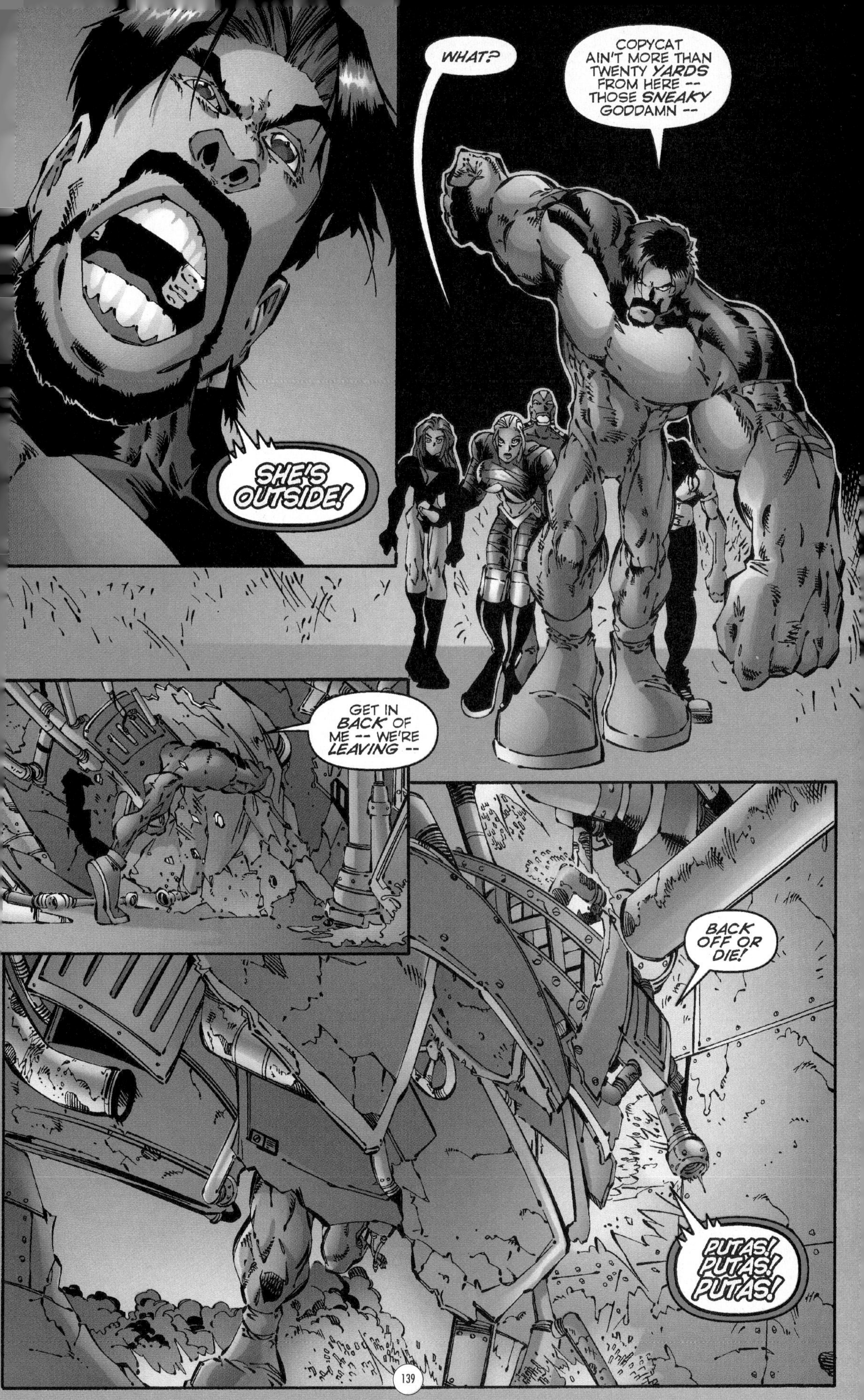
SHE'S OUTSIDE!
WHAT?
COPYCAT AIN'T MORE THAN TWENTY YARDS FROM HERE -- THOSE SNEAKY GODDAMN --
GET IN BACK OF ME -- WE'RE LEAVING --
BACK OFF OR DIE!
PUTAS! PUTAS! PUTAS!

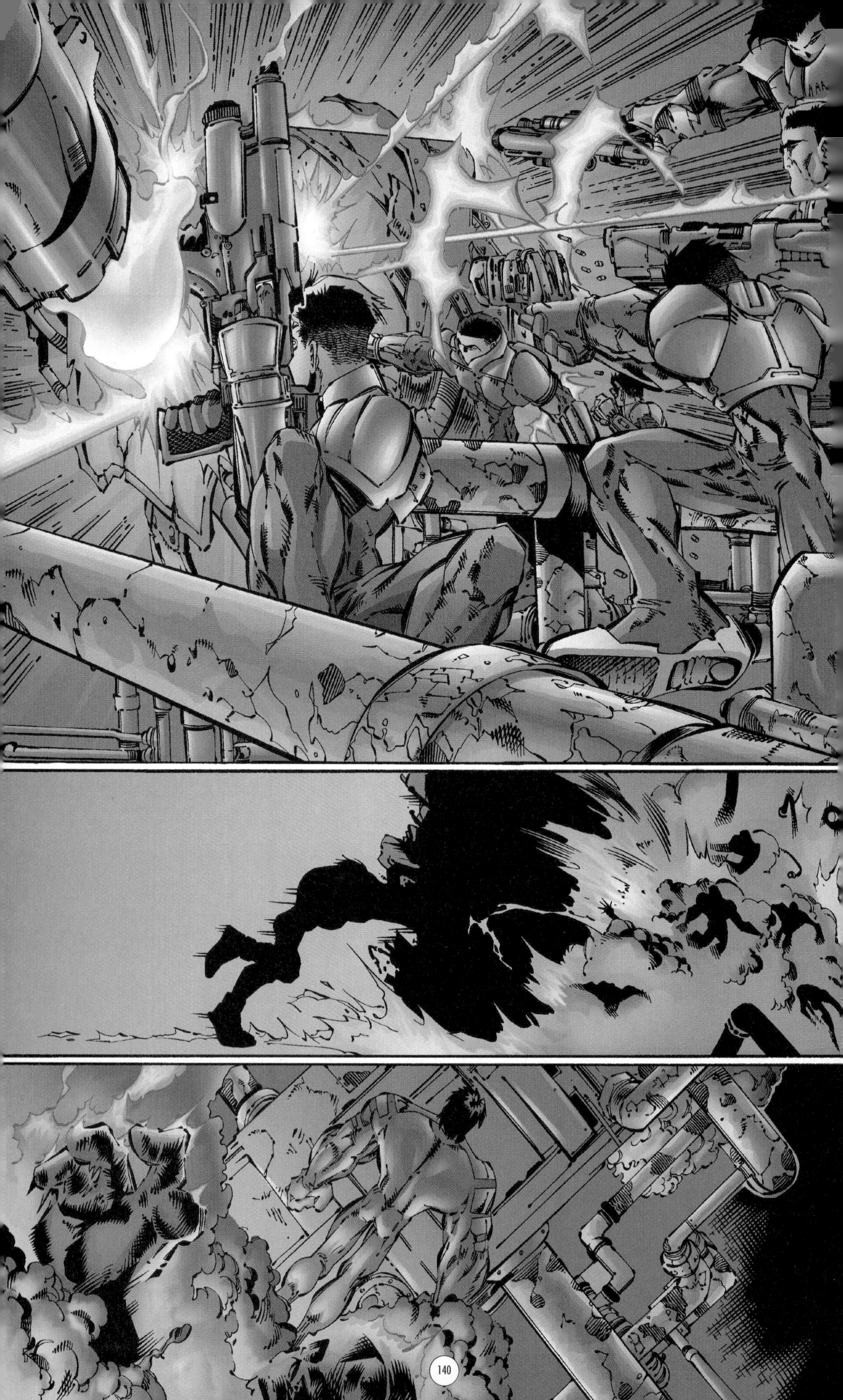

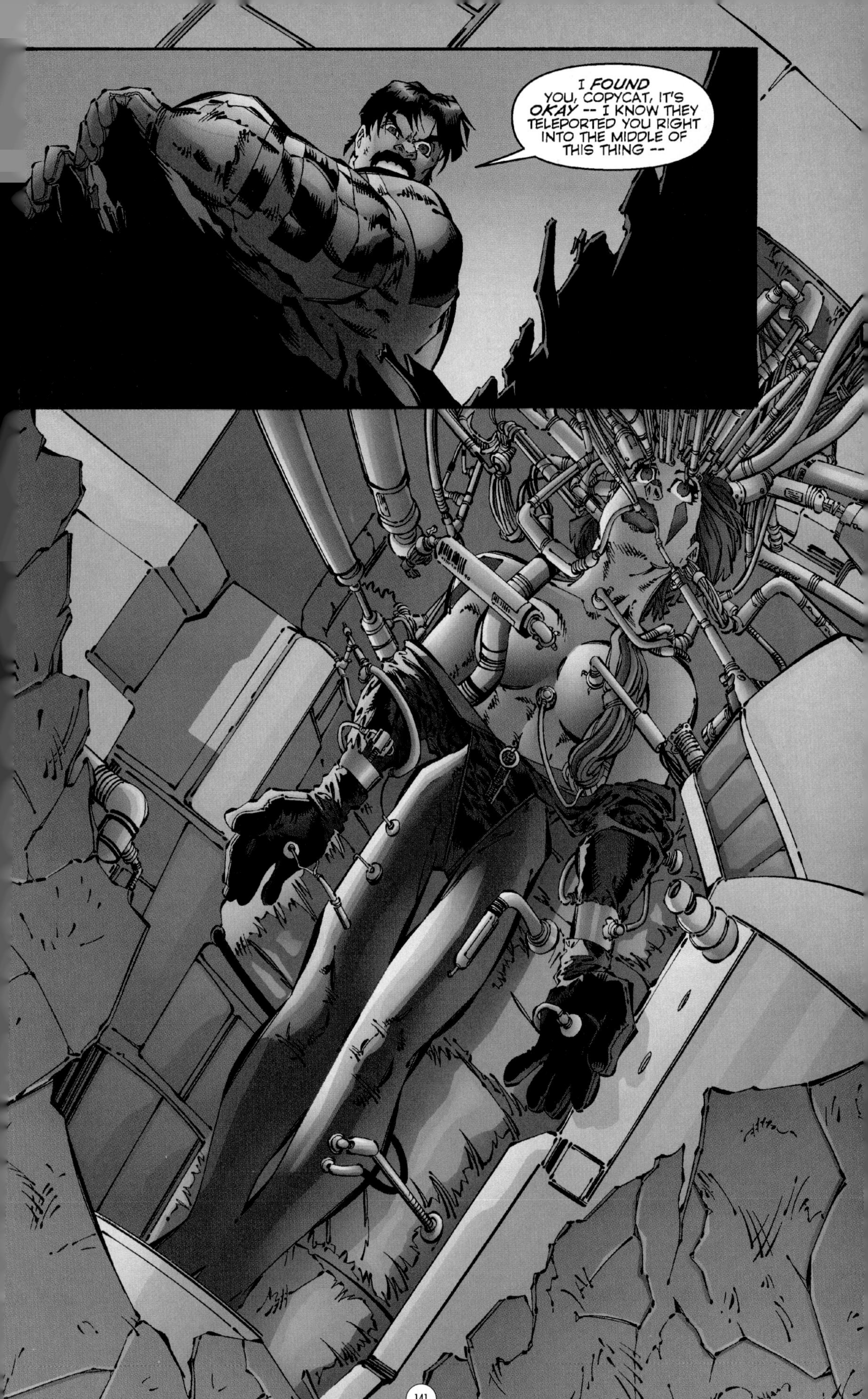
I FOUND YOU, COPYCAT, IT'S OKAY -- I KNOW THEY TELEPORTED YOU RIGHT INTO THE MIDDLE OF THIS THING --

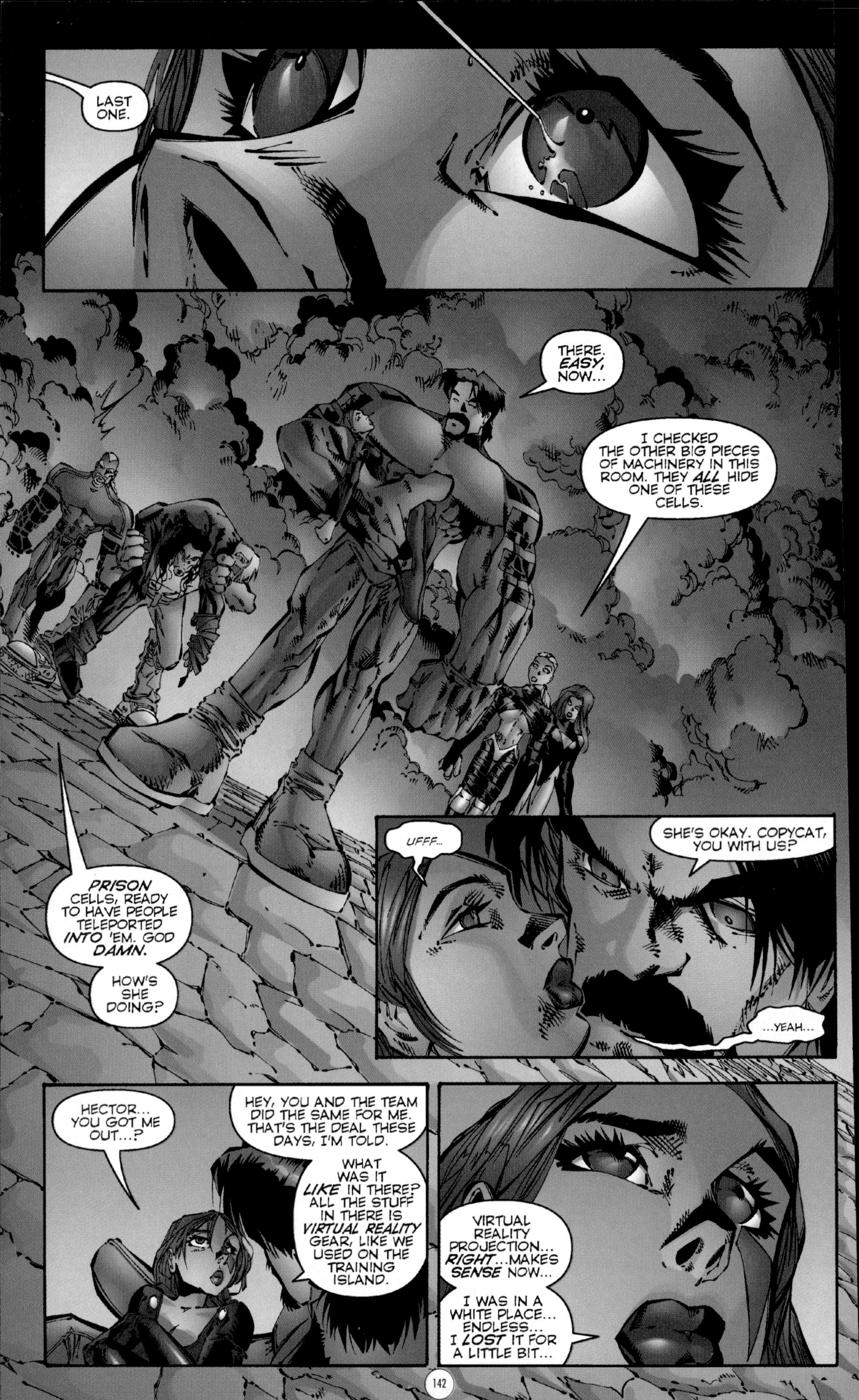
LAST ONE.
THERE. EASY, NOW...
I CHECKED THE OTHER BIG PIECES OF MACHINERY IN THIS ROOM. THEY ALL HIDE ONE OF THESE CELLS.
PRISON CELLS, READY TO HAVE PEOPLE TELEPORTED INTO 'EM. GOD DAMN.
HOW'S SHE DOING?
UFFF...
SHE'S OKAY. COPYCAT, YOU WITH US?
...YEAH...
HECTOR... YOU GOT ME OUT...?
HEY, YOU AND THE TEAM DID THE SAME FOR ME. THAT'S THE DEAL THESE DAYS, I'M TOLD.
WHAT WAS IT LIKE IN THERE? ALL THE STUFF IN THERE IS VIRTUAL REALITY GEAR, LIKE WE USED ON THE TRAINING ISLAND.
VIRTUAL REALITY PROJECTION... RIGHT...MAKES SENSE NOW...
I WAS IN A WHITE PLACE... ENDLESS... I LOST IT FOR A LITTLE BIT...

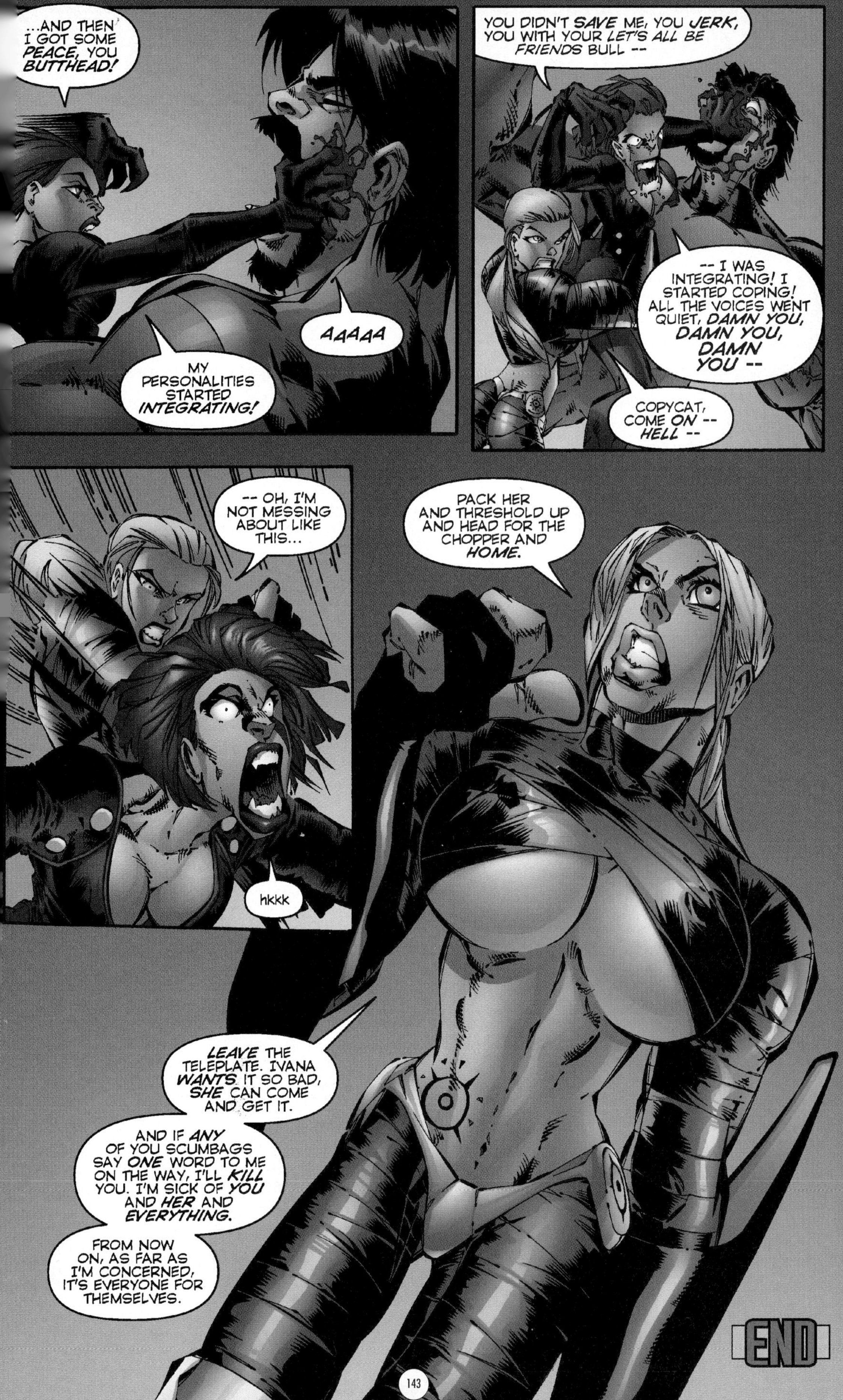
...AND THEN I GOT SOME PEACE, YOU BUTTHEAD!
AAAAA
MY PERSONALITIES STARTED INTEGRATING!
YOU DIDN'T SAVE ME, YOU JERK, YOU WITH YOUR LET'S ALL BE FRIENDS BULL --
-- I WAS INTEGRATING! I STARTED COPING! ALL THE VOICES WENT QUIET, DAMN YOU, DAMN YOU, DAMN YOU --
COPYCAT, COME ON -- HELL --
-- OH, I'M NOT MESSING ABOUT LIKE THIS...
hkkk
PACK HER AND THRESHOLD UP AND HEAD FOR THE CHOPPER AND HOME.
LEAVE THE TELEPLATE. IVANA WANTS IT SO BAD, SHE CAN COME AND GET IT.
AND IF ANY OF YOU SCUMBAGS SAY ONE WORD TO ME ON THE WAY, I'LL KILL YOU. I'M SICK OF YOU AND HER AND EVERYTHING.
FROM NOW ON, AS FAR AS I'M CONCERNED, IT'S EVERYONE FOR THEMSELVES.
END

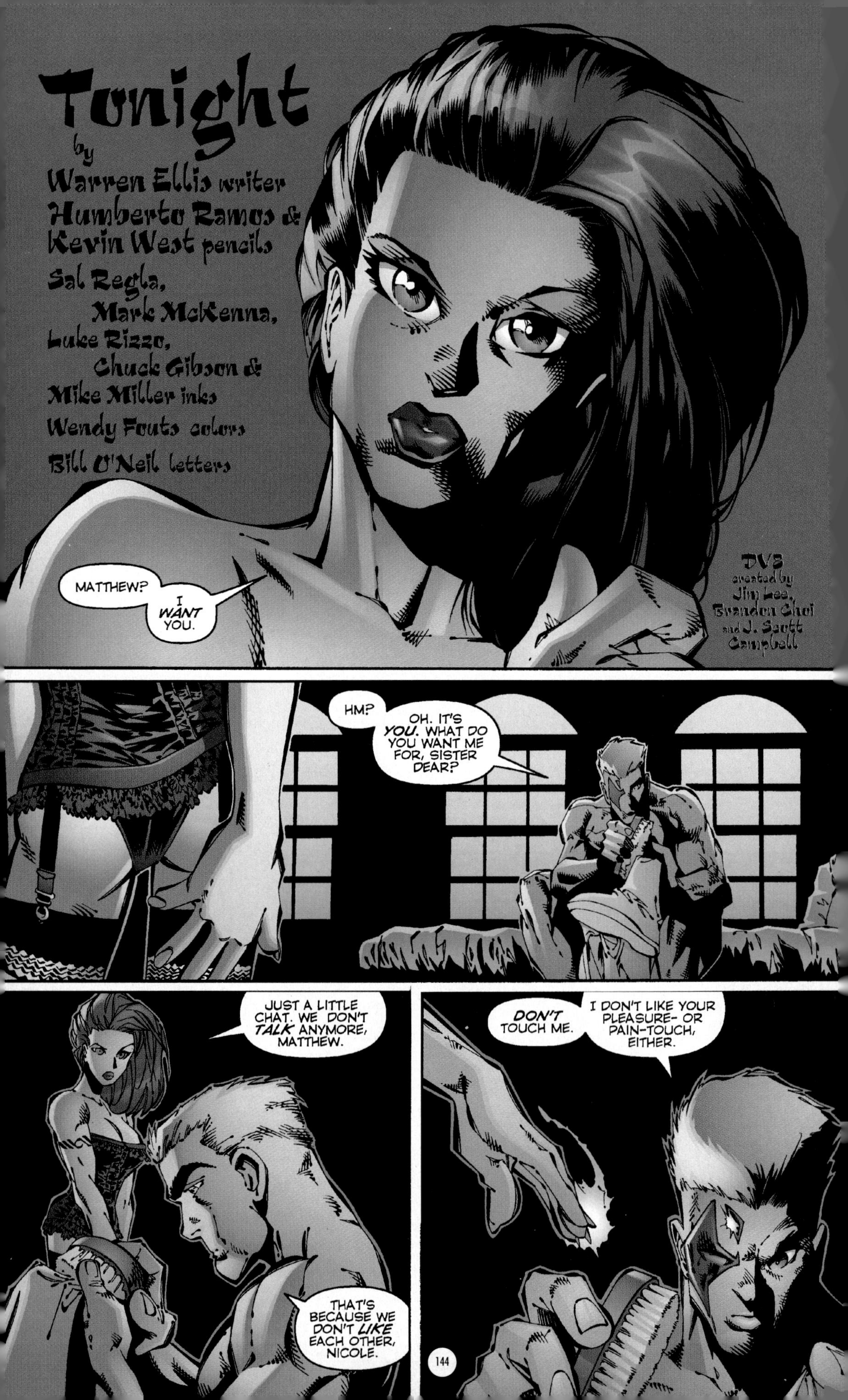

Tonight
by
Warren Ellis writer
Humberto Ramos & Kevin West pencils
Sal Regla, Mark McKenna, Luke Rizzo, Chuck Gibson & Mike Miller inks
Wendy Fouts colors
Bill O'Neil letters
DV8 created by Jim Lee, Brandon Choi and J. Scott Campbell
MATTHEW?
I WANT YOU.
HM?
OH. IT'S YOU. WHAT DO YOU WANT ME FOR, SISTER DEAR?
JUST A LITTLE CHAT. WE DON'T TALK ANYMORE, MATTHEW.
THAT'S BECAUSE WE DON'T LIKE EACH OTHER, NICOLE.
DON'T TOUCH ME.
I DON'T LIKE YOUR PLEASURE- OR PAIN-TOUCH, EITHER.

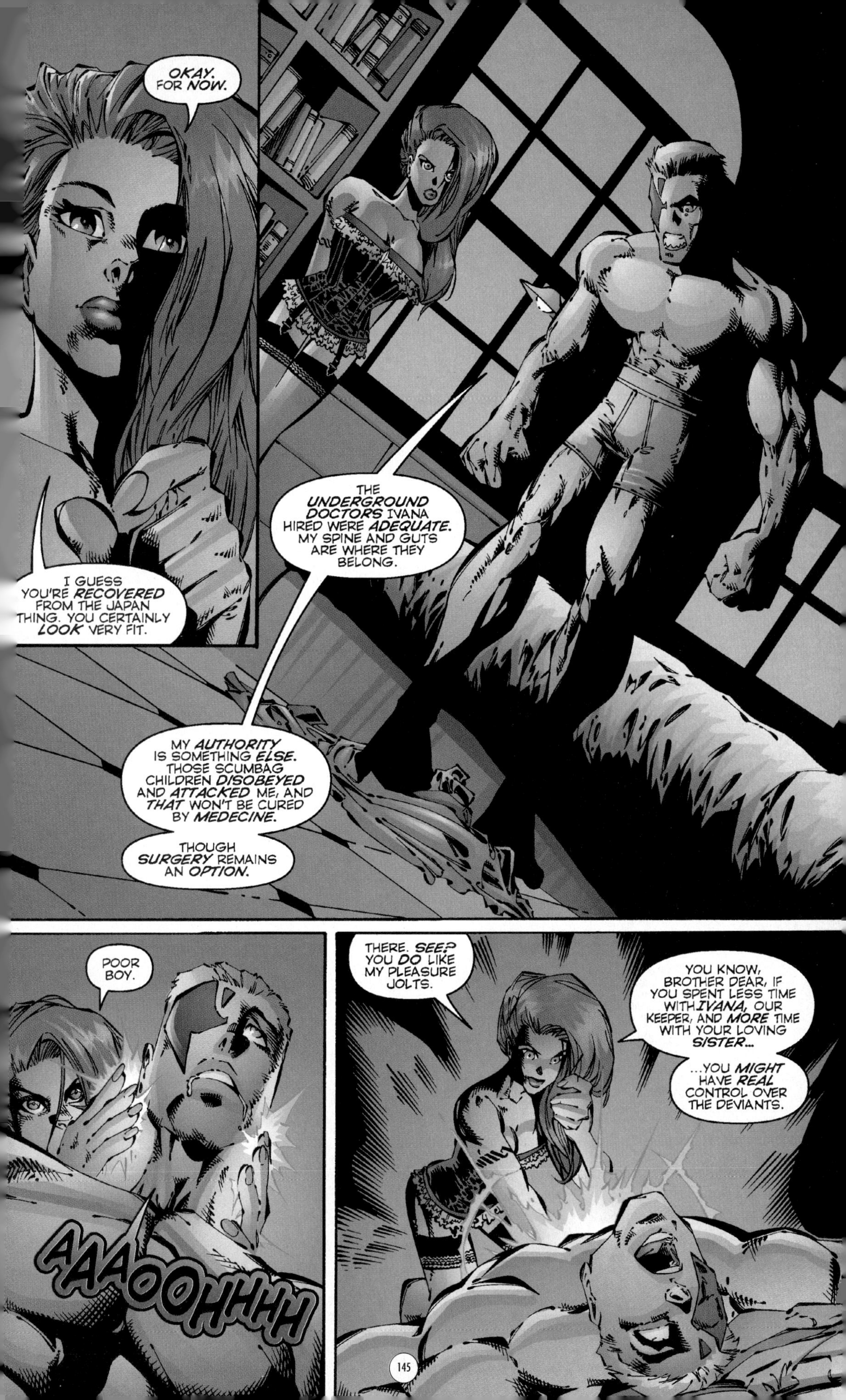

OKAY. FOR NOW.
I GUESS YOU'RE RECOVERED FROM THE JAPAN THING. YOU CERTAINLY LOOK VERY FIT.
THE UNDERGROUND DOCTORS IVANA HIRED WERE ADEQUATE. MY SPINE AND GUTS ARE WHERE THEY BELONG.
MY AUTHORITY IS SOMETHING ELSE. THOSE SCUMBAG CHILDREN DISOBEYED AND ATTACKED ME, AND THAT WON'T BE CURED BY MEDECINE.
THOUGH SURGERY REMAINS AN OPTION.
POOR BOY.
AAAOOHHHH
THERE. SEE? YOU DO LIKE MY PLEASURE JOLTS.
YOU KNOW, BROTHER DEAR, IF YOU SPENT LESS TIME WITH IVANA, OUR KEEPER, AND MORE TIME WITH YOUR LOVING SISTER...
...YOU MIGHT HAVE REAL CONTROL OVER THE DEVIANTS.

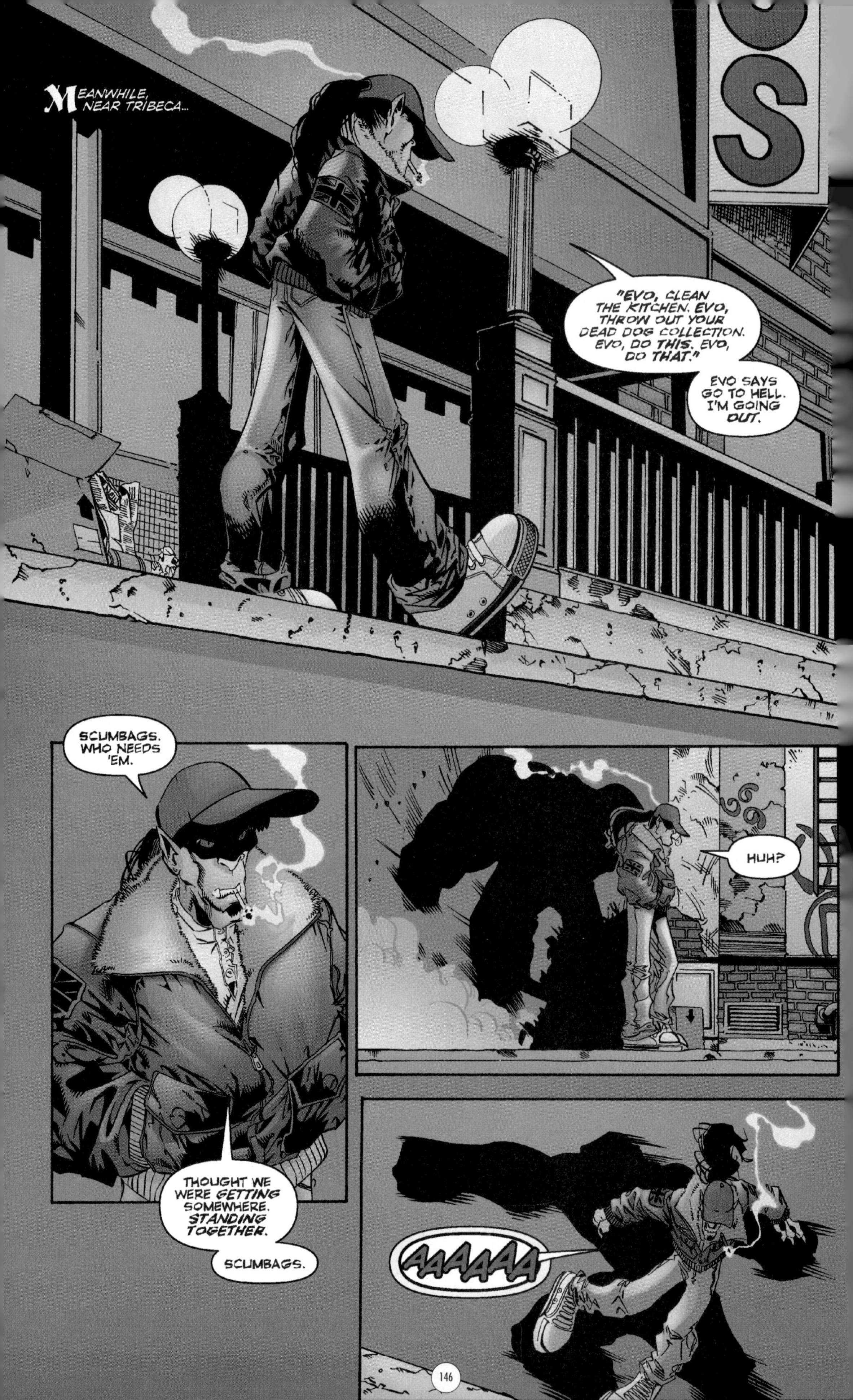
MEANWHILE, NEAR TRIBECA...
"EVO, CLEAN THE KITCHEN. EVO, THROW OUT YOUR DEAD DOG COLLECTION. EVO, DO THIS. EVO, DO THAT."
EVO SAYS GO TO HELL. I'M GOING OUT.
SCUMBAGS. WHO NEEDS 'EM.
THOUGHT WE WERE GETTING SOMEWHERE. STANDING TOGETHER.
SCUMBAGS.
HUH?
AAAAAA

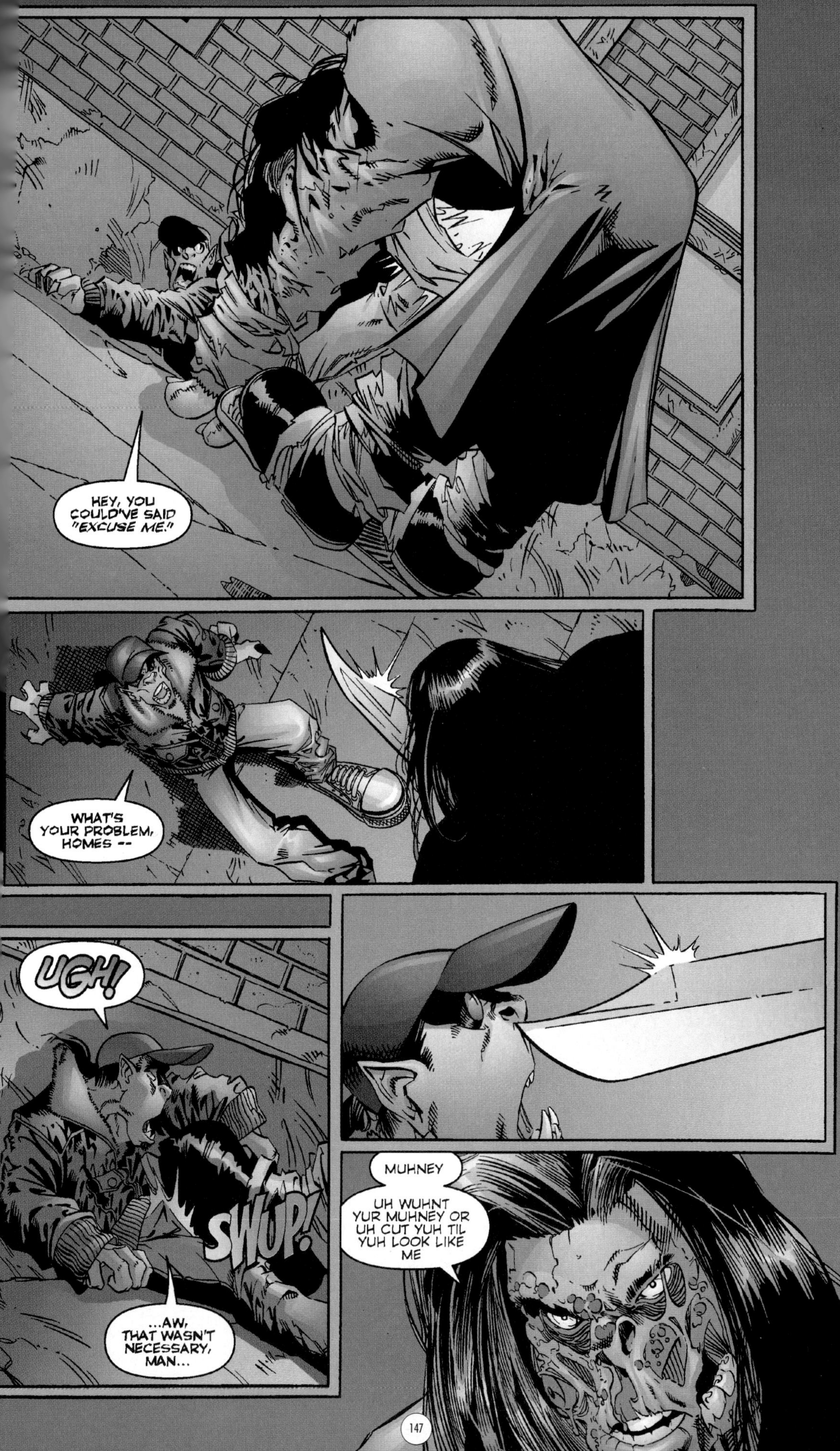
HEY, YOU COULD'VE SAID "EXCUSE ME."
WHAT'S YOUR PROBLEM, HOMES --
UGH!
SWUP!
...AW, THAT WASN'T NECESSARY, MAN...
MUHNEY
UH WUHNT YUR MUHNEY OR UH CUT YUH TIL YUH LOOK LIKE ME

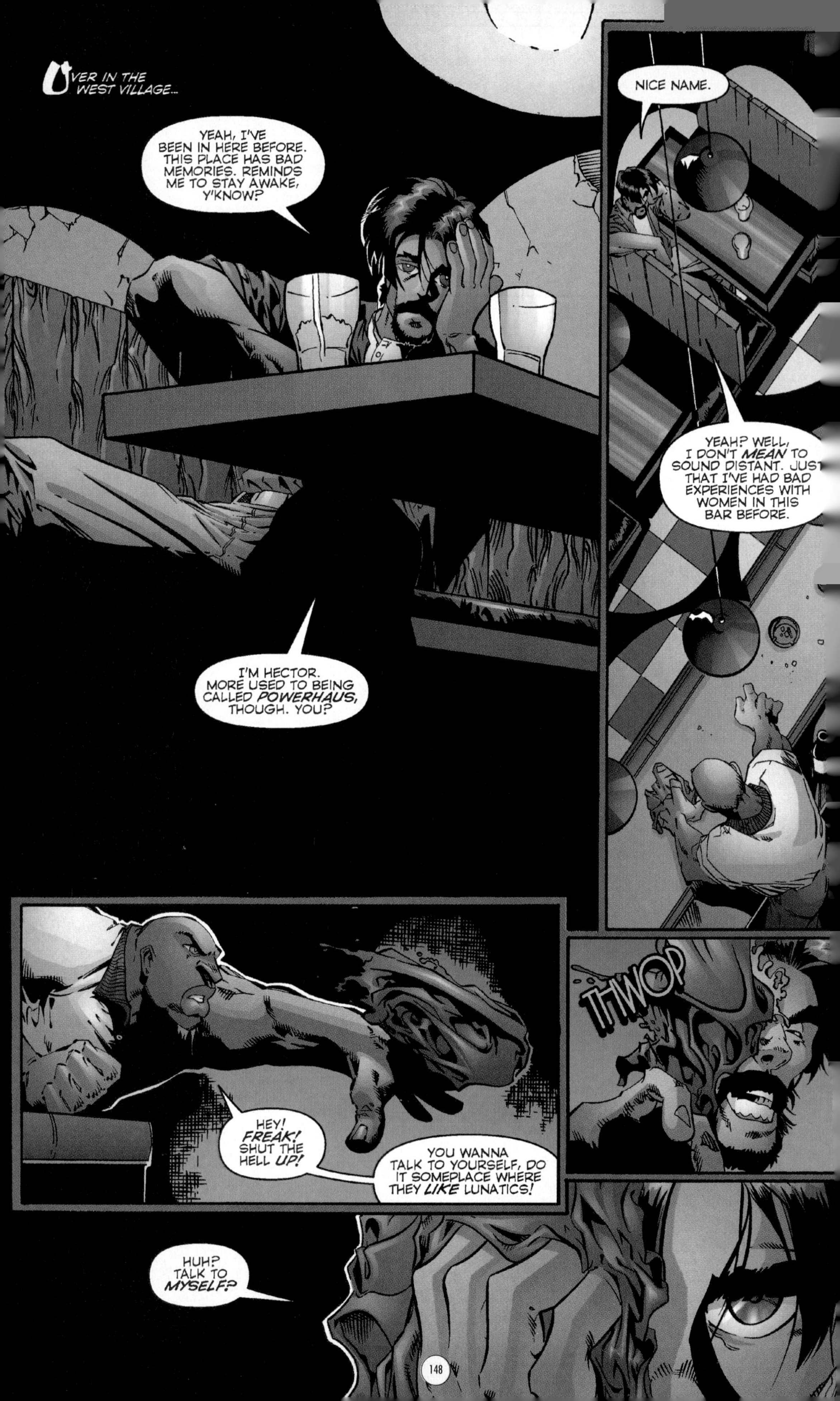
OVER IN THE WEST VILLAGE...
YEAH, I'VE BEEN IN HERE BEFORE. THIS PLACE HAS BAD MEMORIES. REMINDS ME TO STAY AWAKE, Y'KNOW?
I'M HECTOR. MORE USED TO BEING CALLED POWERHAUS, THOUGH. YOU?
NICE NAME.
YEAH? WELL, I DON'T MEAN TO SOUND DISTANT. JUST THAT I'VE HAD BAD EXPERIENCES WITH WOMEN IN THIS BAR BEFORE.
HEY! FREAK! SHUT THE HELL UP!
YOU WANNA TALK TO YOURSELF, DO IT SOMEPLACE WHERE THEY LIKE LUNATICS!
THWOP
HUH? TALK TO MYSELF?

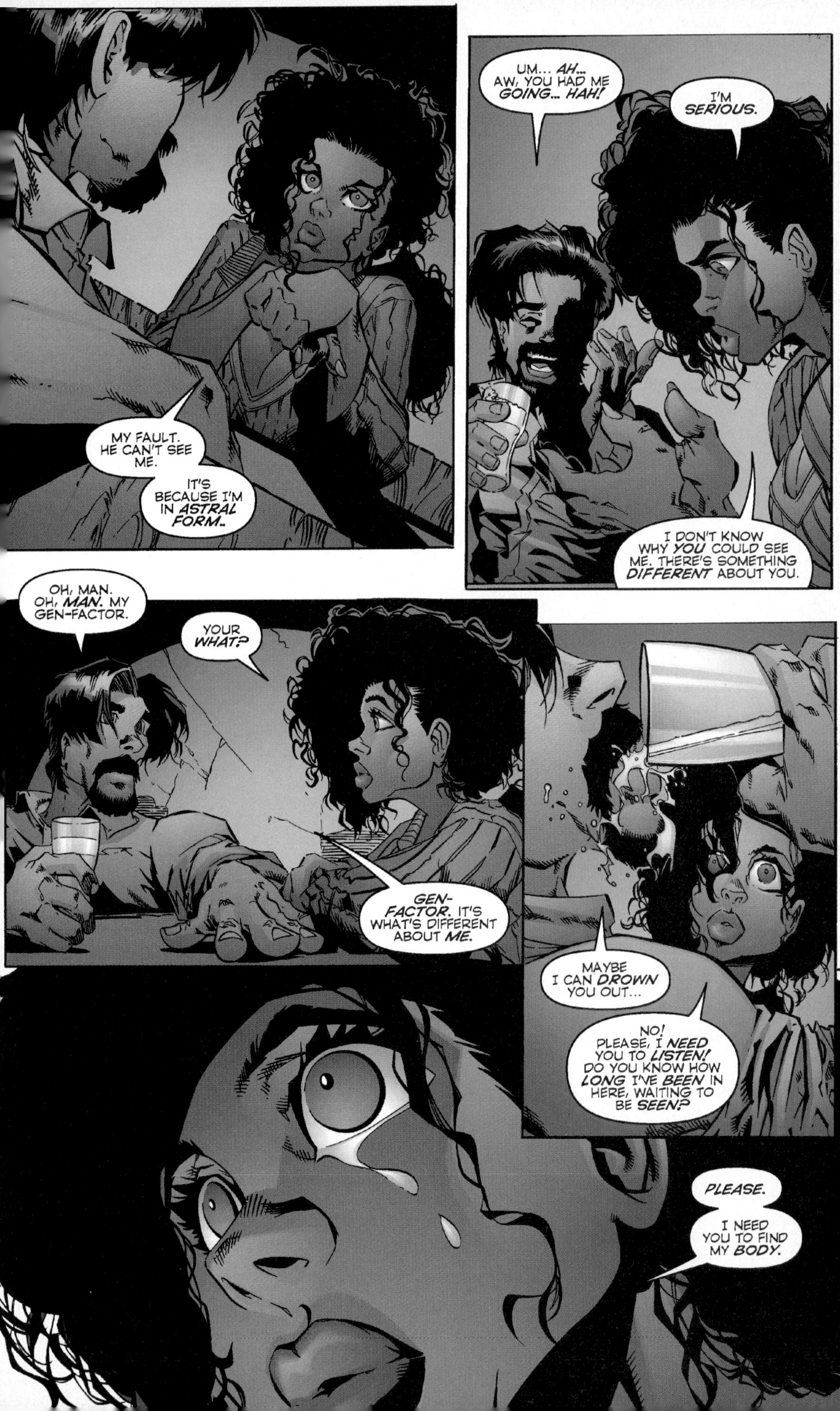
MY FAULT. HE CAN'T SEE ME.
IT'S BECAUSE I'M IN ASTRAL FORM..
UM... AH... AW, YOU HAD ME GOING... HAH!
I'M SERIOUS.
I DON'T KNOW WHY YOU COULD SEE ME. THERE'S SOMETHING DIFFERENT ABOUT YOU.
OH, MAN. OH, MAN. MY GEN-FACTOR.
YOUR WHAT?
GEN-FACTOR. IT'S WHAT'S DIFFERENT ABOUT ME.
MAYBE I CAN DROWN YOU OUT...
NO! PLEASE, I NEED YOU TO LISTEN! DO YOU KNOW HOW LONG I'VE BEEN IN HERE, WAITING TO BE SEEN?
PLEASE.
I NEED YOU TO FIND MY BODY.

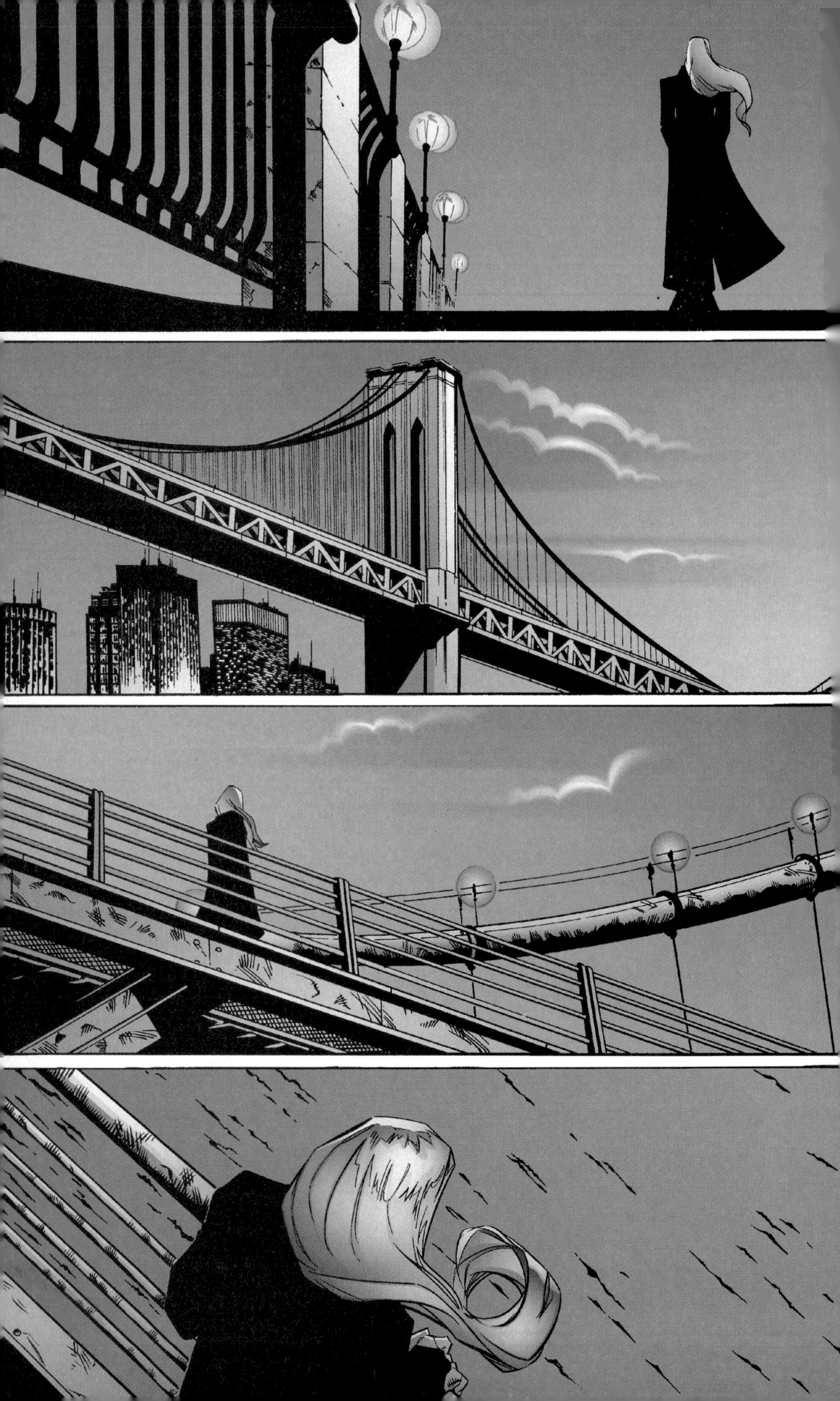

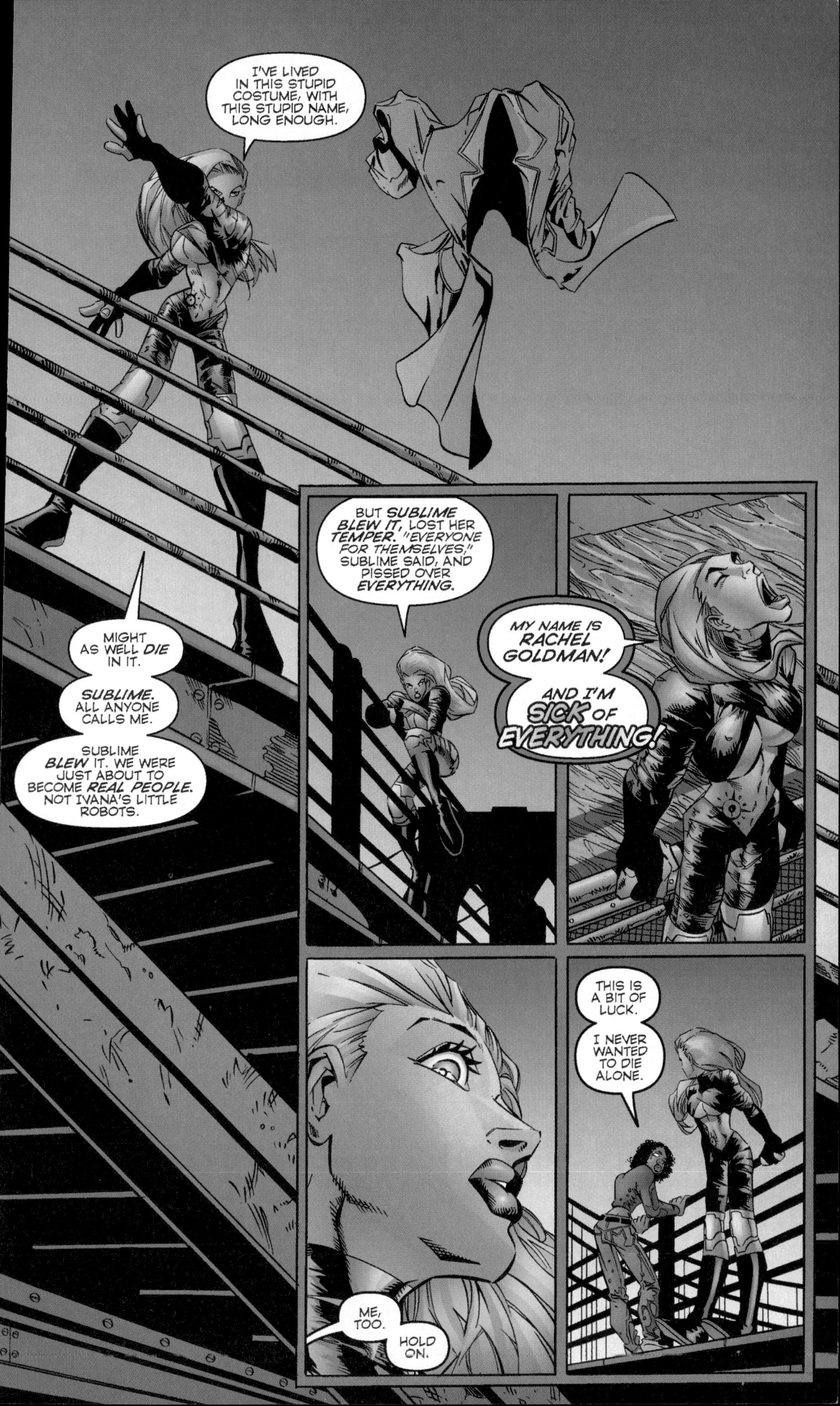
I'VE LIVED IN THIS STUPID COSTUME, WITH THIS STUPID NAME, LONG ENOUGH.
MIGHT AS WELL *DIE* IN IT.
SUBLIME. ALL ANYONE CALLS ME.
SUBLIME *BLEW* IT. WE WERE JUST ABOUT TO BECOME *REAL PEOPLE.* NOT IVANA'S LITTLE ROBOTS.
BUT *SUBLIME BLEW IT,* LOST HER *TEMPER.* "*EVERYONE FOR THEMSELVES,*" SUBLIME SAID, AND PISSED OVER *EVERYTHING.*
MY NAME IS RACHEL GOLDMAN!
AND I'M SICK OF EVERYTHING!
ME, TOO.
HOLD ON.
THIS IS A BIT OF LUCK.
I NEVER WANTED TO DIE ALONE.

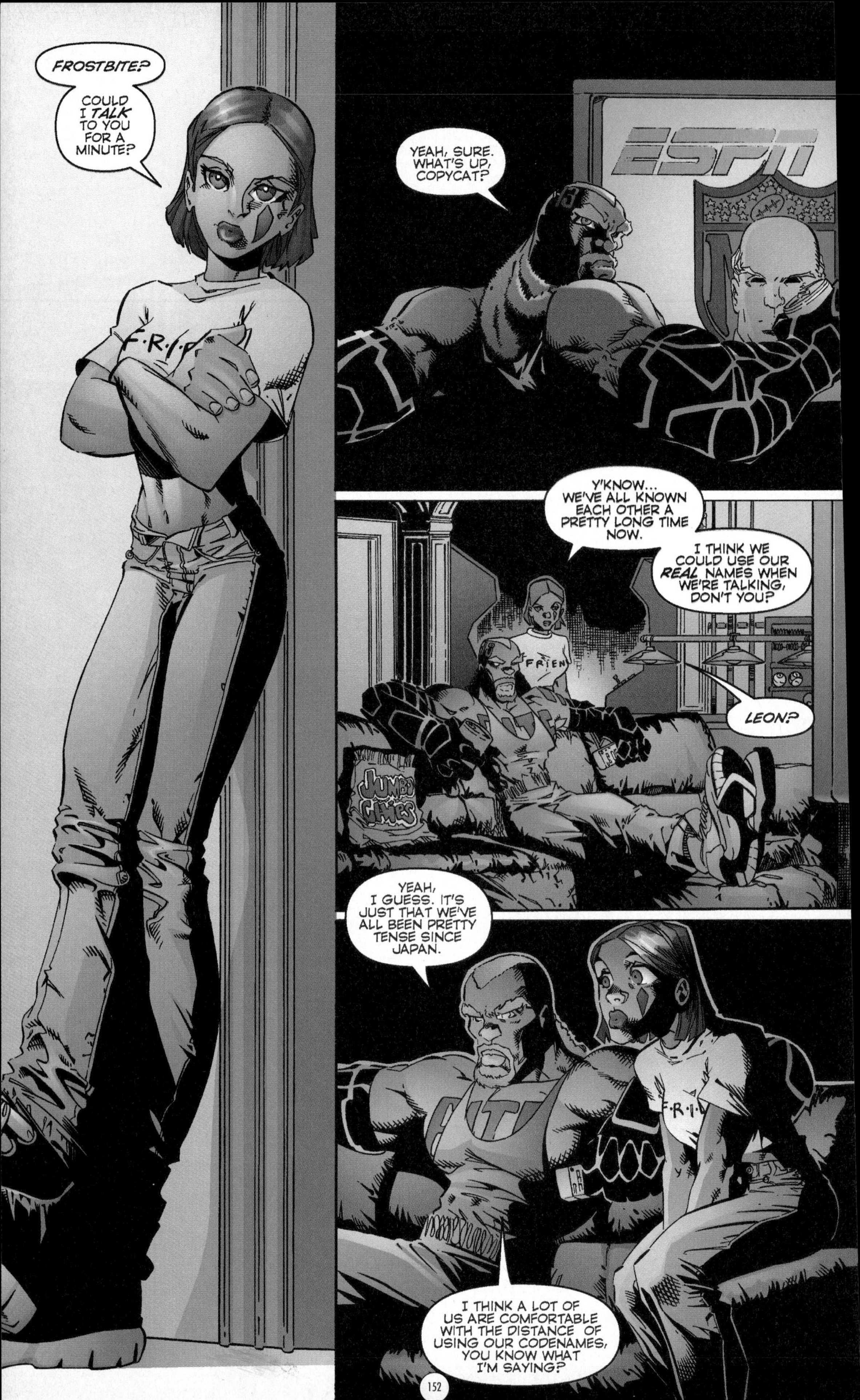
FROSTBITE?
COULD I TALK TO YOU FOR A MINUTE?
YEAH, SURE. WHAT'S UP, COPYCAT?
ESPN
F·R·I·
Y'KNOW... WE'VE ALL KNOWN EACH OTHER A PRETTY LONG TIME NOW.
I THINK WE COULD USE OUR REAL NAMES WHEN WE'RE TALKING, DON'T YOU?
LEON?
FRIEN
JUMBO CHIPS
YEAH, I GUESS. IT'S JUST THAT WE'VE ALL BEEN PRETTY TENSE SINCE JAPAN.
I THINK A LOT OF US ARE COMFORTABLE WITH THE DISTANCE OF USING OUR CODENAMES, YOU KNOW WHAT I'M SAYING?

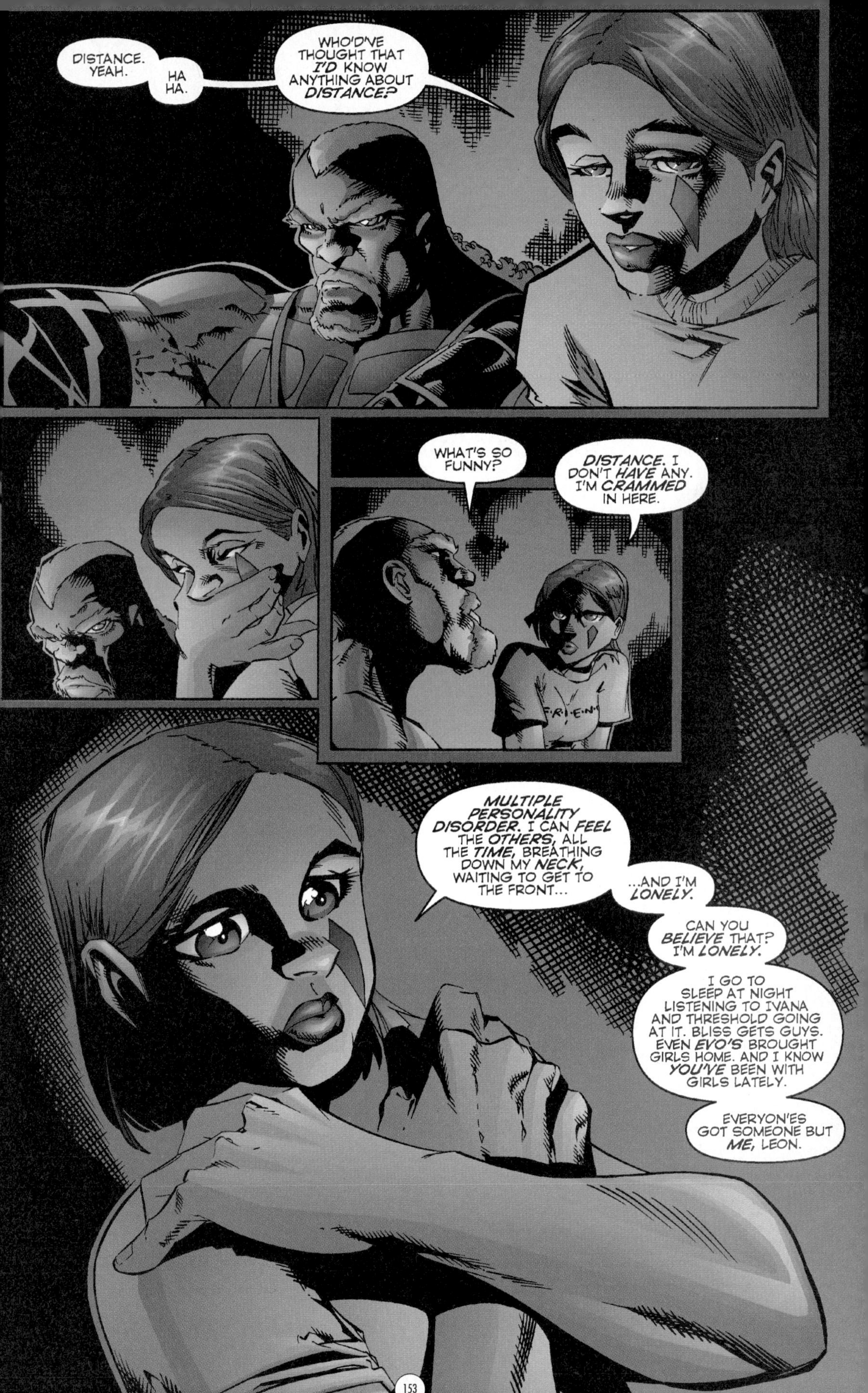
DISTANCE. YEAH.
HA HA.
WHO'D'VE THOUGHT THAT I'D KNOW ANYTHING ABOUT DISTANCE?
WHAT'S SO FUNNY?
DISTANCE. I DON'T HAVE ANY. I'M CRAMMED IN HERE.
F.R.I.E.N.
MULTIPLE PERSONALITY DISORDER. I CAN FEEL THE OTHERS, ALL THE TIME, BREATHING DOWN MY NECK, WAITING TO GET TO THE FRONT...
...AND I'M LONELY.
CAN YOU BELIEVE THAT? I'M LONELY.
I GO TO SLEEP AT NIGHT LISTENING TO IVANA AND THRESHOLD GOING AT IT. BLISS GETS GUYS. EVEN EVO'S BROUGHT GIRLS HOME. AND I KNOW YOU'VE BEEN WITH GIRLS LATELY.
EVERYON'ES GOT SOMEONE BUT ME, LEON.

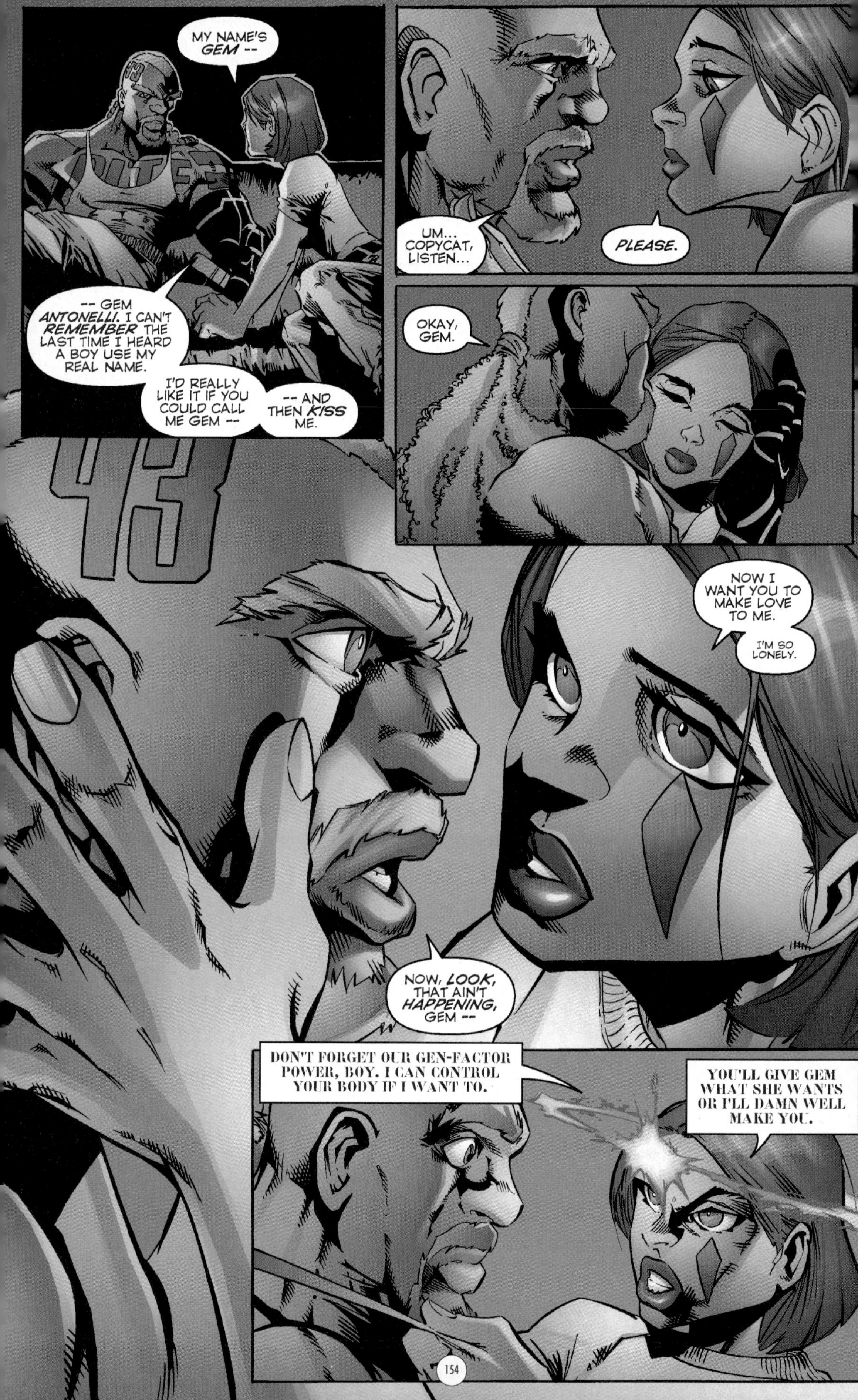
MY NAME'S *GEM* --
-- GEM *ANTONELLI.* I CAN'T *REMEMBER* THE LAST TIME I HEARD A BOY USE MY REAL NAME.
I'D REALLY LIKE IT IF YOU COULD CALL ME GEM --
-- AND THEN *KISS* ME.
UM... COPYCAT, LISTEN...
PLEASE.
OKAY, GEM.
NOW I WANT YOU TO MAKE LOVE TO ME.
I'M SO LONELY.
NOW, *LOOK,* THAT AIN'T *HAPPENING,* GEM --
DON'T FORGET OUR GEN-FACTOR POWER, BOY. I CAN CONTROL YOUR BODY IF I WANT TO.
YOU'LL GIVE GEM WHAT SHE WANTS OR I'LL DAMN WELL MAKE YOU.

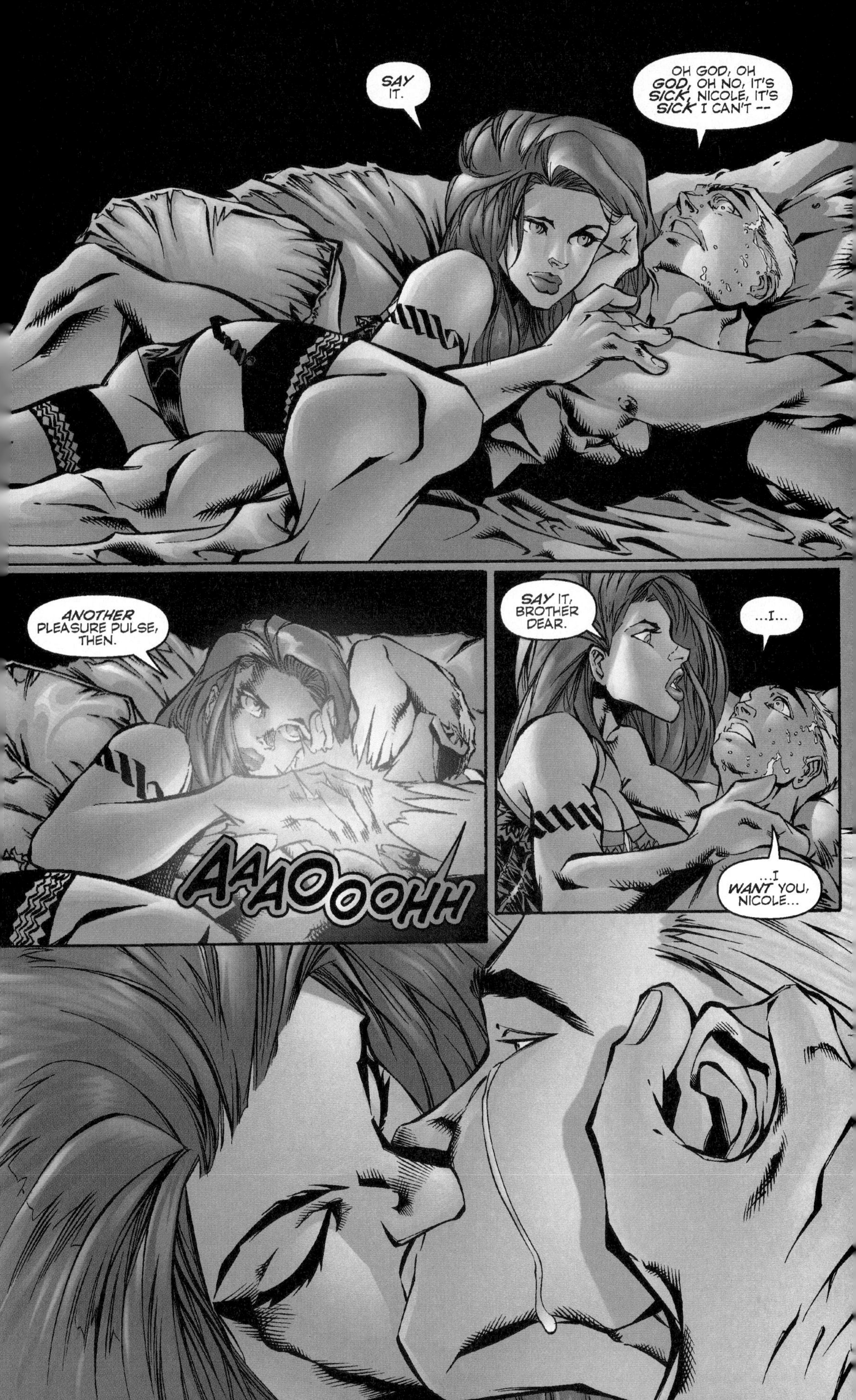
SAY IT.
OH GOD, OH GOD, OH NO, IT'S SICK, NICOLE, IT'S SICK I CAN'T --
ANOTHER PLEASURE PULSE, THEN.
AAAOOOOHH
SAY IT, BROTHER DEAR.
...I...
...I WANT YOU, NICOLE...

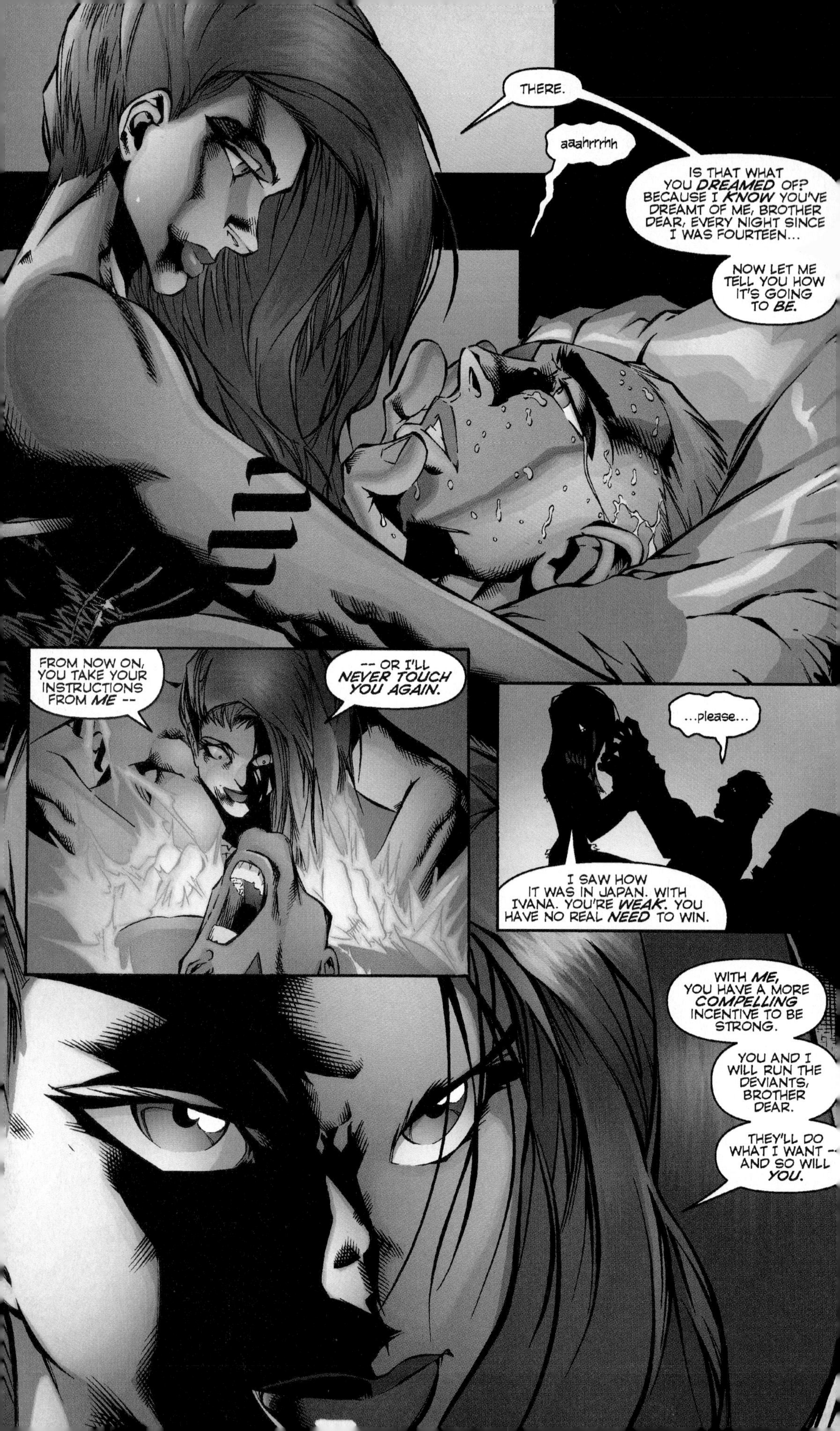
THERE.
aaahrrrhh
IS THAT WHAT YOU DREAMED OF? BECAUSE I KNOW YOU'VE DREAMT OF ME, BROTHER DEAR, EVERY NIGHT SINCE I WAS FOURTEEN...
NOW LET ME TELL YOU HOW IT'S GOING TO BE.
FROM NOW ON, YOU TAKE YOUR INSTRUCTIONS FROM ME --
-- OR I'LL NEVER TOUCH YOU AGAIN.
...please...
I SAW HOW IT WAS IN JAPAN. WITH IVANA. YOU'RE WEAK. YOU HAVE NO REAL NEED TO WIN.
WITH ME, YOU HAVE A MORE COMPELLING INCENTIVE TO BE STRONG.
YOU AND I WILL RUN THE DEVIANTS, BROTHER DEAR.
THEY'LL DO WHAT I WANT -- AND SO WILL YOU.

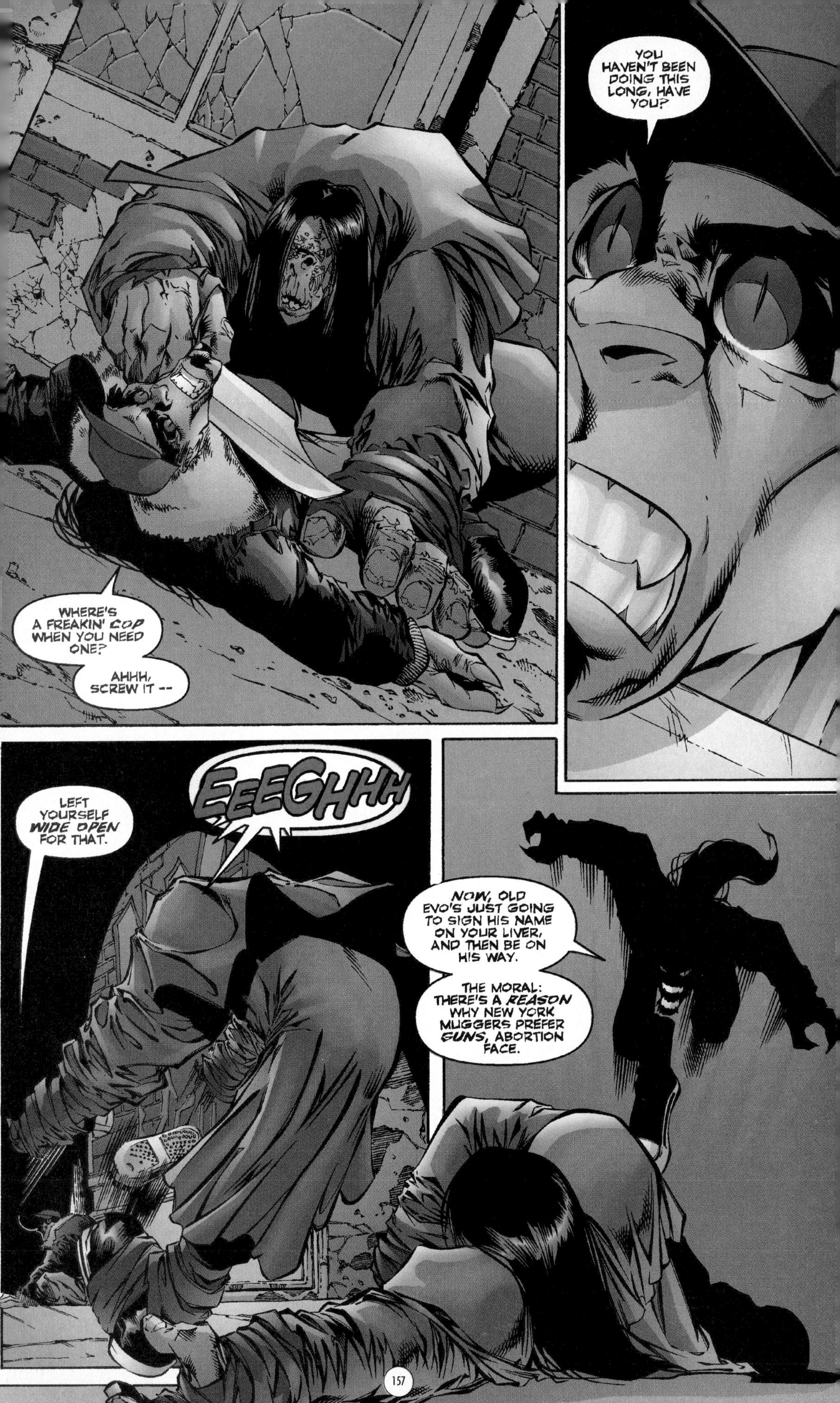
WHERE'S A FREAKIN' COP WHEN YOU NEED ONE?
AHHH, SCREW IT --
YOU HAVEN'T BEEN DOING THIS LONG, HAVE YOU?
LEFT YOURSELF WIDE OPEN FOR THAT.
EEEGHHH
NOW, OLD EVO'S JUST GOING TO SIGN HIS NAME ON YOUR LIVER, AND THEN BE ON HIS WAY.
THE MORAL: THERE'S A REASON WHY NEW YORK MUGGERS PREFER GUNS, ABORTION FACE.

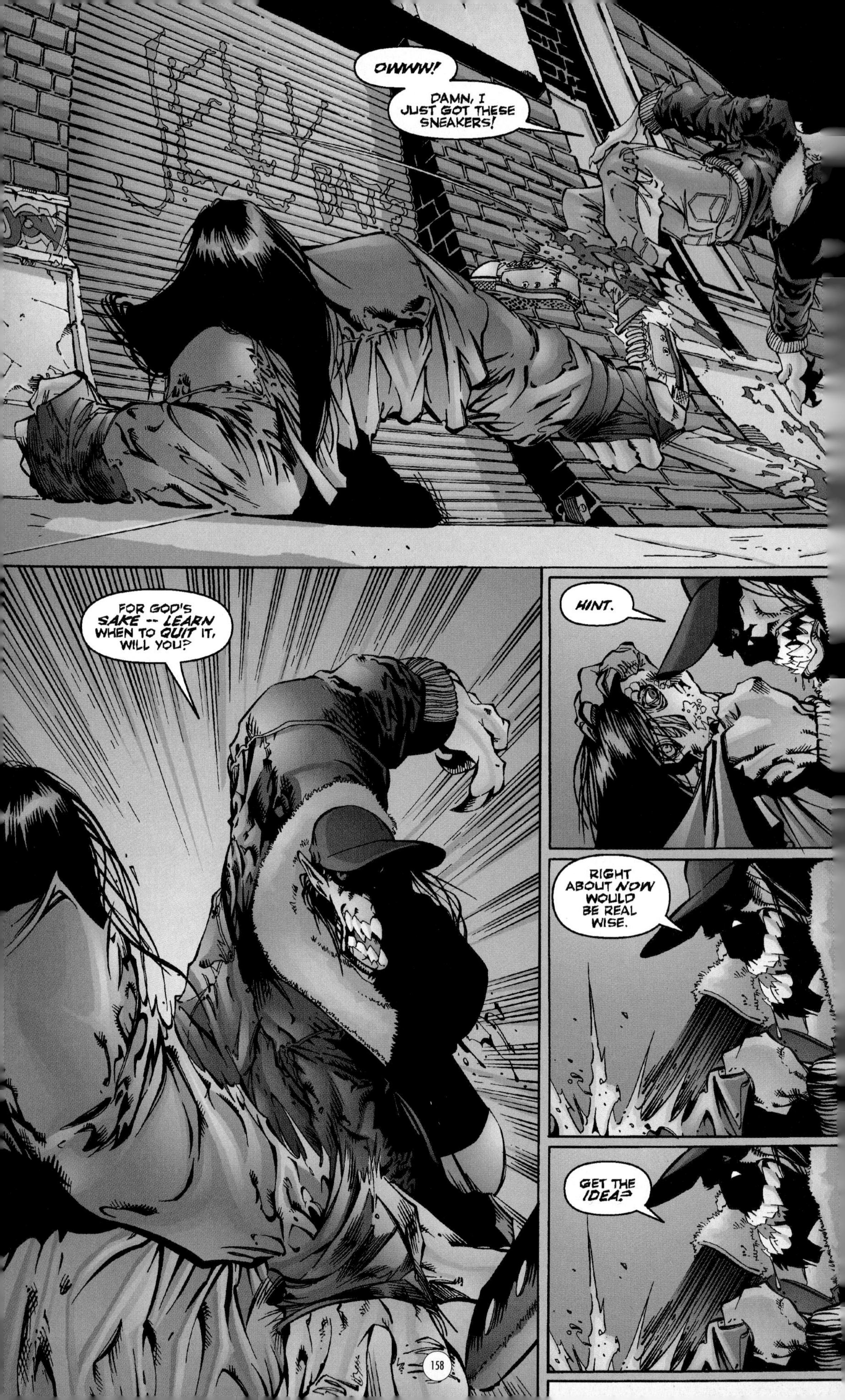
OWWW!
DAMN, I JUST GOT THESE SNEAKERS!
FOR GOD'S SAKE -- LEARN WHEN TO QUIT IT, WILL YOU?
HINT.
RIGHT ABOUT NOW WOULD BE REAL WISE.
GET THE IDEA?

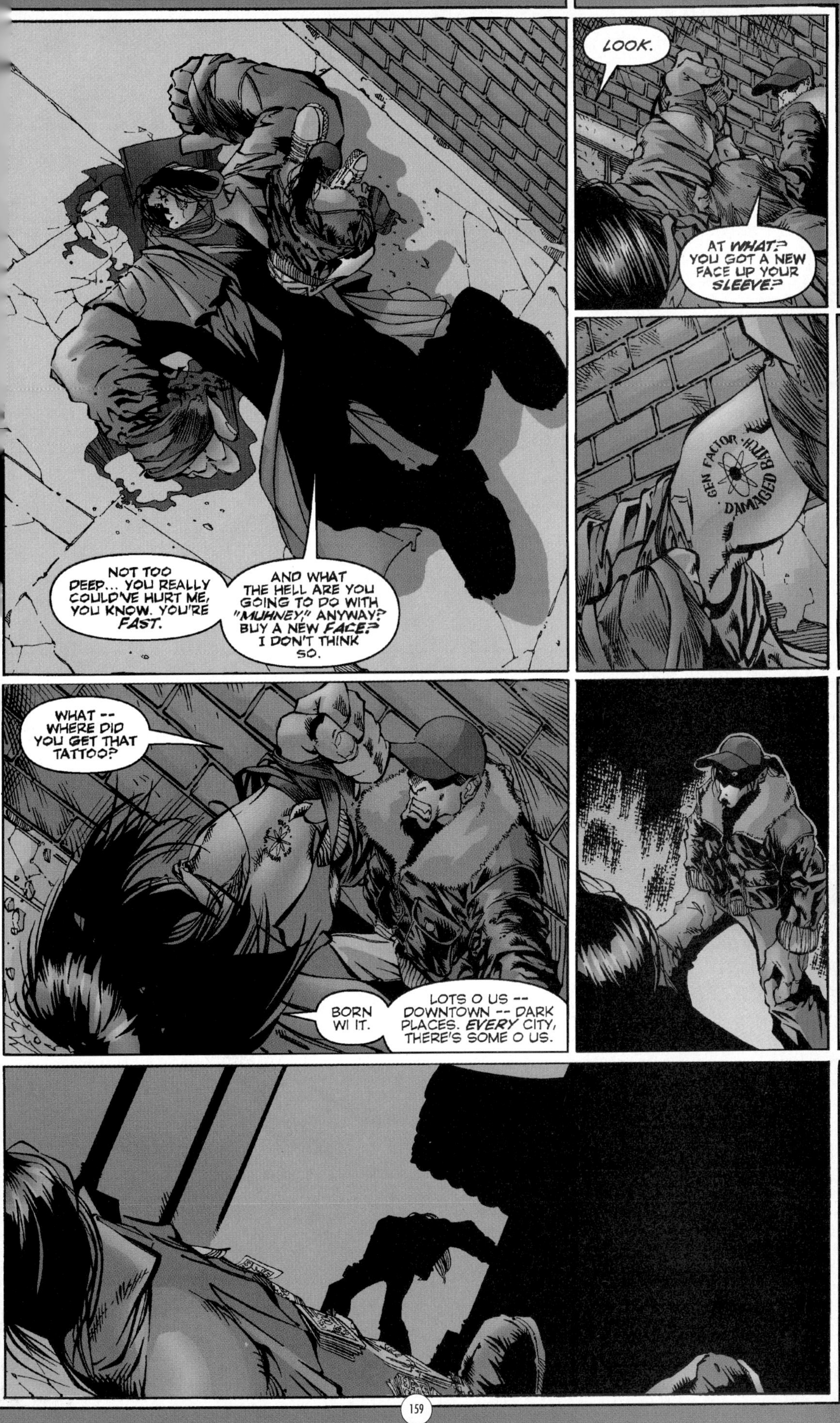
NOT TOO DEEP... YOU REALLY COULD'VE HURT ME, YOU KNOW. YOU'RE FAST.
AND WHAT THE HELL ARE YOU GOING TO DO WITH "MUHNEY," ANYWAY? BUY A NEW FACE? I DON'T THINK SO.
LOOK.
AT WHAT? YOU GOT A NEW FACE UP YOUR SLEEVE?
GEN FACTOR DAMAGED BATCH
WHAT -- WHERE DID YOU GET THAT TATTOO?
BORN WI IT.
LOTS O US -- DOWNTOWN -- DARK PLACES. EVERY CITY, THERE'S SOME O US.

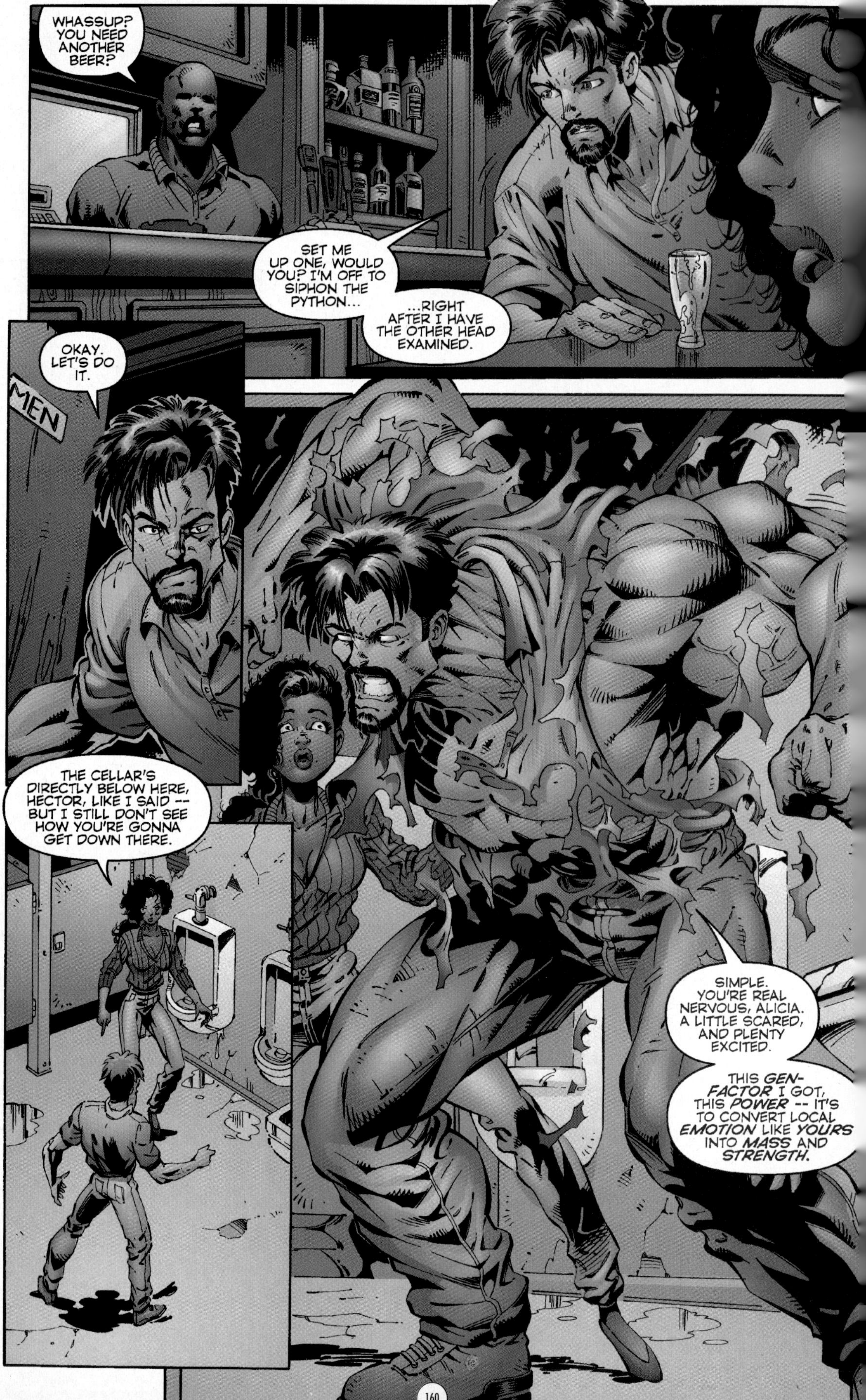
WHASSUP? YOU NEED ANOTHER BEER?
SET ME UP ONE, WOULD YOU? I'M OFF TO SIPHON THE PYTHON...
...RIGHT AFTER I HAVE THE OTHER HEAD EXAMINED.
OKAY. LET'S DO IT.
MEN
THE CELLAR'S DIRECTLY BELOW HERE, HECTOR, LIKE I SAID -- BUT I STILL DON'T SEE HOW YOU'RE GONNA GET DOWN THERE.
SIMPLE. YOU'RE REAL NERVOUS, ALICIA. A LITTLE SCARED, AND PLENTY EXCITED.
THIS *GEN-FACTOR* I GOT, THIS *POWER* -- IT'S TO CONVERT LOCAL *EMOTION* LIKE *YOURS* INTO *MASS* AND *STRENGTH*.

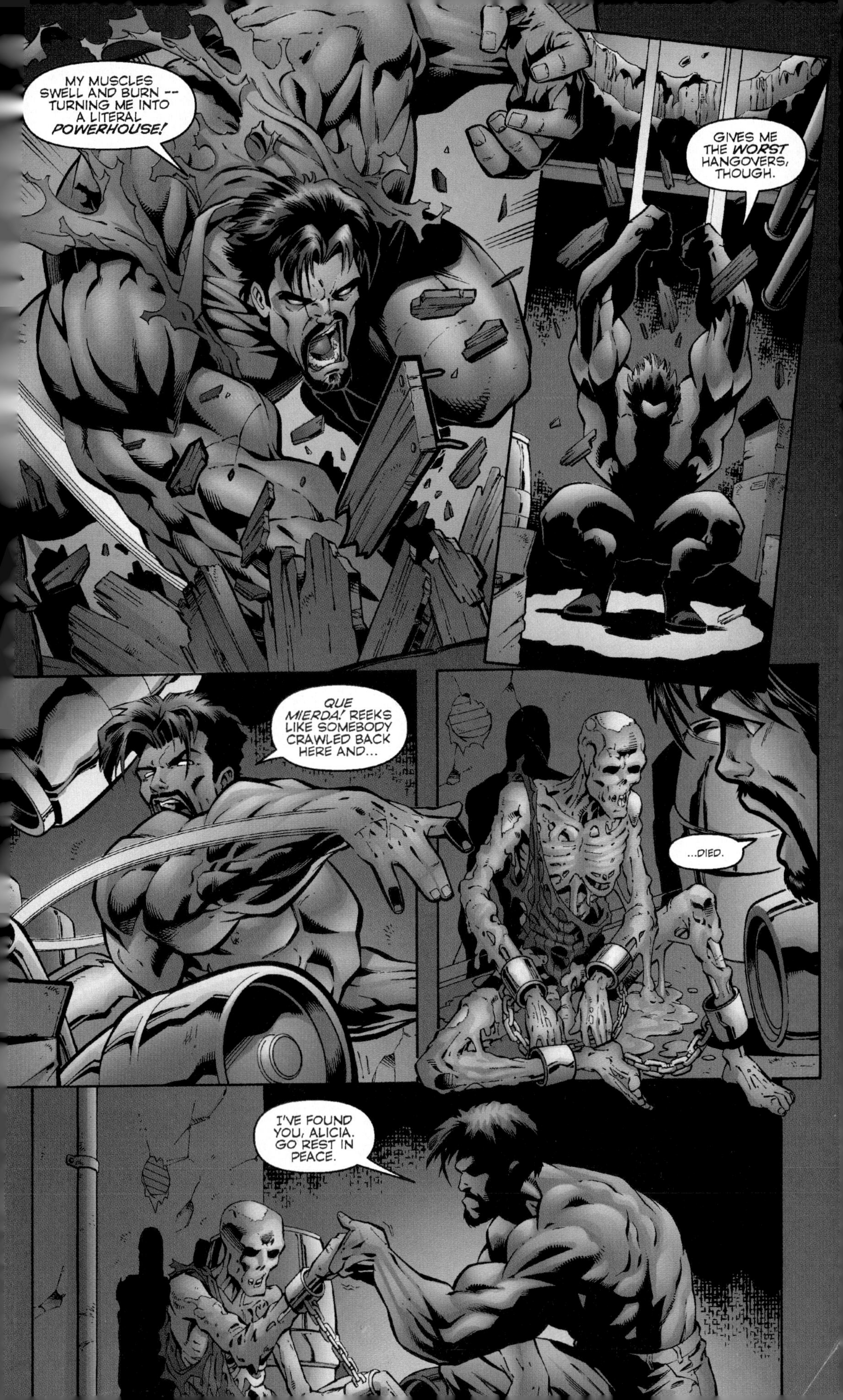
MY MUSCLES SWELL AND BURN -- TURNING ME INTO A LITERAL POWERHOUSE!
GIVES ME THE WORST HANGOVERS, THOUGH.
QUE MIERDA! REEKS LIKE SOMEBODY CRAWLED BACK HERE AND...
...DIED.
I'VE FOUND YOU, ALICIA. GO REST IN PEACE.

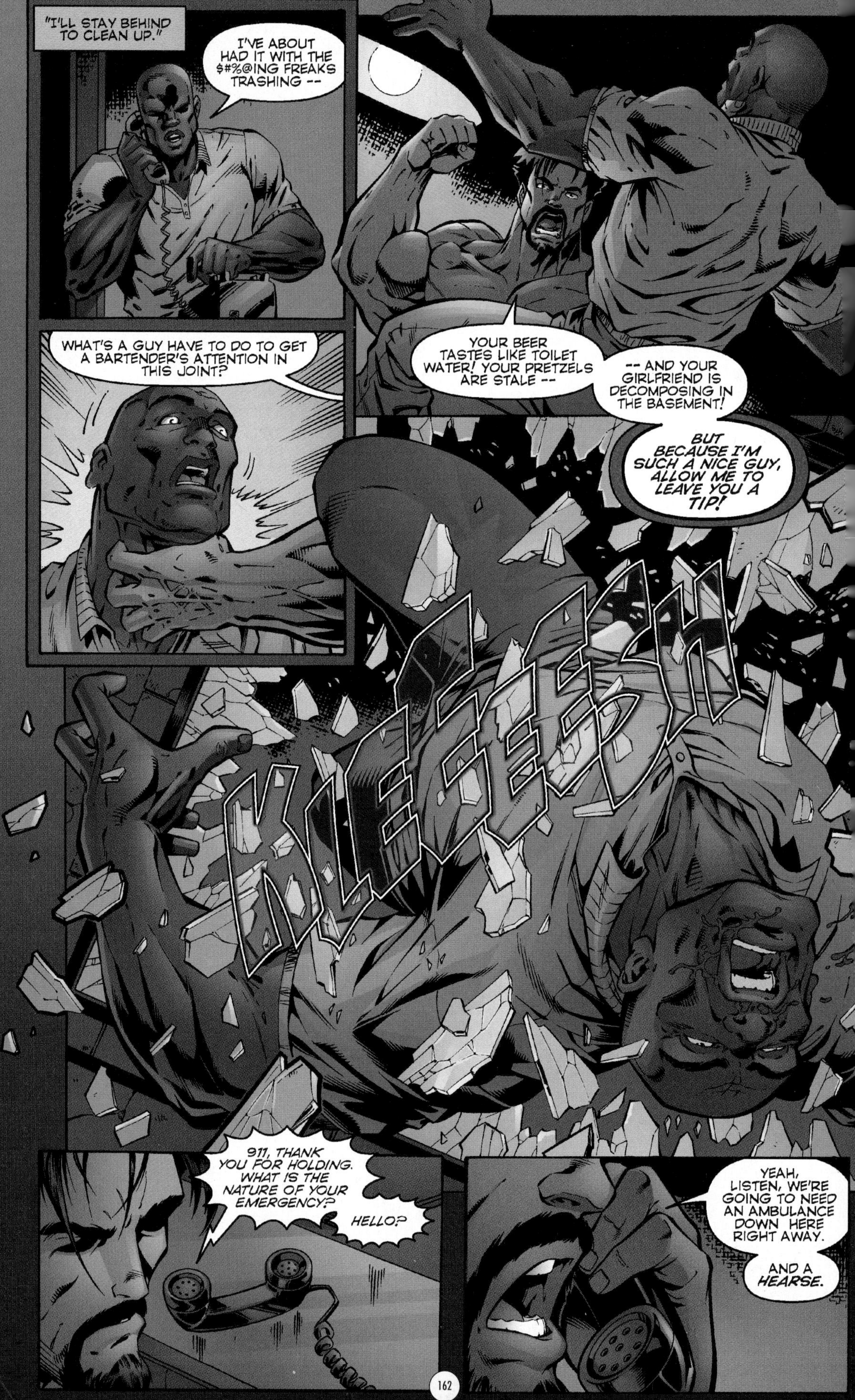
"I'LL STAY BEHIND TO CLEAN UP."
I'VE ABOUT HAD IT WITH THE $#%@ING FREAKS TRASHING --
YOUR BEER TASTES LIKE TOILET WATER! YOUR PRETZELS ARE STALE --
-- AND YOUR GIRLFRIEND IS DECOMPOSING IN THE BASEMENT!
WHAT'S A GUY HAVE TO DO TO GET A BARTENDER'S ATTENTION IN THIS JOINT?
BUT BECAUSE I'M SUCH A NICE GUY, ALLOW ME TO LEAVE YOU A TIP!
KLEEEESH
911, THANK YOU FOR HOLDING. WHAT IS THE NATURE OF YOUR EMERGENCY?
HELLO?
YEAH, LISTEN, WE'RE GOING TO NEED AN AMBULANCE DOWN HERE RIGHT AWAY.
AND A HEARSE.

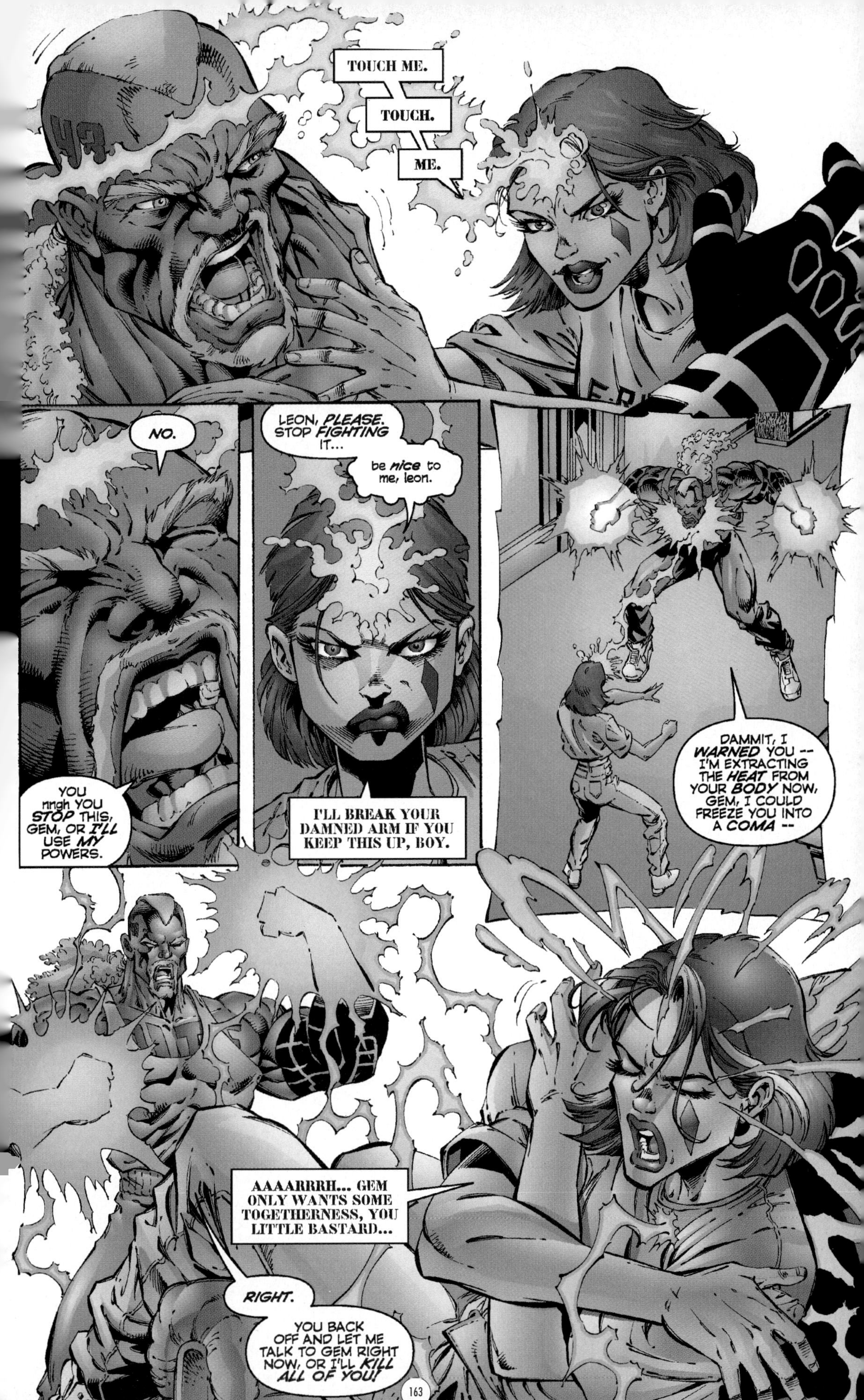

TOUCH ME.
TOUCH.
ME.
NO.
YOU nngh YOU STOP THIS, GEM, OR I'LL USE MY POWERS.
LEON, PLEASE. STOP FIGHTING IT...
be nice to me, leon.
I'LL BREAK YOUR DAMNED ARM IF YOU KEEP THIS UP, BOY.
DAMMIT, I WARNED YOU -- I'M EXTRACTING THE HEAT FROM YOUR BODY NOW, GEM, I COULD FREEZE YOU INTO A COMA --
AAAARRRH... GEM ONLY WANTS SOME TOGETHERNESS, YOU LITTLE BASTARD...
RIGHT.
YOU BACK OFF AND LET ME TALK TO GEM RIGHT NOW, OR I'LL KILL ALL OF YOU!

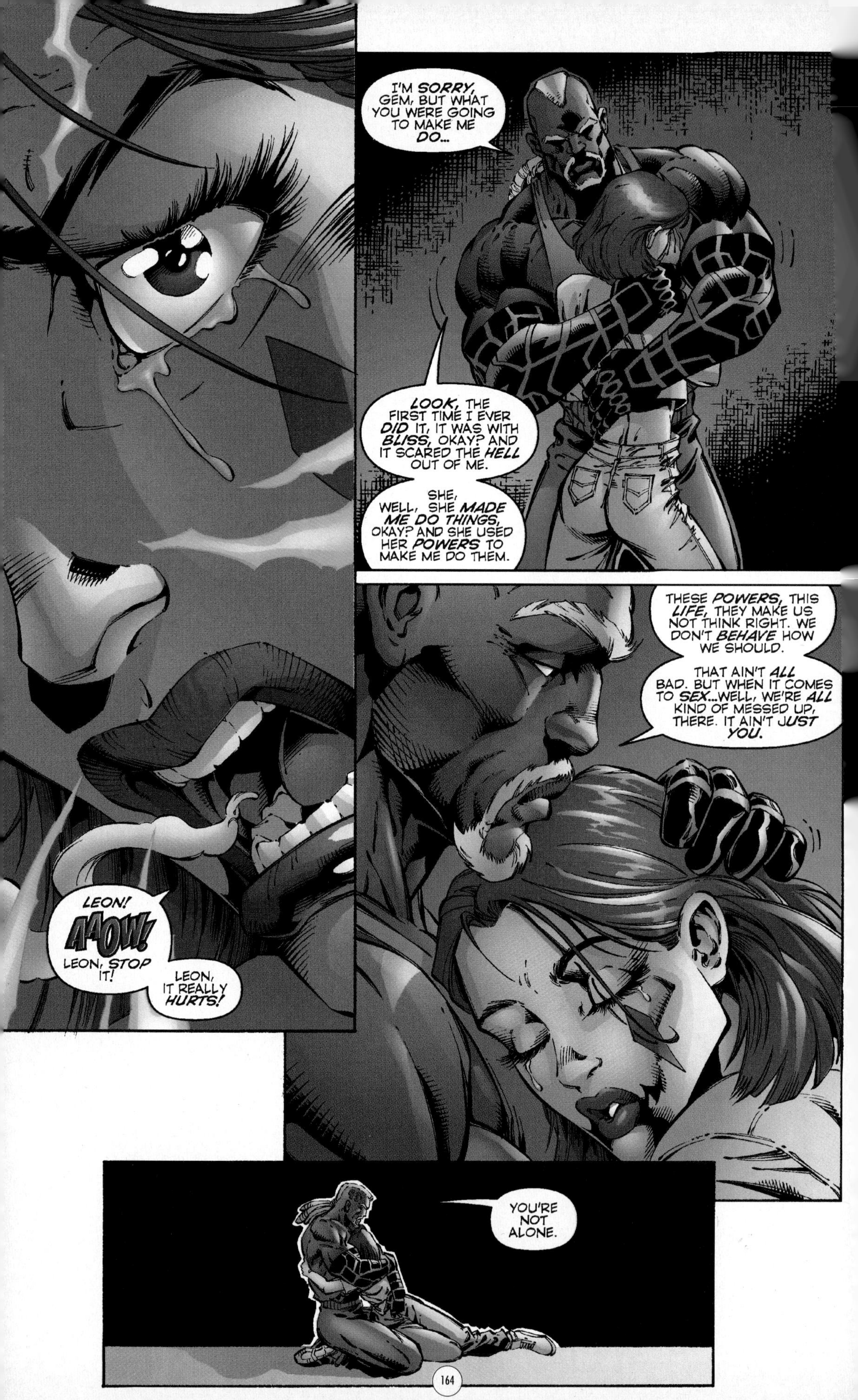
LEON!
AAOW!
LEON, STOP IT!
LEON, IT REALLY HURTS!
I'M SORRY, GEM, BUT WHAT YOU WERE GOING TO MAKE ME DO...
LOOK, THE FIRST TIME I EVER DID IT, IT WAS WITH BLISS, OKAY? AND IT SCARED THE HELL OUT OF ME.
SHE, WELL, SHE MADE ME DO THINGS, OKAY? AND SHE USED HER POWERS TO MAKE ME DO THEM.
THESE POWERS, THIS LIFE, THEY MAKE US NOT THINK RIGHT. WE DON'T BEHAVE HOW WE SHOULD.
THAT AIN'T ALL BAD. BUT WHEN IT COMES TO SEX...WELL, WE'RE ALL KIND OF MESSED UP, THERE. IT AIN'T JUST YOU.
YOU'RE NOT ALONE.

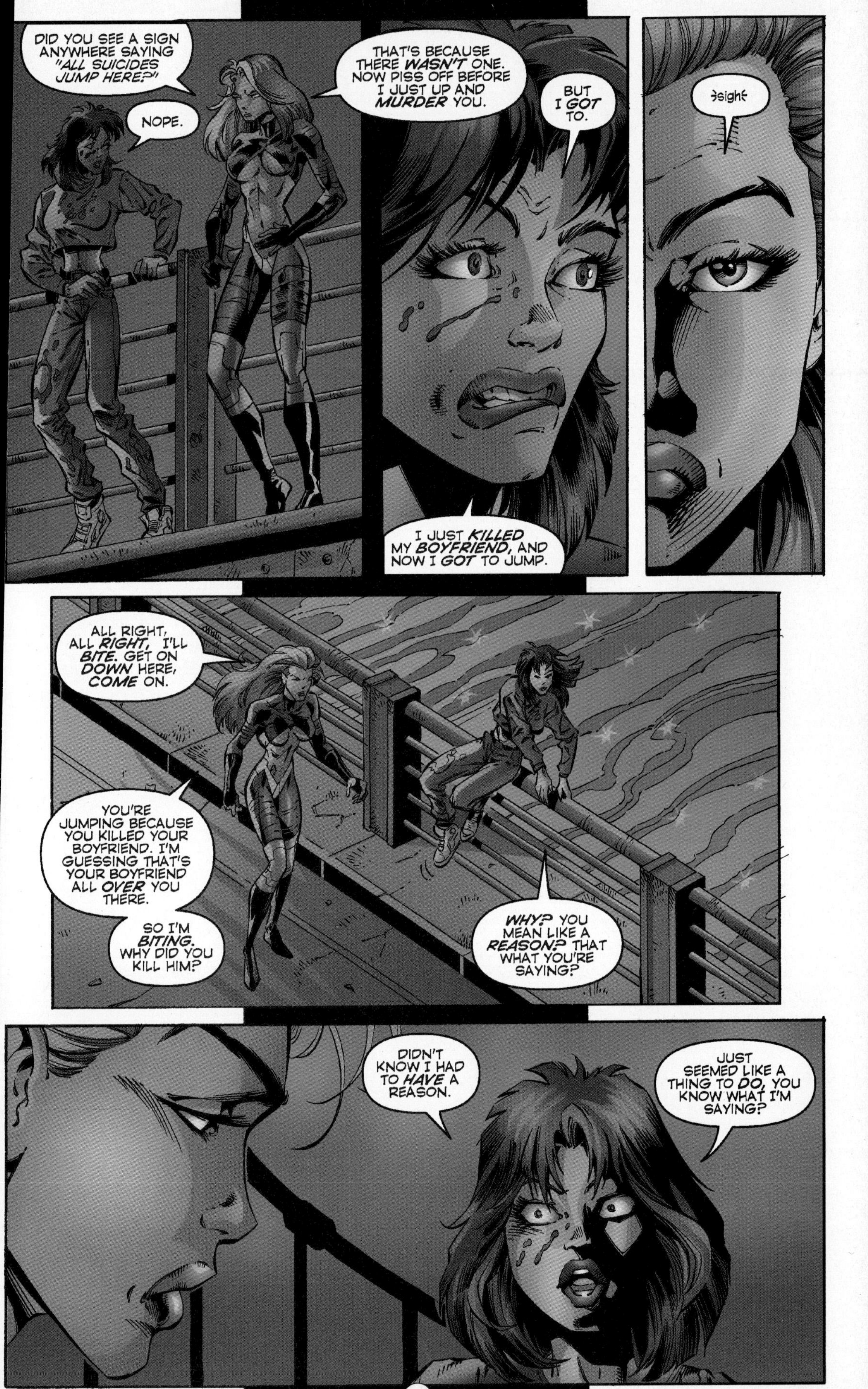
DID YOU SEE A SIGN ANYWHERE SAYING "ALL SUICIDES JUMP HERE?"
NOPE.
THAT'S BECAUSE THERE WASN'T ONE. NOW PISS OFF BEFORE I JUST UP AND MURDER YOU.
BUT I GOT TO.
I JUST KILLED MY BOYFRIEND, AND NOW I GOT TO JUMP.
sigh
ALL RIGHT, ALL RIGHT, I'LL BITE. GET ON DOWN HERE, COME ON.
YOU'RE JUMPING BECAUSE YOU KILLED YOUR BOYFRIEND. I'M GUESSING THAT'S YOUR BOYFRIEND ALL OVER YOU THERE.
SO I'M BITING. WHY DID YOU KILL HIM?
WHY? YOU MEAN LIKE A REASON? THAT WHAT YOU'RE SAYING?
DIDN'T KNOW I HAD TO HAVE A REASON.
JUST SEEMED LIKE A THING TO DO, YOU KNOW WHAT I'M SAYING?

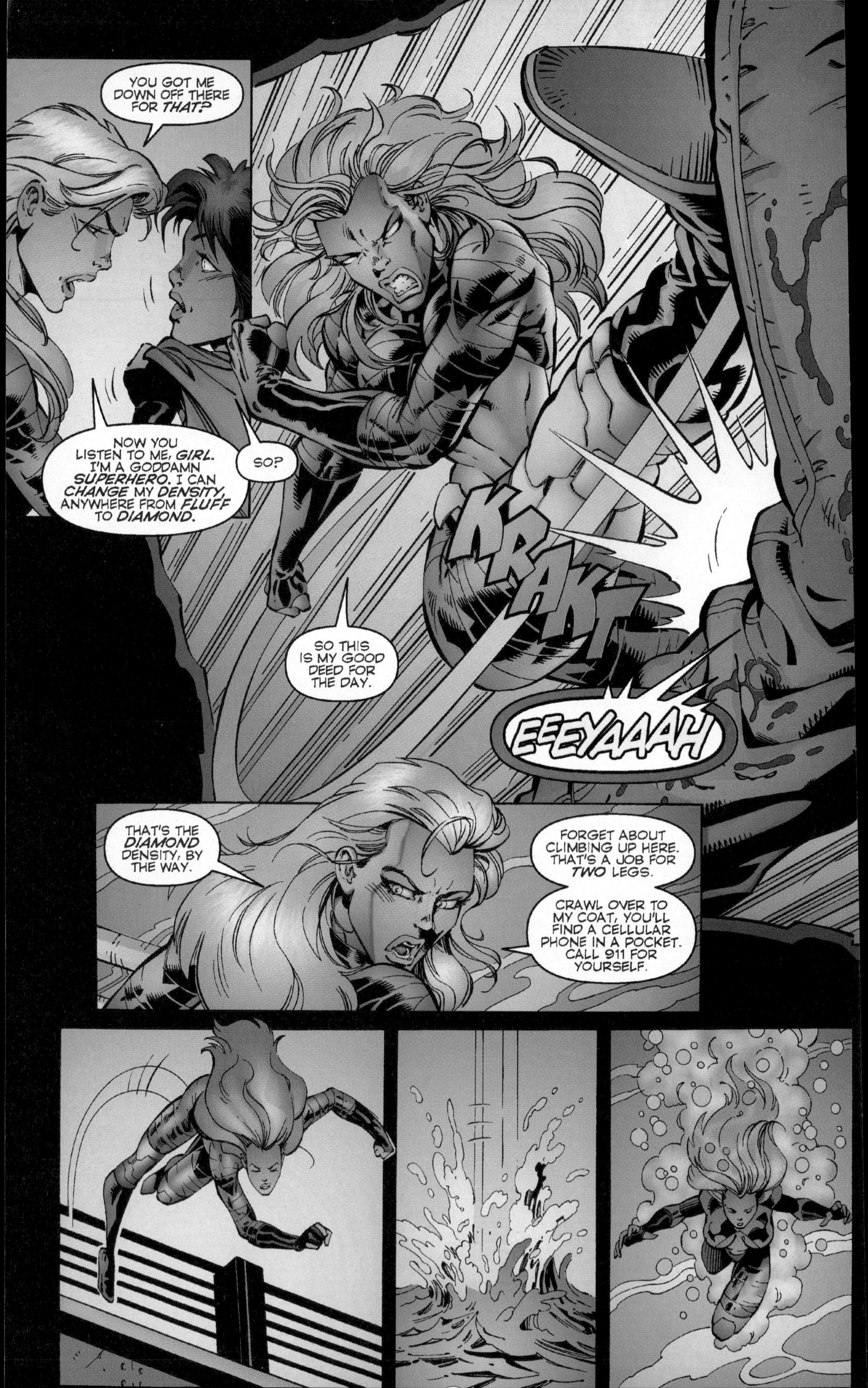

YOU GOT ME DOWN OFF THERE FOR *THAT?*
NOW YOU LISTEN TO ME, *GIRL.* I'M A GODDAMN ***SUPERHERO.*** I CAN ***CHANGE*** MY ***DENSITY,*** ANYWHERE FROM ***FLUFF*** TO ***DIAMOND.***
SO?
SO THIS IS MY GOOD DEED FOR THE DAY.
KRAKT
EEEYAAAH
THAT'S THE ***DIAMOND*** DENSITY, BY THE WAY.
FORGET ABOUT CLIMBING UP HERE. THAT'S A JOB FOR ***TWO*** LEGS.
CRAWL OVER TO MY COAT, YOU'LL FIND A CELLULAR PHONE IN A POCKET. CALL 911 FOR YOURSELF.

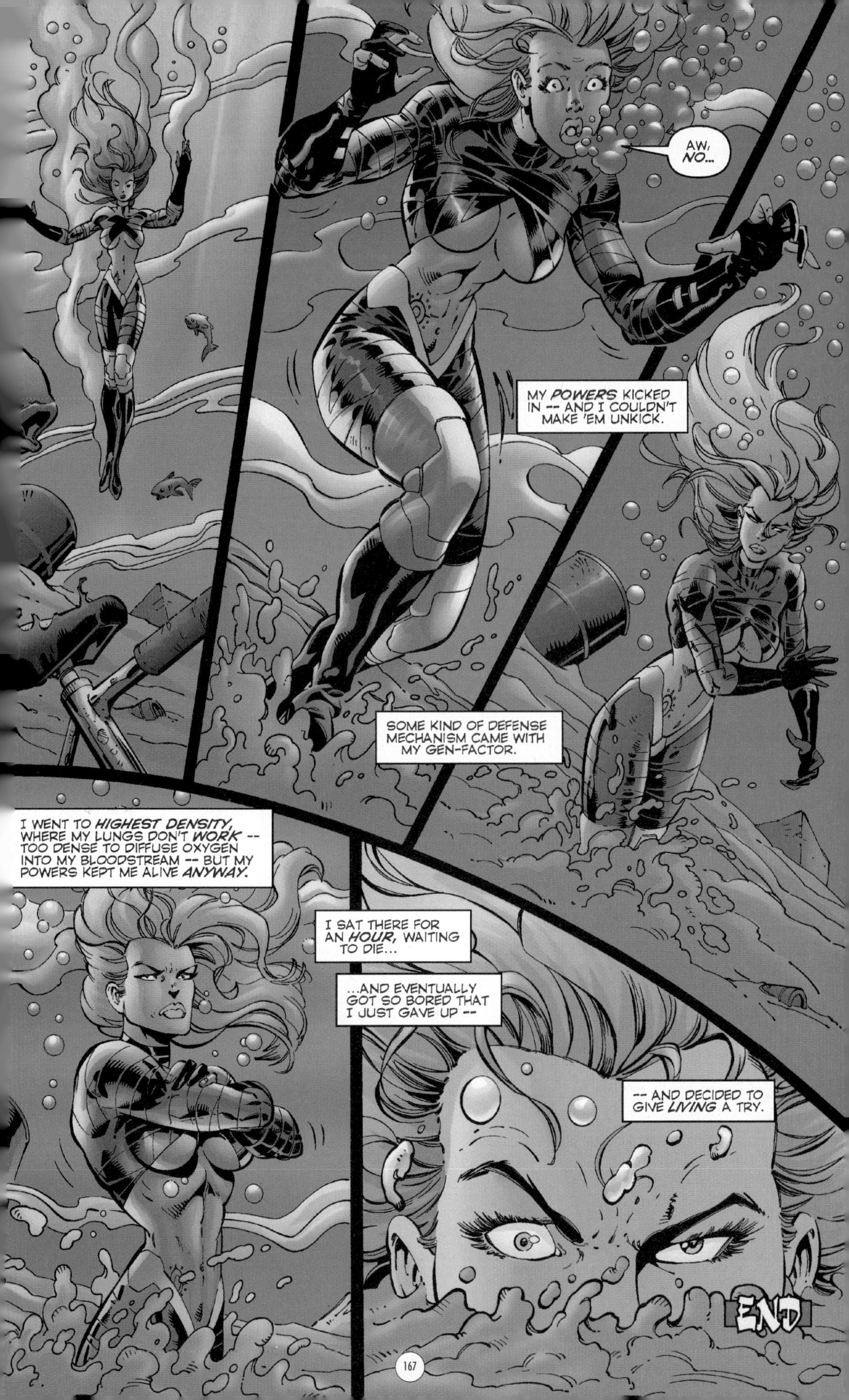
AW, *NO...*
MY *POWERS* KICKED IN -- AND I COULDN'T MAKE 'EM UNKICK.
SOME KIND OF DEFENSE MECHANISM CAME WITH MY GEN-FACTOR.
I WENT TO *HIGHEST DENSITY,* WHERE MY LUNGS DON'T *WORK* -- TOO DENSE TO DIFFUSE OXYGEN INTO MY BLOODSTREAM -- BUT MY POWERS KEPT ME ALIVE *ANYWAY.*
I SAT THERE FOR AN *HOUR,* WAITING TO DIE...
...AND EVENTUALLY GOT SO BORED THAT I JUST GAVE UP --
-- AND DECIDED TO GIVE *LIVING* A TRY.
END

DV8

COVER GALLERY

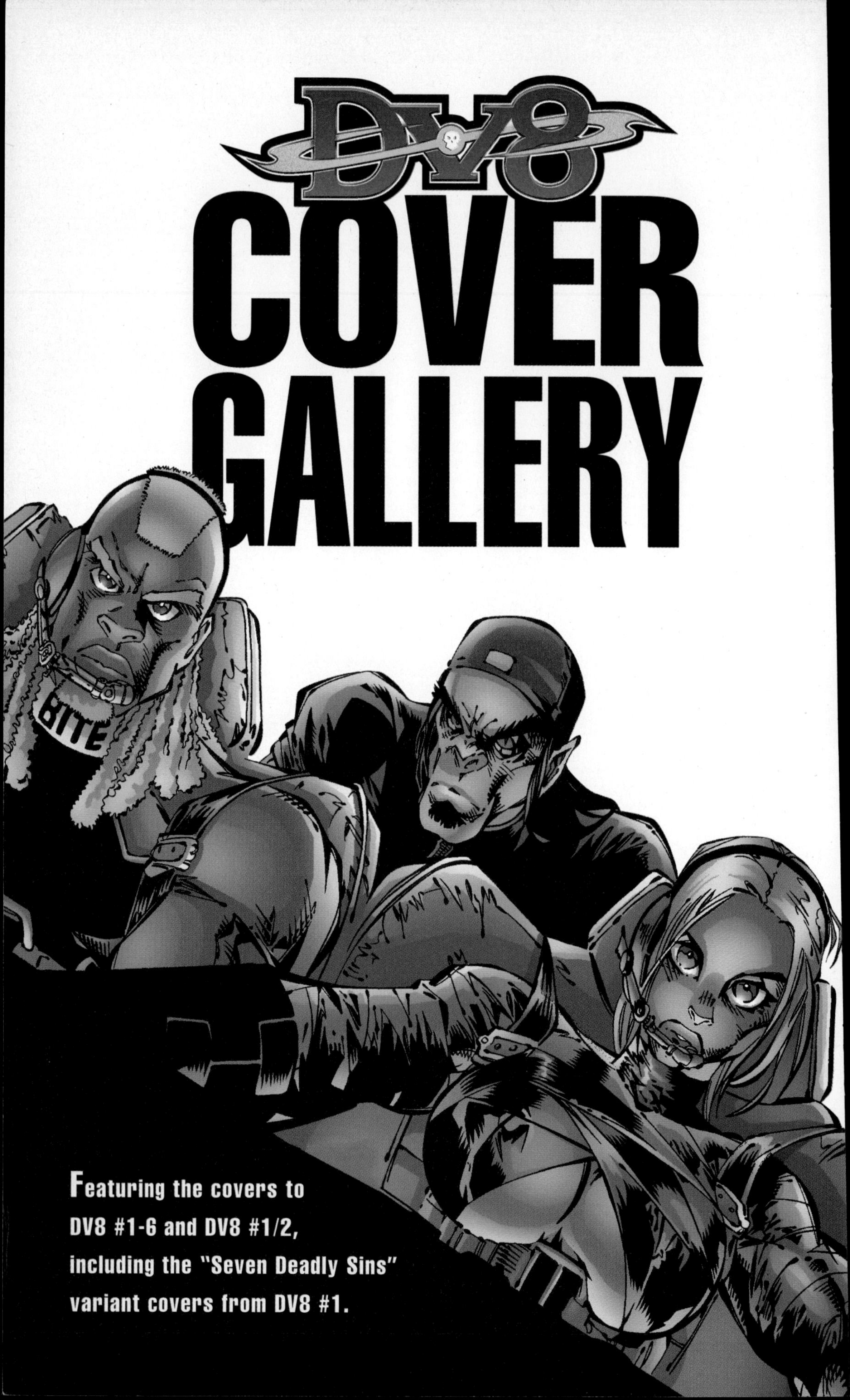
BITE

Featuring the covers to DV8 #1-6 and DV8 #1/2, including the "Seven Deadly Sins" variant covers from DV8 #1.

Original cover to DV8 #1
Art by Humberto Ramos
and Sal Regla

Variant cover to DV8 #1 — "Envy"
Art by Michael Lopez
and Edwin Rosell

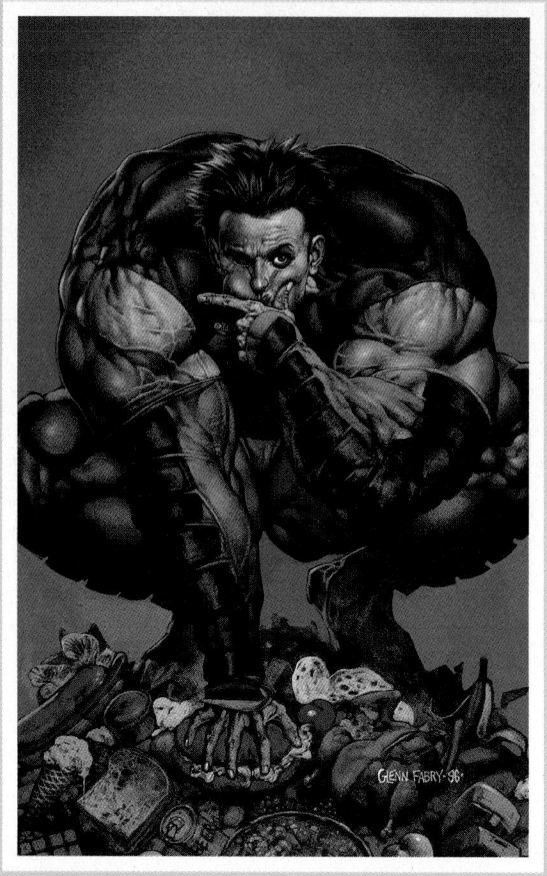
GLENN FABRY-96

Variant cover to DV8 #1 — "Gluttony"
Art by Glenn Fabry

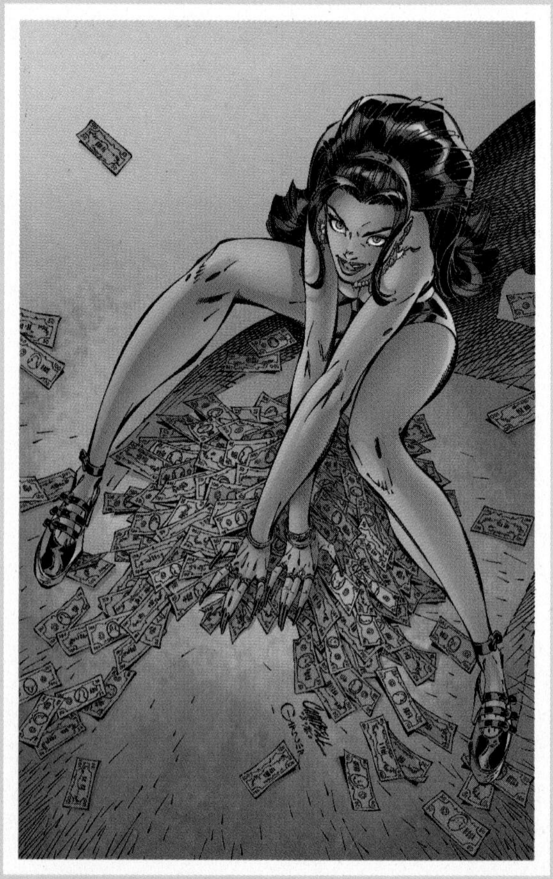

Variant cover to DV8 #1 — "Greed"
Art by J. Scott Campbell and Alex Garner

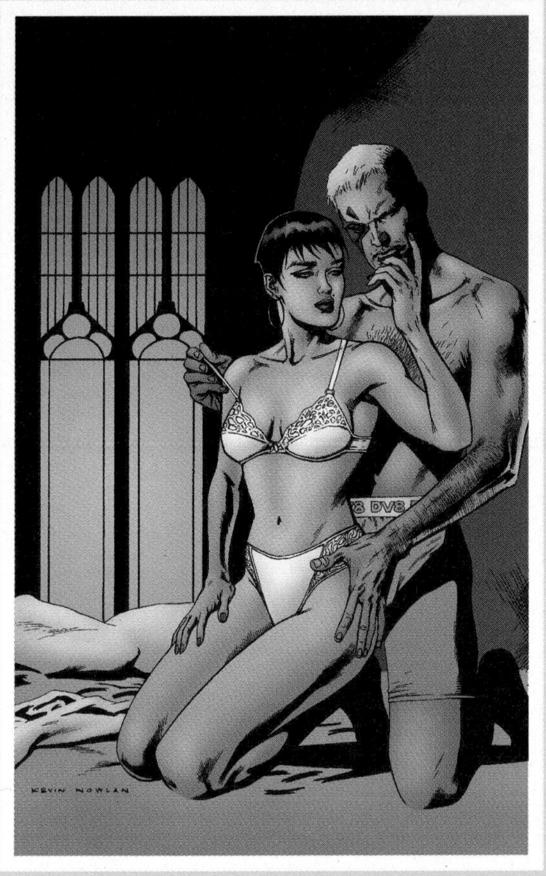
DV8
KEVIN NOWLAN

Variant cover to DV8 #1 — "Lust"
Art by Kevin Nowlan

Variant cover to DV8 #1 — "Pride"
Art by Adam Hughes
and Dave Stevens

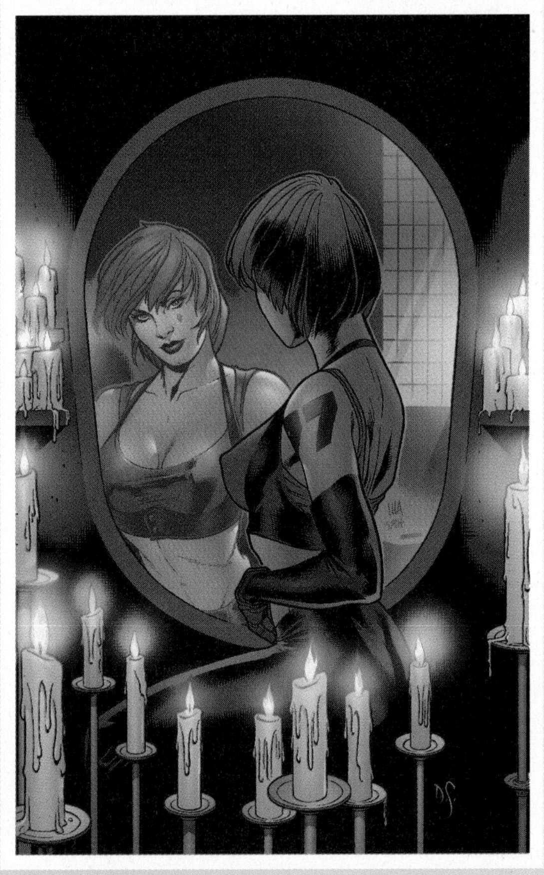

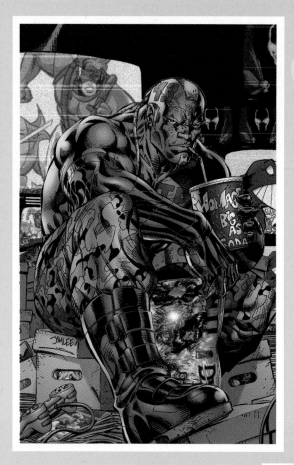

Variant cover to DV8 #1 — "Sloth
Art by Jim Lee and J.D.

Variant cover to DV8 #1 — "Wrath"
Art by Liberatore

Cover to DV8 #2
Art by Humberto Ramos
and Sal Regla

Cover to DV8 #1/2
Art by Juvaun Kirby
and Edwin Rosell

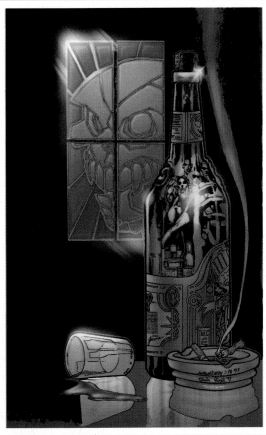

Cover to DV8 #3
Art by Michael Lopez and Troy Hub

Cover to DV8 #4
Art by Humberto Ramos
and Sal Regla

Cover to DV8 #5
Art by Humberto Ramos
and Sal Regla

Cover to DV8 #6
Art by Humberto Ramos
and Sal Regla

WILDSTORM COLLECTIONS

THE AUTHORITY: RELENTLESS
Ellis/Hitch/Neary

THE AUTHORITY: UNDER NEW MANAGEMENT
Ellis/Millar/Hitch/Quitely

THE AUTHORITY: EARTH INFERNO AND OTHER STORIES
Millar/Quitely/Weston/Scott/Leach

CRIMSON: LOYALTY & LOSS
Augustyn/Ramos/Hope

CRIMSON: HEAVEN & EARTH
Augustyn/Ramos/Hope

CRIMSON: EARTH ANGEL
Augustyn/Ramos/Hope

CRIMSON: REDEMPTION
Augustyn/Ramos/Hope

DEATHBLOW: SINNERS AND SAINTS
Choi/Lee/Sale/Scott

DANGER GIRL: THE ULTIMATE COLLECTION
Campbell/Hartnell/Garner

DIVINE RIGHT: BOOK ONE
Lee/Williams

GEN13
Choi/Lee/Campbell/Garner

GEN13: #13 ABC
Choi/Lee/Campbell/Garner

GEN13: BOOTLEG Vol. 1
Various writers and artists

GEN13: GRUNGE THE MOVIE
Warren

GEN13: I LOVE NEW YORK
Arcudi/Frank/Smith

GEN13: INTERACTIVE PLUS
Various writers and artists

GEN13: STARTING OVER
Choi/Lee/Campbell/Garner

GEN13: WE'LL TAKE MANHATTAN
Lobdell/Benes/Sibal

GEN13: SUPERHUMAN LIKE YOU
Warren/Benes/Andrews

GEN13: SUPERMAN
Hughes/Bermejo/Nyberg

KURT BUSIEK'S ASTRO CITY: LIFE IN THE BIG CITY
Busiek/Anderson

KURT BUSIEK'S ASTRO CITY: CONFESSION
Busiek/Anderson/Blyberg

KURT BUSIEK'S ASTRO CITY: FAMILY ALBUM
Busiek/Anderson/Blyberg

KURT BUSIEK'S ASTRO CITY: TARNISHED ANGEL
Busiek/Anderson/Blyberg

LEAVE IT TO CHANCE: SHAMAN'S RAIN
Robinson/Smith

LEAVE IT TO CHANCE: TRICK OR THREAT
Robinson/Smith/Freeman

THE MONARCHY BULLETS OVER BABYLON
Young/McCrea/Leach/Pleece

MR. MAJESTIC
Casey/Holguin/McGuinness/D'Anda

OUT THERE: THE EVIL WITHIN
Augustyn/Ramos/Hope

PLANETARY/AUTHORITY: RULING THE WORLD
Ellis/Jimenez/Lanning

PLANETARY: ALL OVER THE WORLD AND OTHER STORIES
Ellis/Cassaday

PLANETARY: THE FOURTH MAN
Ellis/Cassaday

STEAMPUNK: MANIMATRON
Kelly/Bachalo/Friend

STORMWATCH: FORCE OF NATURE
Ellis/Raney/Elliott

STORMWATCH: LIGHTNING STRIKES
Ellis/Raney/Lee/Elliott/Williams

STORMWATCH: CHANGE OR DIE
Ellis/Raney/Jimenez

STORMWATCH: A FINER WORLD
Ellis/Hitch/Neary

STORMWATCH: FINAL ORBIT
Ellis/Various

WETWORKS: REBIRTH
Portacio/Choi/Williams

WILDC.A.T.S: GANG WAR
Moore/Various

WILDC.A.T.S: GATHERING OF EAGLES
Claremont/Lee/Williams

WILDC.A.T.S: HOMECOMING
Moore/Various

WILDC.A.T.S/X-MEN
Various writers and artists

WILDCATS: STREET SMART
Lobdell/Charest/Friend

WILDCATS: VICIOUS CIRCLES
Casey/Phillips

WILDCATS: SERIAL BOXES
Casey/Phillips

ZERO GIRL
Kieth

AMERICA'S BEST COMICS

ABC SPECIAL
Moore/ Various

LEAGUE OF EXTRAORDINARY GENTLEMEN
Moore/O'Neill

PROMETHEA: BOOK ONE
Moore/Williams III/Gray

PROMETHEA: BOOK TWO
Moore/Williams III/Gray

PROMETHEA: BOOK THREE
Moore/Williams III/Gray

TOMORROW STORIES: BOOK ONE
Moore/Nowlan/Veitch/Baikie/Gebbie/Barta

TOM STRONG: BOOK ONE
Moore/Sprouse/Gordon

TOM STRONG: BOOK TWO
Moore/Sprouse/Gordon

TOP TEN: BOOK ONE
Moore/Ha/Cannon

TOP TEN: BOOK TWO
Moore/Ha/Cannon

STAR TREK COLLECTIONS

STAR TREK: OTHER REALITIES
Various

STAR TREK: THE NEXT GENERATION ENEMY UNSEEN
Various

STAR TREK: THE NEXT GENERATION FORGIVENESS
Brin/Hampton

STAR TREK: THE NEXT GENERATION GORN CRISIS
Anderson & Moesta/Kordey

STAR TREK: VOYAGER ENCOUNTERS WITH THE UNKNOWN
Various

STAR TREK: NEW FRONTIER DOUBLE TIME
David/Collins/Roach

To find more collected editions and monthly comic books from WildStorm and DC Comics, call 1-888-comic book for the nearest comics shop or go to your local book store.

Visit us at www.dccomics.com

WS0011